The Edge of Hell

Gods of the Undead, A Post-Apocalyptic Epic

By Peter Meredith

I0598252

Fictional works by Peter Meredith:

A Perfect America
The Sacrificial Daughter
The Apocalypse Crusade War of the Undead: Day One
The Apocalypse Crusade War of the Undead: Day Two
The Horror of the Shade: Trilogy of the Void 1
An Illusion of Hell: Trilogy of the Void 2
Hell Blade: Trilogy of the Void 3
The Punished
Sprite
The Blood Lure: A Hidden Land Novel 1
The King's Trap: A Hidden Land Novel 2
To Ensnare A Queen: A Hidden Land Novel 3
The Apocalypse: The Undead World Novel 1
The Apocalypse Survivors: The Undead World Novel 2
The Apocalypse Outcasts: The Undead World Novel 3
The Apocalypse Fugitives: The Undead World Novel 4
The Apocalypse Renegades: The Undead World Novel 5
The Apocalypse Exile: The Undead World Novel 6
The Apocalypse War: The Undead World Novel 7
The Edge of Hell: Gods of the Undead, A Post-Apocalyptic

Epic

Pen(Novella)
A Sliver of Perfection (Novella)
The Haunting At Red Feathers(Short Story)
The Haunting On Colonel's Row(Short Story)
The Drawer(Short Story)
Eyes in the Storm(Short Story)
The Witch: Jillybean in the Undead World

Prologue

Nekhen, Egypt

The Upper Nile 1925

The sand on top of the burial site was the same awful dun-colored grit that covered most of the miserable country. He hated the sand with a passion. It seemed to get in everything: in his bedroll, his boots, in his underwear, in the crack of his ass, in the web of lines that had developed around his eyes from squinting through the perpetual glare, and always the sand coated his nostrils.

Of course, nothing was worse than the sand in his food. Jonathan Dreyden had lived with sand in his food for the last three months and now he chewed like an old man: carefully, slowly, even fearfully. He had lost twenty pounds; partially from the desert sun which was turning him into a dried-out husk of a man, tough and stringy, and partly because he had simply lost his once hearty appetite. Crunching down on sand once too often would do that to a man.

Beneath the sand at the site of the dig was—he didn't have to guess—more sand. This time a hard compact layer several feet deep. It had the consistency of concrete but not the charm.

The burial site was out in the middle of nowhere west of the Nile and south of the "city of the dead," the necropolis at Nekhen. They were far up the river almost to the country of Sudan where things were sketchy at best; Jonathan always kept his 1911 model Colt .45 at his side, except that is, when he was cleaning the damned sand out of its inner workings.

As the project wasn't of immense proportions, it took weeks of back-breaking labor for the small crew to hack through that second layer.

It was ugly, harsh, thankless work. "And this is why God gave us heathens," Robert Montgomery said, elbowing his father gently in the side. His father, the current Earl of Blackburn, was standing beneath a great umbrella held by another of the dozen or so local Egyptians who toiled under the blistering sun in their *gallibayas*, the long, loose robes that the Egyptians all seemed to wear.

"I suppose," Lord Blackburn replied, in the soft spoken manner he used whenever Jonathan was near. The tone was, as always, picked up by Robert. It made him mean.

"Jonathan, dear," Robert said. "Do you think you can move them along a little quicker? This heat is simply miserable and I wouldn't want *my father* having a fit on account of it."

My father. It was never 'our' father, and it never would be and Robert made sure Jonathan knew it. Jonathan was an embarrassment. He was a living scandal. He was proof of the sin of adultery. He was a bastard in a time when the word meant something, and, what was worse, he was an American bastard.

Robert would never let either his father or Jonathan forget it.

It was the reason that Jonathan had accompanied them on the expedition. He was there so Robert could treat him like a servant, so he could make sure Jonathan would never forget his place in proper society.

Robert was jealous of his half-brother. Jonathan was the spitting image of his cheating father: tall, broad shouldered, keen eyed and sharp-witted. His hair was the same sandy-blonde and his eyes the same sky blue. They were both quiet and contemplative. They both treated those of lesser birth with the same respect as they would the king.

On the other hand, Robert had the same unfortunate qualities that his slightly inbred mother possessed—close set, suspicious eyes that were the color of mud, a thin hooked nose and the heavy lips frequent among the Hanoverians from which much of the British royalty was descended. They were the lips of a grouper, Jonathan thought.

"I'll get right on it," the bastard drawled. The sound of his voice seemed to grate on Robert's nerves—it was one of the reasons why Jonathan refused to change his American idioms. Even when he spoke to his father he could barely bring himself to use the terms: Lord or Lordship, it just didn't feel right.

Jonathan glanced at one of the locals, Mustafa Al-mara. "Let's pick it up, Mustafa!" he yelled, clapping his hands. He also made sure to raise a quick eyebrow so that the foreman knew it wasn't him giving the inhumane order. The crew was already glaring as they worked, casting evil eyes at Lord Blackburn, who was up in years and somewhat oblivious to the danger around him.

The local Mohammedans bowed and scraped and made sure to appear subservient; however, they hid nothing from Jonathan. They were as dangerous as any pirate crew and Jonathan would rather dine with jungle cannibals than turn his back on them.

Still, as an American, he was safer than either his father or his half-brother. The Egyptians had been granted independence from the British only two years before and they were still in a stew over things.

The locals, muttering under their breath, worked the remainder of the afternoon away until one cried out and began pointing. "What is he jabbering on about?" Robert demanded. "Jonathan, be a dear and find out." Robert did not like the idea of stepping away from the shade of his umbrella. As he had mentioned a dozen times, the idea of coming home looking like a "sun-ravaged Indian" was appalling to him.

"He's saying something about a scorpion," Jonathan remarked, causing Robert to back even further away.

His father, on the other hand, hurried forward with a leather-bound text under his arm. "Your lordship, please,"

Robert said. "Let Jonathan take care of it. Scorpions are simply abysmal. If there's one thing I hate, it's a scorpion."

"It's not a real scorpion, Robert," Lord Blackburn said over his shoulder. "They would've hacked it into pieces with their implements. No...it's...it's..." His words faltered as he saw the faint outlines of the ancient blocks that had been uncovered. They were sun-baked mud bricks, about a foot in length and width, and on each was stamped a crude scorpion. "Clear the dirt away, quickly!" Blackburn cried, following Jonathan down into the excavation pit. He was excited. He ran a hand through his white hair and it stayed sprung, but he didn't care.

One man picked up an iron shovel but Jonathan stopped him. "No. Use the trowels and the small brooms. You don't want to scratch any of these; they're far too valuable." He was not a scholar or a classically trained Egyptologist, however, both his father and brother were and three months stuck in the desert with them endlessly discussing the possible meanings of this hieroglyph or the symbols carved on that cartouche had made Jonathan almost an expert.

"Yes," agreed Lord Blackburn. "We don't want to make the same mistakes as that fool Quibell. How does one unearth something as famous as the *Narmer Palette* and not take adequate notes? Speaking of which. Robert! Get your pen and paper. And make sure you use a fresh nib. This could be big." He was as excited as a boy at Christmas.

Due to the heat, Robert moved languidly. He seemed apathetic as he gazed down at the bricks that were slowly being unearthed. "I'm failing to see the *bigness* of this, father. If you're thinking this is the tomb of the *Scorpion King*, I'm afraid you're going to be sadly mistaken. Yes, the bricks are very nice, the placement, excellent and the workmanship topnotch, but this is not a pharaoh's tomb. Look."

He pointed all around the excavation site. "No obelisks, no colossi, no cartouches, no funerary complex.

I'm not saying that this isn't a major discovery or I should say, possibly one. It is right where a proper reading of Mespero's *Pyramid Texts* said we would find 'something' but this is no pharaoh."

Jonathan wanted to agree, but doing so would have earned him only a scathing look of condescension from Robert.

"You are probably correct," Blackburn said. "But that doesn't mean we don't do this in proper fashion. We should move forward as if there's a thousand pound gold sarcophagus within. Remember Tutankhamen!"

The story of the boy pharaoh was still new in 1925 and was responsible for the great wave of amateur archaeologists who had descended on Egypt like flies on a carcass in the last three years. A fortune in gold and precious relics had been unearthed in what had been thought to be only a servant's tomb. Tutankhamen's tomb had appeared so insignificant that time had swallowed it up allowing the tomb to remain intact and undisturbed for forty-three hundred years.

The talk of gold and precious relics lit a flame in the laborers. They had a lust in their eyes and they worked with much more enthusiasm than they had been. Jonathan read the gold fever in their faces and he made sure they saw his hand on the butt of his Colt. They knew he was a marksman; once a week he practiced with the pistol, blasting targets in the empty desert. Still they spoke in low, conspiratorial tones.

As early evening came on, Jonathan pulled Mustafa aside. "I don't like the way the men are acting. They're being sneaky. What are they saying when we aren't around?"

He was putting the foreman in a bad position; however, there was something in the air that only he suspected. Robert had such a superior attitude that he couldn't fathom the "savages" turning on their "betters" and Lord Blackburn was too engrossed in the find to even look up. Jonathan had a feeling things weren't right. He had relied on those feeling to get him through sixteen months of war on the Western Front and his sixth-sense hadn't left him.

"It is nothing," Mustafa answered in his heavily accented English. *It* came out sounding like *eat* and *is* was *ease*. "They grumble. They make jokes. If I could, I would beat them, but these are not those times. Am I right?"

"I guess not," Jonathan replied, not liking the answer. It didn't fit.

The sun lingered in the desert and it was after supper when it finally torched the lower edge of western desert skies, turning everything golden. By that time, the workers had uncovered the entrance to the tomb: a single slab of white granite. Another scorpion had been chiseled on it.

"How extraordinary," Lord Blackburn, exclaimed. "I've never heard of such a thing. A single glyph. What do you make of it, Robert?"

Robert looked up from his sketch. "Perhaps whoever is buried here didn't need more. Maybe he was so famous that a single glyph was all that was needed to proclaim who he was. Either that, or he was so insignificant that the single glyph was all he was known by."

"I think it's a warning," Jonathan said. There were danger bells going off in his head and it didn't just stem from the local thugs. Something else was wrong; in fact, nothing seemed right.

"If you say the words *Pharaoh's Curse*, I'm going to brand you a coward here and now," Robert said with a smirk that was almost a dare.

Jonathan's eyes narrowed, taking in his brother's smug face. "No, I wasn't. The scorpion had many meanings with these sorts of glyphs and nearly all of them suggest danger. Have you considered that the person buried here might have died as a result of some sort of disease?"

The outbreak of influenza that had swept the world following the Great War had been too recent and too fantastically cruel to discard Jonathan's idea out of hand. Eighteen million people had succumbed, enough for even Robert to hesitate.

"Possible…possible," he said. "But would a disease last three thousand years in this sort of dry heat? I really doubt any could."

"I, for one, am willing to take the chance," Lord Blackburn said. He was a stout old man and, apart from his dalliance with 'that American woman' as Jonathan's mother was always referred to, his heart was never in question.

Robert was quick to agree: "As am I." He looked at Jonathan as if he had won some sort of contest.

"Then by all means," Jonathan said. Now that he had agreed, he was hoping they would crack the vault right there and then, but his father would not hear of it. He wanted a good night sleep so they could be fresh and alert. Bright-eyed and bushy-tailed was how he put it.

Jonathan knew he wasn't going to be either bright eyed or bushy tailed. The scorpion glyph bothered him to no end, as did the sly look the laborers kept slipping their way. Lord Blackburn had purposely kept his expedition quiet. He hadn't wanted to advertise a possible new find which would only generate unwanted publicity and unwanted legal headaches. He was, in essence, out on a limb. It was why Jonathan had made sure the workers knew he carried the Colt and knew he could use it.

That night Jonathan regretted the fire that had been burning outside their tents for the last three months; the desert could become deadly cold at night. That night the crackle and snap of the fire masked sounds that pointed to deception, thievery and perhaps even murder.

Jonathan woke up when the moon was straight above, casting everything in the pale light of the dead. He did not move except to slide his right hand beneath the roll of his winter coat that he used as a pillow. The Colt was there, a hard, deadly lump, a constant reminder that he was always one breath from his last.

He had his hand around the grip, his finger caressing the trigger. Something had woken him. Maybe the howl of a jackal, maybe the hoot of the desert owl, maybe the scrape of a pry-bar against granite that hadn't seen the light of day in thousands of years.

As he laid there, his ears straining, there was another scrape of metal against stone; his suspicions were confirmed. He bit back the curse that was on the edge of his lips and then, silent as an adder, he slipped on his boots. Next, he checked the load on his .45: seven in the magazine and one in the chamber.

With a deft hand, he pulled on the white laces that held the flaps of his tent closed and slipped out into the dead of night, the gun in his hand, the dark air settling on his skin, tenting it up in a thousand goosebumps.

There was a glow beyond the fire; a slight one out toward the excavation site. It was wholly expected. The laborers were robbing a grave that was, in a sense, Lord Blackburn's to rob. The moral distinctions aside, Jonathan couldn't allow it. His father had paid for this dig and, as such, he had the legal right to whatever was found at the site.

He stepped through the sand, lifting his feet and placing them silently; he was a shadow in a land of shadows. He advanced down into the pit that had been dug that day and saw that the Mohammedans had torn back the granite covering of the crypt and that there was a flickering glow from inside. Echoes of excited whispers drifted up to him.

Jonathan eased to the door and peeked around the corner of the granite wall and saw the men as shadows dancing on the walls; they were deep already, heading down into the earth where something dreadful awaited. Their minds were clouded with a fever that only the lust for gold could bring on, making them oblivious to the real, palpable danger in the air.

It wasn't poison and it wasn't a disease. It was foreign, alien, evil.

The little hairs on the back of Jonathan's neck lifted right up as he followed the men downstairs of pure marble. Unlike other tombs he had been in, this one was ageless: no dust, no cobwebs, no mouse droppings. The way was incredibly clean, the tile: hand-finished marble, looked new. Both the walls and the floors were unadorned and stark white. It seemed impossible, especially with Jonathan's preconceived notions of the ancient Egyptians as being only one step up from dirty savages.

He followed in the dark until he came to the first chamber: a simple square room, unadorned save for a doorway straight across from the one that Jonathan was standing in, and a single block of black stone, six feet per side, sitting smack dab in the middle of the room. There was a lip that ran all around the stone, suggesting there was something within it. Four of the men were grunting over crowbars, trying to lift it, while a fifth held a lantern for them to work by.

"Stop!" Jonathan barked, advancing into the room with his .45 pointed. The men froze, their hands coiled around their metal tools. "Step back, nice and slow," he added. When they didn't budge, he gave the gun a little flick to the side, the universal language of: move or you'll get shot.

The man with the lantern turned his head, never taking his eyes from the big bore of the pistol, and called out something in Arabic. In seconds, a light appeared from the other doorway and two men came to stand just shy of the room. The first was Mustafa. He held his empty hands out to Jonathan. Another of the workers was so close behind him that they seemed chained together somehow.

Jonathan was confused until the second man put a knife to Mustafa's throat.

"He says that you are to hand over your weapon or he will kill me."

"Sorry, Mustafa, old boy, I can't do that. Tell him to drop the knife or I will shoot him in the face, and no one wants that."

Mustafa translated and in answer, the man with the knife dragged the foreman back into the shadows. The other workers in the room followed despite Jonathan waving the gun and demanding that they stop.

He followed after, cursing under his breath, afraid that they would make him shoot one of them before they would listen.

The passage was clean and neat like the first one; however, that feeling of dread he had experienced earlier came on stronger with every step he took. It ran up his nerves and he was shocked to see that his gun hand was trembling. A year and a half fighting the krauts and he had never shaken like this. It made no sense.

Ahead, the workers were jabbering so quickly that he couldn't make out a single word; however, he could tell that they were scared as well. They weren't afraid of Jonathan. There was something in the tomb with them, something alive that couldn't possibly be alive. They were just beginning to understand.

Jonathan wanted to run away, only he couldn't get his feet to respond; he was being drawn forward against his will. Very quickly, he was at the doorway of a second room, this one a long rectangle. At the back was a sarcophagus; a big one, as if a giant was being held inside. He knew there wasn't a giant in it; like Russian nesting dolls, there would be a smaller sarcophagus in it and a smaller one in that, and so on.

He had always found the idea tedious; however, just then, he was glad for all the layers. The more barriers between him and whatever was in the sarcophagus the better. They would delay *it* from getting out—there was a palpable feeling now, as though the thing in the sarcophagus could see them through the dividing layers.

"Holy God," Jonathan said in a whisper. He wanted to take a step back and yet found himself a step closer. He wasn't the only one; the workers were all edging in toward it, one with a hand outstretched. His brown fingers were shaking uncontrollably as though he was fighting his own body—and then he touched the outer shell of the sarcophagus.

The man screamed high in his throat, and there was a tremendous *Boom!* The sound rolled down the corridor toward them, coming from the first chamber and could only be the sound of the black lid from the block of stone hitting the floor.

One of the men dropped his lantern and ran right past Jonathan as if he and his gun weren't there. Then they were all running, their minds overcome by a fear that was impossible to describe and more impossible to contain. They were mindless in their fear. They ran towards death and it ran towards them.

It was a ghastly thing made of bone and rotted flesh. It had come from the block of stone in the antechamber and it brought with it the stench of decay that was worse than any charnel house. Once during the Great War, Jonathan had come across a mass grave where hundreds of bloated bodies had been left to blister in the sun. The odor of that had left him weak and gagging for an hour.

This was worse. His legs gave out and he fell to his knees. The workers were struck down by it as well; two passed out, falling right over and the rest were on the ground puking up their dinner on the white tile.

The man closest to the horrid creature held up a hand over his head as if to ward off a blow. The thing, the monstrous dead thing stood over the man for a moment and slowly lifted a hand; the ends of its fingers were without even the moldy, ancient remnants of the flesh that stretched over the rest of its body and the bones were strangely sharp as if it had been clawing at the stone lid of its tomb during its long internment.

Those sharpened fingers were like claws and, so fast that the eye could barely follow, it reached out and grabbed the man by the throat and lifted him off the ground. There was a creaking noise as the thing squeezed its hand, driving those claws deep into the man's flesh, crushing his larynx and piercing the fat arteries on either side of his throat.

In the dim light it looked as though the man's blood was black as the devil, as it poured over the creature's fist and down its arm. In seconds, he was dead and cast aside by the creature, which then turned its terrifyingly empty gaze on the next man.

It was Mustafa. He was frozen, staring into the barren eye sockets of the creature. A scream ran out of his throat and yet, despite his fear, he didn't move or make any attempt to defend himself. With one quick swipe of its bloody claws, the creature tore Mustafa's throat out. Again the blood was nightmare dark as it gushed. It drenched the front of his long robe and splashed onto the pristine white tile.

Seeing the blood on the floor was a catalyst. Jonathan had been as paralyzed as the others but now he was suddenly able to think and move. He brought his Colt up and fired until the magazine was empty—he couldn't miss a stationary target from twenty feet away. The bullets, 45 ACPs, were honking big slugs that could put a man on his back in a flash and yet the creature took eight hits without slowing.

In the time it took for Jonathan to change out for a fresh magazine, the last he carried, the creature killed two more of the Egyptian workers. They died in a blink: more blood and shredded flesh.

Strangely, Jonathan was no longer afraid. The power of the gun, the ear-ringing blasts and the heavy recoil had settled his nerves. He was back in combat, something he knew and understood. This time he was more circumspect with his aim. All eight from the first magazine had gone straight into the thing's chest.

Now, he aimed for the head. No blood or brain matter exploded out, instead chips of bone and an ageless dust filled the air. Five bullets fired and most of thing's skull from the eye sockets on up was gone. The last two shots blasted out teeth and unhinged its jaw so that it hung from what was left of its face by the dried husk of its skin.

And still it kept coming.

The remaining Egyptians screamed all the harder and ran back to the burial chamber with the still closed sarcophagus and the eyes within that could somehow see outward. Jonathan ran as well, but he did so with slow steps—he had the feeling that what was trapped in the sarcophagus was a far worse evil than the creature of bone. But with his death imminent, he chose the burial chamber to seek refuge in and for just a moment it seemed like it would indeed be a refuge.

The creature paused in the doorway, with what was left of its head turned toward the sarcophagus. The moment was a short one, just long enough for Jonathan to pick up one of the crowbars the Egyptians had been using. "Arm your selves!" he yelled to the others.

Two of them did. The first man was struck down by the creature, who charged into the room at Jonathan's call to arms. Before the man could even lift the heavy metal bar, the creature drove razor sharp fingers into his eyes deep enough to stew his brains.

Jonathan knew this creature would be his death and yet, fearlessly he charged and struck with his bar while the creature still had its hand in the worker's face. He swung the bar as if he was Babe Ruth and knocked the remains of the monster's skull clear off. He felt a second of elation and then the creature lunged forward and grabbed Jonathan. It was headless and somehow was even more dangerous.

It raised a hand that was dripping with blood and brains; however, it did not strike. Just then one of the Egyptians made a break for freedom. He ran through the doorway and up the passageway toward the exit and right after him was the creature, its death shrouds billowing out from behind.

The man screamed as he ran, but it was cut short and then the creature was racing back. Jack could *feel* it coming, a sensation that he couldn't understand.

He was afraid, but not overwhelmed by the fear; there were enough of them still alive to overwhelm the creature if they all armed themselves and attacked at once. None did. The second the creature had left the room, the thing in the sarcophagus came awake once more and Jonathan felt an unstoppable urge to open the sarcophagus and release it.

All the men did. One actually had his hand on the lid when the creature of bone and sinew came roaring back into the room. Jonathan had been nearest to the door and should have been killed first; however, the creature went right for the man touching the sarcophagus and tore his head from his body. Blood splashed and again Jonathan came around.

The Egyptians did as well. They scattered from the creature like cockroaches and alone, Jonathan charged, catching the creature with his back to him. It had another of the workers by the throat and Jonathan aimed his heavy bar at the thing's extended arm.

With a grisly *snap*, it broke off at the elbow. This time there was no elation on Jonathan's part. If the thing could fight without a head, it could fight with only one arm.

Sure enough, the creature spun and tried to grab Jonathan's throat. He got the bar up just in time. Undeterred, the monster flung the bar across the room with Jonathan still hanging on—he wasn't going to give up the bar for anything.

He landed in a heap and despite a flare of pain in his side, he struggled to his feet. In that short time, two more Egyptians were dead and a third raced for the exit. He made it just beyond the doorway before he was killed.

His death was the only thing that allowed Jonathan to finally destroy the creature. Once again, he was able to attack from behind and he aimed for the thing's remaining arm. It took two swings before it broke off and fell to the bloody tile with a rattle of bones.

Then it was a just a matter of time before the remainder of the creature was utterly dismembered. Jonathan swung and swung the bar until no two bones were connected. He was covered in what looked like flour by the time Robert and Lord Blackburn came down the passage.

"What is the meaning of this?" Robert demanded, his eyes wide and his face stricken by the horror of the burial chamber.

Jonathan, panting and sweating from his labors could only shrug; no other answer would do. The truth would get him sent straight to the booby-hatch; in fact, just then he felt as though a spell in a loony bin might be something that would do him good.

He dropped the metal bar with a clang which seemed to awaken the last of the Egyptians. He'd been standing like a man caught up in singularly bad epileptic fit. It was almost as if he was frozen, but now he was moving...moving toward the sarcophagus.

"We have to stop that man," Jonathan said, starting forward.

"Your killing spree is over, Jonathan!" Robert said, grabbing his half-brother. "You will pay for this, I'll see to it."

Jonathan spun and clubbed Robert in the face with one beefy fist, dropping him straight to the bloody tile. "When I start killing, I'll begin with you."

He left his brother, sneering around a grimace of pain, and ran to the last Egyptian who had given in to the strange demand emanating from the nightmare monster within the sarcophagus. Just before Jonathan could get to him, the man heaved off the lid; what must have weighed hundreds of pounds. As expected, there was another sarcophagus within the first and on the breast of it was a scroll of papyrus. It radiated heat and when the man picked it up he moaned aloud.

He went on moaning until Jonathan cocked him on the side of the head with his rock-hard fist. His eyes twisted in their sockets and he fell to the ground, unconscious.

"What was that?" Robert asked. The sneer had been wiped from his face and he looked uncertain all of a sudden. Jonathan guessed that he had felt the call of the thing in the sarcophagus.

"I think a better question," Lord Blackburn said, "how is *that* happening?"

He pointed down at the bones of the creature that Jonathan had destroyed. They were jittering, coming alive, sliding across the floor and reforming themselves. The sinew and ancient muscle grew back as well, but it grew in no particular order so that a bicep was partially showing beneath the creature's jaw. As well there were pieces of its white burial shroud fused in with everything else.

The creature of bone was alive again and even stronger than before.

Chapter 1

Jack Dreyden

New York University, Manhattan

The residence hall overlooking Union Square, one of twenty operated by New York University, was silent as a tomb. Two days before Christmas and only the orphans were left in the converted apartment building. It was the same every year.

No home to go to, no family, no real reason to go out.

The few true orphans, those who had never been adopted, kept to themselves because it was Christmas! It was all anyone talked about during the last week before the semester ended. *Are you going home for Christmas?* Jack heard that question a hundred times, though only once had it been directed at him. He had lied and said: "Yes, I can't wait."

Lying was better than the pity. It was also better than ever voicing the ugly truth: his father had been murdered when he was the tender age of ten, and his mother slain seven years later when she came home to find two men ransacking her small Pennsylvania home. That sort of truth was best not dwelt upon.

Yet it was never far from his mind, and so Jack Dreyden made sure to immerse himself in his work during the holidays and only rarely pulled his nose from his books. Truly this was how he lived his life on a daily basis, anyway. Jack wasn't really one for socializing, which is why he had turned down the one invitation to a Christmas party he had received.

It was a black tie affair and there were going to be a lot of bigwigs in the *dirt grubbing* business in attendance.

That's how Jack's mom had spoken of her husband's work as an archeologist...when they were both alive, of course. She would jokingly tell friends: *He's always going about, grubbing in the dirt. And don't get me started on his nails!*

Jack knew it probably would have been smart to attend the party. The archeology community was exceedingly small and it paid in the long run to rub elbows and schmooze whenever possible. "I still have time," he reminded himself. He was on course to earn his doctorate in two years, which he felt was plenty of time, perhaps even too much time, to meet the right people to further his career.

The very thought of schmoozing at all left him feeling ill at ease. He wasn't exactly gregarious, especially at this time of year.

He preferred books to people. Jack was just finishing John Strange's, *Caphtor Keftiu: A New Investigation.* He had dog-eared a quarter of the pages and had highlighted so much of it that it made more sense just to re-read the entire book rather than to look for anything specific. He was easing it back into place on the bookshelf when he heard footsteps in the hall.

Normally, the tap of the shoes would have been drowned out by the ambient ruckus kicked up by his fellow students who were all very much concerned with drinking and partying in general and thus were very loud. However, with Christmas approaching, the building was so empty that Jack picked out the sound when the man was still halfway down the hall.

It was a man. The stride wasn't that of a student bopping along in ratty high-top Converse sneakers, or a janitor in worn down work boots trudging as a guy did when he hated his job. It was a man who considered himself of some importance. The man strode down the hall with a purpose and for some reason Jack felt distinctly uneasy, as if the man heading toward him was the bearer of ill news.

On the day his mother had been killed, Jack had been in the school library at Valens High and, as most libraries are, it was empty save for the books, the dust floating in the sunbeams, the sleepy librarian propped up on one elbow, and a few bespectacled nerds.

It was so quiet that Jack heard the important tapping of the principal's shoes as he came to ruin Jack's world—and the sound matched this so closely that a wave of goosebumps went up Jack's back.

The steps ended at his door. It might have been his imagination; however, there seemed to be a distinct danger in the air. He'd been having that feeling frequently since his mother had died. He might have chalked it up to paranoia, except Jack Dreyden came from a family of extremely short-lived people.

His great grandfather, the original Jonathan Dreyden, had died at the age of twenty-eight, leaving but a single child behind. That child, the next Jonathan Dreyden and Jack's grandfather, had disappeared from a dig in the *Valley of the Kings* when he was forty-two. His own father, Jonathan Dreyden the third had been murdered at the ripe old age of thirty-one.

Jack figured that if he somehow managed to live long enough to have a son of his own, he would name him Chuck or Rory or even Arnold; anything but Jonathan. It was why he went by Jack; he felt that his given name was cursed.

With all of this hanging over his head, Jack had grown up with a sense of urgency. He had graduated high school at seventeen, earned a bachelor's degree in ancient history at twenty, a master's in Egyptian Studies a year later and now he was blistering through his doctoral program.

And when he was done with school? He had no idea, except he knew he didn't want to die before he got his first grey hair.

It was this reasoning that had him eyeing the fencing saber he kept next to the front door. After his father had been killed, Jack became difficult for his mother to handle. He'd been angry and resentful. There were times he lashed out, uncontrollably, and there were many days he wept when no one was watching.

The truth that he had kept hidden from everyone was that he had been secretly afraid of the world. He'd been ten years old and his mom had called him Jon-Jon and she had done the best that she could. She had taken him to every new movie, bought him the best games, and made sure that he was always surrounded by friends whenever possible.

But all he could really remember of the year after his father's murder was that he had been afraid of every shadow and every little bump in the night that couldn't be explained away. He'd wet the bed most nights.

Yet, at the same time, he'd been so full of anger that he walked around with his fists clenched like rocks. He sought out fights, always ready to go against the biggest bullies. It seemed impossible that he could feel both anger and fear so intensely at the same time, but somehow he had.

Instead of trying to control his feelings, his mother channeled them.

On his eleventh birthday, Jack had received a sword; perhaps a strange gift for a child with anger issues and yet from that day on, he fenced two to three times a week and never had an outburst again.

Now, the person with the important-sounding tapping shoes knocked lightly on Jack's door; it was almost a secretive sound as if whoever it was hoped that Jack wouldn't be in.

Jack slid off his desk chair, crept to the door and took up the saber. It settled his nerves. "Yes?" he asked.

"How splendid that you're in," the man said in a light British accent. "Open up, it's Robert."

Jack relaxed immediately. He put the saber away, turned the three locks that he had placed on the door and greeted his cousin with a strained smile. As the only son of an only son of an only son, Jack had never known he had a cousin. In fact the entire cousin thing: first, second, third, once removed, five times removed and all that was very much lost on Jack. He understood the terms as they were defined but they had never seemed to apply to him.

Then one day out of the blue, two years after his mother had died, Robert Montgomery had shown up with a sickly grin—what passed for a smile—on his pale, cadaverous face. He was very much surprised that Jack was clueless as to his past. "Yes, we share the same relative," he had said. "Your great, great grandfather, is my great grandfather."

As impressive as that sounded, Robert was somewhat distasteful; pushing a relationship that Jack wasn't keen on having. Despite his pedigree and his fancy accent, Robert had the feel of a used car salesman about him. Jack was polite, which Robert took as friendly, and over the next three years, Robert had come to visit him every six months or so and he always came without warning and always he came with questions; though he masked his intent with a good deal of flowery rhetoric.

Jack didn't think he was up to entertaining just then, especially when Robert started as he always did: "Wild Jack, old sport, you look fantastic."

Jack had never once shown Robert a "wild" side and he knew for sure that he didn't look fantastic or even very good. He hadn't seen the sun in weeks and he was sure he looked pale and unwell.

"Thanks," Jack replied, trying his best to put on a good show. "And how are you? You look splendid. Are you going somewhere special?"

Perhaps for the first time since Jack had known him, Robert looked almost chipper, as though he was just about to jump out of his patent leather shoes. In fact, he wore a manic grin, but it went almost unnoticed as Jack took in the finely tailored tuxedo that Robert wore.

"What kind of question is that?" Robert replied with mock incredulity. "The right question is why aren't you dressed? The party started half an hour ago. You did receive Rebecca's invitation, didn't you?"

Jack grimaced. "Yes. But I don't know her, and I don't own a tux, and sure, the party sounds nice, but I have a ton of work to do, and…"

Robert held up a prissy hand. He was slim with a hooked nose and dark eyes that were almost buried in deep pouches. "Enough with your excuses, Wild Jack. Rebecca is not just my cousin, she's yours as well and I worked hard to get you an invitation."

"She's my second cousin or something, and a half-second cousin at that," Jack shot back. "And I don't want to go to a party that someone has to work hard to get me in to. I'd feel very much like a beggar at their door; a pity-case. No, thank you."

"That's all a bunch of bull spittle as you Americans say," Robert answered. "You're just feeling sorry for your-self because it's Christmas and you don't have anyone, but you have me and you have Rebecca. She's very sweet and you two have so much in common."

"Hardly. She's a linguist, not an archeologist."

Robert acted as though this admission was tanta-mount to Jack agreeing to go to the Christmas party. "She's a linguist who specializes in ancient languages, with an emphasis in ancient Egyptian. You two are peas in a pod."

Jack shook his head. "And a Christmas party really isn't the time or the place to be talking about a subject so archaic and dull. I'm sorry, but I'm not going. Of course, knowing you, you're not here for that anyway."

"Oh, don't be like that," Robert snapped. He opened his mouth but at Jack's look, he shrugged and smiled again. "Ok, so I need a favor. I need some minor work translated." He reached into an inner pocket and pulled out a sheaf of papers. On each were enlarged hieroglyphs. The first one was a partial glyph; Jack could see the edges of the ones on either side that had been cut off by the printer.

Jack gave it a glance. "That might say *st* depending on what went before it or after. If you want an actual trans-lation I would need the entire text to see if what I'm looking at is part of a ligature, a stand-alone phonetic glyph, a logograph or a..."

"Ok, I don't need you to prove your credentials, old chum, I just need a translation." Somewhat reluctantly, Robert handed over a sheet of paper that was scrawled with writing.

"What the hell?" Jack demanded, his eyes flicking over the parchment. "Where did you get this?" The sample was a strange mixture of Sumerian Cuneiform and proto-dynastic hieroglyphs. It was ancient, even compared to most of the early Egyptian texts, and it was so rare that only one version was thought to exist. It began: *Hrr vahl Evi, ah hurrumm fd...* which translated as *Come Mother of Demons, Queen of Souls*.

"I have my sources and I can't divulge them," Robert answered, without really answering. "My father mentioned that you might be able to help with the translation."

"Your father?" Jack had no idea who Robert's father was. "How would he know anything about me?"

Robert rolled his eyes as if he was in the presence of an imbecile. "Because we are kin as you Americans say. He has always looked out for you, whether you know it or not. Speaking of which, I can pay you for your work. Would a thousand dollars be sufficient?"

Suddenly, Jack forgot his anger and the seam of anxiety that had zipped through his gut at the sight of the paper. There had been some insurance money when his father died, really a lot, half a million dollars; however, that had been thirteen years ago and his mother had spent a good chunk on a small house and bills, Uncle Sam had taken an even larger chunk and NYU was getting the rest. Jack had enough money to graduate in two years, but not enough to graduate and also eat.

And yet there were some scary implications seeing Robert with that text. It was a hard choice, but hunger won out. "I guess I can do it for a thousand," he said, and then, almost instantly regretted it. Robert practically jumped with excitement. His eagerness, bordering on stark greed was as unnerving as the idea that he had a copy of the text. Jack suddenly wanted to take back his words, but it was too late, the die had been cast.

Wanting to slow things down and give himself time to think, Jack added: "I'll need at least a day, maybe two."

This reined in Robert's eagerness and he gave Jack a look of suspicion as if he fully expected Jack to be able to snap out a translation of a five-thousand year old text in ten minutes. In truth, Jack could have. He knew its contents by heart, just as he knew there was no way that Robert should have a copy of it.

"Sure," Robert replied, a not-so-happy smile back on his thin lips, barely covering his disappointment. "I'll be back tomorrow evening. In the mean time, mum's the word."

He turned on his heel and his new shoes beat out a snappy rhythm as he went to the door. "Say hello to Rebecca for me," Jack said when Robert was half way out the front door to his apartment. Robert gave him a puzzled look before he remembered their cousin and the party he was supposedly attending.

"Of course I will," Robert said. "Good night."

The moment he was in the hall, Jack locked all three of his locks and then went to the window overlooking Union Square and waited for Robert to leave. When he did, Jack threw on a coat and rushed out as well, the copy of his 'one of a kind' text stuffed in his coat pocket.

Chapter 2

Greenwich Village, New York

Jack went out the back entrance of the residence hall and although it was after eight in the evening, and it was full on dark with the wind starting to rush down the streets in great gusts, there were plenty of people to get lost in. This was one of the best things about New York City: the anonymity.

Eight million individuals made up the city and yet you couldn't tell one from another on a cold, windy night like that. Still Jack tried. As he hurried down the street, he stared with bright eyes at every single person he passed and he had his head bent around back the way he had come nearly as much as he had it forward. He thought it very likely that he was being followed or spied upon.

He was a nothing of an orphan and a nobody of a student, but that didn't mean he didn't have his secrets. And Robert knowing about the ancient text made it feel like someone had safe-cracked his skull.

It was probably his family history stoking the embers of his paranoia, but Robert should not have had that piece of paper. He shouldn't have even known that it existed. It was impossible. Jack knew that Robert was very rich and very well-connected, but not *that* rich or connected.

With his fears in full bloom, he hurried to the nearest subway station and jumped on the 'R' train heading north. He had a particular destination in mind; however, the R wouldn't get him there; the subway was simply a distraction, a way to lose his pursuers—he figured there had to be a team of spies after him, like in the movies.

But why?

The why wasn't something he felt he couldn't fathom just then. What Robert wanted, as far as Jack knew, was worthless. The five-thousand year old papyrus, which no one should have known about, was stored in a safe deposit box in a bank in lower downtown that only he and some unknown bank flunky had ever been to. It was likely worth somewhere around ten thousand dollars—not a kingly sum to anyone, but worth far more than a translation which had a value of about twenty dollars, if that much.

The papyrus was part of an Egyptian funeral text and there were many, many funeral texts running around, each as full of blather and nonsense as the next. You could pull fifty of them off the internet in a blink.

So why pay a thousand dollars for a translation of this one? And why ask the very person you had stolen it from to translate it for you? It made no sense and so he concentrated on something that did: Robert had somehow gotten into his safe deposit box without a key. That meant he had shelled out big money—perhaps even huge money to get at the papyrus and that meant...what?

Jack had no idea; he just knew that he couldn't trust Robert. After all, what did he really know of his cousin? Not much. In fact, were they even cousins at all? There had never been a DNA test taken, and Jack didn't have relatives around to attest that, yes, this was his great, great grandfather's...

He was suddenly shaken out of his reverie: across the platform a down-bound R train had just pulled up. With a last glance around, and feeling very foolish, he leapt up and slipped through the doors just as they were closing. A few people idling on the platform gave him curious looks, but none followed him onto the down-bound R.

Sweating with relief, he rode it all of one stop, left the train slowly so that he was the last one off and then followed a dozen or so ordinary looking people out into the cold night. He knew his paranoia was unfounded and yet his chest wouldn't stop shaking and his nerves ached. Something was wrong in all of this.

"The Waldorf," he said to the cabdriver who pulled up within a second of Jack lifting his hand.

"Sure thing," the cabby said, with a barely raised eyebrow. Jack did not look like Waldorf material. His boots had been his father's and were still a dusty brown as if he had just walked out of the desert; his jeans were faded relics from high school, and his coat was a Vietnam era army jacket that he had picked up for twelve dollars at a military surplus shop.

To top it all off, his wavy blonde hair was a mess and he had who knew how many days' worth of scruff on his chin.

The front desk manager at the Waldorf was of the same mind as the cabbie and gave him a look that suggested that, *no, vagabonds weren't wanted in his hotel*. Even the invitation to the Christmas party didn't seem to help much and was viewed with equal suspicion until Jack lied: "I'm a musician," as if that was all the explanation that was needed.

It helped, a little. The manager's lip curled to an even greater extent, but he nodded and escorted Jack to a second floor ballroom that was bright and posh and practically exploding with Christmas cheer. The people in attendance were dressed to the nines in their tuxes and their formal gowns. They were ruddy from alcohol and dancing.

"Mr. Jonathan Dreyden," the manager said to the headwaiter, who at least had the decency to keep his face frozen in a neutral setting.

"It's Jack, actually." He felt stupid for saying it, but he was feeling jinxed enough without people calling him Jonathan all night, not that he planned on staying.

The waiter didn't care one way or the other. "As you wish. May I show you to your table?"

"A table?" Jack glanced down at his outfit. "No thanks. I'm uh, not really dressed for the occasion. I was actually hoping to talk to someone privately out here in the hall. My cousin, Rebecca Childs?"

"And she is?" The waiter lifted a hand to indicate the entire swarm of people. Although there were placards in front of every seat, the tables were mostly empty, the guests either dancing or mingling. Jack could only shrug.

The waiter looked uncomfortable. "She is *your* cousin, sir."

"Right, but I don't know her exactly; she's a very distant cousin. Uh, maybe her?" He pointed at a woman: tall, statuesque, blonde but with some grey mixed in.

"That's Mrs. Singer; she is the hostess of tonight's event. It might move things along if I ask her." He left before Jack could thank him.

The waiter engaged Mrs. Singer in a short conversation and even with forty yards of crowded ballroom between them, Jack could feel the disappointment coming off the lady at his attire. He stepped back into the hall to shield himself from her glare.

Not a minute later, he could hear the soft step of a woman's shoe and was surprised when a remarkably young lady strode from the ballroom. She was maybe all of twenty and quite stunning with a sharp chin, a thin nose, a spill of blonde hair as thick as a fox's tail that enveloped one shoulder, and the most curious smile; it was mostly a "knowing smirk" but there was also a hint of the devil in it.

"Ms. Childs?" Jack asked, uncertainly.

She had eyes of blue crystal that narrowed as she took in his head-to-toe scruffiness. "Yes?"

"Uh, Rebecca Childs, the linguist? You...you have a doctorate?"

"No," she answered stiffly in a lilting British accent. "I'm Cynthia Childs. Rebecca is my mother. And you are?"

"Jack Dreyden. I think you're my cousin."

Cynthia's eyes widened. "So you're 'Wild Jack?' Robert sure got the wild part correct." Jack couldn't help it and tried to pat his hair down. He had to stop when she stuck her hand out to him. It was a rather dainty hand and, she being so British, Jack didn't know if he was expected to kiss it. Thankfully, she initiated a handshake.

"Robert is the reason I'm here," he confessed. "Is he really my cousin? Do you know? I'm not really up on my pedigree or whatever you call it."

Her smile went a touch sour. "If you are really Jonathan Dreyden then, sad to say, Robert really is your cousin and mine as well. It's something that isn't easy to get used to, believe me. He would be our..." Her eyes went a little out of focus as she counted back the generations. "He's our second cousin once removed. And I am your third cousin."

"Oh." Jack didn't know where that left him exactly. Cousin or not, Robert shouldn't have had a copy of the papyrus. It was wrong on more than one level. The papyrus was singularly unique; perhaps one of the most unique items in the world and it was pretty much the only thing of value that had been left to him by his parents. What's more it came with an obligation.

Two weeks after the death of his mother, he had discovered a key and a letter written in his father's hand: *Deborah—Where we first met. Keep it safe. Do not sell it or give it away. Keep it secret.* This was followed by a series of glyphs, the same strange glyphs that Jack found on an ancient scroll tucked in a glass case in a locker of a bus station in Allentown, Pennsylvania, where his parents had met eighteen years before.

The papyrus had taken four years to decipher. He had to understand the bizarre nature of hieroglyphs as well as Sumerian cuneiform before he was able to even begin.

Although the final translation was somewhat disappointing, Jack had followed his father's wishes and had moved the papyrus to a bank, a much safer location...but obviously not safe enough.

"That was my reaction, too," Cynthia said, seeing his look. "It's not easy knowing that your only blood relation, distant as he is, is a bit of a creep. But now I have you and you are...well you're American, so you have an excuse."

Again Jack's hand went to his hair. "I don't usually look like this. Well, I guess maybe I do, but not for parties."

"I'm sure. Well, it is a new and splendid thing for me to meet an actual blood relation, and I do hope that you are planning on staying. Will you keep me company?" She spoke so rapidly that before he could answer, she was on again: "As you can see, all of these people are the very essence of stuffy, and they're so old! My mother insisted that I come since I'm going into the family business. Just like you, I hear. Robert considers you some sort of savage, but he insists that you are a brilliant savage."

This was his moment to reply to what he supposed was a compliment; however, she had a breathy, airy way of speaking, as though she was always pleasantly surprised by the simplest of things. It was endearing and Jack found himself staring, but then, out of the corner of his eye he saw Robert coming through the crowd toward the main entrance to the ballroom. Jack hadn't been seen yet and he wanted to keep it that way. He started backing away, saying: "I wish I could, but I can't. It was nice meeting you, Cynthia and maybe we can get together, you know, after Christmas."

"My friends call me Cyn. And sure, we're staying here at the Waldorf. I rather believe that my mother would be perfectly happy to see you...as long as you shave and put on proper attire that is."

"Yes, sounds good. I will. Thanks, but I have to go, bye." He practically fled down the hall and took the stairs instead of waiting on the elevator. In minutes, he was back out in the cold and hurrying for the nearest subway. The taxi had been a luxury, one that he couldn't afford a second time. But there was a second reason why he ignored the line of cabs: he had just realized that it made no sense for anyone to be following him.

His father's secret was out. Robert already had the text, it was a done deal and there was only one real question in Jack's mind: *Do I make any money off of the translation or should I hold out on principle and starve?*

It wasn't much of a choice. Jack thought of himself as smart, but he was nobody's genius—there had to be many other scholars who could decipher the writing.

"I'll ask for five-thousand," Jack decided once he was warm and safe in his apartment. Safe being the optimal word. Not only had he triple-locked the door, he had gone around his place inspecting every inch of it for hidden microphones or cameras. There were none, though he studiously kept clear of his computer, knowing that there were ways to hack into it, remotely.

He was able to come to grips with his decision and fell asleep by midnight. An hour later he was up with the unsettling idea that maybe he was no longer in possession of the original papyrus. After all, he hadn't checked on it since he had finished deciphering it over a year ago.

The thought crept into his head, *if it could be copied, it could be stolen.*

"Crap," Jack whispered into the dark. The idea was upsetting and yet on the other hand, it cemented the idea that no one would be after him. Why would they be? Here it was a few minutes into Christmas Eve and he was alone: a nothing orphan and a nobody of a student. He fell asleep with a heavy depression settling into his bones.

The next morning his mood was little improved and he went to his bank fully expecting to find his safe deposit box empty; however, it was not. The papyrus lay in the glass tube in which he had originally found it all those years ago. In keeping with his junior spy routine of the day before, Jack held the glass tube up to the light, trying to see if there were fingerprints on it that were obviously different than his own.

With his experience in fingerprints being confined simply to what he had seen on television, his attempts proved impossible. It wasn't his area of expertise. Handwritten hieroglyphics were. He took out the copies of the text that Robert had given him and his practiced eye quickly saw that the glyphs hadn't been copied by a machine.

"Thank God for that."

The idea that someone had put the papyrus in a copier had been worrying him sick. The next thing he saw was that someone with experience had done the copying and yet there were three odd breaks in the lines that didn't make much sense. There were also four different errors in the copying, small ones, little slips of the stylus that would have led to mistakes in the translation if he hadn't already known what it said.

In spite of the transcribing errors, he knew he would fix them in the final translation. "For five-thousand dollars, I should do it right," he said.

After replacing the papyrus, he left the bank and went straight back to his apartment and began the translation. He first translated the piece with the numerous mistakes left in, just to see if that would change the meaning in any way—he was somewhat disappointed that it did not.

Next, he translated the original text, word for word, double checking himself and mumbling the final version in English: "Come Mother of Demons, Queen of Souls from who's thighs life did spring. Take this sacrifice, Give me entry into the Duat. Bring forth your others as they call and are called."

He sat back, shaking his head. "Why would Robert pay even a thousand dollars for that? What a moron." He laughed, just a chuckle, and then sighed.

"Now what?" he said as he looked around his dreary little apartment. Bored and hungry, and wishing that Christmas was already behind him for good, he made himself a peanut butter and jelly sandwich and then settled back down with a new book. The translated work he left sitting on his desk. Why bother hiding it? If Robert came with a gun or some goons in order to steal it, what good would hiding anything do?

Besides, Jack didn't think Robert would try anything untoward. He wouldn't be happy about Jack demanding more money, but so what? Jack wasn't exactly happy that somebody, Robert most likely, had bribed his way into his safe deposit box.

At six that evening, when the residence hall was again morgue-quiet, Jack heard Robert's shoes tapping up the hall. They were brisker now. Eager. They were also alone. Still, Jack was nervous and took his saber from the door and leaned it against his desk.

"Come in," Jack said at Robert's knock. "It's open." He hadn't bothered with locking his door for the same reason that the translation wasn't hidden.

Robert was dapper as usual: suit, tie, shiny shoes, soft calfskin gloves. "Merry Christmas!" he cried as he came in. His words were cheery, however his eyes were quick. He scanned the small studio apartment and saw the clean white papers on Jack's desk. He also saw the saber and his grin faltered. "What's with the sword?"

Jack shrugged. "I fence, or I used to. Before we get started..."

"Started?" Robert interrupted. "There's nothing really to start. I give you a check and you give me the translation."

"A check is right," Jack replied, feeling strangely cool, especially compared to the day before when he'd been seeing spies in every face. "I've changed my mind on the amount. I think five-thousand would be a better, more appropriate price since what I translated belonged to me to begin with. Someone has been in my bank. I'm not saying it was you, Robert, but you probably know who it was."

Robert's smile became tense. "That's quite an accusation."

"It's not an accusation...yet. Right now, it's simply a statement. It might become an accusation, though I doubt it. You want this translation badly. You offered a thousand without hesitation and you would've gone higher if I had pressed you on it. Once I realized that *someone* had been in my safe deposit box, I realized that a thousand was far too low a price. In fact, it's something of an insult, seeing as we are kin."

The talk of money relaxed Robert and his grin wasn't forced. "Let me assure you that I don't think anyone was in your bank, and yes, a thousand is too low. I apologize. I'm used to driving hard bargains."

"So we have a deal on five-thousand?"

"Yes," Robert said, again so quickly that Jack wondered if he had gone too low once more. It was a little too late to ask for more. Despite the skullduggery on Robert's part, that would have been unseemly.

As Robert reached for his checkbook, Jack glanced a final time at the translation and asked: "Why do you want this so badly? Do you have a buyer who doesn't realize that funeral texts are a dime a dozen?" Robert hesitated and there was something in the way he held his gold-leaf pen that triggered a thought in Jack.

"Wait a minute! You found someone who actually believes in these spells?" A hearty laugh escaped Jack and he shook his head ruefully. "Will they still pay if they find out that the spell doesn't work? Don't tell them, but I've spoken the words in English and ancient Egyptian and nothing's happened. The gate to the Duat never materialized."

"But did you paint the glyphs in a circle of sacrificial blood while wearing the head of a bull like the first Viziers used to?" Robert asked, with a chuckle.

"The bull's head, that's what I forgot. I knew I was missing something."

"Maybe next time," Robert said, adding a flourish to his signature. "Here is your check and now, if you don't mind, I really do have to get going."

"Of course," Jack said. He took the check, stuck it in the top drawer of his desk and then handed over the translation but kept the copies he had been given. There was still a part of him that could hear the echo of his father's warning in his mind: *Keep it safe. Do not sell it or give it away. Keep it secret.* Although it was no longer safe, or secret, there was no sense adding to his guilt.

Robert gave a glance at the copies, looked as though he wanted to ask for them back, but only shrugged and turned his back on Jack and headed for the door. "Enjoy your day, tomorrow," he said and was half out the door before Jack could blink.

"Merry Christmas," Jack answered, happy to be shut of his cousin so quickly and happy that the entire sordid business was behind him. He felt somewhat coated with sleaze at having dealt with him and guilty as well for having sold his birthright and ignoring his father's wishes.

"Those had been instructions for mom, not for me," he rationalized as he opened the desk drawer and picked up the check. It was the largest sum he had ever held in his life; he put it up to the light, giving it a thorough inspection to make sure that there wasn't anything "wrong" with it.

It seemed perfectly fine. He wasn't, however. His guilt grew within him and he ended up taking the copies and the check and stashing them back in the top drawer of his desk. The papers and his guilt weighed on his mind and kept him up deep into the night, which was why he slept in very late on Christmas morning.

The sound of shoes, clacking with importance and severity, woke him. They were coming for him.

Chapter 3

Greenwich Village, New York

The stern sounding shoes came right to Jack's apartment and, even before someone, with what sounded like steel knuckles, rapped on his hollow front door, rattling it in its frame, his first thought was to wonder whether he had unintentionally committed some sort of crime by selling the translation.

"Jonathan Dreyden," a stern voice that was a perfect match for the stern footsteps, said. It was not a question. "This is the police. Open the door."

"The police?" Before the knock, he'd had a raw intuition that it was going to be the police, and yet it was still jarring. He was extremely straight-laced. Unlike the majority of his dorm mates, he didn't have to rush around the room hiding illegal items. He only had to smooth down his blond hair before he opened the door. "Yes?"

There were two men outside his door. One was forty-ish and tall with heroic shoulders, a short afro and a tired, drooping hound-dog face; the other was much older, slightly built, with a perfectly manicured beard, a finely tailored suit, a gold Rolex on his left wrist and dark, angry eyes. The younger of the two spoke first: "I'm Detective Richards of the NYPD and this is Mr. Loret of the..."

"*Doctor* Loret," the older man reminded. The detective gave the doctor a look that said: *Is that really necessary?*

Jack stuck out his hand. "Wow, Dr. Loret of the Brooklyn Museum, curator of the Egyptian exhibit. I've been to four of your lectures and to your museum easily a dozen times."

Loret gave Jack's hand a look of pure disgust. "In preparation for last night's dealings, no doubt. I believe it's called 'casing the joint,' Detective Richards."

"That's enough, Doctor," Richards said. "You are here as a courtesy. There was a break-in at the Brooklyn Museum last night, Mr. Dreyden, and your name has come up as a possible suspect. May we come in and have a look around?" The detective was already, in a sense, looking around. He was gazing past Jack and into his rather small studio apartment. "You're free to say no, though I would just come back with a warrant."

Jack wasn't worried about the legalities of the situation. He had done nothing wrong, at least, nothing intentionally wrong. He was only worried about his reputation in the archeology community. Despite Loret's antagonism, Jack had to show that he had nothing to hide. "I have no idea what this is about, but sure, be my guest," he said, swinging his door wide and ushering both men inside.

Richards went about the room, slowly, his shrewd eyes taking in everything. Loret, on the other hand, began pawing through the books on Jack's desk. Richards opened his mouth to tell him to stop; however, Jack waved him off. "It's ok. It's equally important to me that I clear my name with my colleagues as it is with the authorities. I didn't do anything wrong. I was here all last night."

"Do you have anyone who can verify that?" Richards asked.

"A friend of mine was here until about six, but after that, no." The detective wore a strained grin that suggested that was the wrong answer. Jack began to get nervous, suddenly remembering the check sitting nice and pretty in his top drawer. Perhaps Robert had done something illegal, perhaps he had some hand in the break in—it seemed beyond the realm of possibility that he had actually been the one to break in, personally.

A fat bribe dropped on a bank official was one thing but a break in? No, that didn't seem like Robert's style.

Jack's fears were confirmed when Loret suddenly exclaimed: "Ah-ha!" He held up one of the pages of hieroglyphics that Jack had translated. "This is a clue, detective."

Richards went to the desk and stared at the glyphs, his hound dog face screwed up in puzzlement. "How do you know that's the same stuff? That looks like normal hieroglyphics to me."

Loret made a noise like a strangled snort. "Are you kidding me? Look. See these little wedge shaped characters? That is ancient Sumerian. It doesn't belong; it's just like at the museum."

Jack's stomach had been sinking with every second and he had to resist the urge to begin biting his nails; however, the idea that there was more of the strange amalgamated script caused his anxiety to disappear in a blink. "There's more of these glyphs at the museum? I've never seen them there."

Before Loret could answer, Richards snapped his fingers and shushed him with a warning look. "Are you sure these are the same?" the detective asked Loret.

"Detective, I hold a doctorate in ancient history and several degrees in Egyptology and when I say…"

Richards blinked largely as if he couldn't believe he had to deal with such a smart-stupid person. "Yes or no, Doctor, that's all I want."

"Yes, I'm altogether certain."

The detective rumbled in his throat, a sound Jack took to mean he was considering his options. Eventually, he said to Loret: "Put those down and back away." Richards then took out his phone and began snapping pictures of the desk and its contents but somehow missed the check that was starting to feel like very damning evidence. All he cared about were the glyphs and the various books. He placed them in evidence bags and then started going through Jack's collections of pens.

"He used brushes, camel-hair brushes to be precise," Loret said.

"I don't own brushes of any sort," Jack said, growing angry. It felt as though he was being found guilty of something he had nothing to do with.

Richards sniffed his pens before saying: "Just a precaution. By the way, you do have the right remain silent. Anything you say may be used against you in a court of law."

Jack's anger started to simmer and, almost against his will, his eyes went to his saber; it was just a foot away. "I didn't do anything that may be used against me unless this is some sort of sham investigation. Maybe you should stop right there, detective. You can keep what you have, but you'll need a warrant to go any further."

Loret's eyes gleamed as though this was an admission of guilt. Jack wanted to give him one in the chops just to knock that grin off his face. He barely restrained the urge. "And also you should tell me what I'm being charged with."

"I'd rather show you," Richards said. "Really, I'd like to compare these glyphs with what's at the crime scene. If they don't match, then we can clear you."

And if they do? Jack didn't ask that question, afraid of the answer.

The three of them took an uncomfortably quiet elevator ride down to street level and then took an excruciatingly silent ride in the detective's Ford Taurus out to Brooklyn. The streets were empty and grey; however, in every window that Jack glanced into he saw happy people or festive lights or the outline of a glowing Christmas tree. It was thoroughly depressing.

Finally, they pulled up at the Brooklyn Museum. There was a disquieting number of police vehicles parked out front. *What the hell?* Jack wondered. How many cops did it take to investigate a break-in?

It seemed it took nearly a dozen, including a CSI crew who was taking samples of everything and that included the artifacts that were five-thousand years old. "Jeeze," Jack whispered. Didn't they understand that they were damaging precious, irreplaceable items? He gave Loret a look that suggested that nothing was worth this much damage. Loret kept his lips tight as though he was sucking on a lemon.

Then Jack saw the glyphs. There were two sets, maroon in color, painted in concentric circles around a pair of sarcophagi. He knew these sarcophagi. The one on the left was where the mummy of a Priest of *Thorthirdes* had resided for the last thirty-five hundred years. In the other was the mummy of a vizier named *Hor*, encased in an elaborately painted cartonnage. It had been an utterly amazing piece. Now it was broken and empty like a discarded egg shell. Inside were a few rags of linen and dust.

It was a tragic waste.

Jack's depression was settling into the marrow of his bones, but then his eyes caught sight of the glyphs. Many were the very ones he had translated for Robert, but there were others among them that weren't—others that he had never seen before. He was suddenly eager to get closer.

"What are those?" he asked, heading for the yellow crime-scene tape as if it wasn't there.

Richards grabbed his wrist. "Don't go any closer," the detective said; there was a warning in his voice, backed up by the gun at his hip.

"I can go to the tape, can't I?"

Richards said he could; Jack went to the tape and leaned into it so that he could get an extra three feet closer. "What is that?" The glyphs were interesting; he could read just the closest part of the circles; however, there was something about what they had been written in that made him a little uneasy.

"That's blood," Richards replied. "Human blood."

Beyond the room was a corridor that millions of eager wannabe archeologists shuffled through every year, and in that corridor was another set of painted glyphs set in a circle, and in the middle of the circle was something that made Jack hesitate.

Richards pointed at the disfigured corpse: a man in his mid-forties who had been sliced right up the middle. The skin of his torso was flung out as if it was an open shirt. "Does he look familiar?"

"No," Jack said in a whisper. "How...How did you guys get my name? I mean, why would you guys think of me?"

Loret was quick to answer, as if he wanted Jack to be found guilty. "Robert Montgomery said that you were the only one in possession of these glyphs. That alone is illegal, by the way."

It felt as though the floor was starting to turn to sand beneath his feet. "Robert? Where is he? I...I should, uh, talk to him, maybe in private."

"I'm right here," an older man said. He spoke with a London accent in such a way as to suggest that anyone mumbling through an American accent wasn't much of a person.

The man claiming to be Robert Montgomery was in his sixties, slightly hunched and with an angry, piercing glare to his mud-colored eyes. He had been nearby the entire time; however, Jack hadn't paid him the least attention. Jack had never seen the man before in his life. This wasn't Robert Montgomery.

After a pause in which he tried to gain some sense of the world, and failed, Jack said: "You're not Robert. Robert is...is a lot younger. Black hair; kinda greasy. He's got a bit of a hooked nose. If I had to guess, he looks to be around thirty."

"He's thirty-one," the older man said. "You're describing my son, Robert the Seventh. I am Robert the Sixth. I am the financier of this exhibit."

Jack and the elder Robert locked eyes. They were related though it was hard to see beyond the sharp intellect and the demand to succeed that burned in each of them, but it was there, buried generations deep. The knowledge passed between them in a blink, as did the knowledge that Robert knew that his son was neck-deep in this murder/

break-in and for some reason that Jack didn't understand, the old man wasn't upset in the least.

The elder Robert turned and looked at the crime scene with fresh eyes. They were the eyes of a man calculating, a man scheming, a man *not* disappointed in his son.

"Can I have one second," Jack said to Detective Richards and then pulled the older man away by the arm; it was a frail arm, but Jack wasn't exactly gentle. Something ugly was happening and he had been sucked into the middle of it.

"What did Robert do?" Jack demanded in a hiss.

"He did *it*," the old man said with a grin that never touched his eyes. His eyes were dark as night. "I thought you had somehow figured it out, but it was my boy."

Jack's right hand, made strong by ten-thousand hours of fencing, closed on Robert Montgomery's arm like a vice. "Did what? What did he do?"

The grin was wider now, stretching from ear to ear. Before he answered in a whisper that only Jack could hear, he glanced at the detective, who was watching them both. "He woke the dead, Jonathan. That's what he did."

Chapter 4

Brooklyn, New York

Jack wanted to laugh. He wanted to slap the old man on the back and say: *Good one!* He wanted to pretend that he didn't just get a cold shiver up his spine.

"He woke the dead?" he asked, trying to keep his voice from rising. "Are you saying that...never mind. You are...no, both you and your son are certifiable. The dead did not rise last night, the bodies were simply stolen."

Robert Montgomery's cold grin remained unfazed. He pulled Jack towards the sarcophagus of Hor. "Look. It doesn't take a trained eye to see the signs. No one broke *into* that sarcophagus..." He left the idea unfinished so that it could fester in Jack's mind.

No one with any sense had broken into the sarcophagus, the lid of which could have been simply lifted off. Instead, it was torn open perhaps using what was either a crow bar or the back end of a hammer—both of which were terrible tools of choice.

Don't be stupid, those aren't hammer marks, those are claw marks—the idea popped into his head and another shiver struck him. He looked closer, leaning well over the tape. There was some debris scattered all around the sarcophagus and one good chunk of it was only three feet away. It was part of the sarcophagus, but not the finely painted outer portion that drew the tourists by the thousands, it was the dull brown inner aspect. There were marks on it that made no sense whatsoever. There were deep groves...scratches that appeared to have been made by the boney claws of a skeleton...

"Please stand back, Mr. Dreyden," Detective Richards warned.

Jack straightened, blinking and shaking his head, feeling stupid. "This is some sort of stunt, isn't it?" he asked Robert. "You're trying to set me up. You and your son are in on this together."

"No," Robert said in a low tone. "This is just my son's doing and he's not trying to set you up, he's trying to reclaim his birthright." The pride in his eyes was a gleam that vied with the wickedness that also lurked there.

"Birthright?" Jack exclaimed. None of this made sense to him and likely never would. "I'm done with the games, Mr. Montgomery. Detective!" Jack called, waving Richards over. "I wanted to let you know that the person I translated those glyphs for was Robert Montgomery. Not this Robert, but his son. He came to my apartment last evening and paid me five-thousand dollars for the work. I have a check back at home that will attest to this."

"Would've been nice if you had showed me that when we were there," Richards groused. "Come on, let's get this check." As they left, Robert smiled as if without a care in the world.

Christmas traffic was still amazingly light and they were able to speed across the Brooklyn Bridge and into Greenwich Village in no time, and in no time they were unlocking Jack's triple locks, and in even less time, they discovered that the five-thousand dollar check was missing.

"I'm going to need you to come back to the precinct with me," Richards said, his hands on his hips, the right one very close to his holstered pistol. "And I'm going to get a warrant to search your premises. It would look better for you if you volunteered to let me search. If you have nothing to hide, I would definitely go that route."

Jack wanted to say yes. He didn't have anything to hide that was true, but someone had been in his place. Someone had taken the check and if someone could've *taken* something that person could also have *planted* something, the murder weapon, perhaps.

"I don't know," Jack said, looking around, suddenly suspicious of his dresser—was there an *Idiot's guide to Rituals and Sacrifices* in his sock drawer? And his bathroom door—was there a pile of mummified remains in the shower? And under his bed—was there a bloody knife in among the dust bunnies? And his refrigerator—Jack's skin crawled at the thought of what could be in there.

"Can you give me a minute?" Jack asked. "I'd like to change."

Richards shook his head. "You can change, but I can't leave you alone. Whatever is here is going to be found one way or another."

"Then look, I guess," Jack said. "But…but there was a check here and that meant someone has been in here and they might have, you know, planted evidence."

"I'll take that into consideration," Richards said.

Jack didn't know what he meant by that, but his manner suggested that he believed Jack, at least about the check.

While Detective Richards went through the room, drawer by drawer and inch by inch, Jack stood clutching himself in a perfect state of terror, absolutely sure that Richards would discover something damning, but he did not. He bagged a few more of Jack's books mainly because they had to do with hieroglyphics and they had titles that were indecipherable to him, or so Jack supposed.

When he was done, Jack breathed an audible sigh of relief. "I was sure there would be something here. I mean, why go to the trouble of taking a check and not adding the coup de grace? It seems unlike Robert."

"The old man?" Richards asked. "Or his son? The only evidence I have to implicate either of them is your word and that's not going to go very far."

"Can't you take fingerprints?" Jack asked, but then remembered that Robert hadn't taken off his gloves, even when he had written the check.

Richards' hound dog look deepened. "We can and we will, but first, let's go back to the precinct and take your statement."

That was his very long Christmas day. Jack sat in a Brooklyn police station for twelve hours answering the same questions over and over as the authorities tried relentlessly to trip him up. Eventually, as he stuck to his story, they let him go.

The only evidence they had was the hieroglyphics in Jack's possession which matched those found at the crime scene which wasn't enough to bring charges. Jack was warned not to leave town without alerting Richards and then he was released to find his own way back home.

"Merry Christmas to me," Jack said as he stepped out into the cold. He couldn't imagine his Christmas getting any worse, but it did.

With the holiday schedule in effect, it took him an hour to get back to the residence hall and it was deep dark outside by the time he undid his triple locks and let himself into his apartment. His small room felt different. It felt ugly and foreign. It no longer felt even remotely safe.

Jack went around the room and inspected everything, looking for clues that would point to someone having been there. He found none which didn't make him feel the least bit better. The opposite was true. He *knew* someone had been there and that someone was very, very slick. The idea set up a nervous thrumming in his chest that never left him. He was so anxious that not only did he sleep fully clothed; he also slept with his saber in bed with him.

Footsteps at midnight woke him. The residence hall had never been quieter and so the strange *clack-scrape, clack-scrape, clack-scrape* permeated his dreams. In the span of a second, he was fully awake and listening, but to what he couldn't tell.

This wasn't Robert's fancy shoes and nor were they the thick-soled ones that Richards wore, and they definitely didn't belong to any of the semi-hippie wannabes that infested his floor with their hemp sandals.

He didn't know what was making the clack-scrape sound; he just knew that whoever was making the sound was coming for him. It was a dread certainty and he had never in his life been so scared. His heart quailed, running fast but also bounding within his chest. He found he could barely breathe and when he could, he was nearly overcome with nausea. A horrible smell was accompanying the clack-scrape noise coming up the hall.

The steps ground on, moving closer; his stomach started to heave. The smell was over-powering; it was literally a hellish smell. Nothing on earth was as horrible. It drained his strength and he couldn't resist the urge to heave up the meager dinner he had eaten the night before: hours-old pizza he had bought from a sleepy vendor in Grand Central Station.

He puked over the side of his bed in three great volleys and when he could sit up again there was a sheen of sweat across his forehead and a look of pure terror on his face.

Clack-scrape, clack-scrape, clack-scrape. It was a skeletal sound. The very thought should have sent him into hysterics; however, once he was able to catalog the sound, his mind pulled back from the brink of terror just enough for him to reach over and grab his saber. For the next few seconds, he could only sit there in bed, holding the sword with two shaking hands.

And then the *thing* was right outside his door and he did panic. He jumped out of bed and rushed to his desk where his cellphone was charging. With shaking, fumbling hands, he picked up the phone and tried to dial; however, there was sweat streaming into his eyes and his stomach wouldn't stop heaving, and when the first colossal crash struck the door, the phone fell out of his jittering hands and the screen shattered.

The door was struck again with the sound of thunder and even in his panic, he knew that his triple locks wouldn't stand up to this great of an assault. Unthinkingly, he rushed to the door and put his shoulder to it just as the third strike bent the locks in the frame and nearly sent him flying.

There was now a quarter inch gap between the door and the frame. Through it, he saw something that wasn't possible: there was something…someone dead on the other side. Someone long dead. Its skin, like brown hide, was stretched tight as a drum over its bones. The skin wasn't fully intact and where there were rents and tears, Jack could see the creature was hollow inside.

It was empty. Its innards had been pulled out eons ago and yet it was moving and it was strong.

Jack suddenly realized that the locks would give any second and that even if they didn't, the door wouldn't hold. In that moment, he also realized that he was a dead man. All he had to fight this thing, which was already dead, was his sword, his pathetic, useless sword. The blade was deadly sharp and the edge like a razor, but what good could it possibly be against something that had had all of its blood and organs removed five-thousand years before?

Closer to four-thousand years, the last part of his rational mind said, making him blink. It was an altogether useless point. It was the very definition of the word pedantic and yet Jack clung to this tiny island of rationality. From there he was able to leap frog to another actual thought: *Robert did this to me*.

Yes. The creature had come from the museum, brought back to life by...well, he didn't know how it had been done, but it was Robert for sure who had done it. "And that knowledge does me what good?" he asked as the door was struck a fourth time. Now, he was the only thing keeping the creature...the *mummy* from barging right in.

It was Hor on the other side of the door. Jack had been to the exhibit the year before when it was being advertised as: *Under the Bandages!* They had brought in a medical team to run CAT scans and X-rays on the two mummies and Jack remembered the x-ray images of Hor; the mummy had been missing a foot and the calcified ends of his tibia suggested that he had lived a long time without it.

"Hor?" Jack asked in a trembling voice.

There was a pause from the constant scraping of the bone, and there was even a dampening of the terrible odor. It was almost as if Hor, a creature *without* ears was listening. "Stop, Hor," Jack demanded. "Don't touch the door."

You are not the master, it said, though Jack did not think it actually spoke the words because again, how could it? It had no tongue or lips and no lungs, and that meant it had no breath to form words. Jack heard Hor speak in his mind with a voice like the whispering of wind over desert sand.

"I am the master," Jack said, grasping at straws. "I translated the papyrus. I am the one who was responsible for bringing you back. You should, uh, be grateful. You should be thanking..."

You are not the master. The door was struck again and Jack was sent flying back where he tumbled over his desk, scattering papers and books. He landed in a crouch and, like a child, he wanted to hide in the little foot cubby of the desk with the hope that the dead creature would just go away. He was so afraid that it boggled his mind...in fact it nearly addled his mind, so much so that he almost missed the fact that the fear was unnatural.

Hor was *making* him be afraid. It wasn't simply cause and effect that was making his heart seize in his chest—it wasn't just the fact that he was being confronted by an impossible, undead creature. Hor was doing *something* to him.

A thought rippled through his head: *It's magic*. The very idea should have made him petrified with fear. After all, the only thing worse than a creature raised from the grave sent to kill him was one that could also wield magic. That was some hardcore logic but instead of making him more afraid, as it should have, the thought centered his thinking.

"I don't believe in magic," he said, and then stood, gripping the saber and faced the obviously magical creature in front of him.

Hor, what was left of him, was five feet away on the other side of the desk. It was evil. There was no doubt about that. The evil came off of it in waves. It was in the horrible stench and in the mind-numbing fear and in the deep pits where its eyes had once been. There was a darkness in its eyes that had nothing to do with the light in the room. It was deeper than was possible in the physical universe that Jack understood.

Although he was still undecided over the concept of magic, Jack believed in evil. Hor was the embodiment of evil. It was what had drawn its ancient husk of a body together. Nothing else could have. The meat of its muscles was no longer woven and banded; it was stringy and loose. Its flesh was patched and worn, no longer holding in its innards. The wispy remains of its hair floated above it, defying gravity as did the gauzy, almost ethereal death shroud it had been buried in.

The shroud billowed around it, waving as though rippled by a wind that wasn't blowing on this plane of existence.

Jack did not have time to believe or not to believe his eyes. Hor suddenly flew at him with his hands outstretched, seeking Jack's throat with his claws. Jack reacted from years of training, slashing his saber right to left, hacking at the bones of Hor's wrist.

The razor-sharp blade struck Hor's left hand clear off and when it did, an ugly feeling zinged up the blade. It was a malignancy, coursing like electricity right up Jack's arm, settling into his teeth and tongue, leaving a taste of death there. It was as bitter as the ash that had rained down on Auschwitz.

Before he had a chance to spit it out, Hor attacked again, this time swinging his right hand at Jack's eyes, looking to tear them out.

Again, Jack reacted with trained muscles moving faster than simple pure instinct could have driven them, and again, he caught Hor at the wrist with his sword, sending that hand flying as well.

This, in no way damped Hor's desire to kill. He swung the stumps of his arms as though they were clubs. Jack retreated, keeping his feet, one in front of the other as he shuffled backwards, always managing to keep his weight centered so that he could move quickly in any direction. Hor was evil, and powerful; however his attacks were simple and easily countered.

An ulna whickered past his ear, a dust-dry radius cracked in half. Bones flew all over the apartment as he hacked left and right with his blade. When the arms were in pieces on the floor, he switched to the offense. His first attack laid open Hor's throat, the blade hacking through the remains of tendon and muscle. His second attack slashed through the vertebrae and Hor's skull bounced off the desk and clunked onto the floor where it landed with a hollow sound.

Hor stood there, headless, waving the ragged end of a single humerus around until Jack slammed Hor in the chest with his foot. It collapsed onto the desk and finally ceased moving.

Disgusted, Jack stepped back, aware for the first time that his face was twisted into a grimace, which took an act of will to unknot. He also noted that his right hand stung where the flesh met the metal of his saber's handle. Without taking his eyes off the creature, he quickly pried his hand away from the pommel and wiped it on his jeans. It only helped a little.

"Now, what the hell am I going to do?" Jack asked. His mind was coming back to "normal" and that meant he had to take into account the legal situation he found himself in. Imbued with some sort of evil or not, this was Hor; technically, he was stolen property and technically that meant Jack was in "possession" of said property.

He was sure that was a crime, just as he was sure that no one would believe that he had been attacked. "There's also destruction of property as well. I'm sure Richards will throw that in the mix as…"

Movement to his right caught his eye. It was the ulna that had flown by his head earlier. As though pulled along by a magnetic force, it slid right across the hardwood floors and, while he watched in disbelief, it jumped up to reattach itself to Hor's humerus. A second later there was more scraping as the other bones began to slide back.

A hand passed right in front of him. Jack stomped on it thinking to "kill" it, but the hand grabbed his boot with amazing strength. "Oh!" he cried, hopping around on one foot. He considered stabbing the hand, however it was in an odd position and so he raised his leg up and then crashed his foot down on the floor, sending carpel bones and phalanges dancing on the floor like dice.

They immediately began to slide back toward Hor.

"Oh…jeeze," Jack whispered, feeling suddenly weak again. The smell was back and so was the unnatural fear, and so was Hor, fully formed except for its hand. It lifted its right arm and once again bones started flying. They settled in place and were quickly held there by the remains of its flesh which acted as connective tissue, holding each bone where it belonged.

Before it could rebuild itself completely, Jack ran. It wasn't just the fear emanating from the creature, which was consuming his mind once again, it was also cowardice. There was no use pretending otherwise. Fear had its icy grip around his heart and was squeezing hard enough for his chest to throb. He had fought his best, but now there was no getting around the evidence in front of him: this was magic. He couldn't fight against magic. No one could.

He ran and the grimace was back, cork-screwing his face, twisting his laugh lines into terror-lines. Were there such a thing as terror lines? He had no idea, but he wouldn't discount the idea. Terror had him in such a grip that he was just about mindless. He was down the hall and his finger had jabbed the down button for the elevator a dozen times before he came to his senses, or what passed for senses in his panic-gripped mind.

What if the other mummy was in the elevator when the doors opened? The thought stopped his finger a quarter of an inch away from the glow of the button. The glow meant that the elevator had already been summoned. He could hear it coming. Mechanical, but also supernatural, to a mind under the grips of the fear exerted by Hor.

"Summoned," he breathed. The word was entirely magic. Robert had summoned Hor and the other mummy back from the dead…and he had set them on him. Robert had sent them to kill him. That was magic. Why had he ever questioned the concept?

Again, he fled.

He ran from an empty elevator, sprinting for the staircase and was three flights down before he stumbled, his feet going out in front of him quicker than he could work them. There was pain, in his back and his wrists as he fell. It wasn't bad enough to incapacitate him, but it was enough for him to grab his left arm as he heard a stairwell door open above him.

It was Hor, fully formed and ready to battle again.

Chapter 5

Manhattan, New York

Jack could hear the clack-scrape of Hor's bones on the stairs; it almost stopped his heart. And worse, the evil smell was back, roiling downwards, and with it came the magical mind-sapping fear. It came flowing like a fog seeking the low points in the earth to settle in.

"But I killed you," Jack said in a strangled voice. He tried to struggle to his feet but couldn't. He was too afraid to move, too afraid to make any noise, whatsoever. He wanted only to sit there, in a ball and hope that the creature wouldn't get him.

As he sat there with the bones clacking on the stairs, the whining, sniveling thought wouldn't leave him: *But, I killed you!* It was a childish thought. Childish, but also factual. Slowly, the fact burned through the unnatural haze of fear that was on him and he was able to remember that he had indeed fought Hor and he had defeated him. It had been only a minute before and yet it seemed like it had been hours since that had happened or perhaps never, as if he had dreamed all of it.

"I know I killed him," Jack said, trying to remember the courage he had felt. He couldn't. Something horrible was happening to his mind. He couldn't think through the grip of fear. He could barely remember how he had made it into the stairwell or what he'd been doing ten minutes before. All he really knew was the fear and the idea that he had to get away. And yet the fear was so great he couldn't move. He could hear Hor coming for him but he was paralyzed in fright.

He made to clutch himself and that was when the saber scraped against the concrete stairwell making a scritching sound. It was too loud!

Throwing the sword away struck him as a good idea; Hor hated the sword. Somehow, Jack knew that as a fact. It banged inside his head. *Throw it away! Throw it away!* And he wanted to, only that would make too much noise and he would be heard. There were two forces at work inside of him and both were foreign. Both competed against each other: *Don't move a muscle vs. Throw away the sword.*

He couldn't do both at once and, oddly enough the two demands partially canceled themselves out, leaving enough room in his mind for an original Jack Dreyden idea: *Run away! This is way beyond you.*

Jack had been running before—in a pure panic. Now, he ran with more of a purpose. He was still deathly afraid and the act of fleeing only added to the fear. They went hand in hand; one causing the other to ramp up until he was again racing out of control down the stairs with his heart in his throat.

But at least he was moving again and before he knew it he was outside and the cold had him. It felt like an icy wind slapped him across the face. It wasn't invigorating. The cold was similar to the running; it fed the fear. It settled into his bones and muscles. Jack found himself shaking like a little kid pulled from an iced-over pond.

They are coming.

He could feel them both. Two creatures summoned from beyond the grave. Hor was coming down the stairs and the other one, the Priest of *Thorthirdes* was on the other side of the building. He had been waiting out front, hiding in dark shadows of its own making. Jack could feel the Priest's unnatural presence. It was around the building for now, but it was coming, moving to get him.

That was a horrifying thought, but not a panic-inducing one. The magical grip on his mind was fading with every passing second. They were too far away and there was too much metal and concrete between Jack and his pursuers. He could feel them trying to control him, but it was like a weak radio signal: full of static, cutting in and out, the message garbled.

Jack knew he had to put as much distance as possible between him and the two creatures and so he ran to the street and stuck out a hand, hoping to hail a taxi. Only it was midnight and not just any midnight…this was midnight on Christmas. The streets were deserted.

Again he ran, sword in hand toward a subway station down the block. Halfway there, he faltered in mid-stride because *they* were around the building and coming for him, and he knew in his heart that they would never tire, they would never stumble or slow. They would run him down if it took three days or three years.

With his fear once again beginning to ramp up, Jack made it to the station and flew down the stairs and, for the first time in his life, he jumped the turnstile. If there had been a police officer down in the subway, that would've been just fine with him. They had guns and authority, two things that Jack desperately needed just then.

There were no cops, but there was a train just unloading its passengers. Three of them: a middle-aged couple who were bundled so tight in winter coats and scarves that only their eyes were visible, and a young man with a sleepy look and the smell of weed hanging around him.

"Don't go up there!" Jack cried, trying to pull the three back into the train. They shied away from him and he didn't blame them. He had mad eyes and he was carrying a sword. In New York it was generally a good idea never to talk to a man with a sword.

The doors closed, leaving him alone in the car. "They should be fine," he said, hope in his voice. He had no factual evidence to back the statement up; however, he felt that it was true. The mummies had been after him, alone. He was their target. Any other death would be incidental.

That was logic.

"Logic," he said, as if the idea was a relic from the past. Suddenly, he remembered that it had been logic that he had used to overcome his initial fear when he had first encountered Hor. He needed more logic and sound reasoning...and he needed to know where the hell he was going.

A glance at the map showed him that he was once again on the R, heading uptown. He didn't know anyone uptown, then again, he didn't know anyone in the village, either, not during Christmas break. Jack had all of six friends who were actually closer to acquaintances, and they had all fled to warmer climates until the new semester started. This left him in some very sorry straights. He had not only left his coat, wallet and his keys back at his apartment, but also the scabbard for his sword.

"I must look insane," he said, glancing down at his saber.

Looking insane was a bad thing, but not the worst thing. He was penniless in a city that scoffed at those without money, and he was friendless in a city that ground the lonely under its heel.

He had no idea what to do. One option was to ride the subway all night. With his sword, he'd likely be taken for a madman, which had one benefit: "At least I'll get my own car." Right up until the cops came and hauled him in that is. Now that he was no longer being chased, the police were the last people he needed to see.

For the tenth time that day, he whispered: "Merry Christmas to me," and yes, he was feeling sorry for himself. Attacked by a monster, arrested by the police, no friends, no real home, no family... "No family?" That wasn't entirely true. With a sudden eagerness, he jumped up to study the map of New York's subway system.

It would take a transfer in which he could run into a cop, but there was a train that ran just two blocks shy of the Waldorf Astoria where his cousin Rebecca Childs and her daughter Cyn were staying. "They're family, they have to take me in," he said as he stared into a window and caught his reflection. "Oh, boy."

The glass displayed a disheveled, crazy-man with a sword. He patted his hair down and tucked in his shirt, but he kept hold of his sword. There was no way he was going to part with it.

Holding the sword pressed against his body to keep it hidden, Jack made his transfer, rode the next train a few miles and was soon back out in the night and the cold. Regardless of the frigid temperatures, he paused at the top of the stairs leading out of the subway and not only stared all around him, he also tried to feel all around him. He knew now the ugly evil that emanated from Hor and the Priest of *Thorthirdes* and he knew the smell and the fear.

He felt nothing except the cold and smelled nothing but that peculiar New York City odor; the mixture of old trash, dirty bums, pretzel carts and alley walls stained with urine. For the first time since coming to the city, Jack was almost glad for the smell.

"Speaking of smells," he said and then gave himself a sniff. He seemed to smell normal, but his sword, on the other hand, stank of Hor and the blade was blackened and ugly. Jack jogged to the side of 3rd Avenue where there was a drift of grey snow. He kicked away the sooty top layer and found dazzling white beneath. After cleaning the blade with the fresh snow, his hands were purple with the cold and his nipples were stabbing almost through the thin, khaki shirt he was wearing.

Jack ran to the Waldorf with only the wind chasing him. As he came up on the building, the doorman looked as though he was on the verge of locking the door on him; he had seen the sword.

"I-I w-was mugged," Jack told him, his teeth chattering. "They t-took my wallet and c-coat, but I was able t-to grab my f-fencing sword and r-run." He made sure to hold the sword by the lower part of the blade near the hilt so not to appear as threatening.

"You want me to call the cops?" the doorman asked, leaning away from Jack, still wary of the sword, regardless of how it was held—this was New York after all.

"N-No thank you. I need to talk to one of your g-guests. Her name is Cindy Childs. Y-You c-can hold onto my sword if it makes you feel better." Jack held it out and once the doorman took it, he was allowed into the hotel though he was eyed suspiciously by both the doorman and the lone front desk clerk who stood behind a sixty-foot long marble counter.

The clerk went through his guest list and his strained, somewhat polite smile became even more strained and less polite as he said: "We have a Cynthia Childs."

"She goes by Cyn...we're not that closely related."

The smile had soured into a look of professional un-pleasantness. "I'm sure," he said, with a glance over at the doorman, who held the saber as if he was holding a rabid muskrat. Cyn was thankfully still awake and eagerly invited Jack up to her room.

The clerk accompanied Jack up; however, because of the hotel's weapon's policy, his sword had to be 'checked' as though it were baggage. "Just a precaution," the clerk remarked. Jack said he understood, but felt absolutely naked without it.

Although Cyn's room was on the thirty-eighth floor in the very posh: *Waldorf Towers*, the ride up was so quick that Jack hadn't thought of a thing to say to her. "Merry Christmas," was all he could come up with when she opened the door. It was an uncomfortable moment.

Jack stood in a hunch, holding himself, hoping that his shivering wasn't obvious. Cyn, who wore faded jeans and a tee-shirt, stared at Jack, clearly noting that his outfit did not make sense, not for the time of night and not the season. "Jack, hi. Are you staying in the hotel?" Cyn asked in her lilting English accent.

A shake of his head was all Jack could answer before the clerk spoke: "No, he is not a guest, Ms. Childs, which is why we were a little anxious about letting him come up unescorted. The sword he was carrying didn't help, either."

Cyn actually stepped back. "A sword? Is it for an ex-hibit?"

"No, not exactly," Jack said, and then changed his answer. "Not at all, actually. It's my fencing saber. I was at practice earlier and on the way home I was mugged. They took everything. My wallet, keys, even my coat."

"But left your saber?" Cyn asked. Jack's head wobbled in a manner that could have been a yes, no, or maybe. Her blue eyes narrowed at the lack of answer and Jack expected her to turn him away, but she did not. She opened the door wider, inviting him in. "I understand," she said and then thanked the clerk before shutting the door in his face.

The room, or rather the suite, was fabulous. Posh did not cover it. Everything was scandalously expensive and plush and gilt with gold trimmings. Apart from the foyer there was a sitting room with antique chairs and a French styles chaise, a wet bar, and a TV the size of Jack's front door. Jack went straight for the bar.

"I'll pay you back," he said, unscrewing a tiny bottle of Belvedere vodka with shaking hands and drinking right from the lip.

"Those muggers must have been in the Christmas spirit to leave you a sword," Cyn remarked. Jack nearly choked on the vodka and used his spluttering as an excuse not to answer. "And they must have been crazy going after a swordsman of your size. You could have cut them to ribbons." More coughing was all Jack had as a retort. "And what sort gym offers fencing classes at midnight on Christmas night?"

Instead of answering, Jack finished off the vodka and dug through the bar for an adequate chaser.

"Ok, maybe I wasn't at class tonight," he admitted. "But the clerk and the door-guy were being far too nosy."

Cyn was like a dog with a bone. "Oh, I doubt they were. They probably weren't being nosy enough. Who walks around New York in ten-degree weather, in nothing but a short-sleeved shirt and carrying only a sword, and offering nothing but the most obvious lies as an excuse?"

She's going to kick me out of here in five minutes, if I'm not careful, Jack thought. "I'm sorry about the lies, but there's a lot going on. I think some of it is illegal. I don't know which parts or how I got involved, but I am and I didn't want to get you in trouble."

"So Detective Richards tells me," Cyn said, which had Jack spluttering again, this time for real. Cyn seemed to enjoy it. She wore her devilish smirk as she went on: "Yes, the police have been all over the place asking about you. There's a rumor running around that you have the key to a previously unknown Poly Heiro-Sumerian script."

When Jack could breathe, he asked: "What are the police asking about?"

She was no one's fool. "First tell me about the script."

"It's trouble," he said after a long pause. "It may have been what got my parents killed and my grandfather, too for all I know." And my great-grandfather, he could've added, but didn't. "My father left it for my mother when he died. It was a scroll; an ancient papyrus. If I had to guess by the writing, I'd say it's first dynasty at the least."

Again her intelligent eyes narrowed, taking in his ragged jeans and his tired hand-me-down boots. "It would be worth a small fortune. Why didn't you sell it?"

Jack shrugged. "I doubt it was worth all that much. It's not a long piece, only three-hundred and seventy characters, about ten lines all together. And yes, I know it's worth something, but my dad left a note with it asking to keep it safe and hidden."

"Do you think it was stolen from someone else's dig?" Cyn asked.

"That's what I used to think," Jack answered. It was what made most sense. Throughout history the question as to who actually owns the items excavated from archeological sites had always been ambiguous. Generally, the host country owns the items but allows the financial backers of the discovering team initial access in order to defray the cost of the dig.

It was a good guess that a man in possession of an artifact like the papyrus hadn't come by it legally. Jack knew that he should have turned it over long ago. When he first discovered it at seventeen he hadn't realized the repercussions of owning such an item. At twenty-one when he could no longer claim ignorance of the law, he was caught up in the intrigue of deciphering it.

After all, there had been the cryptic message that his father left—his mind had swarmed with the idea that the text was a clue to an even greater treasure. By the time he was twenty-two and had, with great disappointment, discovered it to be just another funeral text, he was already in the master's program at NYU and if it was discovered that he'd been in possession of a looted item, where would that put him?

Out on his ass, likely.

But, there was more to the text than met the eye. Clearly, it had never been completely secret and what was even more clear was the fact that what was written on it was far more dangerous than just a run of the mill funeral text.

"Used to think?" Cyn asked. "What do you think now?"

"I don't know. Maybe it was..." He paused, wondering how much he wanted to say. What he had seen and felt wasn't possible and he was sure that any explanation would only make him look crazy...or crazier, if that was possible. Cyn's question came back to him: *Who walks around New York in ten-degree weather, in nothing but a short-sleeved shirt and carrying only a sword?*

"I guess I just don't know what to think," Jack answered. Her brows went up. "Really, I don't so don't look at me like that. It was just a funeral text. That's all." Her nose wrinkled as if she had smelled something unpleasant and he shrugged. "Yeah, likely part of a longer text."

At the Brooklyn Museum there had been other glyphs, six others to be precise, intermingled with the twenty-eight glyph alphabet that made up the cross-bred language that had been on the papyrus. Two of the glyphs were apt to be uncommon characters—the equivalent of Q or X in English. The four others were almost certainly names. All of this suggested that there existed more of the strange writing.

Cyn was quiet, thinking. Jack interrupted: "So, the police? What did they want? What did they ask you?"

"They wanted to know about you and our good cousin, Robert. They wanted to know if you two had ever worked together. I told them that I didn't know. They also asked about the glyphs found at the crime scene. They wanted to know if anyone could decipher them, but no one could. That was about it."

"Good," Jack said, feeling somewhat relieved. He'd been afraid that she was going to mention magic or creatures of the night. He shivered at the thought and then went to the window and stared out.

Behind him, Cyn clucked her tongue in annoyance. "It's not good. It's never good for the police to come interview all of your prospective employers. How do you expect to show your face at the new exhibit tomorrow?"

"The what? Oh, yeah, the new *Desert King* display." Along with his invitation to the Christmas Party, he had been invited to the unveiling of a new exhibit at the Metropolitan Museum of Art. The entire tomb of the "*Double Falcon*" had been lifted piece by piece out of Egypt and brought to the museum.

It wasn't a large tomb by any stretch; however it was an important one. By definition, *Double Falcon,* as he was called because of the two facing falcons that made up his *serekh*—an early form of a heraldic crest, was the very first person in history. No name predates his, making everyone who lived before him, in essence, prehistoric.

"I haven't really given it much thought," Jack said. "I had planned on it but, now? I don't know." Actually, he did know. He decided on the spot that he wasn't going anywhere near where there was a mummy, not until he had answers and witnesses and a gun.

"What?" Cyn demanded. "You have to go. This is *our* history. This is one of the tombs our great-great grandfather discovered." Jack gave her a blank look that she read accurately. "Our great-great grandfather was Robert Montgomery, the Earl of Blackburn. He was very famous in his time."

Jack remembered the name Lord Blackburn, a very well-known financier of archeological digs. He had no idea that his real name was Robert Montgomery. "So, our cousin Robert is his direct descendent? That must mean he's royalty of sorts...are you royalty, too?"

She laughed. "No and neither is Robert. Our great-great grandfather was a *life peer*, meaning he had a title, but it wasn't hereditary. I know Robert wishes it had been a traditional peerage and yes, he'd be the heir. Earl Blackburn had three children and each had but a single child and so on until there's just you, me and Robert. Strange, I'd say."

It was more than strange to Jack. "With everything that's happened, I don't know if I can go. I don't mean to intrude, but do you mind if I crash here? On the couch, I mean."

Another laugh escaped her; this one derisive. "There is no possible way I'd let you stay here."

Chapter 6

Jack's mouth came open in disbelief. "What happened to all that talk about family?"

Cyn shrugged and then turned her back on him, going to one of the high-backed antique chairs. Next to it on an end table was a phone; she picked it up and held a finger over one of the buttons. "I do believe in family, but I also believe in protecting myself. You haven't really told me anything, but even a blind person can see that you are mixed up with something dangerous. For example, the police asked more than once about ritualistic sacrifices. It's a good guess that somebody died, didn't they?"

"Yeah," Jack answered. "I don't know who it was. He was cut wide open and the glyphs were written in his blood, but I didn't do it. You have to believe me."

"Actually, I don't," she said, her finger edging closer to the buttons. "I can call the police with one move. I don't want to, but I will. Now, tell me everything...all of it or get out."

Jack saw that for a woman who was barely out of her teens, she had a spine of steel. She would kick him out into the cold if she had to—and she probably would once she heard his tale. Again, he turned to the window. The city, even on Christmas was bright and wonderful...and deadly cold. He had nowhere to go. There were homeless shelters scattered about the city, but where they were located, he had no idea. It wasn't a good choice either way. He'd heard that they were dangerous places and, perhaps worse, they filled up fast when the temperature dropped so low.

His only other option was to chance riding the subways for the rest of the night, but what would he do once morning came? Where would he go? He grimaced and caught the ghost of his reflection in the window; he was truly pathetic looking. "Fine," he said.

For the next twenty minutes, he told her everything: from the moment he had seen the papyrus right up until he fled his building. She didn't interrupt once, but the second he was done speaking she pressed a button on the phone. The simple jab of her finger was like being stabbed in the back.

It wasn't the cops who she called. "Good evening," she said into the phone. "I had a guest visit me earlier this evening…yes, the one with the sword, and speaking of which, I need it brought up to my room. Of course, I understand about hotel policy and in most cases it would be a wise policy, however the sword in question has some significance to it. I need to examine it. No, no sir, I'm not in danger. In fact, it would please me for you to accompany the weapon into my room, personally."

She hung up and then stared evenly at Jack. "Before you ask, I don't know what to believe. You rattled off that story so quickly that it's obvious that you believe what you said. The goosebumps on your arms attest to that." He started to relax and then she added: "Of course you could be insane, there is that."

He noted that her hand had not come off the phone; she could still dial the police in a quarter of a second. The hand remained there until a knock sounded on the door. She backed to it, keeping her blue eyes full on Jack. He hadn't budged.

The front desk clerk, officious as always, came in holding the saber by the blade; he wore gloves. When he handed it to Cyn, he didn't make a move to leave, but only stood there, eyeing Jack coldly as Cyn inspected the sword. From an outside point of view, the two of them were being foolish. The clerk was just that, a clerk. His authority rested in his rather meager rank. He was pudgy about the middle and had a soft face with just the beginning of a double chin, while Cyn was stylishly thin—Jack had more strength in his right arm than she did in her entire body.

But Jack wasn't a killer and he was only dangerous when threatened. He stood, meekly, trying his best to look like an innocent bystander who had been pulled into something terrible.

Cyn held the saber gingerly with a frown creasing her otherwise smooth face. "Do you smell that?" she asked the clerk, holding up the sword. He gave it a sniff and the lingering odor was enough to make his left eye jitter in an involuntary quadruple wink. With a cough, he pulled back.

"That is disgusting," he declared. "What the hell did you rub that in?" Jack remained quiet. There was no adequate answer that he could give—the smell was literally unearthly and just thinking about the source caused a fresh crop of goosebumps to break out on his arms.

"And the edge is blackened," Cyn said, turning the saber to the light. "That's not possible." It was possible... possible just not believable. Cyn put the sword down on one of the end tables, glanced once at her palm before wiping it on her jeans, her face squirming with disgust. For a long sweep of the clock, the room was quiet.

Jack said nothing, hoping that she was well on her way to believing that which could not be believed. The clerk stood there in the uncomfortable silence with his face marred by a lingering disgust over the smell and confusion over the entire situation, which had to be unique. The confusion spiked when Cyn suddenly ordered: "Take off your boots."

"My boots?" Jack asked. The demand, though unexpected was not onerous, especially since he had been fully expecting her to point at the door and order him out. He pulled his boots off and offered them to her. She didn't take them.

"Let me see the treads," she said. Again, a strange demand, but he acquiesced and flipped them over. On the bottom of the right one was a discoloration. She gave it a sniff and her fair skin went a shade green. The clerk gave it a sniff and shivered. That seemed to be the clincher for his cousin.

"Ok," she said to the clerk. "I believe that will be all." He'd been dismissed; he glanced once at the sword, perhaps thinking that due to the hotel's policy he should take it back, but Cyn had an imperious, regal air that was hard not to knuckle under to. He left and again there was a silence between them until she said: "I believe you."

She sounded reluctant to admit it. Jack was just as reluctant to nod in reply.

"What were they?" she asked, suddenly looking her age, suddenly looking vulnerable; the regality gone. "Ghouls? I mean, I suppose I know they were mummies, but living ones? How…or why? Or…" She broke off, shaking her head.

"I don't have a clue why," he answered. But was that true? He had experienced the magic surrounding Hor first hand. As a scientist that was empirical evidence of the existence of said magic i.e. a power that was superhuman…a power that some people craved. His cousin Robert Montgomery seemed like the kind of man who would crave that sort of power.

"I think someone is after power," Jack said. "Magical power, I guess."

She laughed without any sort of happiness or mirth behind it. "Power? Oh, my Lord. Maybe, this isn't real. Maybe you are crazy. That makes much more sense and it's much easier to believe, but...but the sword suggests otherwise." She went to the saber and picked it up. "You can feel it," she said in awe. "You can feel something very bad about this sword. It's like it's been dipped in something…something evil." Her shoulders twitched as she put the sword down and for a second time she wiped her hands on her jeans.

"I'm having trouble believing it, too and I lived through it." He walked over to the saber and put his hand just over it. There was an ugly feel coming off the blade that reminded Jack of the powerful fear that he'd been feeling. Stepping back, he found that he was grinning and didn't know why; it made him feel as though he was just on the edge of raving, as if the tight grin was holding back a much worse lunacy.

Cyn gave another shudder and said: "Maybe a good night's sleep will...I don't know, make everything a little more sane." This moment of wishful thinking on her part was followed by a long silence between the two.

Finally, Jack said: "I should go somewhere else." This was his problem, his very crazy problem, and there was no need to dunk Cyn in the black depths of it. "If you could lend me like, fifty dollars, I'll get a room or something. I'll pay you back, I promise."

Her chin started going up and down just the tiniest bit as though a big part of her, a part suppressed wanted to agree that it was indeed best if he left and never looked back. However, she said: "No. That wouldn't be right. Either you're crazy and thus in need of looking after, or you're telling the truth and..."

"And you should stay far away from me," he filled in. "Really, either way, crazy or truth, it would be best if you kept far away from me." He began to struggle his boots back on his feet when she stopped him.

"No, we're family. It's a thin bond, but it's a bond of blood and distance won't break it. There's something bad happening, something that is very likely greater than what we know. If Robert has somehow brought these creatures back to life...my Lord, it's crazy even thinking it, but if he has done something, then we may be the only ones who can stop him."

Jack's hands were in the midst of struggling with his knotted laces; they froze as he asked: "How is that?"

Cyn pointed to the sword as though it was Exhibit A. "First off, we're the only ones who have a clue that something supernatural is occurring. By the time the authorities figure it out, it'll be too late." Jack shrugged, suggesting the logic was weak, but not actually incorrect. She went on: "Secondly, you've already fought the mummies. Yes, they seem to be invulnerable; however, you know things that no one else does. A strong logical mind can overcome the fear and the smell, and will allow a person to defend themselves."

"Defend themselves for a time," Jack acknowledged. "But not forever."

She began pacing, acting as though she didn't hear his negativity. "And third: we know who's behind this and we're not hampered by the rule of law as the police are. We can do *something* about this."

Jack's eyes went to squints at the word: *something.* "Ok, now it's my turn to get a little nervous. You are jumping into this a little too quickly, don't you think? If someone had come to me with this story a week ago I would have laughed him right out of my room."

"I doubt that," she answered. "The sword alone suggests something unnatural occurred. And your boot and..." She broke off so suddenly that Jack felt that his suspicions were vindicated.

"And what? You know something, don't you? You know more about what's going on than you are telling me."

She nodded reluctantly. "Your papyrus was not one of a kind. My mother received one from her mother. It had the same cryptic message attached. When I turned twenty, my mother showed it to me. I was excited just as you were. I figured it had to be directions to another tomb, or to a treasure, or a lost city of gold."

Jack grinned, remembering how he had thought the same thing and how it had filled him with excitement—right up until he deciphered them. "I was pretty crushed when my papyrus turned out to be only funeral texts. What did yours say?"

Cyn shrugged. "We never deciphered them. I guess I shouldn't say we; I never tried. I'm only now mastering hieroglyphics and I haven't even started on Sumerian cuneiform."

"But your mom should've been able to; there was a primer with your text, right?"

"Sort of one," she answered. "The warning was written on a separate piece of paper. It was written in English and then right after it were more of the glyphs, but no one has yet been able to make heads or tails of it."

A warning bell went off in Jack's head. "No one? Who else has seen it? Did Robert? He did, didn't he? Son of a bitch!"

"No, it wasn't Robert; he's not an accredited Egyptologist. He's too lazy, or at least I thought he was. My mum showed it to Robert's father. He, at least, has a doctorate, but still couldn't decipher it. How did you do it?"

Jack was slow to answer. Cyn was family, in a very, very distant way, and she was going to let him stay the night on her couch, but he felt he had already broken his father's wishes to his great detriment. "I, uh, guess by plugging in the glyphs over and over again until they began to make sense." That's how he had started, at least; it hadn't worked.

"Hmmm," Cyn said, her eyes crinkling at the corners. "You don't trust me? I guess that's good in a way. A little too late, but good." She checked her watch and Jack checked his right after. "It's late," she declared. "You may sleep on the couch. I will be in the bedroom and, I'm sure you understand, I will be keeping the sword with me. Trust, you know, has to be earned."

"Good night," he said as she shut and locked her door. He didn't blame her. Had he been an accomplished liar, she'd be at his mercy. "But what if she's the liar?" he whispered after the lights were down. "What if she is trying to get information out of me?" He laughed and said: "Then she's doing an excellent job."

He had told her everything except for the location of his papyrus and the key to the primer—the now useless primer at least as far as Robert was concerned. His cousin had an entire three-hundred and seventy character text spelled out for him; Robert could translate anything now, including Cyn's papyrus.

"I need to see that text," he said, getting up. He tapped on the door. "Cyn, I need to see the papyrus you were given. It may tell us what Robert is going to do next."

"Ok, I'll just pull a five-thousand year old scroll out of my bum. I don't have the scroll here. It's back home. My mum might have a copy on her lap top, but I don't know if I want to get her involved, especially at midnight on Christmas. I know her; she'll find it without precedent and dismiss our fears out of hand."

Jack felt the pull of urgency. *Something* was going to happen; maybe it was even happening right at that moment. The idea wouldn't leave him, making sleep hard to come by. He tossed and turned on the couch and at two in the morning when the scream of a siren drifted up thirty-eight stories, he went to the window and saw the splash of red and blue lights heading north on 5th Avenue.

The Metropolitan Museum of Art was to the north.

And so too was Harlem and the Bronx and three million people. It was farfetched to think that the police lights were related to him in any way and yet he watched them until the intervening buildings hid them from view. Jack fell asleep sometime an hour later and dreamed of Robert squatting in the dark. He was hunched over a naked man who was tied spread eagle; the flesh of his abdomen was spit wide open, however, his organs hadn't been *much* damaged.

His skin had been slit using a scalpel and a delicate touch—fresh, hot blood was what the spell called for. The man was a living inkwell. At first, Robert used the finest brushes dipped in the blood that pooled on top. Later, he dug the brushes in deep as if the blood on top was no longer any good.

The man, the night guard at the Metropolitan Museum of Art, screamed his mind inside and out—no one could hear him. His partner was long dead, torn limb from limb. The museum was empty of the living all save for Robert. He didn't consider the guard as one of the living, not when there was so little time left for him.

Jack woke in a sweat, his heart like a hammer, one that was trying to pound its way out of his chest. He found himself on his feet beside the couch and couldn't remember if he had leapt up or had been dreaming while sleep-walking. His mind echoed with a scream and he didn't know if it had been his own scream or the guard's.

"There was no scream," he told himself. He knew he was a liar.

In spite of the scream still reverberating in his mind and the horrifyingly vivid dream and the anxiety that was eating him up, Jack fell straight back to sleep. He was exhausted in a way he had never felt before; it was as though his soul had exerted itself in some strange Olympic style event. He was internally tired.

Chapter 7

Manhattan, New York

For the second day in a row, Jack slept in, although this time it wasn't footsteps in the hall that woke him, it was Cyn running around the suite.

"We're late!" she cried. "I slept in. I forgot to set the alarm and my mum is heading over. You have to hide."

Jack was still blinking and bleary. The truth was he didn't know where he was and he barely knew Cyn. She was scurrying around with his sword in one hand and his faded boots in the other, but what mostly caught his eye was the fact that she was wearing an extremely short pair of pajamas.

She's your cousin, he reminded himself. A second voice in his head added chirped up: *She's your very, very distant cousin*. That was also the truth. Still, he averted his gaze as she hustled him into her bedroom, just as a knock sounded on the door.

"Just a moment!" she yelled. She then turned to Jack with a hard look of warning in her eye. "Don't say a word. Cousin or not my mum might just bloody well gut you if she finds you here."

"Sure," he whispered. She shut the door on him and he tiptoed into the bathroom to stand in the tub with the curtain drawn, just in case.

He could hear a mumbly sort of conversation coming through the two walls but what was being said, he didn't know. What he did know was that the sword hadn't lost any of the evil smell on it. His nose wrinkled at its proximity.

There was the sound of a door shutting and then moments later; Cyn was in her bedroom calling out: "Jack? Where are you?"

"In here," he answered and then, once he had stepped out of the tub, turned on the water, going for maximum heat. "What did she say about your text? Does she have it on her?"

Cyn came to stand in the bathroom doorway looking puzzled at Jack's position. "What are you doing?"

He was kneeling over the tub, feeling the water as it steamed out of the faucet. He wanted the temperature to be just this side of scalding. "Washing the sword. I hate the smell."

She stopped him. "Don't. It's one of our few clues as to Robert's criminality. Without it we have a stinky boot and your word. So stop. And about the text, she says she has it on her laptop, and she's going to bring it with her to the exhibit and confront Robert the Sixth with the evidence that she thinks points to his culpability."

Jack glanced down at the blackened blade. He hated that it had such an evil feel; it had saved his life and deserved to shine once again. "I probably should go with you, then. If I don't, Robert will just shift blame in my direction and try to duck out of his role and who knows what that really is."

Cyn checked her watch. "We have an hour and a half. Please tell me you have something to wear besides these *Indiana Jones* rejects, such as a suit and tie?"

"I do," he said, irritably after a glance at himself in the mirror. He didn't think his clothes were so bad. Weren't faded jeans, in? And since when did Indiana Jones wear jeans? He didn't. The old boots and the khaki shirt might have had a little *Indy* inspiration, but certainly not the jeans. That was just silly. "What are you going to wear? A princess gown?"

Her lips practically disappeared at this and her blue eyes were like very sharp and very angry diamonds...the look lasted for only a few seconds and then she pouted. "I don't know. I had a slinky black number picked out, but my mum was in a pantsuit and if we run into Robert, you know, Robert the Seventh, then I don't know if I want to be in heels."

She stared into her closet, until he unhelpfully noted: "It's also cold out." She pushed him out of her room.

"Just trying to help," he said to himself as he went to the window where far below the New York traffic was back in full swing, the cars looking like beetles as they crawled through the streets. He stared for just a brief second before his mind turned to his dream and from there it leapt to the police car that he'd seen the night before. "They had nothing to do with each other," he said. "And really nothing to do with me. The dream was meaningless." He did not believe in dream interpretation, nor did he believe in clairvoyance or pre-cognition or dream-catchers or Big Foot or any of that hokum.

"I also didn't believe five-thousand year old mummies could come alive and kill people." That was too true to be argued with.

In his gut he believed the dream. Thinking about it left him with a nervous trill that made his stomach flutter. He was anxious to get going and at the same time, he didn't want to leave the safety of the hotel; he liked the idea of hundreds of people between him and the mummies.

"I am being such a chicken," he whispered, turning from the window and catching sight of his sword. Despite the smell and the evil emanating from it, he was glad to have it. "But I can't be walking around with it." He called the front desk to see if they had a cardboard tube or a long umbrella that he could borrow and was surprised to find out that the Waldorf had an entire shipping department available to their guests and in minutes, something was sent up.

Even though he knew someone was coming to the room, he still hesitated when a soft knock came at the door. Cyn poked her face out from the bedroom; her eyes were wide.

"It's ok," Jack told her. "I called downstairs for something to hide the sword in." He tried to sound confident; however, he was cautious as he opened the door. It was a young man in a maroon vest holding out a shipping tube. He gave Jack an odd look as he slid the sword in it. "Thanks, it's a perfect fit," Jack told him.

Then there was an even odder moment when the young man stood there with an air of expectation. It stretched out uncomfortably before Jack snapped his fingers. "A tip, yes, I forgot. I don't actually have any money, but I promise to get back with..."

"Oh, please, Jack, you're being ridiculous," Cyn said. "Give him this." In her hand was a five-dollar bill. It was a strange feeling taking it from her. It reminded him of when he had been a kid and his mom would give him money for the ice cream truck. "Thanks," he said before handing the money to the young man.

"It's nothing. Now, if you don't mind, shut the door." She kept shifting her gaze to the hallway.

"Yeah, sure. You ok? Are you nervous?"

"Maybe just a little. Now that the sun is up, I find the idea of mummies coming to life extremely far-fetched. I have to say that I am embarrassed for having entertained the idea and yet, I feel..." She rubbed her stomach as though she was becoming nauseous.

Jack was right there with her. "I lived through it and I'm still having trouble telling myself it was real." He tried a confident grin and changed the subject. "What happened to your choice of shoes? I thought you weren't going with heels."

She had on a simple white, button up shirt and black slacks that clung to her slim figure a little too nicely. On her feet were a pair of four-inch high stilettos. "Well, I just figured that *I* shouldn't be in any danger. If something happens, it'll likely happen to you. Besides, aren't these shoes cute?"

Her logic was spot on; he was the only link between the break-in at the Brooklyn Museum and Robert the Seventh. "Yeah, they're great," he growled. It was logical that his life was in danger but that didn't mean he liked it. "Almost ready?"

She was made up and bundled in a heavy, knee-length coat seven minutes later. They called down for a cab and one was waiting for them when they passed through the grand front entrance of the Waldorf. The cold was biting and the wind carried an icy edge that seemed to slice right to the bone. Even the short distance to the cab was nearly enough to send Jack into shock, but he refused to let it show—for some reason he didn't like the idea of appearing weak in front of Cyn, who looked even prettier in the bright light of day with her blonde hair spilling onto her shoulders and the color high in her cheeks.

He knew he was a little too aware of her beauty and once again he had to remind himself that she was his cousin.

Besides, his life was in danger. He needed to focus his attention outwards. During the cab ride to his apartment, Jack tried to feel for the presence of Hor or the Priest of *Thorthirdes*. Nothing came to him. He also tried to remain hyper-vigilant. Casually, he threw an arm across the back of the seat and looked back to see if they were being followed.

When he turned once more to the front, he saw that Cyn had a pale gold eyebrow raised. "What are you doing?" she asked; her eye flicked to his arm that was just above her shoulders.

The truth that he was *making sure they weren't being tailed* seemed more than a touch melodramatic; in fact, it seemed like something a teenaged douchebag might say. "Just stretching," he said. Too late, he realized that sounded like a lame excuse to get close to her.

"Would you mind stretching in another direction?"

"Sure."

Embarrassed, he stared out the window until they pulled up to the residence hall. As she paid, he stepped out and gazed all around him, again trying to 'feel' the presence of the undead creatures. It was there, but fading into the background of the city. Life was washing the ugly feeling away.

"Do you feel that?" he asked Cyn when she came to stand next to him with the city rising all around them, grey but not lifeless. For the most part, people were still in holiday mode and although the streets weren't nearly teeming at full capacity there were still a few hardy souls scurrying by.

She pulled her coat tighter against her shoulders. "The cold? Of course I do."

The cold wasn't registering on Jack's senses; he was too focused. "No, not the cold. Remember the feeling coming off the sword? It's here, but it's weak and getting weaker."

Cyn was quiet for a time and her eyes lost their focus. She then shrugged. "I don't feel it. Come on, let's get inside before you freeze to death."

They entered the building, both of them quiet, gazing all around. Cyn was nervous; Jack less so. The fading presence was sharper inside, but it wasn't nearly as strong as it had been the night before.

In the elevator it faded to practically nothing; however, once on the seventh floor, it came back strong enough to set Jack's nerves on edge. "Tell me you feel it now," he said.

"A little, but it's not very strong."

"What about the smell?"

The smell seemed particularly heavy to him, but Cyn only made a face. "For the most part I smell old marijuana...like rancid bong water. Ugh! Isn't it illegal in the States?"

"Apparently not in college housing." The smell of the stale weed was indeed unpleasant and it mixed with the stench of Hor to create something bizarre and mean to the senses.

Slowly they went down the hall until they were just a few feet shy of his apartment door. It sat partially open, the sprung locks visible. There were heavy dents in the door and the paint was scratched and grooved in places. The evil feeling was particularly strong on the door.

"This backs up your story," she said, pointing at the locks and the door. She made to open the door, but he stopped her.

"Let me," he whispered. "I don't think those creatures are near, but that doesn't mean Robert isn't." She took a step back and he swung the door open, making sure he stood off to one side.

There was someone in his apartment. He was just a dim figure leaning against the wall facing the door. Jack flinched and was just starting to fumble for the sword tucked away in the tube when he saw that the figure was larger than Robert and seemed to be far more rumpled than he had ever seen his dapper cousin.

"Detective Richards?" Jack asked. "What-what are you doing here?"

The detective stepped forward and he was indeed very rumpled, as though he had slept in his clothes, if he had actually slept. His eyes were bloodshot and his hound dog face drooped even more than ever.

"I came to talk to you and saw that your door had been smashed in. Legally, I'm allowed to be in here, probable cause, you know. Care to tell me what happened? It looks like there was quite a struggle."

Jack's chair was tumbled, his lamp was broken and papers and books were strewn everywhere.

Since the truth would mean a quick trip to an insane asylum, he had to come up with a lie. Strange ideas started jumping into his mind, but all that came out of his mouth were a collection of vowels and random words: "I-I, uh, I...I m-mean we, m-me an-and, uh..."

He might have gone on in that monosyllabic mumble until he was arrested for obstruction of justice, but Cyn came into the apartment then.

"What Jack meant to say is that he was attacked last night by a large man." She seemed perfectly reasonable and so Jack, who was never very good at lying, started shaking his head, vigorously, as if he had never heard anything more true. She went on: "They tussled until Jack grabbed his sword and ran out of here."

"Ms Childs," Richards intoned. "How interesting that you should show up here. Interesting, but not exactly helpful. Now, I would love to hear your version of events, but first I need to hear from Jack. You were attacked? Do you know by who?"

It was more of a what—he couldn't say that. "No, sir. It was dark and all I know was that he was big and dressed in, uh, like black clothes."

"Like a ninja?" Richards asked.

"A ninja?" Jack didn't know if the detective was being serious or if he knew that Jack was lying and was just messing with his head. "No—no it wasn't a ninja. I didn't know who it was. But he smashed in the door..."

Richards held up a hand. "At what time?"

"Around midnight, I guess. He just bashed in the door and charged in and we sort of wrestled like Cyn said. And then I grabbed my sword and ran."

The detective leveled a look of skeptical puzzlement at Jack before asking: "You had a sword, yet you were the one who ran? That seems very backwards to me."

It seemed very backwards to Jack as well. It felt as though he had painted himself into a corner until Cyn remarked: "Remember you said that you thought he was reaching for a gun?"

Again Jack began an eager nodding. "Right, right. He reached into his coat and I just ran. And...and I didn't have anywhere to go. All my friends are out of town and so I went to see Cyn."

"Did you consider calling the police?" Richards asked. "It's kind of our job to deal with this sort of thing." Jack started to stutter into another poor lie, but the detective waved it away. "Maybe you should get your lies straightened out before you go any further."

Cyn strode into the room, her face set in hard lines. "Listen, officer, it's not illegal to have your flat broken into or to be attacked. He came to my place and was very distraught. I let him stay the night on the couch and now we're here. There's not much more to the story. Now, if you don't mind, there is a grand opening at..."

"The Metropolitan Museum of Art?" Richards asked. "I'm sorry to say that it will be postponed, because there is more to this story than anyone is letting on. Especially, him." He pointed an accusing finger at Jack. "Ms. Childs, were you with him all night? Was he within eyesight until morning?"

She didn't answer right away but, eventually she said: "No, but there are cameras everywhere in the hotel; I'm staying at the Waldorf Astoria. I'm certain that they will corroborate our story. Isn't that right, Jack?"

Although she had a smile for him, he could see the cool distrust in her eyes. She knew that he could have left the hotel room at any time after she had gone to bed. "I didn't leave the room," Jack stated, being completely honest for the first time. "So yeah, please check the tapes. And also, I think we deserve to know what's going on."

He knew before the detective spoke that he was going to say there had been a ritualistic, sacrificial murder at the museum—and more mummies were missing. He wasn't wrong.

Chapter 8

The Metropolitan Museum of Art, Manhattan

Once again, Jack was standing just on the other side of yellow tape, pressing it forward so that it was on the verge of snapping. More than once Richards barked at him to back away—he would have, if that was an option. He *had* to decipher the glyphs; he *had* to know what the hell was going on.

The evil smell and the chest rattling sensation that he had been feeling was ten times as bad in the museum. He had even gone light-headed and had nearly fainted dead away and had to suffer the embarrassment of being caught by Cyn.

"It's the smell," he said; it was making him gag.

Her pert nose was wrinkled but she wasn't fainting. "It smells like a body pulled from a bog." It was far worse than that, in Jack's opinion.

In spite of the cancelled grand opening of the exhibit, the Egyptian wing was crawling with people. A minimum of thirty police officers were going in a dozen directions, inspecting every floor, door, wall, glass casing, framed picture, and velvet rope.

There were also ten world renowned Egyptologists offering advice, fretting over everything, freaking out that displays were being trashed and, while they were doing all of this, were also shooting eye-daggers at Jack and grinding their teeth. He couldn't blame them. The police were making a hell of a mess. Pottery and papyri, limestone stellas and sandstone statues, ebony jewelry boxes inlaid with gold and ivory were being lined up in the long hall—all supposedly evidence in some way and all handled in such a way that the exhibit's curator looked as though she was going to have an aneurism. And to top it all off, what wasn't being pulled from their display cases was being covered in fingerprint powder.

"These are ancient and priceless artifacts; these are ancient and priceless artifacts!" one of the Egyptologists kept repeating.

"I think I need to find a new profession," Jack whispered to Cyn.

She didn't disagree, and she also didn't stand very close to him when she could help it. "At least you're no longer a suspect," she said out of the corner of her mouth. Richards had sent a detective around to the Waldorf to examine the security tapes, proving that Jack's alibi was airtight.

"I don't know about that," he answered. "They took my sword. I bet they don't know what to think." He felt naked and vulnerable without his sword—even with all the police around, he didn't feel in the least bit safe.

Cyn grimaced. "*I* don't even know what to think. We have entered a world in which five-thousand year old mummies are coming back to life. That, dear cousin, is a batty world that I don't much care for."

Richards came over and, without saying a word, lifted the tape and gestured for them to duck under. "Follow me and do not touch *anything*." He led them down the hall, their shoes echoing on the marble floor. "Do either of you recognize him?" The detective had a finger pointing at a corpse that was naked, spread eagle and bled so white that he matched the cold marble in color. He was sliced open, right up the gut so that all of his organs were on full display.

Jack recognized him. It was the man he had dreamed of the night before. Once again, his head started going light and he had to step away and stare up at the ceiling until he stopped seeing spots.

"You faint at the sight of blood, Dreyden?" Richards asked. He wasn't concerned; he was suspicious.

"No...at least not normally. Though I guess I don't come across this much blood on a daily basis and certainly not like this, anyway." Jack swept his arm to indicate the room, which was painted in blood. Around three exhibits: two glass cases and a sarcophagus, there were double circles and more of the Heiro-Sumerian glyphs. All hand drawn in blood—the coppery smell had his stomach roiling.

Cyn looked a little pale as well. She said: "I don't know this man, although I might have seen him when I came by three days ago. My mum and I were given a private tour."

"Along with Robert Montgomery and his son," Richards stated, watching her closely. "And do either of you know where the younger Robert is? No one seems to know." The two cousins shook their heads in unison and Richards followed the question with another, this one totally unexpected: "And do you think we'll find his blood on that sword of yours, Mr. Dreyden?"

It took Jack a second to answer: "No, w-why would you ask that? Was there blood on the sword? There shouldn't be."

"What should be on the sword, Mr. Dreyden?"

The question was as out of the blue as the last. Jack's mouth came open and he made little noises that wouldn't have amounted to an entire word if they had been smushed together. He had no idea what to say. Richards watched him struggle with what should have been an easy question before asking: "Would you be surprised that we found epithelial cells that were five-thousand years old on it?"

Again words failed him and Cyn answered: "I think anyone would be surprised and Jack is practically speechless in surprise, or so it seems." She gave him a hard look that he understood as: *Pull it together!*

"Yes, I am surprised," Jack finally said. "And I don't believe it. You've been in possession of the sword for two hours. There's no way any carbon dating could have been done in that time, which leads me to believe that you're trying to trip me up in some fashion. I don't appreciate it. In fact, it seems I should exercise my Fifth Amendment right and not say any more since I did not do this. I had nothing to do with this. Nothing whatsoever."

Richards' hound dog face broke into lines as he smiled. "Nothing? Really? You do realize that it's a felony to lie to a police officer. It's called obstructing justice, so you may want to reconsider your answer. I know for a fact that you're involved with this. The sword proves it. You were right about the carbon dating, but we did run some of the particulates through a mass spectrometer. Any guesses as to what we found?"

Jack had a few good guesses: natron, which was a carbonate salt collected from the edges of desert lakes, resin found in trees that grew along the Nile, linen fibers from the Abeston flax, something that was hardly native to New York City. All the items needed to embalm a mummy.

"I-I guess certain oddities, or rare, um, plant fibers, but I work with such stuff and..."

"Save it for the judge," Richards said, advancing until he was almost nose to nose with Jack; he was suddenly furious. "I plan on bringing you up on charges if you don't come clean with me this instant. I have you on conspiracy to commit murder, obstruction of justice, and more than likely a dozen international antiquities laws. Yes, we know about your safe deposit box and we're just waiting on a judge to issue a warrant."

For the third time that day, Jack's head began to swim. How could he come clean with a story that was altogether unbelievable? The truth sounded like a child's sick fairy tale. He was stuck, that was the real truth. He would have everything pinned on him and he would go to jail and all of his hard work might as well be flushed down the toilet. Now, it was his turn to get angry.

"Come clean?" he asked, his lips twisting. "Sure, I can come clean. I was attacked by an Egyptian mummy…"

Cyn grabbed his arm and hissed "Jack! Don't say a word. We'll call your lawyer. I'm sure the police don't have anything on you."

"My lawyer?" he asked, a furious, uncontrollable laugh barking from him. "I don't have a lawyer. I'm not like you, Cyn. I don't come from money."

He was fuming, but she didn't take offense. She was honestly puzzled and she asked with her head cocked: "You didn't receive an inheritance from your father? Or your grand fa…Oh, right."

"What do you mean, oh right?" He was very aware that Richards was right there watching them, but he had been caught by her words and the way her eyes suddenly opened wide.

"Nothing," she answered, looking uncomfortable. "Don't worry about it. I will pay for your lawyer. What this bobby is doing is bullying, plain and simple."

Richards shook his head, no longer looking angry. He was back to being his usual tired, somewhat emotionless self. "It's not bullying, Ms. Childs. It's the truth. Your cousin is neck deep in trouble and I'm just trying to figure it all out and it isn't helping that he keeps lying to me. Yes, lying, don't start with the denials, Jack. You are simply the worst liar I've ever run into and you should take that as a compliment. A good liar is a practiced liar. A very good liar is one without a soul."

"Thanks, I guess," Jack said.

Cyn gave him a warning look; she didn't trust Richards, he supposed, but Jack was screwed three ways from Sunday—he had to trust somebody. The detective acted like she wasn't there. "Listen to me, Jack. If you haven't done anything wrong, then tell the truth…even if it is weird. Trust me; I'm expecting weirdness out of this."

Cyn made a pleading sound in her throat, but Jack didn't pay attention. The truth was that he was tired of the lies. Richards was correct: Jack was the worst liar in the history of liars. He hated lying; it made him feel greasy and dirty, and so he told the truth, the entire truth. Right off the bat, Cyn groaned and stared up at the ceiling as if praying for lightening to come down and strike Jack in order to shut him up.

No lightning came down to save him from himself and he went on, starting with the illegal papyrus and finishing with the weird feeling that came over him when he had come into the museum. As he spoke Richards nodded politely and said things like: *Go on*, and *Really?* and *Is that right?*

When Jack was done with his tale, which took longer than he had expected, Richards only stood there gazing at the ancient artifacts that were being catalogued and photographed and packed up to be brought back to the evidence locker at the police station.

"So Robert can raise Egyptian mummies? That's what this is all about?" he asked after a time. When Jack nodded, emphatically, Richards' softly lined hound dog face tightened up. He ordered: "Come with me," and stalked away, his steps surprisingly fast.

He strode through the museum until he came to the main building; only then did he look up at the signs that directed people to this exhibit or that. He saw what he wanted and took two rights until they were among the Incan exhibits. Cyn gave Jack a puzzled look; he could only shrug his shoulders in response.

There was another police presence here; this one much more subdued: a single bored looking officer standing before a taped off display that consisted of nothing but a glass case—a broken and empty case.

"So you say that Robert can bring Egyptian mummies back from the dead?" Richards asked.

It was obvious that an answer of 'Yes' wasn't going to cut it and yet, Jack didn't have another answer even though he could read the plaque on the exhibit: *Incan Mummy—Mountain Sacrifice* and he could see the glass that was shattered all over the floor.

"That's what I thought," he said. "But this doesn't make any sense. Where are the glyphs and the ritual circles? How is this possible? It doesn't make any sense."

Richards rubbed his eyes shut for a moment and then looked straight at Jack as he said: "Nothing about this entire case makes sense. Absolutely nothing. The evidence is sketchy and all over the board and doesn't add up, and my two main suspects believe in spells and the undead and superstitious crap."

"You wouldn't be saying that if you had inspected the sword, yourself. Did you, Detective?" Cyn asked.

He shrugged. "I gave it a cursory look. There wasn't anything obvious about it."

"Then you don't know what you're talking about," she said. "That sword was…wrong. There was something *bad* about it."

He gave her a little smile that suggested that her terminology of 'bad' wasn't either scientific or legalistic. "And if it is where does that leave me? I have one suspect who admits that he's in possession of stolen property and another who can't be found. Now, I have asked that first suspect to come clean with me and what does he give me? Monster stories. And what do you have? A 'bad' sword. Let me tell you, that's not exactly helpful."

"And what if he helps in some other fashion?" Cyn asked. "Jack is the only person…other than Robert, who can decipher the glyphs at the scene of the crime."

Richards looked confused. "I thought Robert didn't know this, uh, ancient hieroglyphic sort of language."

"He's not stupid," Cyn chided. "He may not have a degree in Egyptology, but he has been raised within the culture. You pick up things. Besides, Jack did all the work; it doesn't take a genius to be able to substitute characters from one text to another."

Richards glanced around at the rather dull—in Jack's opinion—Incan exhibit, before he asked: "And what good would an interpretation of this mumbo-jumbo do any one?"

The archeologist in Jack wanted to reply simply: *It is knowledge*. It was ancient knowledge and for that reason alone it made sense to decipher the writings that Robert had painstakingly, in more ways than one, written out in blood. Instead, he replied in a manner that a detective would understand: "Perhaps it mentions what he is hoping to accomplish with all of this. Or it might give us a clue as to what he's planning next."

"Or it just feeds into your psychosis," Richards remarked, though, by the slow way in which he did, he didn't really believe himself. "Maybe it wouldn't hurt."

"I'll need the contents of my safe deposit box," Jack said, feeling strangely nervous and excited at the same time. He was dying to interpret the glyphs both for the police and for himself. He hadn't been given money as an inheritance as Cyn had, he'd been given something greater: a pounding desire to discover, to know more, to unearth secrets that the world had buried away for all time.

Secrets that only he was supposed to know.

Chapter 9

The Metropolitan Museum of Art, Manhattan

Reluctantly, as though he was being dragged to the edge of a cliff, Richards agreed to allow Jack to decipher the glyphs. Jack was sure that the detective would never admit it himself, but there was a pull in everyone, a need to know what shouldn't be known.

Too bad that it would remain unknown as far as the detective was concerned. Jack decided that he would interpret the words for himself, but he would never give up their true meaning. These were words of power. It was crazy…very, very, outrageously crazy to think that such things as spells and charms and circles of power were real things, but he had seen Hor with his very own eyes and smelled the otherworldly decay with his own nose and, yes, he had nearly died as a result.

The words he was supposed to decipher were as evil as they were powerful. They could never be allowed out into the world. They had to remain secret.

Jack gave up the key to his safe deposit box to a uniformed policeman and then was subjected to a long wait in which he and Cyn and Detective Richards sat on opposite sides of the hall on low marble benches that were smooth and elegant but also hard and uncomfortable. The silence between them was equally uncomfortable. It became almost palpable, as though it was a real thing. The air was thick with the silence, like jungle air, Jack thought.

Richards' presence was to blame. He had read them their rights and had officially 'detained' them so that they were essentially under arrest, but without the formality of handcuffs.

It was after three before the policeman returned with the glass case that had, for the last five years, sat in Jack's bank. The sight of it caused a harsh whispering to break out among the museum dignitaries. Richards ignored them altogether and Jack tried not to shrink into his green army coat as they tried to wither him with their looks of outrage.

"Please, don't try to open the scroll," Jack begged when Richards started to unscrew the glass case. "Please, it's too delicate. I transcribed everything into the notebook."

The detective looked suspicious until Cyn assured: "It's standard operating procedure to both photograph and transcribe. Besides, Jack obviously thought this was a secret. I doubt he had a fake notebook right next to the real scroll."

This logic saved the scroll from being pawed over and possibly ruined by the detective. He did, however, hover around Jack as he began making notes in his book. Jack knelt a foot away from the twin circles that went around the broken sarcophagus. "You said these are funeral texts," Richards said. "Are these the same sort of writings from *The Book of the Dead*?"

"You know about *The Book of the Dead*?" Cyn asked, surprised.

He held up his phone. "I googled it."

"Then you know that the original Egyptian name for the text," Jack said, without looking up, "is transliterated *rw nw prt m hrw* and is read as the *Book of Coming Forth by Day*. Another translation would be the *Book of Emerging Forth into the Light*. Of course, there is no one Book of the Dead. Each tomb thus far uncovered has its own 'book' so to speak."

Richards glanced at his phone and then stuck it in his pocket. "Its own book? That seems like a lot of work."

"Well, the Egyptians were all about death," Cyn said. She too was hovering. Richards just over Jack's left shoulder, Cyn over his right.

"Can I get some room, please?" Jack asked. He was sketching the glyphs from the floor, something that had to be exact, and the two of them were making him nervous. "You two are making me jumpy and I don't want to screw this up. One little squiggle out of place can change the meaning, completely. Thanks. And Cyn is right; the Egyptians were utterly obsessed by the idea of life after death. But, really it was more than that. They didn't just want to be immortal, they wanted to be gods."

Richards moved in closer, again. "Is that what that says?"

Jack waved him back. "I don't know what it says, yet. So far, I think it's just a standard magic spell."

"Oh," Richard said, sounding disappointed. "More spells, great."

"Yes, the spells were intended to assist a dead person's journey through the *Duat*, or underworld, and into the afterlife," Jack said, speaking in a monotone as if reading from a very dull textbook. "They were written by many priests over a period of about a 1000 years. Now, what makes these glyphs so interesting is that, although they are far older than the traditional funerary texts, they were written on papyrus."

Judging by his facial expression, Richards didn't find this interesting in the least. "Is that right?"

"That is right," Cyn said, frowning. "And it's highly abnormal. The earlier 'Coffin' texts and the 'Pyramid' texts were all painted on objects and not on papyrus. Very strange. Clearly these works are more important than we first took them to be."

Even though by saying "we" and using the plural "works" she had practically admitted that she was also in possession of an illegal scroll, Richards didn't notice. He was good and bored by the discussion just as Jack had hoped he would be, and when he turned away to make a call, Jack slid his sleeve up and began to scribble glyphs onto the inner portion of his arm. He knew that he wouldn't be allowed to keep the notebook when he was done and there were glyphs he had never seen before.

He was positive that they were names. In the ancient world names were extremely important; true names held power out of all proportion to the syllables uttered. Jack didn't understand why, he just knew on a gut level that they did. The night before, Hor had been stopped by the sound of his name.

When Cyn saw what him scribbling on his arm, she shook her head and then pulled her hand from her coat pocket and showed him the phone she had kept hidden; she quickly took a few pictures and then hid it away again.

"I recognize the glyphs on the outer ring," she whispered. "They came from my mum's papyrus; I can tell by their order. Is the inner ring from your papyrus?"

He gave her a tiny, covert nod and then spoke out of the side of his mouth. "Yes, but there are glyphs within it that I've never seen before. Here at the top of the inner ring. It is very close to another glyph meaning *add* or *more*. My guess is that its meaning is likely something like: *combine* and it matches the glyph at the arch of your spell. It makes me think these spells can be used alone or together. I've never seen that before. It may be a first."

"And what does it mean that Robert also called an Incan mummy to life?" Cyn asked. "That shouldn't be possible without any of the ritual circles, in other words without any of the spells."

"None of this should be possible," Jack answered. "And I don't know what it means, but I have a guess. The Incan mummy might have been called by accident. If you take a look, the one mummy that had been in this case was called with a very specific name—*Amanra*." He pointed at the second ring of glyphs at an odd symbol of a bird standing next to what looked like a rake—it was copied three times in a repeating pattern.

Jack then went to the closer of the broken glass casings and pointed out a sun over a mountain glyph situated in the outer ring that surrounded it. "It means thee or thou, sort of a generic term."

She nodded slowly. "That's how easy it is? That sort of scares me more than anything. If Robert can call some no-name mummy, what else can he call?"

"Maybe anything. This third mummy may be the key to how the Incan was called. Robert thought he was only bringing up this one mummy, but see the lines of blood are thinner and the calligraphy sloppier—a few of the glyphs are ambiguous and one is downright nonsense. Look." Jack pointed at the poorly rendered glyph. "It should be a man with the wings of a bird, basically a version of the word *Ba,* which was an element of the soul, instead Robert had simply repeated the previous glyph: a triangle with a quarter moon over it."

"What are we looking at?" Detective Richards said from behind the pair. Jack nearly jumped out of his skin.

He considered lying, but a lie would have been valueless in this situation. "Right there. Robert drew two of the same glyphs: *feast* and *feast,* side by side. You would call it the hierogliphical equivalent of a typo. It might explain how the Incan mummy came to life."

Richards looked as though he was about to make a joke, but then he just waved Jack to explain further.

"Ok, the two rings of the power circle have different functions. The inner ring is the spell that I was in possession of. It opens the portal to the netherworld. The second ring actually acts as a barrier or a protection so that only the being called forth will come through."

"And that's how come we have a missing Incan mummy?" Richards asked, speaking through a sigh.

Jack gave him an apologetic nod. "Essentially. I'd like to examine the body of the guard. I couldn't see how he died...I mean..." Jack stumbled to halt.

"How could you have possibly seen how he died if you were snug in your hotel?" Richards asked with a dangerous tone.

Was it time for another horrible attempt at lying or was it better to go with the altogether crazy truth. Jack's broad shoulders sagged. "I dreamt of all of this last night. I didn't say anything because I know it sounds completely insane, but really, I know I sound crazy no matter what. I'll take a lie detector test if you need me to."

"Oh, I don't need a lie detector to know you're crazy," Richards said. "I was just hoping that you'd be helpful in your craziness. I think it's time you two left, unless you have something relevant I can use in this investigation? And don't tell me about any more dreams. Dreams are not admissible in court. What I need to know is who did this and where your cousin is."

Jack bounced his shoulders in a shrug. "I wish I could help you with that, I really do, but the glyphs don't mention him or point in any direction."

"Then you've wasted my time," Richards growled, poking Jack in the chest. "Go sit on that bench until I call for you."

Jack's notes were taken, including the primer. "You didn't actually translate any of that, did you?" Cyn asked when they were sitting on the bench.

"No way. I was going to try and fake my way through it, but once I copied the new text into my notes I just doodled fake glyphs." She laughed at this, high and sweet, earning a glare from both Richards and a number of the experts. "Maybe you shouldn't sit so close," Jack suggested. "I think my career is pretty much over before it really got started. I don't want to suck you down as I drown."

She patted his leg and then, oddly, gave it a squeeze. "If this was over, I probably would, but it's not. Robert has managed to open a portal to hell. My gut says so even if my brain is refuting all the evidence that is being presented to me. It's the sword. It defies logic. And so does Robert's actions. He can open a portal into hell, but why would he want to? What does he gain from it?"

"He's already wealthy," Jack replied, "and I really doubt that he's trying to impress a girl, so that only leaves power as a justification for murder."

"That's pretty weak," she said. "There's only so many mummies and so many museums, certainly not enough to raise a zombie army to take over the world. There's not enough to even take over Iceland, not that anyone would want to. I've been to Iceland. It's empty and the people are nice but so dull that you want to pull your hair out by the roots."

Jack felt he could use a little dullness in his life. "Ok, it's not Iceland he's after. Maybe he's trying to take over New York...assuming he's still in New York. There's a pretty large Egyptian exhibit in Philadelphia. I took a day trip down there last summer."

"Was it any good?"

He see-sawed his hand back and forth as he answered: "Naw, not really. The usual: pottery and clay tablets with hieroglyphs. And the mummies. There were four of them. If I had to guess, I'd say he's going there next."

"But where is he now?" That was an unsettling question. "He was staying at the Waldorf in the penthouse suite, of course. That's Robert, you know. Wherever he is, it won't be in any flea-bag hotel. It'll be somewhere fancy. We should inform Inspector Richards of where he should begin his search."

"It's *Detective* Richards," Jack told her, "and who knows if he's even looking. I'm the one right in front of his nose talking hocus-pocus. I should never have said anything. I should've played ignorant like Robert's dad. You should've seen..."

Jack abruptly stopped talking as an image came to him—it was a memory, actually and only a fragment of one: he was in the Brooklyn Museum and had just pulled Robert the Sixth aside to ask him about his son and what he knew about what was going on. Nervously, Jack had glanced at Detective Richards, and saw the policeman watching him, his dark, hound dog eyes alive with much more intelligence than he let on.

And then as Jack had turned back to Robert, he had caught just a glimpse of Dr. Loret and for once the curator wasn't in a prissy anger; he was nervous.

Chapter 10

Lindenhurst, Long Island, New York

Two cars: a blue, Ford Taurus and a Lindenhurst police cruiser, paused side by side. The cruiser had been leading but was now stopped before a large wrought iron gate that sat astride Loret's driveway, blocking them. It was after eight and their headlights lit everything in front, brilliantly but left the rest of the world deep in shadows.

"I thought you'd like to do the talking," one of the officers said in a carrying whisper to the Taurus.

Both of the local policemen were young and excited. Lindenhurst was a sleepy village on Long Island, about an hour from the city. It was a place where *nothing* of importance had ever taken place and the few crimes that did occur were always exceedingly banal: one or two drunk drivers per year, a stolen bike back at the beginning of summer and in September some bored teens were caught smoking pot on the beach; they had pleaded down to trespassing and had gotten off with a very small fine.

For the officers, an inquiry in a murder investigation was the highpoint of their careers.

Jack and Cyn watched from the back of the Taurus as Detective Richards got out and went to the speaker beside the gate and hit the button. There was a very long pause during which Richards thumbed the button every three seconds. He was just checking his watch for the second time when there came a nervous voice over the speaker: "Yes?"

"Dr. Loret? This is Detective Richards of the NYPD. I have a warrant to search your property. Please open the gate."

"A warrant?" There was another long pause, followed by: "Just a second."

Richards thumbed the button once more. "We are looking for Robert Montgomery the Seventh. Any attempt on your part, Dr. Loret, to hide him or to attempt to help him in any way to escape is aiding and abetting a fugitive." He stood there for a few more seconds and when nothing more was heard from the box, he strode back to his car and leaned in the window.

"You were right, Jack," he said. "He's definitely in there."

"Then why aren't you breaking down that gate?" Jack asked; he was getting nervous, which always made him edgy. "He could be getting away."

This made the detective laugh; it was a genuine laugh and his smile was actually warm. It made his hound dog face actually handsome for the brief few seconds that the smile braced up his cheeks. "Robert is not going any-where. He might run out the back, but he'll leave his car behind and we'll scoop him up right quick, you'll see."

He had been far less confident three hours before when Jack had explained: "I know where Robert is. Re-member the check I told you about?"

Richards had gazed at him with eyes as hard as stone before saying: "Despite the fact that I don't have a fancy and utterly useless degree in Egyptology, I'm not an idiot. I remember everything about this case."

"Yes, of course. I didn't mean to imply anything; I just meant to preface my remarks. So, about the check, Robert saw me put it in my top drawer. You see what that means?"

"No," Richards said, blandly.

"It means I was wrong. I thought someone had broken into my place, but they really hadn't. It was really..."

Richards had interrupted: "You mean you weren't attacked by an undead mummy?"

"I was," Jack insisted, trying to hold in his anger. "I'm talking about before then. Do you remember how Loret went right for my desk when you two came to visit? Of course you do, sorry. You remember everything, and so you also remember how Loret looked nervous when I pulled Robert's father aside. Before that he was as snide as can be, but just then he didn't know how Robert's dad was going to react. Loret was working with the son, that's what I think. He probably let Robert into the museum that night. He probably also did something about the security cameras, too."

The detective's eyes drifted up as he began nodding. "The cameras had been turned off and the alarms disabled," he said. "I thought it was an inside job at first, but nothing of real value had been stolen and the uh, circles and glyphs suggested a nutcase had done it." He was quiet for a time and then started to shrug his shoulders. "I don't know. It's possible."

"No," Jack had snapped. "It's all very impossible, but that doesn't mean it didn't happen. If you accept the idea that this is real, then everything I've said falls perfectly inline."

"And if I believe that you're trying to steer me away from your accomplice, then what?" Richards asked. "You see, that is a much more likely scenario. I don't have to believe in magic for that scenario to be true. I just have to believe that you and Robert or whoever are plum crazy."

Richards had a smug look on his face, but there had been doubt in his eyes that Jack picked up on. "Only you don't fully believe that, either. The problem, Detective, is that you're stuck in the middle, you know that this is a supernatural phenomenon but you're trying to understand it from the viewpoint of the natural or the normal."

Cyn agreed. "You have to change your paradigm; you have to open up your mind. I know it sounds somewhat hippy-like, but trust me this has nothing to do with peace and love. This is all about murder and blood sacrifices."

"Ok, fine," Richards said, slowly. "Let's say there are mummies running around New York, where are they? And why did Loret bring in the police? The doors to his museum were wide open; that's how we were called into this to begin with."

Jack grunted out a small laugh. "I don't know where the mummies are now. They could be in the back of a van parked under a bridge for all I know. But I have a pretty good guess why the doors to the museum were open. Loret was probably not prepared for what he saw. Maybe he didn't really believe that Robert could do what he said he could do. Maybe he was only humoring him while collecting a big check and then…"

"Then the mummies actually came alive," Cyn said. "I know I'd bloody-well freak."

Another laugh had escaped Jack, this one completely without humor. "You'd do more than freak. You have no idea what kind of fear comes off of them. It takes over your mind. It fills it so that you can't think. I bet Loret just took off screaming."

Richards' deep brown face froze, his lips slightly parted, his eyes, once again lost as he contemplated, not just Jack's words but also the obvious veracity in his face. Finally, the detective had made a sound that lay somewhere between giving up and pain. "Fine, I'll bring in Loret. Nothing else is working."

That had led to a slew of phone calls and discussions with two different district attorneys and, in the end, a warrant to search Loret's property.

But now Jack was nervous. A feeling of dread was creeping into his bones to settle there like ice. And he was suddenly sure that he had made a huge mistake by bringing the police to Loret's home. It was a big home, basically a mansion. The very high and prominent edges of it could be seen just over the tips of the trees.

It was dark and it was cold and *anything* could be in there.

The gates started to swing inward. They were eerily silent. He got the shivers; they ran right up his back as though he was attached to a wire. Cyn patted him on the thigh, strangely high up, distracting him, momentarily. Richards climbed into the Taurus and Jack noted that his sleepy hound dog look wasn't nearly as sleepy as it normally was. He was keyed up.

"When we go in, stay behind us and don't say a word. While we search, keep your hands to yourself, no matter what. Everything you touch will be compromised."

He drove as he spoke. The driveway was a good fifty yards long, winding gently between very high trees. It was probably a gorgeous property…in the daytime. The shadows around them were very deep; Jack grew more and more freaked.

"Detective," he said in a strangled, high voice—he hated that voice and he hated the ice flowing in his veins and the butterflies spinning in tornadoes in his stomach. "Uh, Detective, I think we should get out of here. Robert knows. He knows I'm here."

"He knows we're all here," Richards replied. "I rang the flippin' doorbell. Relax, it'll be ok."

But it wouldn't be okay. Jack knew it in a way that wasn't normal. He knew it like he could never have known it only the week before. Somewhere he had changed and he didn't know how. It defied all logic and every second of his schooling, but for some reason, he could sense what no one else could, whether by his nose or by the strange, uncomfortable knot behind his breastbone. He *knew* things.

He knew that they were driving straight into a trap.

"Please, turn around." He heard the beggy sound to his voice and he hated it. He wanted to rage against it, however they were just pulling up in front of the Doric columns and the marble steps and the eleven-foot tall etched wooden doors.

Richards ignored him. "Being a nerd sure does pay well," he said opening the door. "Come on." Neither Cyn nor Jack had budged. She was taking her cues from Jack and he was feeling the unnatural, magical fear that Hor gave off. It was muted with distance, but was getting closer.

The two Lindenhurst policemen were already at the doors, each with their right hands on the butts of their guns. Jack wanted to laugh at them and their useless weapons.

"Come on," Richards growled again, opening Cyn's door. She climbed out, not knowing what a bad idea that was and Jack found himself sliding out as well.

Hor was closer. He was in the woods and there were others of his kind with him and Jack could envision them: the Priest of *Thorthirdes*, the Incan mummy, the twins from the glass cases and finally Amanra. None gave off nearly as strong a vibe as Hor. Whether he led them or whether Jack was simply more in tune with him, he didn't know.

But Hor was a force.

He was coming in from the woods as were the others. Coming from every angle. Coming to trap them. Jack was starting to feel sick.

"Open up!" Richards ordered, hammering on the doors with a beefy fist. The sound echoed as if there was nothing and no one in the house.

"Detective!" Jack said, grabbing his shoulder. "We have to go. We have to get out of here right now." He was almost hysterical and he absolutely hated the sound of his own voice; however, it was now or never, they either ran or they died.

Richards jerked the hand off his shoulder and then beat on the door again.

"We gotta get out of here," Jack said to Cyn. Unbelievably, she edged away from him and the crazed look in his eyes, trusting the men with the guns more than her own blood. Jack was suddenly furious. His first impulse was to leave her, to run to the Taurus and jump in and drive out of there as fast as he could and had it been anyone else, he would have.

"Cyn!" he hissed, grabbing her arm as once more, Richards hammered the door.

"Open up, Loret!" Richards barked. "Don't make me take down your front door. I have a ram in the c..." Richards stopped suddenly, his breath frozen in his lungs as the insane horror that Jack had been feeling finally reached him and the others.

Cyn sniffed the air and then spun, slowly to stare out at the forest where everything was black and shadowed and the world wasn't formed yet, needing only light or imagination to bring it to life or to a semblance of life. What was in the forest wasn't truly alive and nor was it exactly dead.

"Oh, my God," Cyn said in a hollow whisper, her blue eyes huge in her head.

"What the hell is that?" one of the officers cried as six living nightmares came out from beneath the shadows of the trees, bringing with them an aura of fear that few could stand up against. "What the hell is that?" the same officer screamed.

Cyn looked like she was about to run, but before she could, she was trampled and crushed into one of the doors as the two policemen almost fell back into her; they were both clawing for their guns. Richards was a quicker draw. His Beretta was already out and aimed, but even he had finally awakened to the fact that he was dealing with creatures that didn't recognize the authority of either his badge or his gun.

"Stop!" he bellowed, showing that he had a reserve of courage greater than most.

The creatures didn't stop. They came on, their bones clinking, the power of their fear growing. One of the police officers sobbed, his gun out but turned sideways as though he wanted to give it up without a fight. The other local deputy-dog, in his panic, couldn't free his weapon and had given up on it. He had turned and was clawing at the door, standing over Cyn, whose knees had buckled and who was screeching with her hands covering her face, trying to block the sight of the living dead.

When the creatures marched over the edge of the yard, Richards, his eyes squinted into slits, finally fired his gun. His hands were shaking and he hit Hor, high up on his shoulder but he might as well have shot him in the toe for all the good it did. He fired a second and a third time, missing with the last.

And then Richards was as useless as the others. The fear had him in its grip and, worse, the creatures were close enough now so that their other-worldly stench came off of them in waves. Cyn passed out, falling against the doors. One of the police officers was gagging unable to breathe, while the other puked a load of brewed up coke and cheese burger. Richards swayed in place, his gun wobbling in his hand as though he was a three-in-the-morning drunk trying to figure out how to work his car keys.

Then Hor mounted the marble steps and in the blank sockets of his eyes there gleamed an evil that no human could resist.

Chapter 11

Lindenhurst, Long Island, New York

Jack hadn't wasted a second and had turned away from the advancing creatures. He felt the fear like icy fingers crawling up his back, making his shoulders twitch and his bladder feel loose, but for him, it was somewhat of a familiar feeling and as horrible as it was, it now came with an edge of anger to it.

He was tired of being afraid.

Furiously, he hammered his shoulder into the door. The first strike barely rattled it in its frame. The second, stronger hit, sent a crack running up one of the solid panels. "Son of a bitch!" he thundered as he threw his entire weight into the junction of the two doors. Now there was a gap. Hor was on the stairs and the other five creatures were arrayed behind him, pressing forward, greedily, hungrily.

Jack's fear ramped up as did his anger—as did his adrenaline. It pumped into his system, giving him strength. The fourth hit was powerful enough to split the wood around the striker plate. The two doors blasted inwards; Cyn fell forward into the house with one of the police officers toppling over her. Jack, too, had fallen in; now he spun around to see Hor standing over Detective Richards.

Hor was a monster, and draped in its rotting skin, it was foul beyond understanding. The stench alone had Richards wilting and close to passing out. He would be an easy kill and Hor would gain strength from his hot blood. Hor took the final step with an arm cocked back, its bony claws ready to tear out the man's throat.

Jack, trying to fill his voice with all the authority he could muster, yelled: "Stop!" The monster that was Hor stopped and, as Jack stared fiercely into the endless eye sockets in its grinning skull, something passed between the two of them. It was an understanding of sorts. It was un-spoken, but not unfelt.

It was a challenge and the stakes weren't just Jack's life; his soul was on the line. Hor laughed into Jack's mind and it felt as though something inside of him, his soul, perhaps, was coming unglued and he had the ugly impres-sion that Hor would suck it out of him and claim it for his own. "No," Jack growled.

Yes! Hor answered and, just as the last time they had faced each other, the sound did not come from his empty suit of bones. It just bloomed in Jack's head loud and strong. *I prevailed once before*, Hor spoke. In his mind's eye, Jack could see himself running from his apartment in childish fright, his eyes unblinking and huge and filled with tears, his heart pounding, his bladder just on the verge of letting go.

"That was before," Jack said, feeling the remains of his courage start to unravel at the edges. "This is now and you will not come in, Hor. You cannot come in." As he spoke, Jack reached out and tugged the second police offi-cer into the house.

You are not the master, Hor declared and advanced. Before him, Richards was down on his knees, trembling.

"I am the master!" Jack practically screamed. It wasn't a manly scream and what he had screamed certain-ly wasn't true. He was hardly even his own master. And yet, the very idea of a "master" struck a chord. Hor had a master even beyond Robert Montgomery. "By Osiris, you cannot come in."

Again Hor hesitated and his tremendous presence in Jack's mind grew less and yet, it was not gone. Slowly, Jack reached out and grabbed the back of Richards' coat. Jack could feel Hor; the creature was wary, careful. Invok-ing the name of the god of the underworld was not some-thing done lightly unless one was a fool...or desperate.

In this case, Jack was both. "Stay," he ordered, as if talking to a mean dog, and then, when Hor didn't reach out and kill him, he yanked Richards inside.

Somehow Cyn had managed to gather her wits about her and slammed the door shut in Hor's bone-face. The wood immediately thundered under a blow. "Help me!" she screamed.

Jack threw his shoulder into the door and a few seconds later, Richards did as well. The detective's once brown face was grey and his mouth hung slack but at least he was somewhat aware; Jack could see the wheels of his mind starting to turn slow circles once again. The other two policemen had still not recovered. One was on his knees crying and holding himself and the other was unconscious.

"Get up!" Cyn yelled. She lashed out and kicked the man who was lying face-first on a carpet runner. They were in an open foyer, which like the rest of the tremendous house was as dark as the night.

The officer began to stir and moan and smack his vomit-covered lips. His fellow officer, the one who was still covered in tears, tried to shake him into full consciousness but Jack barked: "Forget him." He then pointed at the nearest piece of furniture; a few feet to Cyn's right sat a marble-topped credenza of Italian origin. "Push that over here, quick!"

Before the officer could get the heavy piece moving, the door shook again. Even with three people bracing it with their bodies, it came open a few inches and the stench of Hor streamed through the crack. Cyn began to gag and Richards moaned, weakly.

"Ignore the stink," Jack told the others despite the fact that his own throat was now so tight that his words came out in squeak. "Ignore it! It only exists in your mind." He didn't know if that was true, exactly, however he knew the smell and the fear could be overcome. "I've fought him before and lived. Ok? Remember that and fight it."

"I can't," whispered the police officer who was supposed to be pushing the credenza. "I-I can't do this. It's...it's too heavy." He looked to be on the verge of passing out.

Jack slapped his hand against the door. "No, damn it! That's a cheap knock-off. Push it, man, it's light." The officer tried again, but he was out of his mind with fear and his strength was being sapped. They were all failing. The power of Hor and the other undead was growing; it was becoming tangible, not just the smell, which was clogging in their nostrils and lying like poison on their tongues, it was also the night that was becoming deeper, seeping through the windows and the cracks of the door like smoke, blocking out even the feeble light from the stars.

The foyer was so dark that Cyn's pale face seemed ghost-like and Richards' normally dark eyes were so hung with shadows that they were starting to resemble Hor's.

"The light!" Cyn cried. Her hand was up and pointing and Jack thought that she was pointing at him. "J-Jack, the light! Turn on the light, please." She sounded like a child who was afraid of what was under the bed and was begging her parents to turn on the hall light.

He followed her pointing finger and saw a light switch next to the door. With a quick move, he slapped it up and was immediately blinded as the foyer chandelier, a great glass and crystal monstrosity, blazed into light. It was shocking to the eyes, but welcoming to the soul.

Somehow, the light had power over the undead. The weight on the other side of the door disappeared in a blink and it slammed shut. Even the magical fear retreated, leaving behind only the natural terror of the living dead.

"What the hell was that?" whispered one of the officers. It was the officer who'd been crying and there were still tears on his lashes.

"They were monsters," the other officer told them, saving Jack from basically saying the same thing but with an extra hundred words of useless explanation. They were monsters. By all classical definitions they were most definitely monsters.

Richards inched up the door and tried to peer through the peephole. "Are they gone?" the teary-eyed officer asked.

"I can't tell," he answered.

Furtively, they went to the windows in the foyer to peek out but all they saw was a darkness of such depth that it couldn't be natural. Richards rushed off to a sitting room that afforded a view to the east. He came back looking shaken. "That darkness, it's everywhere. It's all around the house. And it's deep, like impenetrable deep. Like the world ends right there, right off the porch."

The look of abject fear on the detective's face was enough to get Jack's stomach swirling again. "Quick, the credenza," Jack whispered. He and one of the officers shoved it across the marble tile to hold the door closed.

"Will that stop them?" Cyn asked. She too was whispering and the others were hunched over, trying to appear smaller, perhaps hoping on some level that Hor and the other undead creatures would find them insignificant and go away.

"We should brace it with something else," Richards said, pointing down the hall at the great room where the ceiling was thirty feet high and where there seemed to be a good deal of furniture. The second officer, the one who had passed out, was on his feet now and, despite that he was still shaking from the inside out and his breath hitched in his chest like child, he helped to drag over a large, elaborate couch.

Cyn seemed confused by its satiny purple and white cushions and the ornately carved woodwork. "That's a French Provincial piece," she noted as if fancy couches were only found on Mars and not in a rich man's home. Jack didn't really understand what she was confused about. Yes, the couch didn't go well with the credenza, especially as it was rammed full into its side, but why the odd look?

"We need weapons," she said to Jack. That was true; the three officers had their guns drawn, but Jack and Cyn had nothing. "This way." She pulled him by the hand; his was cold and damp with sweat while hers was soft as expected but also somehow warm. They clung to each other. She led them deeper into the dark house, speed-walking as if she knew where she was going.

"Have you been here before?" he asked, remembering his paranoia and remembering that there had been someone in the house when all of this started and remembering that he didn't know Cyn very well at all.

She shushed him and hunched lower. "No," she answered in an even lighter whisper than before. "We need to find Loret's study. That's where his weapons will be; these guys are all alike." The lower floor had fourteen rooms, but only one with a desk the size of a pilot whale.

"You see?" She pointed in at the study. "All these dusty old farts have to prove that they're still manly men."

The theme of the study was *warrior-king meets metrosexual*. Flanking the door on both sides were full suits of medieval plate armor, on the walls were shields, crossed swords, battle axes and colonial era muskets, while on the desk was a pitcher of herbal tea, a grooming mirror, and a bottle of lotion that cost nearly as much as Jack's rent.

Cyn went right for the largest of the battle axes. It was a heavy, two-headed beast of a weapon...that she couldn't get off the wall. She strained at it until Jack pointed out that it was bound to the wall by nails and very thin wires. Before attempting to take it down, Jack fingered the edge and then shook his head. "You don't want that one, it's dull as hell and besides, it's too heavy for you."

"I need something heavy," she answered, desperately. He understood. These weren't normal creatures and it didn't seem like normal weapons would hurt them.

"No, you need something quick. These creatures are faster than you'd think. Take one of these." He rushed behind the desk to where a pair of crossed swords with intricate guards were hanging from the wall. Despite the danger, he couldn't help to grin. "They're rapiers, probably from Spain. They're a little heavier than I like, but they'll do."

He had just cut the air with one, enjoying the expertly crafted balance of the sword when there came a cry from the front of the house: "I see one! On the porch."

Jack grabbed Cyn's hand and, together, they ran for the front door just as there came a crash of glass and a scream of terror.

They were at the front of the house in seconds, just as guns started going off and windows began crashing in-wards as the undead creatures burst into the house. Richards and the two officers were blasting away, filling the house with such noise that for a few seconds, the sound drowned out the mounting fear.

But Jack knew it couldn't last. The bullets weren't slowing down the undead creatures. They came on—two from the front of the house and one from each side. Hor wasn't with them. Jack could feel him at the back of the house, waiting for them to try to make a run for it, while the Priest of *Thorthirdes* was just outside the front door with the same purpose.

They weren't stupid. They knew that it was just a matter of time before the officers would realize that their weapons were useless against beings pulled from the pits of hell, and then the terror would be too great and they would flee.

It happened quickly. One of the officers was out of his mind. He screamed something, threw down his gun as if it had suddenly bitten him and tried to run. Jack grabbed him and shoved him against the wall. "Don't, it's a trap. They're in the back, too." The officer was too far gone; his eyes were almost all whites and there was foam at the side of his mouth. He tore out of Jack's grip and ran.

Jack took a step after him, but Cyn grabbed his coat and screamed into his face: "What do we do?" She was close to losing it as well.

"Get upstairs," Jack said, pushing her towards a sweeping set of stairs. He turned as Richards' gun ran out of ammo. The detective fumbled for another clip with one of the mummies bearing down on him. Jack saw that even if he got a new clip in his gun in time, he would still die.

Leaping forward, Jack slashed with the rapier at the outstretched bone-hands of the mummy, taking them both off in a shearing strike and, once again, feeling the ugly, negative vibe run up his blade. The feeling warped his face into a grimace and brought a nasty taste into his mouth. It was very similar to what he had felt when he had fought Hor in his apartment—only it was weaker.

The mummy was the Incan. It was weaker, both physically and spiritually. In three, lightning fast cuts with the rapier, Jack struck off both of its arms and sent its skull bouncing away.

"Or maybe I'm stronger," Jack said to himself as he spun and whistled the sword at another of the creatures, again going for the hands first. He moved with such blazing speed that the second mummy was decapitated in moments.

"To your left!" Cyn yelled.

Amanra was closing fast, swinging a deadly clawed hand. Jack was already moving, dancing back to the edge of the stairs. He had caught sight of Amanra in his peripheral vision even before Cyn's warning. In a flashing blur, he took Amanra's arm off at the elbow and was just set to follow up the strike with another when there came a cry from the back of the house which was followed up by the sound of flying feet.

The officer was coming back, running from danger and into more danger. The four people he had abandoned were now pinned with their backs to the stairs with two skeletal creatures in front of them. The officer ignored them all and ran to the front door. He was beyond help. His eyes were spinning in his head and his mouth was stretched wide in a soundless scream. His panic lent him strength and he threw aside the French provincial couch as if it was a cheap futon and the heavy credenza was thrust aside with equal ease.

"Don't!" Jack cried, foolishly taking his eyes off of Amanra. He watched as the Priest of *Thorthirdes* caught the man in the doorway and tore out his throat with one swipe of its claws and he couldn't take his eyes off the scene as a geyser of blood gushed out to spray the priest, and he saw the wickedness in the priest's black sockets blaze and, just before Amanra attacked, Jack watched the priest his mouth wide...wider than humanly possible, and sink his grayed teeth into the officer's throat.

And then there was movement to his left, blackened claws raking through the air. Jack threw himself back, but too late. The ancient and splintered bones of Amanra's fingers tore through his army coat and through the shirt beneath and opened up Jack's flesh.

He screamed.

Chapter 12

Lindenhurst, Long Island, New York

The pain was enormous, far out of proportion to the four, quarter-inch deep gashes that ran across the top of his chest just below the hollow of his throat.

What he was feeling wasn't normal or natural, or even real. It couldn't be real. It was poison and acid and fire all at once. He could barely breathe from the shocking pain. All he could do to protect himself was to stumble backwards as Amanra came on, again bringing his arm back.

Faster than a whip, it came at Jack's throat, but just then, the heel of Jack's foot struck the stairs and he found himself falling as the bloody bones whirred an inch from his skin.

There was laughter in his head and a scream in his ears. The scream wasn't his own. The Priest of *Thorthirdes* had tossed away the body of the Lindenhurst police officer and now there was fresh, red blood dripping from its five-thousand year old teeth and strings of man-flesh hanging from the bone of its jaws.

The other police officer had hit a mental limit. He was staring at the priest with eyes that were glassy and bugging out of his head. And he was screaming fit to wake the dead. It was such an insane scream that it was a second before Jack noticed that one of the lesser mummies had its hand a foot deep in the officer's belly.

The weathered, leathery skin of its face was stretched into a gruesome smile as it slowly twisted its arm. It was going to pull something out of the officer; Jack knew it and he had a passing thought: *That's going to be me*, as

Amanra attacked a third time, stabbing with its hand instead of clawing.

Then there was a line of silver cutting between them and the hand tumbled from Amanra's bone and gristle covered arm.

"Oh, God," Cyn groaned. Her rapier was no longer the beautiful sweep of shining steel. Like Jack's, the edge was black and her face held disgust and horror at what had been transferred through the metal and into her hand.

She should have followed up the stroke with another to render Amanra at least temporarily harmless but she seemed incapable and Jack would have been bitten had it not been for Richards, who lashed out and planted his size thirteen square in the hollow chest of Amanra, sending it flying back to rattle its bones against the credenza.

The pain in Jack's chest was still so immediate and overpowering that he could stand only with help. Richards supplied that help, grabbing him by the collar of his army coat and dragging him to his feet—they were retreating up the stairs without interference from the bone-priest.

It stood at the bottom waiting, while around him the hands and skulls and the pieces of the other mummies came together. Jack felt the same overwhelming desire to run as he had the first time he had faced Hor. Their battle had been in vain. They couldn't win. They could only hold off death for a time, and not a very long time at that.

Hor was coming.

He was their leader, their king. His presence was a force that could be felt in Jack's mind and in his heart. He was coming and this time there was nowhere to run.

Unhindered the three of them fled up to the second floor, where they began opening door after door. Jack didn't know what the others were looking for, probably a way out or a weapon of some sort. He was looking for Robert. His cousin was the one who had started all of this and Jack felt that he was probably the only one who could end it.

And he would, Jack would make sure of it. When he had a sword in his hand, Jack was very persuasive.

Only Robert wasn't behind any of the doors on the second floor and, worse, Hor and the priest and Amanra and the others were coming. Jack felt it deep in the marrow of his bones and in the hard spot behind his breastbone.

"In here," he said in a whisper to the others, pointing to the master bedroom. "They're coming, I can feel it."

Cyn surprised him by saying: "I can, too."

"I can't," Richards said in a strangled voice. "Is that bad? Does that mean I'm next?"

"No, of course not," Jack told him, despite not knowing the truth of anything. He pointed at the bed, a huge four-posted king and asked: "Can we move that?"

The three of them ran to the bed and heaved it in front of the door, Jack cringing as he did: the pain in his chest was still like fire.

"Now what?" Cyn asked. When Jack and Richards only shrugged, she stared at the bed as if it had been a mistake to have moved it. "Then what are we going to do? They'll get in. You know that they will."

The door shuddered under a blow. The three of them glanced back and forth at each other, each hoping that someone else would come up with a plan.

"We can put the dresser in front of the bed," Richards suggested. "All three of us are strong enough to hold them back." As if to belie that statement, a stench reached them that caused them to back away from the door.

"No," Jack said, his free hand clutched to his chest which throbbed and ached. The wound made him feel dirty, as if it was already septic and was quickly poisoning his body. "No, we need a real plan."

The door *bammed!* again and now there was a split in the wood. It wouldn't last. The wood would come apart and then the stench would be mind-boggling. Before too long, Jack would be dead from the poison coursing through his blood and then Cyn would be overcome by the stench and that would leave just Richards, if he could manage to hold out.

He would die as a raving lunatic. An hour alone, trapped in the bedroom with the undead constantly clawing at the door would snap his mind like a twig.

This meant that they would need a real plan.

"What do we know about them?" Jack asked, speaking mostly to himself. "Not much," he answered.

He went down the list of what he knew about the mummies: They were REAL! That was the hardest thing to come to grips with and it was also the hardest thing to get beyond. His mind wanted to fixate on the idea.

"They're real...and?" he asked. The door thrummed from another blow. Richards went to the dresser and started heaving it toward the edge of the bed. Cyn stood between the two men, holding her rapier in two hands; the tip wobbled as her hands shook.

"And they were summoned," she said, answering his question. "Which means that they can be sent back."

The door was hammered again—and now there was a gap in the wood. Hor was just beyond it staring in at them. A black shiver went up Jack's spine. It was a shiver from the deepest part of him.

"We can't send them back," Jack said, turning from the dreadful gaze of the hell-creature. "We don't know the proper spell...yes, spell. It's the right word. A spell brought them here..." He broke off as he realized that was wrong. It wasn't just one spell that had done the job, it had been two.

The first was the spell that had been written on Jack's papyrus and the second was the one that Cyn's mom had been in possession of for years until...what had caused her to give it up? "That doesn't matter," he said to himself. He glanced up to see Richards looking a shade of grey.

Pieces of wood flew out from the door to land on the bed and in his afro. "I need help holding them off," Richards said.

"No," Jack said, forcefully. The answer to their predicament wasn't in something so mundane as a door; that was for certain. The answer had to be in the supernatural. But that didn't mean that it was beyond their understanding or beyond the realm of law…everything had boundaries; everything had limitations and rules, even magic.

It was true, they didn't know the spell to send the monsters back to hell, but they did know the spell to summon them. Could it be worked in reverse? Again, no, but could they work the spell to their advantage? The true answer: possibly. Robert had added to Cyn's spell so that meant he could, too…he hoped.

"Cyn, I need you to make one of the ritual circles," Jack said, pointing at the empty spot on the hardwood floor where the bed had been. "You still have your phone?"

She shook her head, but at the same time she reached into her pocket and pulled out her phone. "A ritual circle? It won't work...it can't work," she said, her head never ceasing its side-to-side motion.

"We don't have a choice," Jack told her, taking her by the shoulders and pointing at the floor. "Draw it upside down...you know, inverted and only draw your portion. My part opens the portal to the netherworld and yours is a protection spell to keep unwanted things from coming out into the world. It should work in reverse, keeping them out of the circle."

"Should work?" Cyn asked in a breathless whisper, her eyes staring at the blank floor.

From the far end of the dresser, Richards asked: "What the hell? You...you...you're going to draw on the floor and you think that'll save us? Don't do it, Ms Childs. Don't. Do anything else but that. We gotta figure a way out of here. Check those windows and see if we can get out onto the roof."

Jack whipped his rapier around and pointed it at Richards. "You need to shut up. It's a straight shot out of the windows thirty feet down to brick. And *they're* out there. The weaker ones. I can feel them. So, no Cyn, don't listen to him. Draw the circle now before..."

Another crash and the top half of the door broke inwards and now the stench filled the room completely. Cyn wavered and dropped her rapier and Richards slumped on the other side of the dresser.

"Ignore it," Jack told them after a shaky breath. "It's bad, but we've smelled it before and we've felt the fear. That's all they got. Those are all the tricks they have." This wasn't true.

Hor was almost literally skin and bones, yet he pushed against the remains of the door with the strength of ten men, sending the bed and the dresser screeching back almost far enough for him to get in. Richards and Jack threw themselves against the far side of the dresser, stopping it for the moment.

"Draw the damn circle!" Jack yelled.

Cyn looked around: pictures on the walls, a tall mirror, a lamp, side tables finished in black lacquer. There wasn't a previously overlooked pint of blood sitting out. "With what?"

There was an obvious answer.

Jack had dropped his rapier when he had thrown his weight against the dresser, now he picked it up and in a quick, precise move he swept it across Cyn's left bicep opening a shallow cut. It was such a deft move that he figured the pain would be minimal and yet she shrieked and dropped to her knees.

"What the hell!" Richards cried.

"I had to," Jack said. "Cyn, I had to. I'm sorry, I really am, but you were the obvious choice. We needed blood and..."

"It burns!" she screamed. "It's burning me!"

The blade of the rapier was black. Like Amanra's claws, the blade was now poisonous. "You're not dying, Cyn. It'll fade. The pain will fade." It was a partial truth;

the slashes across his chest were a misery to him, but he could function.

"Please, draw the circle," he begged; the door was edging further and further open. "Use your fingers as a brush...yes, there you go." She was shaking and still crying, but she managed to pull up the pictures from her phone and began to draw the first glyph. "There you go. Great. Spread out the glyphs but not too far. Now you'll need to change one of them. The one with the ant. Don't draw the leg on it. That changes the meaning from *one* to *none*."

Richards, who was sweating and trembling, asked: "Will this work?"

"Yes," Jack answered. It had to. If it didn't, none of them would get out alive.

The door opened another inch and Hor stuck one leg inside the room. The linens that he had been wrapped in were torn as was the skin covering his thigh bone. The flesh looked like a dried-up rag with a few scraggly black hairs dangling from it. For some reason the sight of it made Richards give up on trying to hold back the door.

He stood up, went wobbly for a second and then pulled out his gun. Without his help, Jack couldn't hold back Hor. The monster pushed the door open one handed, scraping back both the dresser and the bed with ease. Behind him, the hall was filled with clouds as if a storm had sprung up under the roof.

"Draw faster!" Jack yelled. Cyn was on the far curve of the circle, with her back to them; she whimpered every time she put a shaking hand to the wound Jack had given her. He knew the pain she was feeling because he was feeling it too, just as he knew her fear, but at least he could face the creatures and at least he had a weapon in his hand. She only had bloody fingers and crazy scrawled characters and a wild hope that a few ancient glyphs would protect her. She had little faith in the circle and every second or two she would steal a frightened glance over her shoulder at the darkened doorway.

Richards started firing. He kept pulling the trigger until his gun was empty and their ears rang. The bullets had very little effect: a few bones were chipped and some crypt dust was added to the black swirling darkness but, other than that, the gun was almost useless with the exception of causing Hor to pause before he stumped in to the room.

When he finally did, Jack swept up his rapier ready for the onslaught; however, Hor didn't attack right away.

The creature moved to the right, the bare bones of his one foot scraping on the wood. After him came the Priest of *Thorthirdes* and then Amanra. Last was the Incan mummy who stayed in the doorway, completing the trap. They brought the darkness from the hallway in with them so that there was a roiling cloud cloaking their shoulders.

"Draw faster," Jack hissed through gritted teeth.

"One minute," she shot back. They didn't have a minute. They didn't even have ten seconds. With a shrill hissing, the creatures attacked.

Chapter 13

Lindenhurst, Long Island, New York

"Stop!" Jack yelled. "Hor, stop." It didn't work this time. Hor didn't even hesitate. "Oh, boy," Jack said, as the creatures rushed forward, attacking from three sides. Against all logic, Jack attacked as well. Swinging his rapier like a wild man, he sprang forward. He had no form, no precise footwork and no concept of defense. All he cared about was whistling the blade back and forth as fast as he could.

A second later, Richards joined him. He had Cyn's rapier and together he and Jack hacked off a few hands and fingers and kept the creatures at bay for thirty precious seconds. Just long enough for Cyn to finish the circle.

"I'm done!" she cried, standing right in the middle of the circle she had created. To Jack it looked awful small and the characters were far from precise. In other words, he was about to put his life on the line with the only thing between him and a bad death was a hunch and some splashes of blood that may or may not be actual characters.

"Don't step on any of the blood," he warned Richards and then hopped over the edge of the circle where he wavered and pinwheeled his left arm as though he had leapt to the top of a mountain with sheer sides and a thousand-foot drop. Richards pushed his arm away and smushed in close; with three adults in the circle there was precious little room. They stood with their backs to each other and their swords out.

Hor and the priest and Amanra came forward and now the room was altogether black. The only thing that Jack could make out was Hor's bone-grin. It was lit from within by a spectral glow, which made Hor seem deeply hungry. He came right up to the circle and leered in; he was so close that Jack could see his skull perfectly well. It was scarred and pitted with its great age and there were ancient dust particles in its teeth and along the sutures that held the different bones of its skull together. The dust was fine as cigar ash as though someone had carelessly, or perhaps cruelly, tapped their stogie over Hor's corpse at some point and then hadn't bothered to blow them away.

It opened it mouth wide and, just like with its eyes, there was a blackness that went deep down its throat, miles deep. The blackness went down to where Jack did not want to go.

"Hrr vahl Evi ah hurrumm fd," Jack stated in a wandering and shaky voice. "Hrr ah huroon ksa hrer, uh, uh, oh jeeze, um, mkr, hrr fd fdhra."

The glow of Hor faded, his mouth closed and then he slid silently back until he was enveloped in the dark.

"What are you saying?" Richards asked. "What is that?"

Instead of answering, Jack repeated in a stronger voice: "Hrr vahl Evi ah hurrumm fd. Hrr ah huroon ksa hrer, mkr, hrr fd fdhra." The darkness and the horrid smell, and the heart-rattling fear grew around them, becoming almost palpable. The very air in the bedroom became heavy and dank, like a cemetery fog. It was an angry black fog.

"The monster...it's in my mind," Cyn said. "I can feel it in my head...and it knows my name. It knows me."

Jack raised his voice and, for a third time, spoke in a language no one had uttered in eons. There was a brief shimmer to the air and a light sound of wind rushing away from them...and then nothing. The room looked just as it had—a dark storm with the occasional glimpse of grinning skull.

"What the hell are you saying?" Richards cried. "Why do you keep repeating nonsense? We should be...we should be doing something to get out of here before it's too late."

"Don't move, Detective," Jack said, putting out his hand. Hor came stumping out of the darkness to stand directly in front of Jack. It glared, the black sockets where his eyes had long ago rotted away swelled and grew as did the darkness around him. Hor seemed to be gaining in strength. And the other mummies came closer as well and they brimmed with anger, their bones rattling.

In spite of this fury, Jack found himself grinning. The spell was working. He could feel it as though there was an invisible curtain all around them. Hor swelled up only inches away; however, it couldn't cross the barrier.

"It wasn't nonsense," Jack said. "It's the spell. That's what the glyphs say. I was just saying: My will for none to cross. My will for none to walk in the light of day..."

"It's in my head!" Cyn repeated, urgently.

"It's ok, Cyn," Jack said. "He can't get us, so try not to think about it. We should all just try to relax." Cyn nodded but in a manic, spastic manner. Richards didn't appear to have heard Jack at all. He was once again under the influence of the fear and looked on the verge of running. It would be his death if he did.

Jack tried to rally them. "Don't listen to Hor, listen to me, instead. We're going to make it out of here. The spell is working! Can't you feel it? Richards, come on. Don't be afraid, he can't get us. He can't hurt us!" Jack spun, very carefully, in place and took Richards by the shoulders and began to turn him so that he wasn't staring out into the blackness.

He did the same thing for his cousin, saying: "It'll be ok, Cyn. Come here, turn around. Put your head on my shoulder."

For the next few minutes, the three of them huddled close as the creatures did everything they could to get them to break, mentally. The fear grew and the smell was dizzying and the darkness became hellish. But, for those few minutes, Jack was unflappable and soon the darkness grew less and the air began to clear; *they* were weakening!

And then there was the scrape of bone coming from the hall—the creatures were leaving. It was almost too good to be true. Fearing that this was a ruse or a trap, the three humans stayed in the circle for five minutes after the last of the mummies left the house.

During those long minutes, Jack lost the excitement he had been feeling over his first successful spell casting, if that was even what he'd done. He really didn't know and he was having a very difficult time concentrating. The pain in his chest grew steadily until it felt as though it were on fire. Soon, the ugly, poisonous sensation in the four gashes spread deeper into his body. It felt as though he was breathing through lungs that were filling with steel wool. His head was swimmy and the floor of the room had begun to rock.

Cyn was also feeling the poison. Her left arm hung cold and practically useless. Her face was dead white and her eyes went in and out of focus.

Richards was physically healthy; however his mental state was suspect. "This is real, isn't it?" he asked, walking around the bedroom, making sure not to touch the blood on the floor. "I…I can't believe it, and you know what? No one else is going to believe it, either. What am I going to tell the Lindenhurst PD? I got two of their men downstairs. One was eaten. You all saw that, right? That's not some-thing you can just pretend didn't happen. There's going to be an investigation. I'm…I'm screwed."

"Yeah," Cyn said in a breathy whisper. "But first, I think I need to go to the hospital. Jack, too. You look like you might faint."

Jack didn't think going to a hospital would do him any good. No hospital in the world was going to have an antidote for the poison that was spreading through his sys-tem. Just like the wicked feeling that had rushed up the metal of the swords he had used against the undead crea-tures, the poison in his wounds was pure evil.

A hospital would be a waste, but he didn't think he had any other choice. "I need air," he said and then stumbled out of the room. Moving helped and the idea of getting out of the house gave him a burst of energy that carried him down the stairs; however, the energy was utterly sapped when he saw the two dead police officers in the foyer. Their corpses looked as though they had been mauled and the look on their frozen faces was one of eternal terror.

"I'm sorry," he said to them and then went out into the cold night. The air stung his wounds, but helped to clear his head—nothing could help his lungs. He coughed with no strength as he stumbled for Richards' Ford Taurus and only when he thumped against the hood with a strange metallic sound did he realize that he was still carrying the rapier.

"Get in," a soft voice said in his ear a second later. It was Cyn, making Jack wonder whether he had passed out standing up. She opened the door for him and he crawled in.

Richards didn't head straight for his car. He paused at the top of the porch stairs, perhaps to make sure that it was indeed safe to come out of the house. Jack could have told him that the creatures were long gone; they registered only as a vague evil to the northwest and the strength of the feeling was diminishing.

After the pause, Richards went to the Lindenhurst police cruiser and came away with a 12-gauge shotgun and two boxes of shells. He wanted to hand the gun to Jack, but Jack was slumped against the far door, his eyes going in and out of focus. Even if he hadn't been in the process of dying, he really wasn't interested in the gun. He had the rapier. Yes, it had the terrible smell to it and the aura of evil was uncomfortable, but it had also proven itself in battle where guns had yet to do so.

Cyn had been listless, but she grew eager at the sight of the weapon and she took the gun and began studying it.

"It's very simple. The shells go in there," Richards said, pointing to a slot on the side of the weapon. "It holds four shells total. You don't have to pump it, or anything like that. Put three shells in the bottom and one in the chamber. Just brace yourself for the kick because it packs a wallop if you're not careful. But also don't be afraid of it, or it'll get the better of you."

"I think I understand," she answered. "But hopefully we won't need it right? We can call the other cops on Robert, right? They can take care of him, right?"

Richards got in the front seat and started the car. He didn't answer right away. He drove for a few minutes along the forested road and Jack could tell that he was still processing what he had thought was impossible. Coming to grips with the sudden infusion of insanity in their lives wasn't an easy thing to do, though Richards did have the good fortune to have gone through it with two other people.

The detective was quickly getting his wits back.

"I'll drop you two off at the hospital and I'll go after Robert. If I kill him, will those things leave?"

"Maybe...really, I don't know how to get rid of them," Jack said. "I don't even know how we stopped them. Some writing in an ancient language? That worked? It's starting to feel unreal again."

Cyn began nodding. "I know what you mean. Hor was inside my head. That couldn't have been real. That had to be a dream or my imagination. Or I'm on drugs. I must be. Hor was in my head and he spoke to me and I understood him."

Jack remembered the same confused sensation. "It was like he was speaking English and that's impossible. He was Egyptian and...and besides, English hadn't even been invented yet when he was alive."

They were quiet for a few minutes as that sunk in. The empty road ended at a much busier street. There were people walking their dogs and there were other cars driving about and the streetlights had pleasant fairy halos around them. It was all wonderfully normal. It made Jack smile, although it was just a twitch at the corners of his mouth. He didn't have strength for more.

Richards paused, not knowing which way to turn. "They went west, toward the city," Cyn said.

"How?" Jack asked. Just the one word sent him coughing again.

"I can feel them, too," she answered. "I don't know how. And...and I had the same dream as you had last night, Jack. I saw that security guard getting killed and I didn't know what to say. I thought it was crazy that you'd had the same dream. I mean, it made me feel crazy and then Hor...I felt him just like you did, when we were in front of the house."

For just a few seconds, Jack was able to forget the deep pain in his chest and the thousand needles invading his lungs with every breath. It wasn't just happenstance that Cyn could feel Hor and that she had the dream. There was a connection somewhere in Cyn's words...or maybe it was in her blood.

First Robert Montgomery, then Jack Dreyden and now Cynthia Childs. The last three heirs to the fortune of Lord Blackburn. "Although I'm not much of an heir," Jack mumbled under his breath. The only thing Jack had actually received from his great-great grandfather was the papyrus—a spell to open a portal to the netherworld.

And Cyn would eventually receive the spell to control who...or what came through the portal. And that left Robert.

"What spell does he have?" Jack asked. "What power..." He couldn't go on. The pain in his chest flared and it felt as though his lungs had begun to collapse around the needles.

"Drive!" Cyn ordered.

Richards took a left, heading west. He kept glancing back at Jack with an increasingly worried look on his face. Jack wanted to ask him what he was seeing. Did he look like he was dying? It certainly felt like he was dying and it wasn't going to be one of those gently passing into the light sort of deaths either. Jack knew in his heart that when he went, there'd be a gaping hole in the universe and that he'd be sucked in where his screams would never be heard again.

Amanra had touched him with his diseased claws and Amanra would claim him when he was finally quit of this life, and Amanra would own him.

"Faster," Cyn urged. In her worry over Jack, she was managing to ignore her own pain, and the odd fact that her wound was still bleeding. It shouldn't have been. Jack had been very precise with his cut: a third of an inch deep and an inch long. It should have bled just enough to draw the circle and the runes. But it was still going, running like a faucet.

Richards picked up the speed and even lit up his dash lights and started his siren. "We'll be at St. Joseph's hospital in two minutes. Can you hold on?"

Jack nodded, or at least he thought he did; he wasn't all that sure. The lights and the siren were beginning to blur, making everything in his vision turn into a tartan mess.

Then they were at the hospital. Jack felt himself being lifted out of the back of the Ford and the only thing he knew for sure was that the four lacerations on his chest hadn't closed either. He was sitting with a lap full of blood that poured everywhere when he was placed on the gurney.

"What the hell?" someone asked. "Did a bear get at him?"

Richards opened his mouth for what was likely going to be the first of many lies, but Cyn beat him to it. "We don't know what it was. It came out of the dark."

"Yeah," Richards agreed.

Jack passed out at that point. His eyes rolled up in his head and he was gone into the black where he thought he'd be living forever; however, he wasn't out for more than an hour. He woke with what seemed like a dozen people standing over him. There was a tube down his throat and another in his arm. The smell of burnt flesh was strong in his nostrils.

He couldn't breathe. His lungs weren't working properly. There were still gobs of pain in his chest—the thousand needles had become ten-thousand. And yet it was the smell of burning flesh that had Jack the most afraid. What new hell was in his system that would cause his flesh to burn?

A masked doctor saw that he was awake and apologized: "Sorry. We're almost done."

Jack didn't have an idea about what there was to be sorry for until he heard a hiss and felt a sharp sting in his chest. The smell of burnt flesh grew stronger and Jack realized, with some relief, that they were cauterizing his wound. It hurt like a bitch, but it was at least a natural pain.

"Almost done," the doctor said, two more times, each apology accompanied by zinging sting and the smell. "Ok, all done. At least with this part." The doctor had kind, fatherly eyes and they crinkled in Jack's direction as he smiled behind his mask. Jack couldn't smile back; his pain and his fear were too great.

"This is a real stumper, Mr. Dreyden," the doctor said, stepping back. "Your wound just wouldn't close and so we were forced to oh, damn...one of the bleeders just opened up again. You're not a hemophiliac, are you?" Jack shook his head and then grimaced as he was zinged again. "Are you taking drugs? Do you work with chemicals or exotic plants?" Jack kept shaking his head.

The doctor made a noise of disappointment. "And you don't remember seeing what attacked you?" Again Jack shook his head as a monitor above his head started beeping. "O2 sats are getting low," the doctor noted. He turned to a nurse. "Get me an arterial stick. I'm going to go check on the girl."

Jack grunted out a noise and reached out with his left hand. "How's she doing?" the doctor asked. "Better than you, but only by a little. The wound in her arm won't close. It's a relatively minor laceration; however, we're seeing some necrosis around the edges, meaning the flesh is dying."

Jack nodded. There was no need to ask if his own flesh was dying; he could feel the death of a million cells every second. He could feel the *evil* working in his blood. He could feel it not just invading his lungs, he could feel it working its way to his heart.

He felt as though he was on the Titanic as it sank beneath the frigid waters of the Atlantic and the band was playing, but they weren't playing anything uplifting, they were playing *The Devil Went Down to Georgia*. The line: And he was looking for a soul to steal...went round and round in Jack's head.

His soul was on the line and he had no way of fighting back.

Cyn was two beds down and when the nurses finally took a break from trying to save their lives, she stole out of bed and came to see Jack, carrying her IV in her good arm. They'd been in the hospital for just over an hour and already she had dark circles under her eyes and she was so pale that she looked as though a doctor with a pocket full of leeches had been working on her. Even her blonde hair was lank and tired appearing, like a mop propped up in the corner of the broom closet.

Jack didn't like the look in those shadowed eyes, they said far more than the doctor's professionally hooded ones had and they said exactly what he didn't want to hear and the tears didn't help. She was in obvious pain, but the tears were for him.

"I have a confession," she whispered. "I'm sorry, but it wasn't my mother who showed our scroll to Robert's dad. It was me. I-I thought that we could figure it out together and I really didn't know what the scroll would do. You have to believe me."

Of course he believed her and he truly wished he could forgive her, verbally that is, but the tube that they had snaked down his throat wouldn't allow it. He actually had an issue with the entire concept of forgiveness. Since his mother had died, he had slowly drifted from the agnostic state in which he had been raised to being a straight-up atheist.

He had been angry at the loss of both of his parents and, in petulant irony, he had blamed the very God he claimed not to believe in.

That was then. Lying in the hospital with what could only be true evil spreading through his veins was an entirely different story. The evil in him was pure and raw, and for the first time he was physically aware of his soul. It made the idea of being an atheist foolish.

Which gave him an idea.

He motioned to Cyn, pantomiming writing on his hand. "A pen? Sure," she answered. She never got him a pen. Within two seconds of searching for one, she was caught out of bed and forcefully relocated back to her gurney.

Growing desperate, Jack thumbed the button that called a nurse. The nurse was a new one to Jack: she had a wide, pleasant face over a thick frame. "What do you need, hun?" she asked, sounding so much more like a waitress than a nurse. "Do you need something for the pain?" Jack answered by sketching out a quick and slightly inaccurate *sign of the cross*. "You want to talk to a priest?" the nurse asked.

Jack nodded with enthusiasm, although in truth he didn't care what sort of clergyman they had available. Right then he would've tried his luck with any sort of minister or rabbi, or hell, even a Jehovah's Witness would have sufficed. He was far too desperate to be picky.

Chapter 14

Lindenhurst, Long Island, New York

It was after eleven and the town of Lindenhurst wasn't exactly a hotpot for excitement, especially not priestly excitement. Still, it was a Catholic hospital and, somewhat like a doctor, there was always a priest on call. Generally...really exclusively, when a priest received a call after dark, he came prepared to administer *Last Rites*.

Jack had no idea what these rites entailed. In fact, he knew far more about the dead religions of ancient Egypt than he did about the any modern day theism, but he was more than willing to give Christianity a shot if it would save his soul. He knew that wasn't much of a foundation for belief, but he didn't need or want "faith."

He needed facts; hard, very true and very real facts.

Hell had proven itself to be real, now his life depended on heaven stepping up and coming through for him. He was ready to believe—really, he was halfway there already; however, if the priest came with only a bunch of empty promises of happy sky-fairies ruling the clouds, *but* only in some sort of mythical afterlife, Jack knew he was screwed.

The priest, a portly middle-aged man with the dark complexion and sing-song accent of someone from India, took thirty-four agonizing minutes to get to the hospital. Jack was in the ICU at that point. His respirations were down to six a minute and his heart was beginning to shudder and misfire like an old, rusted-out Ford Pinto.

He fought to stay conscious, afraid that if he drifted into the yawning black chasm of his mind, he'd never come back again, regardless of what sort of magic the priest had at his beck and call.

And yes, despite his scientific upbringing, or perhaps because of it, he was hoping and praying for the priest to bring some good old fashioned white magic to the table. Jack even envisioned a light show, complete with golden auras and cherubs playing long, brass-beaked trumpets and celestial choirs, ringing through the halls of the hospital and the priest casting out the evil invading his body with a voice like thunder.

Instead he got Father Paul, whose only nod to the miraculous side of things was in his eyes—he had deep brown eyes and they were utterly compassionate and gentle. Other than that he was a small, soft man with jowls folding over his unyielding priestly collar, and he had a quiet, cheerless way of talking as if he was expecting only sadness and death.

All in all, he was a bit of a disappointment to Jack, who had been hoping for more of a fire and brimstone sort of priest. *Perhaps a half-drunk Irishman would've been better*, Jack thought, unkindly.

"I am Father Paul Nalikar. Do I have your permission to administer Last Rites?"

If Jack could have screamed in frustration and pain, he would have. He knew very little about religion, but he had seen enough movies to know that there was no coming back once a priest laid some of those old fashioned *Last Rites* on you. Once they broke out the rosary beads everyone knew that it was time to roll credits. It meant that Jack was done for, and everyone, including God knew it.

Reluctantly, he nodded. His body was dying, but there was still his soul to worry about. He could feel it slowly being eaten even before his body had breathed its last.

Father Paul wasted no time. Speaking rapidly as though he was afraid Jack would expire before he could finish, he machine-gunned the words out: "God the Father of mercies, through the death and resurrection of his Son, has reconciled the world to himself and sent the Holy Spirit among us for the forgiveness of sins; through the ministry of the Church may God give you pardon and peace, and I absolve you from your sins in the name of the Father, and of the Son, and of the Holy Spirit."

The priest crossed himself and kissed a purple stole that lay across his shoulders. He began speaking again and his lilting, accented voice was a drone that lulled Jack into a stupor. He heard something about saints, "the Blessed Virgin Mary," and the salvation of his eternal soul—and then he was gone; not unconscious and not dead. He simply fell asleep. The pain radiating from his chest had become loose and somewhat disconnected and the fear that had gripped him lost its hold and the exhaustion of his mind and body became too great and out he went.

He was zonked for two straight hours and only another, painfully realistic dream woke him: He found himself in the deepest dark of his life. It was like being in the blackest storm cloud and yet his feet were on the ground. He stood in finely trimmed grass—*manicured*, he thought. Within the rolling blackness, there were chiseled stones as though he was in a rock garden. He wanted…no, he needed to look around, but his eyes fell on Robert Montgomery. His cousin was kneeling in front of another man who was cold and naked, spread eagle just like the guard back at the museum. Robert, with the delicate touch of a surgeon, was sacrificing another victim.

Jack knew the man.

"Dr. Loret," Jack said in a gravely whisper, as he came awake. Immediately, he grabbed his throat. It was mighty sore, as if he'd just had his tonsils removed by someone using a rusty pair of kitchen scissors. When he swallowed, it was a bit like swallowing hot sand.

There was a woman sitting by his bedside in what Jack took at first to be blue pajamas. It was a moment before he realized that they were hospital scrubs and it was another second before he recognized where he was.

"You're awake," she stated and then left the room, making sure that she didn't break eye contact with him until she was out the door.

"Yeah, I am," he said to himself. He was completely puzzled and at the same time completely relieved…well almost completely. There was a heavy sense of dread gripping his heart. Robert was not done with whatever crazy scheme he was up to. It meant more danger and more death and it meant that Jack's soul wasn't necessarily as saved as he wished it could be.

The anxiety grew to become so all-consuming that he couldn't just lie there doing nothing. He needed to get out of the bed and find out what had happened to Cyn and Richards. He had to find his clothes and his boots and his sword, but he still had an IV in his arm, nine EKG leads attached to various parts of his body and a tube sticking out of the end of his penis. When he pulled back the covers and saw this last tube, he whispered: "Whoa," wondering how the tube got there and if it was going to hurt coming out.

Likely so, he figured. He might have been rested and, somehow alive, but he was still in pain. His throat—very much so, his penis—moderately so, though most of that might have been all in his head, and his chest—a throbbing ache that was a thousand times better than it had been not long before.

He was still staring at the tube coming out of his penis when the door to his room came open and Father Paul came in followed by Cyn and a doctor that wasn't familiar until he smiled, and then Jack remembered the crinkling eyes of the ER doctor. Jack dropped the sheet down, quickly, with an odd sensation of guilt as if he had done something wrong by noticing the tube.

"Hi there," the doctor said. He had the looks of an actor, and the easy bedside manner he affected was so warm that it felt rehearsed. Somewhere in the back of his mind, Jack's paranoia began its familiar warning rumble. "I'm Dr. Rayman. You gave us quite a scare last night. You went downhill so quickly that we were afraid that we were going to lose you."

As he spoke, he pulled the sheet down and glanced under the bandage on Jack's chest. It was a quick peek, like a man checking his hole cards in a game of *Texas Hold'em*. "Hmm," he said. "Healing nicely. It's almost as if you hadn't been on death's door not so long ago. Your case is very intriguing, sort of like a puzzle that's missing some pieces."

He gave Jack an open, interested look as though he thought it would be polite for Jack to fill in some of those missing puzzle pieces. Before Jack could begin to think of something to say, Cyn shook her head the tiniest bit; warning him to remain quiet. She stood close to the priest, practically touching him. It was clear to Jack that she had been healed as well; she was back to her "old" self: utterly beautiful, composed, and, as always, there was a secret brewing behind her eyes.

When Jack failed to voluntarily give up the answers the doctor was looking for, he became more direct: "So, would you care to explain how you were injured?"

"No, I-I don't know if I can," Jack said, fumbling once again with the beginnings of a lie. It didn't help that there was a priest three feet from him, a priest with either magical powers or a direct link to God. Either way it didn't seem like a smart idea to start lying with him in hearing distance.

"Like I told you earlier, Dr. Rayman," Cyn said, before Jack could say anything too stupid. "There's an ongoing investigation into all of this. You'll need to speak to Detective Richards if you want answers because we're not at liberty to speak openly. I have his number if you need it."

The doctor grimaced as though pained by the answer. "You want to know something ugly?" The word *ugly* had been unexpected and Cyn and Jack shared a nervous look. "People lie to me every single day. *No, I wasn't drinking when I ran into the back of that parked garbage truck. No, my husband never touched me, I fell down the stairs. Sorry, Doc, I don't know how that wine bottle got wedged up my butt. I must have slipped and fallen on it*. People come in here every single day and lie their heads off, mainly because they're embarrassed. I can tell that you two are definitely lying, but not because you're embarrassed and that's what worries me. You're lying because you're in deep trouble. Yes, I've seen those lies, too…only I've never seen them when a cop's involved. That makes me nervous."

Cyn shrugged, but it was a lie as well, and not a very good one. "Well, it…it shouldn't make you nervous. Detective Richards is not actually involved, per say. He is heading up a criminal investigation and he has the situation well in hand."

"Really?" Dr. Rayman asked. "And the two bodies that are being brought in to the morgue, is that part of the situation that he has so well in hand? We don't get murdered cops in Lindenhurst every day."

This almost derailed Cyn, who could only repeat: "Like I said, we're not at liberty to discuss the case."

"And we really need to be going," Jack said, catching Cyn's eye. The dream was still fresh in his mind and with it was an echo of fear running along his nerves. "There are things we have to attend to," he went on, "so, if I can get these tubes out, I'd really like to get going."

Rayman's face turned stony. "You two don't seem to understand my situation. If you were smuggling dope or were two-bit hoodlums who had robbed a 7-11, I wouldn't care what you were you up to. In fact, I'd want you out of here as soon as I could honestly release you, but that's not what's happening, is it?"

Again, Jack glanced to Cyn, who was thin-lipped; the calculations behind her eyes were so obvious that Rayman gave her a tired look and said: "Just don't. Before you come up with some stupid lie, let me tell you that I can detain you if I wish. I can put both of you on an infectious disease hold for three days. Those wounds you came in with had all the hallmarks of necrotizing fasciitis. That's a flesh-eating bacterium that will eat you from the inside out and only a three-week long regimen of some heavy-duty antibiotics has any chance of stopping it, and that's under the best of circumstances."

A third time, Jack shifted his eyes toward his cousin, hoping that she'd be able to come up with something to counter the doctor. Her cheek started to quiver and her mouth started to work as though it was on the verge of speech, but nothing came out.

"Really?" Dr. Rayman asked in amazement. "I tell you that an almost incurable flesh-eating disease is ravaging you and neither of you is willing to talk? You're leaving me no choice here. I can't take the risk of spreading whatever pathogen it was that you were carrying."

Father Paul put up a brown hand; it was as soft and gentle appearing as the rest of him. "Maybe they'll talk to me. Would you allow that?"

The doctor shifted his eyes towards Jack's monitor, which beeped softly every few seconds; the numbers were all within the proper parameters. He shrugged and said: "Sure, Father. I'm not trying to be the bad guy here, I'm just trying to keep the public safe and what I saw tonight...well I guess I don't really know what I saw, and that scares me."

When the doctor left, Father Paul gave them a very white-toothed smile; he then began to beam and seemed almost giddy. "He trusts me," he said about Dr. Rayman. "But I don't think he trusts God, which is a shame, especially after what occurred here tonight. It was a miracle! I really believe that. I walked into your room, Mister Jack, expecting to go through the regular routine of catering to the dying or the dead. I don't mean to be blasé about *Last Rites*, but I am only the intermediary between the Lord and the person lying in the bed. It can be disheartening at times to be called on like this night after night. But tonight..."

He laughed, a quick happy sound and his teeth flashed again, brighter now that he was speaking of the miracle.

"You were basically dead, Mister Jack. That is a fact that cannot be denied. I come to this hospital five, six times a week and sometimes two or three times a night, so I know what it means when the alarms are turned off on the monitor and there is nothing but the blinking lights and all the numbers are gradually winding down to zero. It means you are almost dead."

The huge grin splitting his face while he was saying this was rather jolting to Jack, who felt the need to answer it back with one of his own. He was too anxious to do a smile proper justice and it stayed on his lips for only a brief flash. Father Paul didn't notice, he had begun pacing in his excitement, his hands held up near his face as though suspended by invisible wires.

"I began the rites with the imparting of absolution," Father Paul went on, staring at the stark, white wall. "At first you just laid there and then, so quickly, your heart rate began to climb! I saw it with my own eyes. It started at around thirty and then just climbed and climbed. The more I spoke the further it went up...and your respirations did as well, and then when I anointed you with the sacramental oil...oh! You jerked and there was a strong smell. It was like the smell from a cesspool or a mass grave. It was there and so strong that my eyes watered, but then it was gone and I smelled honey and olives and the air was clean. And that was when you groaned, Mister Jack and raised your hand."

"I did?"

"Of course you did," the priest said, his grin was now so wide his laugh-lines bent to touch both ears. "You raised your hand to God! It was miraculous. It was a real miracle, one that I long wished for. That is a weakness and a sin, I know, but I've so longed to feel the hand of God and to feel his presence and his power."

Despite the impending doom hanging over his head, Jack smiled as well. Father Paul's obvious joy was infectious and Jack stuck out his hand. "I'm so sorry; I haven't even thanked you for saving my life. If it wasn't for you, I'd..."

"No, do not thank me, you should thank God!" Father Paul cried. "It was *His* intercession that saved you. I did nothing. I was only the conduit. I was the servant. One does not thank the servant, one thanks the master."

Father Paul waited, eyeing Jack with expectation until Jack said: "Thank you, God." It was a clumsy attempt at gratitude mainly because the room felt empty as though God had already moved on, if he had even been there at all. Jack had slept through his miracle healing and already the suspicious, paranoid doubter in his mind was back.

It might have been the antibiotics that Dr. Rayman had you on, an inner voice remarked. Jack glanced up at the IV running into the crook of his arm, and saw that piggybacked to a bag of normal saline, was an antibiotic with a name fourteen letters long that he wasn't going to begin trying to pronounce. He only knew it was an antibiotic because the word: Antibiotic was written under the fourteen-letter word.

Jack ignored the voice in his head, but he couldn't ignore the sudden fear that suddenly swept him. It was a huge feeling; it was a tidal wave of terror. It gripped him around the heart and squeezed, making his monitor ring out in a long strident tone.

It went on and on until Dr. Rayman rushed in. "What the hell?" he cried as he fell straight over Cyn, who had fainted dead away.

The word *hell* caught in Jack's mind. *Robert has done it again*, he thought. That was the only explanation he could think of to both his and Cyn's simultaneous reaction. Robert was using the spells once more, and something very big was demanding to come through, something monstrous.

Chapter 15

Calvary Cemetery, Queens, New York

Jack's heart was a bounding mess. He sat in the back seat of Richards' Ford Taurus with one hand on his chest, feeling the organ inside skitter and throb. Sitting next to him, her face just as white as a snow bank, was Cyn. She alternated between staring out the window at the passing city and staring at Jack.

She had the frightened eyes of a kitten about to be gassed.

In the front seat, Richards drove, his hound dog look morphed into a scowl. He had, in his own words: *Lied his ass off*, concerning the crime scene at Dr. Loret's home. "I told my lieutenant that we were dealing with a highly-financed gang of devil-worshipping art thieves. I'm pretty sure that he didn't believe me, not that I blame him. It was as cockamamie a story as I've heard anyone tell, but it was the only thing I could think of that fit even remotely with the facts."

Next to him sat Father Paul who was the only one of the four who was completely at ease. On his lap, sitting primly like a pet cat, was a bible and on top of that was a cross that he had taken from a wall in the little chapel that was tucked in a corner of the maze-like hospital. In his pocket was a bottle of blessed oil and another of Holy Water.

"I think lying may be the wrong approach here," Father Paul said. This was the second time in the last half hour that he had said those words. The first came after Jack's heart attack. He was sure that it wasn't really a heart attack and that it was only a panic attack or some sort of event brought on by stress, but it sure had *felt* like a heart attack. He had honestly thought he was on the verge of dying.

Dr. Rayman had tried to calm him by saying: "You're too young for a heart attack." And yet he hadn't taken any chances and had administered nitroglycerin to Jack. The nitro had done nothing as far as Jack could tell.

"Try to relax," Father Paul said. "The Lord is looking out for both of you."

"He had better be," Cyn had said from a chair in the corner of the room. She had been brought around by a whiff of smelling salts. She was itching to say more, but waited until Dr. Rayman left the room. The moment he did, she told Father Paul everything in a rushed condensed version that made the events sound as though they had been lifted from a movie.

From time to time, the priest had glanced at Jack as if to verify he was not being pranked. When she had finished with: "And now something's happened. We both felt it, Jack and I did. It's something big or the start of something big, I don't know."

"What are we going to tell Dr. Rayman?" Jack had asked. That's when Father Paul had first used the line about lying. Cyn had gotten around the necessity of lying by calling Detective Richards and begging him to get to the hospital as fast as he could. He didn't even ask why, and three minutes later, the Ford's siren could be heard, quiet at first, but with growing urgency.

When he arrived, he took one look at their faces and began ordering the hospital workers to disconnect Jack and to fetch his clothes, and he wasn't lying when he told Rayman that lives were at stake.

"So, what are we looking at?" Richards asked as they sped west, towards the city.

"I dreamt that Robert was sacrificing Dr. Loret," Jack answered. "He was drawing the glyphs and the circles, but I couldn't see where, exactly. I think it might have been a park somewhere in Brooklyn...no wait, it was Queens. I could just make out the tips of the Empire State Building and the Chrysler building. The angle suggested that he was straight east of 34th Street. That's Queens, right?"

Richards nodded, his scowl deepening. "There aren't that many parks in Queens, at least not close in. There's Juniper Park. In your dream did you see baseball fields?"

"Maybe," Jack said. "The grass was trim but thick, sort of like an outfield."

"This seems all so fantastic," Father Paul said, his easy look of contentment still upon him as he caressed the leather cover of his bible with his soft brown hand. "It is hard to believe that your story is real and yet, I am sure that it is. I feel it in my bones and I see the truth in your faces."

Jack touched the rapier that sat point down between his legs. When they had first jumped into the police car, he had been loath to touch it, but as the buildings had gradually grown and the suburbs had given way to the city, and his fear had built, he pulled the weapon close.

"It's real, Father," Jack said. He then pointed to the bible and asked: "Is there a special prayer or a passage in there to help us fight the undead? Or what about..." He words stopped and his throat began working up and down as a feeling of dread struck him and hot bile built up inside of him.

They were on the Long Island Expressway, in the middle of Queens. On their right was Flushing Meadows Park; it was dark and cold and the grass was a dull brown. On their left was a cemetery—the grass was browned but deep and plush, even in winter and there were tens of thousands of headstones.

Jack felt his heart begin to tremble.

Father Paul did not notice his discomfort or the fact that he was on the verge of passing out again. The priest was speaking about prayer in general. "We can pray for those in need of guidance and we can pray for courage in the face of our enemies, but as for actual battle, there is little that is uplifting, though most consider the *Psalm of David* adequate. The Lord is my shepherd; I shall not want. He maketh me to lie down in green pastures: he leadeth me beside the still waters. He restoreth my soul: he leadeth me in the paths of righteousness for his name's sake. Yea, though I walk through the valley of the shadow of death, I will fear no evil: for thou art with me; thy rod and thy staff they comfort me."

"I think I'm going to need more of that fear no evil stuff," Jack said. "I think it was a cemetery that I saw Robert in, not a park. Everything was dark and there were what I thought were parts of rocks sticking up out of the ground."

"They were headstones?" Cyn asked. Jack nodded. She stared out the window, shaking her head as they rode past rank upon rank of graves. Finally she said: "Then we don't go. We let someone else take care of this, like the army or something."

Instead of slowing at the suggestion, Detective Richards hit the gas. "You know, I wanted to quit this earlier. After I dropped you off at the hospital, I wanted to beg off sick and let someone else shoulder the yoke, but I didn't, because what if the next guy did the same thing? No, we don't run. We have a chance to nip this in the bud. We need to take out Robert now before he can call any more of these things back to life. Really, it shouldn't be that hard. We know what they can do: fear, darkness, poisonous touch. These are all things we can fight against and we can fight against the monsters as well. We have two shotguns with us and two swords and we have Father Paul."

With a friendly smile, the detective reached over and punched the priest in the arm, saying: "Who knows what sort power he has. I for one think we have a real good shot at ending this."

"But what about what Jack and I felt earlier?" Cyn asked. "It was big."

"And the feeling hasn't gotten any better," Jack added, licking his lips, which seemed desert-dry. "The feeling has been coming to me in pulses, there's been three so far, and it feels like it's building to something." Cyn nodded along in agreement.

Father Paul glanced back at the two of them with a confused look. "Perhaps you are making more out of this than is necessary. How many mummies...you know, em-balmed people can there be in New York? I'm betting the number is not over twenty and can he raise them all at once? I doubt it, but even if he could, twenty is a manage-able number."

Again Jack licked his lips; twenty mummies were far from manageable. It was a huge number to Jack. They'd had their hands full...more than full with six of them. He was about to say so when his heart skipped a beat. "Oh. The focal point has shifted. It's west of here and a little south."

"That's the Calvary Cemetery," Father Paul told them. "Take the next exit and go south on Laurel Hill." The four of them grew quiet, and now, even Father Paul looked nervous. The night was deep and the cemetery was like an immense playground for the dead, but instead of swings and slides, there were tombstones and mausoleums and hallowed shrines holding the moldering bones of not thousands of corpses and not tens of thousands of corpses, but hundreds of thousands.

Cyn had her phone out and looked like a corpse her-self with the white light shining up to highlight the ex-treme paleness of her face. "It says here that Calvary Cemetery has 850,000 people buried in it."

Jack leaned over and looked at the phone. "That's impossible." She showed him the link. He felt like he had been punched in the gut. "The Incan mummy," he said.

"Yeah," Cyn replied.

"But that was an accident," Richards said. "He proba-bly wouldn't make the same mistake, twice, and even if he did, it's like the Father said, how many mummies can there be?"

They reached the gates of the cemetery and found them flung wide and yet nothing had ever looked less inviting. The night was moonless and dark, darker than usual; however, the cemetery seemed darker than was physically possible. The shadows were not just deep, they looked endlessly deep as if they could swallow you whole, as if you could get lost in them and never find your way out.

Jack found himself staring into them; certain he would see a living corpse in every one of them, waiting for him to come closer. The shadows were so sinister that he failed to notice the circle of glyphs spelled out in blood beneath the cast-iron sign spanning the entrance.

When Cyn nudged him and pointed, he couldn't help feeling relief. The cemetery was dark, sure, but it wasn't crawling with half a million zombies. "I don't see any empty graves," he said. "Maybe we got lucky and he screwed up."

"You should go check it out," Cyn said, nudging Jack and trying to hand him her phone.

He refused to take it, pulling his hands back. "Me? Why me?"

"Because you're the expert," she told him, placing the phone in his lap. "You're the only one who knows this language well enough to catch a mistake. Besides, you can take Father Paul with you."

The euphoria of the healing miracle appeared to be fading quickly and now the priest had a shine of sweat across his brow. "That is blood, is it not?" he asked, staring at the glyphs.

"Yeah," Jack said, taking a deep breath. "Come on." With the rapier in hand, he opened his door and took a tentative step out. The first thing that struck him was just how quiet the night was. There were no sounds at all coming from the cemetery. There was the low rumble of the Ford and nothing else, seemingly for miles.

When he took a step, the crunch of gravel under his foot felt magnified and it also felt unwelcome. Jack had the distinct sensation that he didn't belong. Calvary had always been a place for the dead, but now it felt as though it was *only* for the dead. It felt as though all 850,000 sets of rotted and sunken eyes were watching him as he began almost tiptoeing towards the twin circles that Robert had drawn at the entrance.

Next to him, Father Paul was also treading as lightly as he could, taking comically exaggerated steps in order not to disturb the gravel and the eerie quiet of the cemetery. "I didn't think it would be like this," he admitted in a whisper. "I honestly didn't think I would be afraid."

To Jack, even the priest's whispering was loud and he wondered how he had been saddled with the unarmed Father Paul. Despite her size, he would've preferred Cyn. Not only did she have a tenacious manner to her, she also clung to the gigantic shotgun that Richards had taken from the Lindenhurst police cruiser. From the moment they had climbed into the Taurus, she had laid the gun across her thighs and held it there in a firm grip.

"It's going to get worse," Jack told Father Paul. "Just remember that it's all in your head and that you can fight it. Now, if you don't mind, I have to concentrate."

Jack turned on the phone's light and shone it down on the glyphs. The outer ring was a dull brown, while the inner one glistened. "He calls for protection first, before he opens the portal," Jack said to himself. "But there's something missing. There were three heirs but there's only evidence of two spells. There has to be another one, but what does the third spell do? And look, the arch-glyph, the one at the top center is different. This sun rising with the three lines below it, what's it mean? Three more spells or the same spell three more times? Or maybe it's describing a boundary?"

He stood for a few minutes biting the inside of his cheek, however the answer didn't jump out at him and his anxiety grew steadily. He gave up on that riddle and squatted down just on the outside of the rings. It made sense for him to analyze "his" spell first. He knew it by heart and spoke the words in a mumble under his breath, stopping just short of finishing the incantation…just in case.

Other than a few curved lines that should've been straight and a couple of smudged wedges, the opening spell was well done, especially considering the medium that was being used. "He's getting better," Jack murmured.

Then he started in on the protection spell. Three words had been changed; or rather one word had been changed three times. "It should say 'one' walks in the light."

"Is that significant?" Father Paul asked. The priest held his bible tight to his chest in his left hand, while in his right he held a weighty crucifix with his brown fingers curled around the lower part of the cross as though it was the pommel of a sword.

"Very," Jack said. The symbol of 'the one-legged ant' denoting a single individual had been replaced by a circle meaning 'all.'

It seemed that Robert had tried to raise all of the dead in the cemetery, but had failed. Yes, there was an eerie, unnatural feeling in the bone yard, but there wasn't any evidence that a single grave had been disturbed. The plots were all covered over in sod and the mausoleums were silent houses of the dead.

But what explained the dreadful feeling of being watched from beneath the earth? And what was with the sour air of expectation that he sucked in with every breath?

"Wait here," Jack said to the priest. He walked under the wrought iron sign and stood just inside the cemetery and tried to feel with that unknown part of him that had sprung into being two days before. He could sense that Hor and the other mummies were near. Jack could feel them to the southwest.

They were close maybe a mile, which meant that there was still time to run. At this time of night, they could be in New Jersey in an hour and in Pennsylvania an hour after that, and on the west coast a day after that, if they took turns pushing the Ford for all she was worth.

He dearly wanted to. With all of his shaking heart he wanted to run away, but he had the sinking feeling that the planet just wasn't big enough anymore. If he could feel Hor, didn't that mean that Hor could feel him as well? That was little kid logic and yet it couldn't be denied that Hor could find him anywhere he went.

Jack crossed back over the threshold of the cemetery and felt instant relief. It made the idea of heading back in that much more difficult. He walked around the circles and said to the priest: "Let's go."

Seconds later they were back in the car and the fear he'd been feeling receded that much more, it allowed him to say: "We still have a chance. Robert tried to raise all of them…"

"What?" Cyn almost screamed. "All of them? Why? Why on earth would he do that?"

"He tried and he failed," Jack said. "Look! The graves aren't disturbed. But I think he's trying again. I can feel Hor and the others. They're still in the cemetery."

A shiver went up Cyn's back and her shoulders twitched. "Me too," she admitted. "That way." She pointed in the direction Jack's heart knew they would find the living dead.

"Then we go after him," Richards said. "We go after him with the intent to kill him. Is everyone agreed?" He had his beefy arm flung over the headrest of Father Paul's seat; however, he wasn't talking to the priest; he wasn't even taking his opinion into consideration.

"I'm in," Jack said, trying to forget the extent of the soul-crushing fear that he had endured or the pain or the fact that he'd been at death's door not long before. Cyn sat in the back seat with all eyes on her. She sat cringed inwards, so much like a child that it hurt Jack's heart to ask: "What about you?"

She started to nod and it went on for half a minute until the action made it to her lips: "Yes. I-I…this is at least partially my fault, so yes, let's kill him." Her British accent was cool and clipped, but it didn't hide her fear.

Father Paul began to offer reasons why they should consider mercy or a different path besides violence, but

Jack stopped him by holding up a hand. "Give me this speech when you see what he's done or when Hor has his bony fist five inches deep in your chest or when you see what's left of Loret. Then go ahead and tell me how forgiveness and love will win out. Until then…keep that bible ready, we're going to need it."

Chapter 16

Calvary Cemetery, Queens, New York

Father Paul nodded to Jack, but said nothing. His confident look spoke volumes that was a cinch to read: the priest had a direct hand in an *actual* verifiable miracle not three hours before and he had all the faith in his Lord that he would ever need, enough faith to overcome the bugwumps and the closet monsters and the things that hid under the bed when the lights went out…or whatever their Indian equivalents were.

Jack knew better than to trust the look. His confidence would fail and so would his faith, but there was also a chance that it would fight back—the faith that is. The confidence was only seconds from being wiped away forever.

Just as Jack knew it would, the look vanished the moment they crossed over the threshold of the cemetery and the thousands of dead eyes in their crypts turned toward the car. That very second, every inch of Father Paul's exposed flesh was tented up by goosebumps and when he swallowed, it was with a clicking sound.

He wasn't the only one suddenly stricken by terror. They all were. It was impossible not to feel the unnatural, magical hell-fear that saturated the night. The feeling was akin to the dread that Hor had been able to create, only it was tremendous in scope and shivered the very air.

The only thing that kept them going forwards was the fact that there wasn't a single disturbed grave in sight. The grass had been browned by the chill of winter but it hadn't been overturned by clawed hands and the doors to the various mausoleums hadn't been hammered open, and, most importantly, there weren't hordes of undead charging the Ford.

If the evil in the air could be ignored, then the cemetery was just that, a cemetery—a place where teens came to scare each other or make out, or a place where loved ones came, perhaps on Veterans Day or Christmas or a birthday, or, more often than people knew, on a *deathday*, to pay their respects.

But the evil couldn't be ignored.

The four of them rolled into a darkness that wasn't God-created. It was a roiling black cloud that ate up the headlights of the Ford and swirled among their feet, freezing their bones and causing their hands to hook into claws and their teeth to chatter.

Cyn turned from Jack, holding the shotgun toward the window. He put his back to hers, expecting to be attacked at any second. In the front seat, Father Paul began to pray: "Our Father, who art in heaven, hallowed be thy name; thy kingdom come, thy will be done, on earth as it is in heaven..."

Richards interrupted him: "Father, maybe you should stop that." The blackness had grown thicker, heavier, angrier. It was now as substantial as London fog and it stopped their high beams as if the lights were shooting into a wall.

"I am of a different mind," the priest said. "I rather think that I should keep going if my prayer is agitating whatever is causing this. As well, I find it reassuring." He began again from the beginning. Jack wanted the priest to keep going, hoping that the culmination of the prayer would bring with it some sort ecclesiastical outburst that would drive away the darkness.

It did not.

The darkness was unaffected other than the swirling and the increasing depth. Jack wasn't the only one disappointed. "I'd turn off the headlights," Cyn suggested in a quiet voice.

"Yeah, I think you're right," Richards said. Now their running lights were all the illumination they had, forcing Richards to drive at a snail's pace. Jack was glad for the lack of speed. They didn't have far to go and he had a sinking feeling that they were driving into a hornet's nest of trouble.

Father Paul had moved on and was voicing the *Psalm of David*, when Cyn whispered: "We're close. We're bloody close." Her lips were blue and jabbering up and down and her eyes were wide, unblinking ovals and yet when Richards stopped the car, she was the first out, holding the shotgun against her stomach instead of her shoulder.

The improper stance was enough to get Richards out of the car. "Brace it like this. Good, now remember, you don't really aim a shotgun; pointing is good enough at close quarters...and it's gonna be really fricking close."

As they couldn't see three feet in front of their faces, Richards wasn't wrong. Jack climbed out of the Ford and swished at the darkness with his rapier causing it to only swirl and spin. Father Paul was last out and the other three turned to him.

Cyn waited, impatiently as the priest only stood there. "Do something," she hissed. "Try a spell or something. *They* are out there watching us."

"I'm a priest, not a sorcerer," he answered. "We don't have spells or voodoo. Our strength comes to us through faith and payer."

A sound that might have been the scrape of an old leaf blowing across the ground or the scuff of a dried-up bone on concrete had Cyn spinning to her right, once again thrusting the shotgun out in front of her. "Then pray for some bloody light!"

"That I can do." Father Paul raised the bible and said in a loud voice: "All powerful and ever-living God, cast out from our hearts the darkness of sin and bring us to the light of your truth. We ask this through our Lord Jesus

Christ, your Son, who lives and reigns with you and the Holy Spirit, one God, for ever and ever. AMEN!"

"Whoa," Jack said. As the priest spoke, the darkness was swept back as if blown by an unfelt wind and now, they could see the cemetery just as Jack had envisioned it in his dream—the graves were still undisturbed; Loret was naked, spread eagle split open from throat to testicles and Robert Montgomery, still arrayed in the same suit he had been wearing the last Jack had seen him, knelt over him with a camel-hair brush in his red hand, putting the final touches on the last of the glyphs.

Richards' shotgun swiveled to take Robert in his sights. "Stop! Put the brush down or I swear I will end you!"

The brush paused on a down stroke and Robert glanced up. There was something wrong with his eyes that even the night couldn't hide. They were twitchy and appeared to be filled with blood. "This is your fault, Detective. And yours as well, Wild Jack. This entire episode wasn't supposed to occur in this manner. I never wanted to include any of you in this, especially you my dear cousins...of course, I couldn't have done it without your help, either."

Jack stole a peek at Cyn. The truth seemed to have wilted her and the shotgun wavered, coming off her shoulder. Her chin swung Jack's way, but she wouldn't look up from the tops of his dusty boots.

"Put the brush down!" Richards ordered a second time, his finger slipping into the trigger guard. "You are under arrest, Robert. Put the brush down and no one will get hurt."

The detective should have ignored his training and his humanity. He should not have hesitated or issued a warning, and above all, he should have killed the man on his knees, who was armed with only a paintbrush. If Jack had a gun instead of a sword, he would have pulled the trigger without a qualm, because, unlike Richards he could feel Hor and the other undead creatures.

They had been swept back with the darkness, but now as the shadows advanced once again, they crept closer. The dark hid them until they were only steps away.

Cyn shot first.

Jack watched as if seeing the world in slow motion as she tugged her chin around to the right; the shotgun came around even slower. She could sense the creatures as well as Jack could. "Detective!" she cried.

Richards took his eyes off Robert for a split second and the moment he did, everything snapped back to normal speed and all hell broke loose...literally. The Incan appeared out of the darkness and was on Cyn so quickly that she didn't have time to haul the heavy gun to her shoulder. She fired from the hip. There was a blinding light and a roar of an explosion that was shocking to the ears.

The force of the blast, coupled with an unseen headstone sent the hundred-and-five pound girl falling over backwards, her gun going off a second time, luckily it was pointed at the stars and not at any of them.

"Help her!" Jack cried, pushing Father Paul toward Cyn and then spinning to face Amanra...or so he thought. The magical blackness was coming back stronger than ever and all Jack could see of the mummy was a flash of bleached bone as claws whistled at him.

He threw himself backwards to avoid the strike that would have taken out his eyes and left him blind...or rather more blind than he was. The darkness made the next few moments a nightmare of leering bone-faces, sharpened claws and ear-shattering explosions.

Jack whipped his rapier back and forth, fighting, using only the strange "feeling" he possessed that emanated from behind his breastbone. He could tell the direction of his enemies and if they were *closer* or *further*, but not how close or far, so that half the time he flailed at nothing.

A half minute went by without him being gutted and he found that if he used his ears in conjunction with his ability to "feel" his opponents, he was able to hone in on them. A lucky strike took Amanra's right arm off and then Jack was so close that he was able to see the monster well enough to send a kick into its chest, knocking it over the front of the Ford.

Under the pale glow of the running lights, Jack dismembered Amanra in two more swings. Flush with victory, he spun around and headed to where the twin shotguns were tearing up the night. Every time they fired, they appeared to Jack like the breath of dragons. He almost forgot that neither Richards nor Cyn could see him and one shot *fizzed* so close that Jack felt his hair blown back by the blast.

"It's me!" he yelled as he cowered behind a tombstone. "Don't shoot!"

"Where's Robert?" Richards bellowed.

Caught in the swirling darkness, Jack was completely turned around; he barely knew which way up was. "I don't know he was...." He stopped as he heard mumbling off to his left.

The words were dreadfully familiar: "*Hrr vahl Evi ah hurrumm fd. Kulhrr hrer hrrfhk. Ahk kul, ahk fd, ahk thul ah fherd...*" Jack knew these words. Jack had even spoken them aloud when he had been working on deciphering the scroll that his father had left to him. The words and the bloody glyphs opened the portal to the netherworld!

"Father Paul!" he screamed. "Give us some damned light!"

There was a moment of hesitancy and then Father Paul began in a wavering voice: "All powerful and everliving God, cast out from our hearts the darkness of sin..."

Jack tuned out the priest and with his sword-arm cocked back, he let the sound of the ancient words—"*Hrr vahl Evi ah hurrumm fd. Kulhrr hrer hrrfhk. Ahk kul, ahk fd, ahk thul ah fherd.*"—lead him to Robert; however, before he could find his cousin in the dark, Hor appeared before him, a ghastly apparition. His presence was a tumor in Jack's mind causing him to reel back swinging at the darkness with his sword, this way and that.

The cuts were so feeble that Hor's laugh bounced back and forth in his mind, echoing, echoing, echoing… beguiling him and stunning him at once. He staggered, knocking into unyielding objects: the Ford, a tombstone, a leafless tree that had lived its life, sucking the remains of the dead from the earth.

And then, when Jack couldn't tell up from down, the darkness suddenly drew back and with it went the pounding laugh in Jack's mind. Jack put out a hand to the nearest thing to him: a weathered tombstone with only the name Orin Haymech and the date April 4th 1863 chiseled upon it. After a hundred and fifty-three years the surface of the granite was so smooth that the lettering was visible only at an angle and even then it was barely visible.

He gazed around him like the survivor of a car crash would. The ground was littered with bones and ugly chunks of the mummies: an arm here, a torso there, a death shroud caught up in the tree like a child's kite.

His cousin Cynthia was alive and unharmed, standing with her back to Detective Richards; there was a gentle wisp of grey smoke rising up from the bore of the shotgun she held in a tight grip. Her breath was running in and out of her causing the smoke to curl into spirals.

A sound pulled Jack's head around. It was Robert. During the fight in the dark he hadn't budged and still knelt over Dr. Loret. Jack's eyes were drawn to the glyphs and saw that this was the fourth time the spells had been used. Each set of the spells were oriented on the compass and had been drawn at the furthest reaches of the cemetery, north, south east, and west…and this was the last, and when it was done, every corpse within its boundary would come alive.

"*Hrr vahl Evi ah hurrumm fd. Kulhrr hrer hrrfhk. Ahk kul, ahk fd, ahk thul ah fherd,*" Robert said, or rather repeated. The spell was spoken in threes and there was no need to guess that this was the third utterance.

As the last syllable left his lips a harsh, tinny noise rang out from the circle in front of him. It was an ugly sound that made the living cringe and the undead stand up straight as though they had been called to attention by some other-worldly drillmaster. The sound became louder and louder and was joined by other, distant metallic cries, each corresponding to the cardinal points of the compass.

The sound set up a vibration in Jack's chest that ran along his nerves and deep into his bones. His strength left him so suddenly that his legs gave out and he fell against Orin Haymech's stone. The others were in much the same situation. Even Robert was affected by the sound; he backed away from the twin circles that he had drawn with his hands over his ears, his eyes squeezed shut, and his teeth clenched. He too, struck a tombstone and he sagged down against it until the sound gradually became less and faded away.

Then came a moment of dread expectation. Everyone stared at the twin circles and saw that the cement drive within them had disappeared and now there was what looked like a pool of oil. It was slick ebony and so black that it looked wet. But it wasn't endless and neither was it perfect in its blackness. There were motes and imperfections that grew as Jack stared, becoming yellow-grey boils that swarmed up from the awful depths.

"Make it stop," Jack said…it was more of a beg. He could hear the child-like petulance in his own voice.

"I can't," Robert said. His face was still afflicted by the terror that the metallic sound had induced in them.

Jack knew he had to get away. He had to run from there before it was too late, before whatever that had been imprisoned in the pit escaped. And yet he couldn't move. His muscles were jello and shaking and his will wasn't strong enough to overcome the terror that was building.

The surface of the black pool became scummed over as the sick boils hit the slick top and flattened out. The surface didn't balloon as Jack expected, but instead it grew tight and thin. There was a layer of something holding the scum in but it was failing. It grew thin and tighter and tighter until there came a strange sad sigh, a loud *aaahhh* from the earth as though the planet was dying and giving up its soul.

Then *they* escaped.

They weren't exactly spirits as Jack understood the term, nor were they ghosts or even souls. What came from the pool was the essence of evil, condensed and given a human shape and maybe even human memories, but they weren't human, or if they had been, they had been scorched in the void and malformed beyond recognition. They were twisted and tortured. They were chaos. There was nothing to them, they were phantoms of rage.

In a billowing wave they came soundlessly screaming up out of the void, riding a wind of ice and death, and, ignoring Robert altogether, they made straight for Jack. Neither instinct nor skill saved him. He threw himself backward and slashed with his rapier, but the beings had no form. They were creatures of pure malice and couldn't be hurt, at least not until they had a body to possess and Jack's was the closest.

Dozens of them swept past the blade and swarmed down Jack's open mouth and went straight up his nose until his lungs were filled with them, freezing the air there and turning his blood to ice. His heart stuttered, forgetting its rhythm and his chest hitched, but no air could move in or out and slowly the world went grey. He was dying, but the creatures didn't care.

They fought for supremacy. They fought to see which of them was greatest, to see which would be able to wear him like a meat suit.

Chapter 17

Calvary Cemetery, Queens, New York

Jack's hands went numb and the rapier fell. He could barely feel his fingers as they clawed at his own throat. The swarm inside his chest was killing him. The sensation was similar to that of drowning; however, there was no sweet release from the agony by sucking in lungfuls of seawater.

The horrible feeling simply went on and on until an unassuming and almost girlish voice said: "Release him. I-In the name of J-Jesus Christ release him."

Something gold flashed in the night and Jack was able to focus his eyes long enough to see the unwieldy crucifix Father Paul had been carrying, thrust forward. Then came a screaming in his mind that was picked up by his body as the spirit creatures fled.

He screamed uncontrollably until the last of them had been forced from him. Jack sat up, but didn't thank Father Paul—he turned to the side and puked his guts out. Only when he brought up loud croaking burps did he look around and see that not even a minute had passed and that the portal into hell was still open and still gushing forth the warped spirits.

Father Paul stood hunched over Richards, Cyn, and Jack, holding the symbol of his faith out toward the portal. The spirits would rush up, see the crucifix and then veer away, heading into the cemetery toward the hundreds of thousands of bodies just waiting for someone or something to bring them back to a semblance of life.

As they watched, the phantoms slipped around the cracks in the doors of the mausoleums or slid beneath the dirt—and there were just so many of them.

"We need to close the portal," Cyn yelled. The night was no longer quiet. A howling wind rushed up out of the portal and kept her hair spinning so that at times it floated around her face like gold flames. The night was loud but also the four of them were subject to a psychic storm that filled their heads with the crackling static of an unturned and blaring radio.

They all turned to Father Paul, who nodded, but not as the eager strong priest he had been, but more like a frightened boy. He cleared his throat and raised his hands —the bible in his left, the crucifix in his right. "In the name of the Father, and the son, and the Holy Ghost!" he yelled at the top of his lungs. "We humbly prostrate ourselves in your presence, oh Lord, and beg your mercy. Please hear our prayers, Lord and destroy these minions of Satan. Send them back into the void whence they came. In your name, Amen!"

The swirling spirits flared briefly so that their translucent forms lit brightly from within, but only for a flash and then it was as if nothing had happened and they continued to rush out into the world the way they had been.

"How come that didn't work?" Cyn cried. "That should've worked." No one knew, and with the evil in the air and their minds being raped by the static noise, none of them looked capable of properly analyzing the situation.

"Maybe if we broke the circle it would close the portal," Jack suggested, coming up with a solution that was in essence: *What if we shut the door?* They all agreed it was a good plan and then the three of them looked once again to Father Paul. None of them had known the meek priest three hours before, but now they were putting their lives in his hands.

His arms holding up the bible and the crucifix were trembling, his soft brown face drooped, and his breath was ragged. It took a lot out of him just to yell over the gale: "I don't think I can. I am very tired and I don't know why. I am afraid to use up too much of my energy. Mister Jack, you should do it. In my coat pocket is a little bottle of Holy Water. It should do the trick if anything will."

Me? Jack wanted to ask. He was feeling weak as well. His energy and his will to fight drained from him with every passing second. He wanted to argue that someone else should break the circle, but then he saw that he was the only one who was empty-handed. His sword lay a few feet away, but was outside the very small circle of protection that the crucifix afforded.

"I guess," he mumbled beneath the fury, and then fished out the bottle. It was disappointingly small, a few ounces at most. He'd been hoping for something larger, closer to the size of a canteen, something he could have thrown from where they stood, huddled together.

"We need to get closer!" Jack yelled. He was amped up with fear, certain that if he got too close to the portal he'd be sucked in. "And hold onto me. Don't let go!" Hands gripped him as he edged forward with tiny shuffling steps.

They were so tiny and hesitant that Detective Richards stepped on the back of his boots on more than one occasion. "Get moving," Richards growled in his ear.

Jack ignored the detective. His entire being was focused on the yawning pit. As he neared the edge, he saw the phantoms lined up, millions deep, each eagerly waiting their turn to get back into a land of the living, eagerly looking forward to despoiling exactly what they desired and turning it into another hell.

The cold and the wind slowed him, as well. His flesh hardened and stung, his eyes watered, the tears freezing on his lashes, the air in his lungs felt like spikes, and the knuckles of the hand with the outstretched bottle were so cold that they felt as though they were on fire—and yet his palm was warm—the Holy Water was not turning to ice as it should have.

The water danced and jiggled in the bottle as his hand shook from the cold, but through some mysterious force, not a drop left the bottle until he was at the circle of glyphs. The spell to open the portal was the inner ring of blood runes. Just like the Holy Water, Dr. Loret's blood was unaffected by the cold of the portal; it was still fresh and wet.

Loret was a different story. His corpse was frozen solid and hoary with frost and ice. His face was forever contorted in a look of utter shock and agony.

Jack, with his head turned from the fearful cold rushing out of the pit had a perfect view of the doctor and so horrible was his fate that Jack felt a pang of sympathy. But it was a brief feeling. He had run up against the edge of the outer ring of glyphs and the bottle in his hand was no longer warm, it was blistering hot and the contents were frothing and bubbling.

"Now! Now!" Cyn screamed in his ear, while Richards thumped a meaty hand on his back.

Am I supposed to say something? Jack wondered. *A prayer or some sort of religious invocation?* "In the name of Jesus Christ," was all he could think to say, before he upended the bottle.

It was hard to tell what happened next. There was a flash of light and what felt like a discharge of electricity that ran up Jack's hand and into his arm. The bottle broke and, very strangely, there was the sound of glass falling on pavement. It was a merry, tinkling sound.

Jack had his eyes closed and now he saw the earth reclaiming itself, sealing the hole into the void like a puzzle putting itself together starting with the edges and working inward. The last of the phantom spirits came screaming out of the shrinking hole and then it was gone and the night was suddenly quiet. It was a numb sort of quiet; however, as if they had just left a rock concert.

With a nervous finger, Jack touched the cement within the circle...and then yanked his hand back. "It's freezing," he said, and even as he watched, mist began lifting from the ground.

"What did you say?" Cyn asked. She had a pinky stuck in her ear and was giving it a hardy wiggle.

"I said..."

Richards grabbed Jack's shoulder in a tight grip. "Shush," he said in a quiet tone and then pointed. Jack followed his finger and saw that the six mummies had reformed once again and were lined in front of his cousin, Robert, who stood with a hand on a tremendous oak tree. It had a trunk of great girth and threw a deep shadow over him.

"That was something," he said and then laughed briefly, tiredly.

Richards brought his shotgun to his shoulder. "I should kill you right now," he said.

The threat left Robert unfazed. He made no move to duck behind the tree. Perhaps he couldn't. Even with the gloom of the tree hanging over him, he looked exhausted. "I wouldn't if I were you," he replied and then cocked his head. "Listen."

The wind was gone, as was the psychic storm they'd been battling, now there were only natural, earthly noises: a strange scritching, a hollow thump of wood being hammered on, rusty chains rattling. And there weren't just a few of each of these sounds; they were coming from everywhere and they were gaining in strength.

Jack jerked in surprise. There was a strange noise almost under his feet, as if a giant gopher was digging upwards out of some dank subterranean tunnel. But it was no gopher. Something...or rather someone was buried under the cement drive and was now trying to fight their way to the surface.

"Yes," Robert said. "They are coming. All those demons have bodies now and they want out of the ground. They want to see the sun and the moon and the stars. Well, not the sun so much, but they do want out and they are awfully hungry."

"Then all the more reason I should kill you now before they get out," Richards said, still with the gun poised, yet he did not shoot.

Robert shook his head. "Like I said, I wouldn't do that. Right now, I'm their master, but if I die, then they won't have a master and you'll really have a problem, because you can't really kill these things. You might be able to exorcise them one at a time, but that would take a heck of a lot of priests and how many people will die in the meantime? Millions, I would think."

"You raised demons?" Cyn asked. "That makes no...why? Why on earth would you do something so horrible?"

Robert took a deep breath and ran a tired hand through his black hair. "I wasn't lying when I said that it was your fault. I raised Hor simply to see if I could. I mean, I knew it was possible, but I was drawn to the power. I freely admit that, but then Loret," he paused to point at the slowly thawing corpse on the ground, "went crazy with fear, which got the police involved and so I had to tie up loose ends and things just sort of snowballed."

"I was a loose end?" Jack cried, realizing now why he'd been targeted. "I'm your damned cousin! Weren't you the one who was always going on about family?"

Robert lifted a single shoulder in a lazy shrug. "You are the last bastard in a line of bastards. Clipping your diseased branch from the family tree was really a duty. You see, this is my destiny. The spells are my birthright. They all should have come to me."

Jack was ready to start spitting curses, but Father Paul pointed the bible at him and hissed: "We should not be wasting our time like this. We should either consider capturing him or fleeing."

This made Robert laugh. "Capture me? Do you know why I chose this cemetery? Calvary has a unique history that few people remember. In the early part of the last century, influenza and tuberculosis epidemics were so bad that it caused a shortage of gravediggers, forcing people to dig graves for their own loved ones. Many of those people were so poor that they could afford neither coffins, nor shovels. Think about that. How deep do you think they dug with a diseased corpse sitting next to them? What if it was winter and all they had to dig with was a trowel?"

The visual Robert painted seized his four enemies and each turned to stare into the night, realizing that there were likely tens of thousands of bodies out there covered in nothing but a foot or two of dirt.

Movement next to the Ford caught Jack's attention: the grass in front of one of the grave markers suddenly bulged and began to press upward. Jack pointed at it, his eyes growing larger and larger. "Right there," he said as a head pushed up out of the dirt. It was Orin Haymech...dead Orin Haymech.

There was little flesh left on its moldy bones, but it had long, long strands of wet, muddy hair and there was more mud clogging the eye sockets in its skull, and when it turned toward Jack its mouth was filled with grave dirt and worms. They came squirming out to fall on the remains of the black suit he wore. Most of the suit fell apart when Orin stood.

There were many others like him. Some in better condition or with better made clothes that hung on their skinny shoulders. Some were disturbingly fresh appearing.

One lady wore what appeared to be a wedding gown that was still satiny white in parts—her face fell off and dropped into a fold of cloth where her bosom had once been. One man came walking out of the dark still in his entire suit; his pants only staying up because of the suspenders he wore. As he walked, a horrible slop that was part decomposed intestine and half-curdled blood leaked down out of the legs of his pants.

Jack couldn't stop staring as the cemetery came "alive" around them. He was jerked into action as a hand grabbed his shoulder and started pulling him backward. "Come on." It was Richards hauling him away from the corpse of Loret and the bloody glyphs...and the Ford.

There were too many of the walking corpses all around the car to even think of making an attempt at getting to it.

"Wait!" Jack said and shook off the hand that was pulling him away. The rapier, his only weapon, was just feet away; he grabbed it and ran. All of them ran. The living corpses were everywhere; however they were positively swarming back in the direction of the gate, so they had no choice but to run deeper into the cemetery.

It felt like the exact wrong direction to Jack. With all his heart, he knew they had to get out of the cemetery, no matter what, but Richards was leading them and he seemed loath to leave the winding drive that meandered through the grounds. Jack understood to some extent. Although the grass appeared normal, he had a nervous feeling that if they ran across it, hands would reach up out of it and trip them up and then drag them under.

And yet, their feet slapping on the pavement seemed to draw every corpse in the graveyard right to them and eventually they were cut off with hundreds forming a veritable wall in front of them.

With a deep breath and a nervous glance at the brown grass, Cyn cried: "This way!" She charged off down a grassy slope that was, for the moment, free of the creatures. Jack followed with light steps, ready to leap at the first sign of a bony finger creeping up out of the dirt like a blind mole.

Cyn was running strangely, high up on her tippy-toes as her fashionable, but poorly chosen, stilettos kept stabbing into the earth, pinning each foot in place.

She had been heading for the tall, rock wall that surrounded the grounds but in seconds that direction was cut off as well as the dirt in front of it erupted and foul bone-creatures clawed their way into the night. There were literally thousands upon thousands of corpses pushing their way to the surface.

It was a sight that stole their breath.

Few of the corpses wore anything but stretched-over drum-tight flesh and the furry bubbles of black mold. They were horrors. There were some that were terrible and sad. These were the smaller ones. They were the living bones of Irish children who had, for their brief lives, been uncared for and unwanted by society and in death, dumped in mass graves.

"*Not* this way!" Cyn screamed, breaking to her left.

The hell-children followed, while all around more of the dead swarmed, moving to block them from escaping.

These weren't cartoon caricatures of zombies. They could stumble along at a pretty good clip, depending if they had all of their appendages or not. And they weren't stupid, not exactly. They were cunning in their way and very, very evil. They exuded evil; they polluted the very air with the stench of it. It was a noxious cloud that hung over the cemetery, making it difficult for the older men, Father Paul and Detective Richards, to keep up.

They sounded like broken horses and with Cyn limping, it was up to Jack to make sure they made it out of there. Had he been alone, he might have made a run for one of the walls, but since the others would never be able to keep up, he headed for a row of stone buildings; mausoleums built for the rich or well-connected.

With the dead closing in on them, there was no time to be choosey and Jack went to the first in the line. It was a strange little building, somewhat styled after a miniature cathedral, complete with a cross-topped spire and stone cherubs on each corner. In the dark, the granite slabs that made up its walls were dull and dreary; in fact, the entire structure was as spooky as hell and had this been any other night, Jack wouldn't have gone in on a dare.

Now, he was practically begging to get in; however, there was an old hasp on the door with a newish Yale lock clapped on it. Jack took one look at the lock and started on to the next crypt, but Richards held him back. "They're all going to be locked. Give me your sword."

"Why? I need it..."

Richards ignored him and grabbed the rapier out of Jack's surprised hands and slid it down into the very slim opening between the hasp and the door. "It'll be ok," Richards assured and then heaved back on the grip of the sword. It was obvious that he expected the hasp with its rust and its aged appearance to break before the gleaming sword did. In this he was wrong.

The sword snapped right off just above the cross-guard.

"You...it...my sword!" Jack cried, his mouth falling open.

Richards handed him the pommel, muttered: "Sorry," and then stepped back, hoisting the shotgun to his shoulder. Jack turned away just as the detective pulled the trigger.

Now the hasp was broken and with a heavy shoulder slamming into it, the door swung open, squealing a cry like an old woman. Richards didn't barge right in. This was a house of the dead after all. He stood with the gun at the ready, only the dark in the little building was absolute and revealed nothing.

Cyn stepped forward, thrusting the shotgun she'd been carrying into Jack's hands. "Watch our backs," she instructed and then pulled out her phone and lit up the interior of the death house. There wasn't much to see: a lone marble coffin sat upon a granite pedestal while next to it was a viewing bench that had likely never been used a single time. The bench was marble, angular and, because it was flat and literally as hard as rock, was only just functional. The dust coating the room was a quarter-inch thick and likely older than Jack and maybe even older than Richards who, with his deeply pouched eyes, looked to be in his forties.

Jack only caught a glimpse of the inside of the mausoleum before he turned back to the night and the night creatures that were charging down on them. The closest of them was thirty yards away; they only had seconds to get to a place of safety.

"Is it clear?" he asked. "Tell me nothing's alive in there, because we have all sorts of trouble out here."

"Yeah, we're good," Richards answered, his voice coming to Jack in an echoey manner that suggested the interior of the mausoleum was much bigger on the inside. It wasn't and nor was it "clear." There was indeed something alive in it that had no right to be alive; thankfully, it was trapped under a thousand ponds of marble.

The second Jack was through the door, Richards slammed it shut and braced it with his shoulder. It was a solid door, but they had been down that road before. "Break out a good prayer, Father. We're going to need it." He jutted his chin toward the heavy, leather-bound book in Father Paul's hand.

"Have faith," the priest said and then squinted down at the bible, unable to read a word.

"Let there be light, right Father?" Cyn pointed her cell phone light at the bible just as the door shook from the first attack.

Jack, who had little faith in anything just then looked around the single room for something to brace the door with. His eyes fell upon the marble bench. He rushed to it and strained at it until his eyes bulged with the effort, but wasn't able to move it. Then he went to the marble coffin and ran his hands along its dusty surface only to pull his hands away with a squeak when something moved inside of it.

"Do you have anything yet, Father?" he asked and heard the sound of his fear radiate off the walls and come back to him.

"I do." Father Paul cleared his throat, took a breath of the fetid air and began: "Lord in heaven..." It was a long prayer, beseeching the Almighty Father in Heaven for aid in the face of death, and help in destroying the spawn of hell, and for power to drive out the evil in the world.

It was a long prayer because Father Paul kept changing it and adding to it—all in vain. The undead beasts kept piling up outside the walls of the mausoleum and it was all Jack and Richards could do to keep the door closed.

Eventually, Cyn pulled the light from the bible. "It's not working! We need to use the glyphs again. Does anyone have a knife?"

"In my back pocket," Richards grunted.

Cyn had the knife out and after a quick, steadying breath she sliced open the soft part of her forearm. She wasn't timid about it, either. The cut was deep and immediately ran with blood that looked black in the dim light. "Father, I'm going to need you to hold the phone. Alternate between showing me the glyphs and giving me light to work by."

Her hair hung down in her face and without thinking, she swept it up in a bun, leaving a maroon line of blood in her thick blonde mane.

Father Paul looked at the blood in her hair and the blood coursing out of her arm with his throat working. "Blood sacrifices? I'm very uncomfortable with assisting in a satanic ritual but I will do this on the condition that we all agree that we will need some forgiveness when this is over."

"Yes, yes," Cyn agreed. "Just hold the light steady!"

It took three minutes for her to draw the circle perfectly and then she repeated the arcane phrase: *Hrr vahl Evi ah hurrumm fd. Hrr ah huroon ksa hrer, mkr, hrr fd fdhra*, three times.

Although the heavy door had remained intact during the assault, both Jack and Richards were exhausted and happy to leave the door. They grabbed their guns and leapt into the bloody circle. Right away Jack felt that something was wrong.

"This isn't right," he said, bringing his shotgun up just as the door banged open and the first of the living corpses charged into the room.

"Don't shoot," Cyn ordered. "Give the spell a chance."

The bone-creature did indeed pause just on the other side of the ring of glyphs. Though it no longer possessed eyes, it dropped its chin and stared down for a moment and then, slowly it raised a hand that was stained black from the dirt it had dug through to get out of its grave.

It should not have been able to cross the barrier. Its hand should have been turned aside, but it didn't. The bone hand reached right over the ring and straight for Jack's throat.

Chapter 18

Calvary Cemetery, Queens, New York

Jack didn't wait for the creature's touch; he knew their power, their negative life-sucking energy. He pulled the trigger on the twelve gauge and had the pleasure of seeing the bone-thing blast back to the door where it slammed into more of its infernal kind.

The living corpses had a strength to them that was entirely magical in nature. In other words they lacked a real heft to them; few had even stringy muscles left hanging on their rotting corpse, while most had all the mass of a similar sized pile of sticks.

Two shots apiece from Richards' and Jack's shotguns sent bones flying and cleared the door enough for Cyn to slam it shut again. The three of them braced it with their backs as the creatures attacked once more.

"What the hell?" Richards demanded, his voice pitched high and his eyes wide with fright. "What the hell just happened? Did she say the spell wrong?"

Jack shook his head, saying: "She said everything correct. I mouthed the incantation along with her, listening to make sure she hit all the right inflections. There must be something else."

For a few moments the crypt was quiet save for their heavy breathing and the pounding of bony fists on the door, and then the priest, who was the calmest of the four postulated: "Perhaps your lack of faith in the Lord had something to do with it."

Cyn rolled her eyes, while Richards ignored Father Paul's statement entirely. "Maybe she doesn't have the right mojo," he suggested. "It was you, Jack, who did the spell the first time. You should try it again, but hurry, something is different."

Jack felt it as well; there was a gathering power and he knew the cause: Hor was coming. He was the strongest of the undead. So far as Jack could tell, the creatures that had been called "generically" such as the Incan mummy, the Priest of *Thorthirdes*, and the two mummies from the Museum of Modern Art that had been encased in the glass boxes, and all of the undead that had sprung up from the pit were, relatively speaking, weak. They gave off the heart-shrinking fear and they could manifest darkness, only they couldn't do it to the extent that Hor and Amanra were capable of.

Hor was definitely the strongest of all of them. Jack could feel him even among the cloud of evil generated by the horde—and he was coming closer. "Father, take my spot," Jack ordered and, once the switch was complete, Jack took a large step into the middle of the circle of glyphs and stated in the clearest voice he could manage: "*Hrr vahl Evi ah hurrumm fd. Hrr ah huroon ksa hrer, mkr, hrr fd fdhra. Hrr vahl Evi ah hurrumm fd. Hrr ah huroon ksa hrer, mkr, hrr fd fdhra. Hrr vahl Evi ah hurrumm fd. Hrr ah huroon ksa hrer, mkr, hrr fd fdhra.*"

He then waited with his breath caught up in his throat for something to happen. Yet nothing did. Absolutely nothing. No shimmer, no crackling of power, no nothing.

"It didn't work," he said.

"Then it must be the glyphs," Cyn said. She slid her phone over and said: "Check my work."

On hands and knees, he went around the circle checking each glyph as around them the darkness grew and the fear made breathing difficult. Hor was on the other side of the door now and the other monsters drew back.

"It's clean," Jack told them, swallowing loudly. There was fear on the air and on their skin which tented up with gooseflesh and it ran along their nerves, making their stomachs turn and their lips jabber, and the fear was in their lungs, making it hard to breathe.

Jack looked at the others and saw right away that Cyn was on the verge of going rabbit-in-the-road crazy. There was the beginnings of madness behind her eyes. He knew the feeling well. He had gone from logic-minded victor over Hor in their first encounter to a screaming baby in less than a minute. The mind could only take so much before it failed and hers was failing, quickly.

Richards was the eldest and a tough as nails detective who had seen his share of horror; Father Paul had his faith in the Lord that had been proven time and again in the last few hours—the healing of both Jack and Cyn; the banishment of the magical dark; the exorcism of the creatures that had taken over Jack's body.

Jack didn't know what was holding back the fear crawling all over his mind. It was, strangely enough, becoming familiar—and now familiarity was breeding contempt. It sort of felt like a parlor trick…a very good and very powerful parlor trick, but as long as he thought of it as a trick it seemed to weaken it. The fear was there, but so was the fear of being torn apart by the thousands of undead surrounding them. It was a piss-in-your-pants kind of fear, but at least it was a logical fear.

He grabbed Cyn's leg just above the knee and squeezed, causing her leg to shoot out and her mind to re-align, to adjust to a new and unexpected sensation. "It'll be all right," he told her.

"No, it won't!" she hissed just above a whisper. "It won't, not until you figure out what's wrong."

She was right. Jack was the only one who had a chance in hell of figuring this out. He had seen the most, he had felt the most, he had been subject to the most misery of the four of them, and most importantly, he was the only one of them to have created actual magic—what Father Paul had done hadn't been magic. That fell into an entirely separate category.

And, most importantly, the answer was right in front of him. He had done this spell before, with Cyn's help, of course. She had written the runes in her blood and he had spoken the "magic" words. So what was different?

One thing jumped right out at him: with the first spell he had used a poisoned blade to cut her and in the second she had used Richards' knife to lay open her own flesh. The difference wasn't in the poison. Robert hadn't had access to the poison when he had made his initial sacrifice that had brought Hor to life.

The difference was in the sacrifice.

Cyn had used her own blood in order to save her comrades, while Jack had sacrificed her blood for the same purpose, the major difference being he had done it without her permission—he had stolen her blood, just as Robert had.

"I need the knife," Jack said.

After she had cut open her arm, she had snapped the knife shut and then had pocketed it. Now, she brought it out again and held it out. Despite the growing fear, Jack smiled a sick smile as he took it and opened up the blade. It was four inches of gleaming steel; however along its edge was a line of red.

It didn't need to be cleaned. It would work better dirty.

With a quick move he stabbed Cyn in the calf. Even though she'd been cut now for the third time, she was the only logical choice. She screamed and the sound traveled right up the blade, up his arm and turned his heart a shade blacker than it had been. He was stealing her essence and not in some noble pursuit; he was stealing it to live.

She screamed a long string of curses and Richards glared and balled his fists and Father Paul looked indignant as though he wished he could condemn Jack in the harshest of terms.

"Shut up!" Jack demanded and though Cyn was the only one making a noise, he really was talking to all of them and their angry, wordless accusations. "Draw the damn glyphs again! Draw them on the outside of the first circle and don't ask questions."

Cyn glared, but left the door. Jack forced Detective Richards over and took a spot bracing up their meager defenses. It was about to be assaulted by Hor. He knew it. Just as he knew that Hor was going to bring on the fear and the darkness.

"Father, you're going to need to do something about the darkness or Cyn won't be able to see."

"What is wrong with you?" Father Paul asked, doing his best to reign in his anger. "Are you under *their* control?"

Jack's heart was acid in his chest, eating away at what he was sure was an eroding gossamer soul. "Just beat back the darkness," he said. "And prepare for more fear. It's coming even greater. And Cyn? You're going to have to get cracking. Hor is stronger than all of them. The others are shadows of their hell selves, but Hor is the real deal."

Father Paul gave him another sharp look and then opened his bible and not a moment too soon. The dark inside the crypt began to swell. The far wall disappeared first and then the flat, marble bench was eaten up inch by inch, and then Cyn's feet which were tucked up under her, were lost to the shadows.

The darkness suffocated the light. It gobbled it right up and left nothing behind.

In seconds, Jack couldn't see past his nose. "Father Paul, are you going to do something?"

"I-I'm uh, just preparing myself." Fear had a good hold of his throat, so that he squeaked when he spoke, and yet when he began his prayers and there came a contest between him and his faith in God, against Hor and the power of hell. The darkness fled into the corners of the room.

"That did it," Richards said, with a laugh of relief. "Good job, Father."

The contest between the two wasn't over, however. Hor unleashed his fear and it was far more insidious as it mixed with their natural fear of the unholy creatures that swarmed around them. Father Paul could fight one, but not the other; he stood with his back to the door, frozen in place, gripping his bible with desperate strength. Richards was also feeling the effect. He had begun to sweat despite the cold and his face was warped so that his hound dog look, with its long soulful lines, was warped as though Jack was seeing a funhouse version of it.

Possibly because she was busy with an intricate set of drawings as well as dabbing her fingers into an open wound, Cyn was handling the fear better than the other two. She sat within the circle, her legs crossed Indian style so that her wound was right there and the well of blood didn't leak away. Her hands were straight red and her phone, which had been encased in glittery "bling" was smeared in blood.

Since she had a perfect copy of the spell laid out on the floor in front of her, she didn't need to be able to see the pictures stored on her phone and was using it simply to light what she was doing.

"We're almost safe," Jack said to buoy their spirits. He had shrugged off the greater part of the fear, reminding himself that it was a parlor trick after all; it was nothing but a mind game. That's how he had to look at it. It was a game he had to win. It was a fencing match and he had always been more determined and far quicker than his opponents.

"What was that one prayer, Father?" he asked, giving the priest a shake. "The one with the valley? Why don't you tell us that one?"

Father Paul was no longer really pushing against the door; he leaned against it in a little ball, holding himself, but with Jack's encouragement he started mumbling the prayer and when he was done, Richards asked: "Say it again."

He ran through it a second time and gained back even more strength, throwing off the last of the fear. By then, the fear was starting to become the least of their worries—the door was finally coming apart under the repeated blows of Hor and the others. Hor possessed obscene physical strength.

The hinges went first, the rusty screws snapping so that the door yawed at an ugly angle. Richards, who was the tallest, planted himself at the corner and struggled with the door until he was panting. "How much longer?" he yelled to Cyn.

"I'm just checking to make sure everything is perfect. We only have one shot at this, you know."

"Just hurry," Richards said without the usual sharp bite to his words. Jack looked over at him in alarm, and saw that he was grey-faced again and the sweat glistened in his afro.

Jack's first thought was that the detective had somehow contracted some sort of "zombie disease" from the walking corpses. Only, that didn't make a lick of sense. Jack had been scratched by Amanra and had felt the poison, but he had never turned grey and nor had he ever panted. Richards was panting and looked to be on the verge of collapsing.

"Get to the circle!" Jack yelled, taking the weight of the door on his shoulder. "Both of you go." There would be no holding the door single handedly. The moment Richards stepped away, the door practically fell right on top of Jack and Father Paul.

They had no choice, but to let it fall and jump for the circle and the hope of safety.

Just as the first undead bone-creature had, Hor paused upon seeing the writing, giving Jack enough time to chant: "*Hrr vahl Evi ah hurrumm fd. Hrr ah huroon ksa hrer, mkr, hrr fd fdhra.*"

Hor hissed in anger as the air shimmered and there was the light sound of wind rushing away from them. It blew back the spiderweb like strings of hair left on Hor's scalp.

"Too bad, you old bitch," Cyn challenged. "You're not getting past this line so you might as well go put yourself back in your hole or go back to hell where you belong."

Jack put an arm out to hold her back before she put a toe over the glyphs. "Let's just ignore him. He'll go away pretty soon I suspect."

He didn't, at least not right away. Hor lifted one of its bone-claws and tested the air in front of them making it bend and shimmer again. Cyn leaned back from the hand and into Jack; he could feel her heart running fast and hard. He pushed her behind him and then was forced to shuffle to his right as Hor began to test the strength of the circle.

After it had gone round them it stood for a minutes, gathering the dark into its body. "Get something ready," Jack said to Father Paul, meaning a prayer or some white magic to counter the dark that was coming.

Strangely, it wasn't needed.

"Hold this," Father Paul said to Jack, handing him the crucifix; it was warm and heavy. As the priest flipped through the bible with Cyn shining her light over his shoulder, Jack thrust the crucifix toward Hor and was surprised to see the creature recoil.

"Look at that." Jack pointed with his free hand. "He's not coming close." Not only did Hor shy back, but as they watched, he turned around and pushed through the swarm of weaker creatures.

A sudden euphoria struck Jack and he felt like laughing. Hor was the baddest of them, the strongest. Jack was sure that they could overcome the others' magic just as long the circle held. "We did it! We..." His excitement failed him as he heard the sound of a distant siren. It warbled up and down growing closer...and then came the wail of another, and still more. Then there was a gunshot and screams, lots and lots of screams.

"What is happening?" Father Paul asked.

There was no need to answer. The city was being attacked by an army of undead. As they stood in their circle, the sound of battle, a very one-sided battle grew. In minutes there were helicopters overhead and the single *pop, pop, pop* of the occasional gun was superseded by a full-on barrage of a dozen weapons firing at once and the sirens were going nonstop and the screams ramped up to a fevered pitch.

"This is madness," Father Paul stated. "We have to get out of here. We have to help them."

"Hopefully the answer is in your bible," Jack said. "Or we won't be helping anyone." Although Hor had left, there was still a steady stream of living corpses coming into the mausoleum. Most came in, felt the warding power in the glyphs and then turned away.

Every ten minutes or so, one would stalk in, bringing with it the evil stench of decomposing flesh and the utter darkness of hell. Many of these had embers glowing in their cavernous eye sockets. These ones were different from the rest. They were stronger and the hate and wickedness that came off of them was as strong as the stink.

Some tested either the strength of the spell or the mental strength of the four humans. Whenever one tried, Father Paul began a litany of prayers which always caused the beasts to blanch and turn away. Father Paul was tired but did not stop.

Jack glanced to see how the others were holding up. Cyn was pale and small, and yet she still had her spunk and her grit. When the stronger creatures came in, her lips drew into a line on her face. Jack hardly knew her at all, but could see she was determined and there was still fight left in her...maybe too much fight.

"I think we'll be ok," he told her and put his hand on her shoulder.

"Is that right?" she asked and then, without warning, she punched him square in the gut, knocking the air out of him.

Chapter 19

Calvary Cemetery, Queens, New York

Jack's eyes bugged and his lungs spazzed, hitching uselessly. The blow had been so unexpected and struck so fiercely that his legs buckled. Before he could topple over and perhaps ruin the protective circle around them, Cyn grabbed his green coat and pulled him close so that they were nose to nose.

"Why the hell did you stab me?" She was so close that he thought she was going to bite his nose off and the look on her face suggested that she wanted to.

He would have liked to been able to answer her, however his lungs were basically paralyzed. Like a landed fish, Jack could only work his jaws uselessly and it was a few minutes before he could breathe anywhere near close to normal. When he could, he explained: "In order to do the spell, I had to *take* your blood. Father Paul called it a blood sacrifice, and it is, but the blood can't be given freely. It has to be taken by force."

"Oh," she said, not making eye contact as though embarrassed by her violent outburst. "I didn't know, sorry."

"I didn't know either. It was just a guess after all." Jack rubbed his stomach where she had socked him. "That was some punch. I don't mean to be sexist but you hit as hard as some guys do."

She grinned at the compliment. Jack grinned back and then turned to Richards, fully expecting to be razzed about having the wind knocked out of him by a girl; however Richards looked as though someone much bigger than Cyn had knocked the wind out of him.

The grey tint that Jack had noticed earlier had progressed and there was a slick of sweat across his forehead that had nothing to do with holding back the door. He looked sick.

"What's wrong?" Jack asked.

The detective shook his head. "Nothing's wrong. I'm good. Ms. Childs, get the light out of my face and...and..." He broke off, grimacing, and clutching his left arm.

"No, something is wrong," Jack insisted. He figured that Richards had been scratched at some point and had been poisoned by the hell-fever as he thought it.

What he wasn't expecting was: "It's my-my heart," Richards gasped, "I think. It feels like a h-heart a-attack."

Jack sat him down, and then turned to the priest. "Do something."

The priest blinked like an owl. "Do what? I'm not a doctor."

"Maybe it's not a real heart attack," Cyn suggested. "Maybe it's more of their magic or maybe all these crazy feelings triggered it. Either way, you fixed me and Jack. I say you try the same spell."

"It's not a spell, young lady," Father Paul snipped. "Last Rites are a set of sacraments; they're a gift from God. That being said, they are appropriate in this situation since they're used to prepare a dying person's soul for death, by providing absolution for sins through penance, sacramental grace and prayers for the relief of suffering through anointing, and, in the extreme, the final administration of the Eucharist, known as 'Viaticum', which means 'provision for the journey' in Latin."

Cyn raised an eyebrow at being called "young lady," but she bit back an obvious snarky retort and only said: "Ok, well don't let us stop you."

Father Paul broke out his oil, the purple stole he'd worn earlier and a small silver box which held the Eucharist. He had his bible marked with specific passages and, after flicking to one, he started right in. Once more, Cyn kept the light from her phone on the text while Jack went back to holding the crucifix out to whatever creature came into the crypt.

The priest's words were spoken in such a quick mumble that Jack thought he was speaking Latin. He anointed Richard with the oil, spun through a long prayer and then heard Richards' confession.

Both Jack and Cyn turned away during the confession and pretended not to hear the somewhat banal details of the police officer's sins. Then he received his first communion and it was basically over...and it was clear that the sacrament hadn't helped, at least not physically. Although his pain hadn't receded and he was still grey and his eyes were glazed over, Richards at least seemed more relaxed, as though the rites had helped him to come to grips with the fact that his heart was dying.

"Thanks, Father," he said. "My chest still hurts, but I feel better, sorta on the inside, you know?" Father Paul said he understood completely and Cyn lied within inches of the priest by telling Richards that he looked "ten times better."

All Jack could do was smile. He didn't want to bring down the mood by mentioning just how disappointed he was that the priest's power wasn't greater. Father Paul had been able to cure the poison that had been killing Jack, and he had been able to drive away the magical darkness that Hor had created and he had some strength against the fear exuded by the undead, but he had inexplicably failed in other ways such as Richards' healing.

Fixing a run of the mill bum ticker should have been a kindergarten level miracle compared to battling the undead. It didn't make sense especially since there was definitely a power within the priest.

Or perhaps the power was within his faith. Jack didn't know; the only thing he really knew was that he now had more questions than answers. It was true, he was no longer strictly an atheist, but after Father Paul's pathetic attempt at healing, Jack's agnosticism had increased. As far as his understanding went, God was an all-powerful force for good—so why couldn't the priest wield that power? And why wasn't God sending angels down to wipe the undead army off the face of the earth? Or why didn't he just come himself?

Cyn was also deep in thought and the interior of the crypt was dead quiet. The same could not be said outside the granite walls of the mausoleum.

The chaos and the mayhem continued and in fact had grown, considerably, but it was a moment before any of them realized that in the last few minutes the screams and the gunshots and the sirens were all much further away. There were also a lot fewer of the undead creatures coming into the crypt.

Jack could feel that there were maybe twenty or thirty of the creatures outside, lurking, while the great majority of them, a massive army of hundreds of thousands fanned out killing indiscriminately.

Cyn caught Jack's eye and her little smirk that he found so intriguing was miles away. She could feel the beasts, too. "I wish I understood any of this," she said, almost echoing his own thoughts. "What I really want is to just know the rules involved. These ones with the sodding red eyes? What's that about? And why is Hor the strongest? And how on earth do these scribbles make any difference?"

"I wish I knew...hold on, one of the strong ones is coming," Jack said.

Its presence in Jack's mind was like a shadow that loomed larger and larger. Its presence in his eyes was laughable. The spirit creature had a well of power that was deep and primal and yet it had chosen the body of a tiny child.

The corpse was as sad as it was sickening. It had been a girl and couldn't have been more than three years old when she died. She still wore the remains of a lace and silken gown. It was in remarkably good condition as was the flesh covering her bones. The skin was tight as a drum across her angular little face, but it wasn't rent or worm-riddled and instead of deep sockets that sunk down into her skull, she had large brown coins where her eyes had been. They wouldn't fall no matter how she turned her head.

Jack couldn't get over the coins and Father Paul couldn't get over the palpable aura of evil surrounding the thing and Richards began to sweat in fat beads and the grey look had now progressed to his lips.

The quiet in the crypt grew as the little monster came to test the power of the glyphs. It strolled around them, not once as most of them did, but twice and as it did it grinned and though it still had skin, it didn't have a tongue or any flesh on the inside of its mouth and the smell, the natural smell coming up out of its throat was ghastly.

It was one of the worst and longest moments of the night, but then Cyn ended it, sighing as only a very put out pretty woman could and stating baldly: "I have to pee."

This statement deflated the tension in the crypt like the air being let out of a balloon and soon Jack was crying with laughter and Richards was waving a weak hand and saying: "Stop. I can't take it."

"Well, I'm not joking. I have to go the loo something fierce. It's been how long since the hospital? Too bloody long I say. And you, little demon girl, get on with you. I hear your mum calling."

They were all quite amazed when it left. Their laughter turned to intermittent chuckles that gradually died away. Long minutes turned into a long hour. Richards and Father Paul fell into an uneasy sleep. They were all exhausted, only there was very little room in the circle for four people. Richards had his legs drawn in and leaned against Farther Paul like soldiers in a wet fox hole.

Jack and Cyn stood on either side of the two and whispered their conversation. "I going to make a break for the car," Jack said. "Richards needs a real doctor. I don't think he's going to last long like this."

"And where do you think you're going to find this doctor? Do you hear what's happening out there? Robert has set them loose on the city, which makes no sense to me. What does he gain by destroying New York City?"

"I wish I knew," Jack answered. "But he's not just destroying the city, he destroying the world. Those monsters can't die. You saw them."

She shivered and wrapped her arms around herself. "Do you want my coat?" She shook her head, however the shivering hadn't stopped and so he pulled it off and draped it over her shoulders. She looked a mess. The light, stylish jacket and the silk shirt that had once been white was ripped and stained with blood, both hers and his. She had blood in her hair and under her nails, it looked like dirt.

And yet she was still beautiful and captivating and determined.

"Robert is not destroying the world," she insisted. "He's destroying this version of it. When we were growing up, he was always going on about the greatness of the old British Empire and he would tell anyone who'd listen that we were royals who had been screwed out of our titles. If I had to guess, I think Robert's endgame is to set himself up as king of the world."

"A world inhabited by the undead?" Jack asked, and then quickly answered his own question. "No. He can control them and, it's safe to say that since he brought them into this world, he can send them back."

Cyn tapped her chin, thinking. "You don't know that for certain. He might have control of them, yes, but those monsters are going to fight being sent back, especially the ones with the red eyes. The other ones I think are twisted souls, but the red-eyed ones are demons. I'm sure of it."

Jack shook his head at the word "demon." Everything about the situation was crazy but the idea of actual demons running around in little girl corpses was too much to try to wrap his head around. "I guess that whatever Robert is going to do depends on what spells he has access to. Have you ever seen any other writing that looks like that?"

He pointed at the floor; she shook her head. "No, never."

"Me, neither, although it is safe to say that Robert has and his father, too. They have to have at least one more spell. Hey, you know what we should do? We should go after Robert's father. At the very least we could hold him hostage and maybe he has the third spell on him."

Cyn's eyes narrowed. "And what would you do with it? Use it?" When he didn't answer, she glared. "I can't believe you would even think about using one of these spells. They're the blackest of magic. You have to *steal* blood just to use the simplest protection spell and the others...you know that you might have to kill in order to use them."

"Yes, and right now thousands of people are dying even as we speak and by the time the sun comes up that number will be a hundred thousand or a million. So, yes, I'm willing to sacrifice one person to save a million."

Father Paul suddenly spoke, causing Jack to jump, not only out of his skin but out of the circle, as well. Quickly, he jumped back in as the priest said: "Put your faith in the Lord. Has he not shown you miracle after miracle tonight? They should have been all the signs you need to know that the only way to fight such monstrous evil is through the power of the Lord's love."

"That would be a lot more impressive of a statement if Detective Richards wasn't sitting there, dying. I'm sorry, but when it comes to God I don't know what to believe."

The priest did not bat an eye. "What drives out the dark of night? More darkness? No, only the light of heaven drives away the dark."

That was a fine platitude, but so far the light had only managed a few minor victories, and it was still as dark as hell out, but Jack figured that right then wasn't the time for this argument. "I don't know why this is even being discussed. I never said I would use the spells; I said it was an option, only. The first thing we need to do is get out of here. I'm going to make a run for the car. Father, are you with me?"

"Me? I'm not much of a runner; in fact it has been since before the seminary that I ran anywhere. I'm afraid I'll slow you down."

"I'll go with you," Cyn said. "What do you Americans say? I'll ride shotguns?"

Jack didn't like the idea of dragging her back out into danger, but what he liked less was going out there alone. It wasn't just that he was afraid of being ripped apart by the creatures; what scared him more was the idea of dying alone. He was afraid that his soul would be stolen easier if he was alone. It was an odd thought, but one that had him nodding to Cyn, against his better judgment.

Chapter 20

Calvary Cemetery Queens, New York

Jack loaded up his pockets with the last of Richards' shotgun shells. He also went to get the keys to the Ford and only when he held them up to show Cyn did he say: "You ready?"

"Into the breach," she answered, determined. She then gave him the little curious smile which, as it always did, made him wonder what she meant by it.

And then with a deep breath, they stepped across the threshold of the ring of glyphs. Jack expected the creatures outside the mausoleum to immediately charge right in, but they hadn't moved.

He could feel them: two on either side of the door and another fifteen or sixteen ranged in a circle around the building, holding them in place. They had been set as guards by Robert; there was no other explanation as to why they weren't out pillaging and feasting like the others. So the question was: if Jack and Cyn could get past them, would they follow the pair or would they stay and guard the building?

He didn't know which he hoped for.

Cyn knew the score when it came to where the beasts were as well. Without hesitation, she ran out into the night, looking neither left or right. Jack should have been ready; he should have been right on her tail, but he was a second behind and nearly had his face shredded open by a sudden slashing hand as he ran after her.

He couldn't look back. The creatures were charging from every angle. Cyn ran right at one: a stick man made of bones and little else; it swam in the black rags of a suit made for someone who had died in the prime of life.

She blasted it into splinters with one pull of the trigger of her shotgun, while Jack took care of another, this one with the remains of what might have been a burlap sack tied over its head. Jack didn't want to know what was under the sack—he envisioned a mass of worms or snakes instead of a head. He aimed his shotgun at the thing's chest and had the pleasure of seeing it blast back, its feet flying up.

His pleasure evaporated quickly when a muddy shoe with a foot still within it, hit him on the shoulder and left a splotch of something black and stinking. "Oh jeeze," he groaned and gave his shoulder a twitch to dislodge some of the scum, but it wasn't going anywhere.

And then they were beyond the creatures and running up the gentle hills of the cemetery, doing their best not to fall into the many, many open graves that littered the landscape. There seemed to be more overturned dirt than there was grass. It was enough to shake them to their cores and they both ran with their heads going back and forth, marveling in fear.

Behind them came all twenty of the creatures that had been set to guard the mausoleum. Some were faster than others but none were as fast as either Jack or Cyn, but where they lacked in speed, they more than made up for in dogged determination. They didn't have muscles that tired or lungs that burned.

They came on relentlessly without wavering.

The same could not be said of Jack and Cyn. They topped a rise and saw Queens before them…and stopped as their eyes traveled up and down the skyline. At least a dozen buildings were on fire, burning like torches, lighting up the night. All around the cemetery were fire trucks and ambulances and police cruisers with their strobes splashing the night in blue and red.

Even from a distance, they could see that there wasn't a single fire hose being sprayed on any of the fires and there wasn't anyone directing traffic and there weren't men or women pushing gurneys back and forth or administering oxygen or hooking up IVs.

There wasn't a single authority figure in sight.

There were only people running for their lives and people being eaten and people fighting in vain with sticks or knives or baseball bats.

And there were swarms of undead everywhere. They would be knocked down by bat or bullet and seconds later they would get right back up and charge again.

The screams drifted through the night, far away but heartbreakingly urgent nonetheless. Cyn had been reloading her gun as she watched, but the second she was done, she elbowed Jack. "Let's go."

"Yeah," Jack answered and then loped off down the slope. Behind them the undead had nearly caught up and in front there were more. Most of these were little more than parts of people—corpses that had disintegrated over the years until there was so little left of them that they could only drag themselves along with a single arm or they rolled, limbless.

Others were far more intact; however, they were slow coming to the surface, having only just clawed their way out of stout coffins or bashed down iron reinforced doors.

These ones were much quicker and both Jack and Cyn had to waste two rounds a piece clearing a lane to run through.

And then they were at the Ford and Jack was relieved to see that it was still intact. He'd been afraid that they would run all that way only to find that the car had been demolished or otherwise rendered useless.

With gangs of dead charging from every direction, Jack jumped in the driver's seat and gunned the engine. Cyn was in a moment later, her bosom heaving and her shotgun pointed straight into his gut.

"Do you mind?" he asked, gently pushing the gun to the side.

She gave him a sharp look, clearly unaccustomed to anyone finding fault in her. "Are you going to drive or what?"

"Just a second," he said, waiting for the first monster to put its bony claws on the Ford's hood. Only then did he stomp the gas. There was a long *screeeech* as the creature left gouges in the paint and then Jack was tearing across the cemetery, leaving lines in the dirt. It was rough going until he made it back to the winding path and then he left the undead behind.

Cyn was half-turned. "They're way back there. You can slow down." Jack didn't slow; the dash showed that it was after four in the morning and he was afraid that Robert was long gone and his father probably was as well.

He raced straight to the row of crypts, left the car running and jumped out, calling over his shoulder: "Keep them off of us." He charged inside what he considered "their" mausoleum and found both Father Paul and Richards standing within the circle. "Let's go!" he barked. "They're a ways back."

Richards swayed as he stood. Jack hooked a shoulder beneath his arm and hoisted him along. The dozens of un-dead that were bearing down on them leant an urgency that could never be matched. Even with his heart failing, Richards made it to the Taurus in seconds and collapsed in the front seat.

Even before he got the engine going, Jack handed him the mike to the radio. "We need to stop Robert or his father. Get someone over to the Waldorf to arrest them; trust me, he wouldn't bring any of the monsters with him. He would think it was gauche."

"Yeah, I can make a call," Richards said, and then flicked on the radio. They were instantly inundated by harsh static and a dozen hysterical voices, a few of them screaming, a few in tears, a few dying. The detective flicked off the radio and then sighed with such exhaustion that it sounded like the last sigh of a corpse.

"I'll try my phone," Cyn said. "What? Out of service area? That's not possible. Does anyone have service?" Jack had left his phone in his dorm room and Richards and Father Paul's were both as useless as Cyn's.

With the creatures rushing down on them, they had no time left to worry about phones or radios. Jack raced the Ford for the cemetery gates. They were blocked by a single being: the girl with the large hundred-year old pennies over her eyes.

"Run her down, Jack," Richards said in a wheeze; Jack had slowed upon seeing her. "It'll be ok. These are bullet resistant windows. She won't be able to hurt the car."

Hurting the car had been a secondary consideration to Jack. He had always been squeamish over the idea of running over anything, even a squirrel, hell, even a dead squirrel, and so the idea of hitting a child and hearing all of her bones snap like so much kindling made his stomach do a little dance.

But this was no ordinary child.

Gripping the wheel, he stepped on the gas and aimed for the child-demon who made no move to step out of the way. Its ugly perma-grin grew wider as if seeing the car heading right for her constituted a long awaited challenge. Jack figured it was going to be a rather one-sided affair: two tons of rolling steel against thirty pounds of bones and a few ounces of dried flesh.

He knew there wasn't going to be much of an impact, but it turned out that there wasn't *any* impact. Just before Jack ran her over, the girl leapt onto the hood. She slid right up the windshield and should have shot right over the top but she managed to hook a wiper blade and stopped her momentum.

And there she was leering down at Jack with large, strange pennies for eyes. Jack was so shocked that he came within a whisker of striking a fire hydrant squatting on the *other* side of the street. He barely got the wheel around and they thumped up onto the curb, throwing everyone to the side...everyone except the girl.

She went on smiling as she raised a tiny fist made up of tinier bones that had to have all the durability of a like number of tooth picks, and yet when she brought that fist down there was a sharp *crack* and the glass starred.

"Holy crap!" Jack cried. "That's bullet resistant?" There was no time for an answer. The little creature raised that same little fist and Jack had the sinking feeling that the window wasn't going to hold up under too many more punches. He went with both feet as he crushed down on the brake. The Ford's tires screamed as the girl almost flew off the front of the car; she only just managed to hold onto the wiper blade.

"*Ighs ish afar rhe*," it hissed and then opened it mouth wide; where there should have been rows of baby teeth, there was only scabby blackness. Jack knew something bad was coming; they all did. The car was silent, each of the four mesmerized by the dreadful anticipation in the air. The silence lasted not even an entire second, then the girl breathed out a cloud of white.

The cloud washed over the windshield, instantly covering it with a layer of frost and the cracks in the glass grew like lightening, spreading out from end to end. The cold was immediate and intense. A thousand pale hairs stood up on Jack's arms, his breath came out in a wispy imitation of the demon's. Worst of all, the Ford's engine began to hitch as its innards froze.

"Drive," Richards said in a ghostly whisper.

"Yeah, yeah," Jack said, not taking his eyes from the shadow figure of the girl on the other side of the frosted-over glass. His foot found the gas and the engine knocked and rattled louder, but his hand on the unfamiliar gear-shifter stuck the car in neutral and not in drive.

He was confused as the car only revved louder. At first he thought it was more of the demon's magic, but then he saw the problem. "It was in..."

With a crash, the windshield blasted in, covering them in glass that was so intensely cold that each piece seared their exposed flesh, while the air shriveled their lungs. The demon knelt on the remains of the windshield, half in and half out of the car. "*Ighs ish afar rhe*," it hissed once more and again gaped its mouth wide ready to bring up another of the white clouds.

This one would freeze their eyeballs into ice cubes and turn them into frost covered statues...but then a shotgun was thrust over the seat between Jack and Richards.

"Shut it, you little tart," Cyn said and then pulled the trigger of the shotgun. The roar of the gun sent a spike of pain into Jack's ear, but he didn't care. The demon was blasted over the hood of the car, losing most of the skin of its face, its jaw, her right arm, and both pennies in the process.

"That's one way to tell her to sod off," Cyn said, pulling back the gun.

Next to Jack, Richards looked greyer than ever. He reached out and put his hand over Jack's and pulled the shifter down to drive. "Please, go," he said, again in the voice of a man on the verge of death.

Jack floored the pedal and raced away, watching the side mirror to make sure that the girl demon was left far behind. He had seen too many horror movies to make that rookie mistake. Only when he saw the little bundle of rags searching for its pennies was he able to breathe a sigh of relief.

Chapter 21

Queens, New York City

The night blowing in their faces felt strangely warm after the cold created by the demon in the girl's body...at first.

Very quickly they were all shivering, especially Jack, who had given up his coat to Cyn, hours before. They needed a different car and not just because of the cold, there was the undead to worry about as well.

Walking corpses were everywhere. It was all Jack could do to weave in and out of them. There was no way he was going to try to run one over, not after what had just happened, especially without a windshield affording the simplest protection.

The problem was that there just weren't a lot of cars in New York and, even if Jack knew how to hot-wire a car, which he did not, New York cars were generally equipped with the most high-tech anti-theft devices on the planet.

This was one of the reasons that Jack took a gamble and headed to where the street fighting had been heaviest. He ran the Taurus up the ramp to the Long Island Expressway, which was a direct shot into Manhattan. A mile away, strung across the street, were eight police cars, three ambulances and two bus-sized fire trucks. There weren't any people around the vehicles, only bodies and parts of bodies and pools of blood.

The first responders who had taken a stand there had either died or had run away, leaving behind vehicles that were perfectly serviceable and, in most cases, still running. Jack headed straight for an ambulance—it was a heavy machine, able to crush any of the creatures.

And it had what Detective Richards needed if he was to have any hope in staying alive: nitroglycerin to dilate the blood vessels around his heart and oxygen to keep more of his heart muscles from dying. When Jack had his "issue" at the hospital, this was what he had been given. There could have been fifty other drugs to help a man with a heart attack, but he didn't know them.

"Cyn stand guard," Jack ordered as they pulled up. "Father Paul run over to those police cars and get all the shotgun ammo they have and another gun if there is one. I'm going to help Richards into the ambulance."

When he jumped out, the noise and the light and the energy of the city caused him to pause. It was after four in the morning and yet it seemed all of Queens was awake, which was no wonder with all of the car alarms blaring and the sirens wailing and the screams and the gunshots.

Every building for miles around was lit up and there were faces in the windows. Some people stared out with fear stamped on their features and others hid behind curtains like children peeping on their cousins changing. It seemed the largest portion of the population had chairs pulled right up to the glass and were watching the spectacle as nearly a million undead monsters destroyed the city around them; the people watched as if they found everything so entertaining.

Jack couldn't understand how so many people could be so calm.

The creatures knew the people were up there, but they had patience and went about picking the low hanging fruit. They tore down first floor apartment doors or broke into living room windows and they feasted on blood and warm flesh. They were so focused that Jack hoped that his little group would have at least a minute before the creatures noticed them sitting right out in the middle of the street.

It took thirty-four seconds before Cyn fired her first shot.

Jack was just easing Richards into the back of the ambulance when the blast sent a wave of goosebumps running up his arms. "Go," Richards said, shoving Jack away with a soft push. He started fumbling with an oxygen mask, saying over his shoulder: "I got this."

There was a second shot and Jack had to leave him.

He almost ran into Father Paul who was rushing into the ambulance carrying only a single box of shells. It wouldn't be enough, not if they had to fight their way out of the city.

The priest was not the bravest of men. Before that night his nerve had probably never been tested, and he was now running on the last dregs of courage. Being outside a car or a building where there was nothing between a person and a very quick death wasn't easy. It made a man feel naked or perhaps worse than that: *skinless*.

And yet Cyn was calmly blasting away the undead as they came charging at her. They were never fast, but the creatures were determined and there were so many of them. With all the strobes lighting up the area, there weren't shadows in which the creatures could hide; there had to be a hundred of them grinding forward on their bone-feet.

"Hold them off a bit longer!" Jack yelled to Cyn and then turned to the priest: "Find some nitroglycerine and get him hooked to some oxygen." He didn't wait for an answer or acknowledgement; he ran for the nearest police car where there was a shotgun in a rack behind the front seats. It was locked in place which was why the priest hadn't grabbed it. Of course, the keys to the lock were sitting in the ignition.

It took fourteen seconds and three shots from Cyn's gun to free the weapon. Jack then ran around to the trunk and when he popped it open the first thing he saw was a black box that looked like futuristic luggage. Inside that were two sets of riot gear: heavy vests, black helmets, gloves, and arm and leg guards.

He hauled the case out and ran for the ambulance, where he chucked the case into the back and shut the door. There were two more blasts from Cyn's gun and he was just about to yell for her to get back to the ambulance when he happened to glance over at Richards' Ford and saw that not only was Cyn's rapier sitting in the back seat, there was one of the boxes of shotgun shells that Richards had taken from the Lindenhurst police cruiser earlier that night.

Unfortunately, between him and the car were two of the creatures. They were both small but that didn't make them any less dangerous.

Jack ran to his right in a wide loop, taking advantage of his speed, and coming around the far side of the Taurus with a good enough lead to get in the back seat and shut the door on them. The two creatures immediately attacked the glass with their fists, and that was just fine with Jack. He grabbed the box of shells and the sword and scooted out of the near side of the car, yelling to Cyn: "Let's go!"

He ran for the ambulance with the beasts lumbering behind. Cyn beat him into the vehicle and was already re-loading when Jack got in. "It's a might bit sporting out there," she commented. Her shaking hands belied her calm exterior.

"Find me the heat, will you?" Jack asked, guiding the ambulance at break-neck speed down the road. He didn't want to chance taking his eyes from the road and there were what looked like fifty different buttons and knobs on the dash.

She found the heat and cranked it over to full blast. Then she found the switch for the emergency lights and flicked them off so the world was no longer lit in a mad swirl of red and white.

They sped along the expressway until the road started to slope down; to their right was a sign that read: *Queens Midtown Tunnel*. Jack began coasting, feeling dread creep into his belly like a weight.

Seconds later they saw the opening to the tunnel. It was normally lit with a greenish glow; now, it was a black maw that had Jack's fear building. The road down into it was five lanes of hell, jammed with cars, a few on fire, a few with people trapped inside, most abandoned. They appeared fused together, one bumper locked to the next. There were skeleton beings all around the cars, smashing glass or dragging people out by their hair.

"Don't you dare go down there, Jack!" Cyn warned.

Of course not, he thought. Going down there would be suicide and yet he hadn't slammed on the brakes as he should have. Something shadowy, swift and slight had run from behind one of the cars. At first, Jack thought it was one of the smaller creatures, but it was too fast and its gait was too human. It was a boy.

Jack stared past the boy, hoping to see one of his parents and sure enough there was a woman with three-foot dreadlocks hanging on her shoulders, waving a blanket as seven or eight of the creatures charged her. He had never seen anything so fantastic. Where she got the courage from, he had no idea.

On instinct, he swung the ambulance wide to the right and then curved it back in toward the woman who had thrown the blanket over the first of the creatures and was now running after her son. Jack cut right behind her and roared through the undead, no longer squeamish about hitting them. How could he be squeamish when a lone woman armed with nothing but a blanket could have the guts to stand against them?

He blasted the creatures with the heavy duty vehicle and sent bones flying and skulls tumbling.

Barely slowing he turned back up the ramp and came up along the side of the woman and saw that she was more incredible than he had even guessed. He blinked in embarrassed surprise as he saw that she had fought the creatures almost naked. She had on soft-looking pajama bottoms, but was both shirtless and shoeless. He slowed long enough for her to climb in, scramble over Cyn and then he was going again, chasing after the son who was racing away from them.

The son took one look back at the onrushing ambulance and his eyes went huge in his dark face. He tried to push his legs faster, but he was spent and gradually slowed, crying in fear.

He wouldn't get in the ambulance even when his mother screamed out the window: "Andra! Get your butt in here, right this second!"

Andra pointed at the front of the ambulance. "There's one right there."

Jack glanced in the side mirror and saw that there was fifty yards between them and the nearest of the creatures and so he chanced getting out, rapier in hand. "Where is..." he started to ask, but then saw the pile of bones and rotted flesh stuck to the grill.

The creature was still "alive" and trying to free itself from the metal work. With a quick strike, Jack hacked off its head and then used the blade to peel the rest of it away. It fell on the ground, still moving, one arm reaching for a head that it couldn't possible see.

"Get in, Andra. We'll take you somewhere safe."

Somewhere safe was a concept that had lost all of its meaning. The streets were alive with the dead. They roamed everywhere and savagely attacked anything that had the least scent of humanity to it.

The closest bridge to Manhattan, the Queensboro Bridge was a mile north. From an onramp they were able to see the entire sweep of it. There were undead up and down it, all heading west. At the far end, a terrific gun battle was being waged. The police were trying everything they could, from tear gas to machine guns. There was even a water cannon being used to knock the undead back.

"They're not going to last," Cyn said. "One of those sodding big ones like Hor or that girl with the hay-pennies for eyes will come up and put an end to all of that. Oh, please excuse my language. I don't mean to be so vulgar in front of the wee one."

Andra's mother shrugged and drew Jack's coat around her, tighter. "That's all right," she said. "I can barely understand you; I doubt he knows what you're saying at all."

"I understand her, Momma. She's from Harry Potter. They all talk like that in Harry Potter."

"I guess," the mom replied in a somewhat stunned voice. "Do you folks know what they are? Are they zombies?"

Cyn looked to Jack to answer. "No, but they're close," he said, feeling an ache of guilt. These people had nearly been killed because he had decided that five thousand dollars was more important than listening to his father's direct order. "Whatever they are, don't let them touch you, but if you do get scratched, go see a priest. Speaking of which."

Jack pulled back on the door that separated the cab from the working area of the ambulance. "How's he doing?"

"Better," the priest answered. "I believe the nitro is helping, but we should get him straight away to a hospital."

The detective tried to sit up but found that he was strapped to the gurney. He pulled away the O2 mask that had been covering his face and said: "No. We need to get to the Waldorf and find Robert. Consider that an order." His words were stronger and his face was returning to its normal warm brown color. Still, he was in no position to give orders or do much of anything besides rest.

"I will, but I'll make the arrest," Jack answered. "Any more excitement and you'll drop dead and won't be any use to anyone. It'll be ok. I'll take Cyn with me. I just need your badge and your cuffs."

Richards started shaking his head, but Father Paul wagged a finger at him. "This is non-negotiable," the priest told him and then relieved him of his ID and handcuffs.

"Thanks so much for volunteering me," Cyn said. "That was right manly of you."

"We'll be fine," Jack said and lugged the fancy suitcase from the back. "We'll be dressed in these outfits and besides, we'll have Father Paul riding shotgun just in case

Robert has any more surprises. You don't mind, do you, Father?"

There was a moment's hesitation, but he eventually said: "I do not mind, Mister Jack. We'll be confronting the root of this evil and I should be honored to be there, even it means my death."

"Death? Wait," Andra's mom said, tapping Jack on the shoulder until he turned back to her. "Can you drop me and my boy off, first? I have an aunt who lives uptown...or you can point us at the nearest subway and that would be good, too."

"I'm sorry, Mrs..."

She didn't quite understand that he was looking for her name at first, but then she said: "It's just Ms." The way she said Ms, it should have had two Zs at the end. "Ms Sheila Crawford."

Her son piped up as she was about to go on: "Our neighbor, Joey calls me Andra Crawfish. I don't like it, none. But I think he got eaten, so I guess he won't be calling me that no more."

"No, I guess he won't," Sheila said, pulling her son close to her. After a second, when she looked back and forth from Jack to Cyn, she added: "Hey, I want to thank you and all for saving us, but I have to look out for my son. We can't go anywhere near whatever is the root of all this mess. I'm just sorry, but no."

"We really need someone to look after that man back there," Jack said. "But if you can't, I guess I understand."

She shook her head, making it clear she wasn't going anywhere near the Waldorf.

Jack was running out of time and compromised: "I can drop you off anywhere between here and the hotel, but I should warn you against taking the subways. If one of these things gets on a subway car with you and you can't get off before the train pulls away from the station, you'll be trapped and it'll kill you both."

"What about one of the ferries out to Staten Island?" she asked.

"That might work," he said, but he had no idea.

Safe for the moment, Jack and Cyn buckled the strange gear on. It made Jack feel like a turtle...but a safe turtle. Cyn swam in her outfit. Even with the straps pulled as tight as they could go, the arm guards became wrist guards because they wouldn't stay in place and her helmet rattled on her head as though she was wearing a bucket.

She straitened the helmet and declared them ready for battle.

Jack turned the ambulance south and drove out of Queens and into Brooklyn and then across one of the lower bridges into Manhattan. It wasn't an easy ride. The ambulance swayed and rocked as they dodged in and out, and sometimes over, gangs of the undead.

It was the same sad scene played out over and over. Along the way they picked up four more people fleeing from the creatures, one of whom was a policeman who was no longer coherent, driven into madness by the magical fear given off by the creatures. With spit flying, he babbled endlessly about "demons" and "monsters" and could only relax as long as Father Paul prayed in a loud voice.

None of the survivors they rescued would go on to the Waldorf.

Brooklyn had been as bad as Queens with the sole exception that the bridge was almost wide open. Just as before, people hadn't fled at the first sight of the creatures. For the most part they had locked their doors and hunkered down.

The same was true for Manhattan, where the buildings were even taller and the danger seemed far away across the East River. It was closer than most people realized. According to the static-filled two-way radio, the police were fighting for their lives at five main points: the mid-town tunnel, which Cyn had smartly ordered them not to take, the Queensboro Bridge, and three subway stations all located on the Upper East Side.

Lower Manhattan was still relatively empty, though they did pass a few hundred bloody corpses and a few dozen of the bone creatures. They sped down the highway on the east side of the island and were at the ferry station just as the sun was starting to rise.

"Get as far away from the city as you can," Jack told Sheila and the others. "Even if you have to walk across Staten Island and New Jersey, do it."

Cyn gave them all the cash she had on her and Father Paul blessed them, mainly to calm the police officer, who had wild eyes. Then the four of them were alone again and the silence in the ambulance was heavy.

"Here's the plan: we hit the Waldorf and snatch up Robert," Richards said, in a dry whisper. When Cyn raised a soft, golden eyebrow, he amended his statement to: "Ok, you snatch him up, and then you bring him down to me. I've never in my life beat a confession out of a prisoner, but I think I will today."

Chapter 22

The Waldorf Astoria, Manhattan, New York City

Jack was slow to get the ambulance moving. Now that the sun had cracked the horizon, they could see the smoke hanging above the eastern part of the city like a shroud of doom, while behind them, the open stretch of the harbor glinted with morning-gold.

It was practically an invitation to give up and run away and Jack was sorely tempted to. Next to him, with her own gold spilling down the back of her black vest, Cyn kept her face sturdily forward to where they could both feel the undead in a vast swarm, some close, some far, some strong like beacons, but for the most part they were a blur on the mind, a great mass of heart-stopping evil.

Although she kept her face straight ahead, Cyn's eyes went to the side mirror more than once and Jack was sure that if he mentioned something about leaving, her will would fail her and she would be quick to abandon their self-appointed duty.

"Damn," he whispered under his breath, stuck the vehicle in gear and drove north where the sounds of battle grew—it was a good guess that the police lines holding the approaches into Manhattan had fallen. They passed people who were running south. Some carried bags or suitcases stuffed to overflowing and some ran with improvised weapons: canes or golf clubs, and some went crazy when they saw the ambulance and ran at it with faces contorted in fear and begging words on their lips.

Jack only stopped once.

A girl of maybe twenty with a heavy suitcase in one hand was trying to save both her meager possessions and her life. She had the same wild eyes that the police officer had, which meant that she was almost beyond saving. As Jack knew, once the madness set in, only luck could save a person.

And she didn't look particularly lucky. Her face was a teary mess. She was dressed only in a peasant blouse and a short skirt in below freezing weather, and one of the wheels on her suitcase had snapped off, so she was forced to drag it along like an unwilling dog…and there was a long-dead coffin creature after her.

It was nearly all bone with only the thinnest of tissue holding it together. It wasn't even an intact skeleton. It had only a few molars left in its gaping jaw and was missing an ulna, a handful of carpals and all the toes on one foot—and yet it was as deadly as all the rest.

Its power didn't rest in its bones or the ratty connective tissue that couldn't possibly be holding it together. Its power rested in whatever hell-beast had taken up residence in its remains.

Thankfully, the spirit was rather run of the mill and so Jack slid out of the ambulance carrying only the rapier. It had a good blade, although not the sharpest, and yet Jack made short work of the creature. Since it was, essentially, unkillable, it attacked in the thoughtless way they all did—at first. It reached out a bony claw and Jack hacked it off. Then it reached out its other hand and he took that off as well and then followed it up with a slash that toppled the skull right off.

It shattered when it hit the pavement.

"Get in," Jack said, ushering the girl to the back of the ambulance. He didn't really want to take on more passengers since he was heading further into danger, however, he didn't trust the skittish look in the girl's eyes. She was apt to go anywhere if left on her own.

As he opened the back of the ambulance, she began to babble out her story. "They came up out of the sewers… like rats. They were like rats, you know. They could fit in the smallest…"

He wasn't listening. He needed her to get in quickly so he could get out of there. They had wasted too much time already. Robert had at least a four-hour head start, meaning he could have a two-hundred mile lead, or he could have raised the dead in three more of the gargantuan cemeteries located in the city.

"You're safe now," Jack said, giving her a little shove in the bottom, to help her up. "And look, there's a priest. Father, can you give us another version of that psalm about the valley?"

He began the psalm for probably the thirtieth time that night: "Yea, though I walk in the shadow…" Jack shut the door on the remainder and ran around to the driver's seat.

"She was cute," Cyn said.

"Huh?" Jack hadn't thought so, not that he had really paid attention. He had been more worried about the bone-creature to notice anything more than a soft girl and a tangle of brown hair and large pouty lips. Perhaps there had been something about her which had elicited some sort of primal protective instinct within Jack, but cute? "I guess. I really didn't notice."

Her look was unreadable, not that Jack could spare more than a moment to read it. The bones of the creature were sliding back together; it would be whole again in seconds and its next attack wouldn't be so mindless—they weren't stupid; they learned and they had a whole bag of tricks to use.

Jack raced northward where more and more buildings bore the signs of fire and smoke, where there was blood in the street and sad-looking bodies lying in the gutters, unmoving.

There were creatures roaming everywhere. Not as many as in Queens, but enough to keep the humans penned in their skyscrapers. Few had the courage to chance the streets. For the most part, they remained high up, thinking that by being encased in glass and steel that they would stay safe until whatever was happening passed them by or was dealt with by the authorities.

Jack saw very few "authorities." A handful of police cruisers flew by, frequently going in the wrong direction, and a couple of ambulances passed them, their drivers giving the black-clad Jack a hard look as they zipped by. Jack was driving at a quick, but not dangerous pace. He'd been swerving back and forth for the last hour or so and had almost crashed enough times to know that a steady pace was better than a literal break-neck one.

Still, it seemed like no time before they pulled up in front of the Waldorf Astoria. It was, as always, an impressive building, tall and grand, opulent in every sense of the word, from its gleaming marble floors, to its shining brass, to its million dollar frescos adorning its walls.

Jack stuck the heavy helmet on his head and armed himself with one of the shotguns and filled his pockets with extra shells. Then, feeling somewhat silly since he was wearing the heavy black tactical garb and carrying the tremendous shotgun, Jack stuck the rapier through a slot on his belt that was supposed to have been reserved for pepper spray.

The sword looked ridiculous. It looked childish, as though Jack was a five-year old who couldn't decide which Halloween costume he wanted to wear. Ridiculous or not, he trusted the steel blade more than the gun.

Cyn was equally ridiculous appearing. She swam in her heavy bullet proof vest and the shotgun was nearly as long as she was tall.

Their odd appearance was probably why the cowering hotel employees behind the locked glass doors didn't rush to let them in when he hammered on the glass with his armored fist. Flashing Richards' badge, an actual symbol of authority, was the only thing that got them moving. Jack slapped the badge against the glass and barked: "Open up! It's the police."

Cyn, who was, as always, strangely calm even though they were out on the street and twice as vulnerable, smirked as she said: "Very authentic. You're positively making me peckish for doughnuts."

"That's a thing in England? I thought it was just an American stereotype that all cops ate…"

He bit back the rest of his sentence as there was a *clank* of keys on glass and the deadbolt drew back. The door opened and Jack came busting inside, followed by Cyn and a city's worth of cold air.

"Thank God you're here," the doorman gushed; his relief at seeing what he took to be the police evident. "We had called you guys..." He choked on his words as he saw Cyn fully. With her armor hanging loosely and her helmet like a mop bucket on her head and turned slightly to the side, she was so clearly not a police officer that the hotel staff, who were all gathered at the top of the stairs in a frightened knot, began pointing and whispering to each other.

The same snooty manager that Jack had dealt with two days before, came hurrying down as if his meager authority was greater than the two shotguns that Cyn and Jack carried.

"Who do you think you are?" he demanded. "Impersonating a police officer is a crime."

Cyn pulled off the black bucket that was supposedly protecting her head, causing the manager to step back in surprise. He hadn't been expecting the golden hair or the impish smile or the ice-blue eyes. "Where's my mum? Did she check out or leave? Is she still here?"

Jack did a double take at the questions. He had been so focused on getting to Robert that he had plum forgotten that Cyn had family in the city.

The manager, getting over his shock, answered: "M-Miss Childs...I didn't know that it was you. I-I suppose your mother is upstairs in her room. We aren't supposed to leave the building, you know. No one is. It's all over the news. They're saying that no one is supposed to go outside. It isn't safe on account of the terrorists."

"Terrorists?" Cyn asked, looking confused.

"Yes," the manager said. "You don't know what's happening? There's another terrorist attack going on. It's supposedly being contained, but if you ask me it sounds like there's a full scale war going on. We're having a difficult time keeping the guests calm and in their rooms."

Jack, his heart racing faster, grabbed the manager's coat. "What about Robert Montgomery?" he asked. "Did either the father or the son check out?"

The manager began to puff up and looked as though he was about to begin spouting hotel rules once more, when Jack stepped back and leveled the gun at his midsection. "You see what's going on out there? It's not terrorism, you idiot! Robert is responsible for all of that. If he's here, you have to tell us." The manager's uncertain hands began to flutter in front of his tailored vest where the gun was pointed and yet he also began to shake his head, still clinging to his rulebook. Jack pressed the barrel of the gun into his soft stomach, saying: "He's a criminal and anyone who harbors him is a criminal, too, and they're going to pay." Jack was completely serious and the manager finally saw that he had reached the limit of his authority.

"Mr. Montgomery...he is well, I-I don't know where he is," the manager said, and then pointed at the long marble front counter. "I-I c-can f-find out if he's checked out."

"Please," Jack answered, lowering the gun. "And hurry. We don't have a lot of time."

As Cyn went to call her mother and the manager hurried to check on the status of the Montgomerys, Jack went back to the door and waved toward the ambulance, where Father Paul was watching through one of the back windows. The rear door opened and a very haggard Detective Richards slouched out into the cold with Father Paul under one arm and the girl they had picked up hurrying so close behind them that she was tripping on their heels.

Jack pointed to the doorman. "Get the door and hurry, there's one of *them* nearby." He could *feel* one of the creatures a block or two away and hoped that it wasn't looking in their direction. If it was, they were going to have a tough time keeping it out; the front of the hotel was composed of a triple bank of glass doors that wouldn't stand up to an assault from even one of the creatures.

"And we'll need to turn off the lights in here," Jack said. "We have to make the place look as dark and uninhabited as possible. Start with the chandelier." Just up the steps from the doors was a wide open area where guests could meet or mingle; it was lit by a number of ensconced lights and one tremendous crystal chandelier. It was a beautiful piece that was, more or less, a beacon for the undead, screaming: *There are people inside, come eat them!*

"Is Montgomery here?" Richards asked. He was once again grey in the face and shaking from walking up the fourteen steps to the lobby. In his right hand was his 9 mm. It had been useless against the undead, but would do the trick against either of the Montgomerys.

Jack pointed at the manager. "That guy's checking it out for us, but I don't want you to worry about that. If he's here, we'll get him, and we'll make him talk. In the meantime, I want you to rest. In fact..." Jack turned to the doorman, who'd been hovering a few feet away. "Excuse me. Can you also find out if there's a doctor staying in the hotel? I don't care if it's a plastic surgeon or a dentist or whatever. This man is having a heart attack."

With Father Paul's help, Jack led the detective to a nearby French chaise which was embroidered with gold thread. From across the lobby, the manager watched in alarm as Jack laid Richards back and then lifted the policeman's legs up so that his filthy, graveyard-mudded shoes sat on the cushions.

"He seems upset," Richards remarked.

"Who cares?" Jack said. "Just lie back and try to relax." His smile for Richards was a bad bit of acting. He was afraid to go after Robert with just Cyn and Father Paul as backup. There was no telling what craziness they would find up in the penthouse of the hotel.

Cyn came up a moment later with her shotgun hoist on her shoulder as though it was nothing more dangerous than a bamboo fishing pole. "My mum says she's going to bloody kill you, Jack, for dragging me into all of this. So you have that to look forward to once we get Robert."

"You don't look too nervous," Jack answered.

"About me mum? Hardly. She's mad at you not at me."

"I meant about Robert."

"I know. I was just playing. Chances are, he's gone and if he's not..." She shrugged the shotgun from her shoulder. "We have these and a right handy priest. We've faced that sodding Hor twice now and if he's there again we have even more firepower. We should be fine."

Despite her words, her calm demeanor went a touch south when the manager came up, shaking his head. "Mr. Montgomery hasn't checked out. He's upstairs as far as we know." He held out a plastic card. "Room 4207. I have to warn you that you'll be responsible for anything you break and that the Waldorf does not condone this activity and will not be held accountable should either of you or Mr Montgomery be killed. Your funeral expenses are yours and yours alone."

Chapter 23

The Waldorf Astoria, Manhattan, New York City

The elevator hummed upwards, speeding the three of them to a confrontation that only the priest seemed ready to handle. Father Paul had taken a deep breath before stepping onto the elevator and since then he'd had his eyes closed, praying in a soft voice—one that was completely devoid of fear.

Jack figured the fear would take hold of the priest soon enough, just like it always did with everyone whenever they came into contact with one of the undead.

"Do you have a full load?" Cyn asked.

He didn't know, nor did he know how to check. The only way to find out was to feed shells into the lower port until he couldn't fit anymore inside. He slid three in and then laughed, feeling foolish.

"I'm not used to guns," he admitted.

"Neither am I," Cyn said and then worked her right shoulder in a circle. "These big ones sure do land you a right smart kick. I'm going to have a bruise the size..."

The elevator dinged, cutting her off. They were at the top. Both Cyn and Jack leveled their guns as the door slid open without even a whisper of sound. "The Lord will be with us," Father Paul intoned and then crossed himself.

Jack sure hoped so. He went first, holding the gun tight to his shoulder, his hands sweating freely. 4207 was three doors down on the right. Jack nearly blew a hole in the wall when 4205 opened with him creeping by it.

"Jeeze!" Jack hissed as he jumped back.

A tall, somewhat bloated old man stood in the doorway. His eyes were bloodshot and his grey hair went in all directions. He was dressed in a rumpled suit and there was a suitcase sitting next to his leg like an obedient dog. "Is it safe?" he asked. "Can we leave yet?" He didn't seem at all curious about the Indian priest thrusting a crucifix at him, or the barely-out-of-her-teens woman who held an enormous shotgun pointed at his face.

"No," Jack snapped. "Get back inside."

"Yeah, sure. No need to get so huffy." He shut the door, but Jack guessed that he was still just on the other side, listening or staring through the peephole.

Jack flicked up the visor on his helmet and wiped away the sweat that was beading across his upper lip. "Six in the morning and that guy smelled like whiskey. Not that I blame him. Things are pretty..."

Cyn suddenly grabbed Jack's arm. "The smell of the ghouls! It's not here."

After a deep sniff, Jack grinned. "And the evil feeling, it's weak. There's nothing up here." He let out a sigh of relief, while Cyn chuckled as though embarrassed. Even Father Paul relaxed.

"Let us hope this cousin of yours is here," the priest said, "so we can be done with this once and for all."

This put a fade on their relief. It almost felt as though the priest had jinxed their mission with that one sentence. Jack went to the next door down, listened for a minute, and when he didn't hear anything, he slid the key-card into the slot. The light turned green and he rushed in, feeling like a cop-wannabe.

He had seen a hundred cop movies and, taking a cue from them, he checked every door and every corner before moving on. It was a lavish suite of rooms that could have hidden a dozen ninjas, but Jack knew that it was empty from the moment he walked in. The air was stale and so altogether silent that no living thing could be there.

Still, they searched the suite, including the drawers and under the mattresses and couch cushions; they weren't just looking for Robert, they were looking for any portion of the spells that he had used. Save for some expensive clothes and a few toiletries, the place was empty.

"Long gone, I suppose," Cyn said after they had gone through the place twice. "Ok, I guess it's time to face the music. Time to explain things to my mum. And we both know that she'll want to talk to you," she added, lifting an eyebrow in Jack's direction.

"Great," Jack answered without any enthusiasm. He figured that he would get the third degree from her mother and he wasn't wrong.

Father Paul left to check on Detective Richards and Cyn went to change out of her blood-covered pantsuit, leaving Jack in the clutches of his second cousin, once removed.

Rebecca Childs: fiftyish, stern, and sharp-eyed, plied him with question after question concerning the night's adventures. She was especially interested in the two spells. "How did you figure out the language?" she asked in her light British accent as she studied the pictures that Cyn had taken, holding the phone at odd angles or squinting in at it.

"I didn't," he admitted. "I just figured out the primer my father left along with a warning not to show the scroll to anyone. I blew it, badly."

Cyn came into the room and sat on the couch that Jack had used for a bed two nights before. She had on comfortable jeans, a pale sweater and above both she was strapping on the armor—she didn't look up at Jack's admission.

"Yes," Rebecca said. "That is water under the bridge, I suppose. But this primer…we had one also and ours, like yours came with a warning. I tried every combination possible and couldn't figure out how one matched the other."

"That's because they didn't," Jack said. "The key to the primer wasn't the warning. My father used to sign his letters to my mom: *I will love you forever my dear, my child and never leave you.* He'd sign them that way even before they had children. It didn't make much sense to her and when she asked him about it, he would only shrug. But on the warning note he only wrote: Jonathan. I guessed that the rest of his usual message was written in the hiero-glyphic hybrid language."

Rebecca groaned as if she should have seen it. "Yes, of course! Your great-great grandfather used to write the same thing on his letters to his wife, Victoria. Ugh! Right in front of me the entire time. Not that I would ever use the spells. I never used to believe in that sort of thing. It was all such poppycock. But now..."

The room went quiet and they could hear a new crackling of gunfire outside their windows—it was closer than it had been. The suite had an entire bank of glass overlooking Park Avenue and they each went to a window and stared down. The streets were beginning to flood with people.

"They're starting to panic," Cyn said. They had a bird's eye view and could see four different intersecting streets and for the most part people were running in four different directions. Cyn was the first to turn from the window. "So, what do we do? We can't just sit here; the hotel is no sort of protection."

Jack thought it interesting that Cyn's accent had changed in her mother's presence; she was much cooler and refined, even when they were witnessing the break-down of society occurring right below them.

"We alert the authorities," Jack answered. "We should get out of New York first. Right now, as soon as we can and then alert the FBI or the CIA about Robert."

"As if they would believe us," Cyn said over her shoulder.

Rebecca tapped the glass with a manicured nail and then said: "Whether they believe us is immaterial. We have no choice but to present our findings. Now, Cynthia, gath-er up what you need and let's leave as soon as possible."

Cyn ran into her bedroom, threw a few things in a small piece of carryon luggage and then rushed out again in under a minute. They then went to Rebecca's room, gathered a handful of her things and then rode a crowded elevator down to the first floor.

They seemed to stop at every floor and as they did, Jack's fear mounted. The creatures were getting closer, swarming from the north and the east. They were a black cloud in his mind, but there was one blacker than the rest coming closer.

Next to him, Cyn clicked the safety off her gun. He did the same and then they were in the lobby with close to three hundred other people—something had happened.

Jack heard people all around him:

Did you hear?
Did you see?
It can't be true, can it?
This is all a hoax, right?

A thousand questions and no answers...at least no answer that they wanted to hear. Although TV stations had been blacked out, the internet was alive and well and full of fantastic pictures and horrible videos of skeletons and corpses walking through the city streets killing and feasting.

And if they didn't believe the internet, all they had to do was look outside; there were skeletons and mangled creatures trailing graveyard dirt and entrails.

They found Detective Richards and Father Paul where they had left them. If a doctor had come see the police officer, he wasn't around and neither was the girl they had picked up with the ambulance.

"We've got to get out of here," Cyn said in a rush. She pointed north. "One of the big ones is coming. A demon. I can feel it and so can Jack."

"If we leave, we're going to start a riot," Father Paul said, in a low tone. "The people are very much on edge and I don't trust their temper."

Jack glanced around and couldn't feel what the priest was feeling. With the demon so close, his ability to empathize went right out the window. Not to mention, he thought it was the perfect time to panic. There was a demon coming! He wanted to scream it.

"They're going to have to fend for themselves," he said, buckling up his riot helmet. "And get your cross ready, Father, we're going out the front door right now before it's too late. Mrs. Childs, if you can help Detective Richards, please. We'll go straight for the ambulance."

Looking neither left nor right, Jack headed for the stairs leading down out of the lobby. Around them people began to babble more questions, but he paid them no mind, the demon was very close now, almost racing them to the doors, but that didn't make sense unless the demon could feel them as well.

"Hurry!" Cyn cried. She started to pull ahead of them, only just then Jack grabbed her by the collar of her bullet proof vest and yanked her back. They were too late. The demon was crossing the street now.

Jack could see it just fine: Small, not even hip-height, wearing silk and lace, a few limp strands of hair plastered to its grey skull, its mouth, toothless and gaping wide—and two big halfpennies where her eyes should have been. It was the same demon that had nearly killed them in the graveyard. It had healed its body so that it appeared just as it had before, except it had shined up the big pennies covering its eye sockets. The copper gleamed like fire.

"Go back!" Jack cried, his heart beginning to thunder.

Richards saw the creature and nearly collapsed. Father Paul kept him from falling and propelled him back up the stairs, but he did so with his head spun around, looking over his shoulder with fear dancing in his dark eyes.

They had to fight the sudden surge that their rush to the exit had sparked. As though a damn had suddenly let go, people were trampling each other to get out of the hotel; however they stopped when they caught sight of the little girl demon. Jack was virtually stuck two steps from the top, while Father Paul was easing through the crowd, moving like water through the creases when the demon reached out to touch the glass of the door.

It exploded into the crowd with the force of a bomb. Through the remains of the door came a wave of terror that was so mentally shocking that it took a moment for the crowd to react.

They stood dumb with wide eyes as their blood flowed from the many cuts the glass had given them and then, as one, the people began screaming, fighting each other to get back up the stairs. Jack had felt the green, sick fear, but was able to shake it off.

He grabbed Cyn and thrust her in front of him, pushing her up the stairs until a large, powerful hand found a grip on his shoulder and he was shoved down.

Panic had a hold of the crowd. The demon had stepped through the remains of the door sending the people mad, and they swam up the stairs as though they were part of a mass drowning. Mindlessly, they used anything they could to get up the stairs and they crawled over and crushed the bodies of anyone smaller than themselves, and Jack was smaller than the man who had grabbed him from behind.

He felt a foot stomp down on the back of his calf and another was planted on his left kidney; he was being trod upon as though part of the stairs.

The man trampling him was obese, and clumsy; he tripped, falling on Jack and would have crushed him had Jack not been wearing the heavy vest. The man started to fight his way to his feet, but he never made it. He died as the demon opened its dank, black hole and breathed out a frozen cloud of white.

The cloud filled the stairwell top to bottom, ending the screams of the panicked people forever. A hundred men and women died in seconds. The obese man atop Jack took a few moments longer than most. For the most part his bulk insulated him from the intense cold; however, his lungs had frozen solid and his eyes were frosted marbles and unmoving.

He rolled off Jack and began clawing at his throat with fingers that snapped off knuckle by knuckle.

Jack wasn't unscathed by the cold. He had been buried under a three-hundred pound man and still his sweat had beaded into ice and his lungs had contracted—it felt as though he was trying to breathe through a straw. He pushed out from beneath the heavy man and grabbed the frosted over shotgun; even through the tactical gloves he wore, the cold stock of the gun stung his hands as he picked it up.

It felt as though he was moving in slow motion; his muscles were tight and his joints ground together. The demon, on the other hand, came up the stairs an eager black smile on its face. It wanted Jack.

"Jack!" Cyn yelled from above. "Get down!"

Down was much easier than up. Down was as simple as allowing himself to fall, which he did, landing on a woman who had the consistency of formed plastic. There was a loud *bang* and then people began shouting his name. Jack should have run, but he looked back to see that the child-demon had been blown through the doors by the shotgun blast, but it wasn't in pieces and was already picking itself up.

Jack had to do the same if he was going to live. He crawled to the top of the stairs and then was hoisted to his feet by Rebecca and Cyn. It was still a chore to breathe and his head spun as he was propelled along after the crowd.

There had been over three-hundred people in the spacious lobby; they were racing like a stampeding herd for the south side exit onto 49th Street. If Jack could have spoken, he would have told them the way was blocked. There were more of the undead waiting for them.

A sudden rippling scream stopped the forward momentum of the crowd. "This way," Jack said in a feeble voice. He pointed to the long counter where people checked into and out of the hotel. "Cyn, get Father Paul."

She darted through the crowd to fetch the priest, who was still trying to help Richards along.

"Get down." Jack pulled Rebecca to her knees as the crowd surged back into the lobby, this time heading for the 50th Street exit. He was breathing easier and with every passing second, his head had begun to clear. With unexpected understanding, he thought he knew what the creatures were up to. There were undead at every exit moving inwards; they were going to drive the people into one bleating herd stuck in the middle of the lobby and then they were going to feast.

Cyn was back in seconds; Richards was a mess. He was dying right in front of Jack, of a heart attack of all things!

"We'll get you back into the ambulance as fast as we can," Cyn told him, caressing his shoulder and trying not to look as though she wasn't scared that he was going to die any second. "Jack has a plan...right Jack?"

"Yeah, sure." He gave Richards a lying smile and felt weird that it had come so easily. It was an ugly feeling. "All we have to do is…" There was no time for intricate plans and really no time beyond anything more complicated than a role of the dice.

"We'll blast our way out," Jack said, lifting the shotgun and giving it a little shake. When the crowd thins it'll be just the corpse things, you know, the monsters. If we hit them quick, they won't have time to try any of their tricks."

Rebecca narrowed her eyes at Jack. "That's your plan? I'm sorry, but I was expecting, I don't know a little more."

"It is what it is," Jack answered, shortly. "And it'll work as long as we move as fast as we can. We get to the ambulance and we don't look back, and we don't pick up stragglers." It was a cold thing to say, yet no one disagreed.

They didn't have long to wait before the last of the crowd rushed past, tripping over themselves in their fear.

Jack was the first out from behind the counter. He could feel five creatures coming and he wanted to get in the first shot before they saw that he was there—for some reason, he was sure they would recognize him. He didn't recognize them; no Incan mummy, no Amanra, and, thankfully, no Hor. They were just five bone-monsters with rags of forgotten flesh hanging off of them and empty but eternally deep eye-sockets that could drive a person mad and yet, Jack ignored the feeling which had his mind tipping over to a point where sanity was the underside of the boat.

He stepped out, aimed his shotgun and accepted the mule-kick in the shoulder and watched the first of them tumble back, missing its head and one arm. A second later, Jack exploded another, much smaller creature—it seemed to just turn to white powder in a flash of orange. A third one opened its mouth and blasted out a smog of stench that wobbled Jack, but then Cyn was suddenly right next to him, her face hard and sharp. She pulled her trigger and staggered from the force of the gun shot.

The creature she hit had its vertebrae and most of its ribs shot away and it collapsed in on itself like a house of cards.

The fourth and fifth creature were feet away. Cyn, who was staggering under the twin clouds of fear and stink, fired once sending a skull flying in a thousand pieces just as Jack hit the last dead center.

"Let's go!" Cyn yelled to the others. She started to charge through the litter of bone fragments, ignoring, for some reason the fact that one of the corpses was still standing. It was headless and by all natural logic, it should have been harmless; it should have pitched right over and died, except it was already dead.

Cyn sort of shied away from it, but it was a long fiend with arms that stretched out and grabbed her, snagging the back of her armored collar. For something that was made of so little, the creature had the strength of the largest of men; it picked Cyn up and dangled her a foot off the ground.

She tried to bring her gun around but it could see without eyes and grabbed the gun with its free hand and Jack was shocked to see frost run up the barrel. He was shocked, but for only one second and then he fired his shotgun straight across the axis of the thing's shoulders, tearing both arms off by the blast.

He followed the shot up with a kick to what remained of the thing's sternum. Cyn dropped, landing on her feet like a cat. Now, she smirked and charged off through the south end of the lobby and, seconds later they were out in the morning and breathing fresh air.

Cyn smiled at him. It was part relief, part joy at being alive and part…it seemed to Jack, that it was part happiness that he was there with her. He didn't have time to figure out what he thought of that; there was a cry from behind them.

It was Father Paul who was being dragged down, not by one of the undead creatures, but rather by Richards who had either died or had fallen unconscious. Rebecca tried to prop the detective up, but he was too much dead weight and she was too weak to help.

Jack ran back and handed over his shotgun to her. "Cover us!" he ordered, and then took the police officer's shoulders as Father Paul took his feet. Richards was a big man and they moved awkwardly along under his weight, going far too slowly.

They were so slow that the lobby emptied behind them and the demon…the dreadful, little demon girl was able to catch up, having passed through a thinning crowd of screaming hotel guests to come after them.

When he saw the demon he said to Father Paul: "Go faster!" They had a sixty-yard head start and were actually in the ambulance when it caught up. Cyn was just climbing into the ambulance assuming the "shotgun" seat as she had been, and Jack was in the back, pulling the unconscious Richards inside with Father Paul's help.

The only person outside and vulnerable was Cyn's mother, Rebecca.

She saw the monster coming and had to have felt the evil radiating from it. She had seen what it could do first hand, and yet she didn't quail in the face of it. Rebecca shouldered the shotgun, aimed, grimaced in anticipation of the kick that she assumed to be coming, and pulled the trigger.

There was nothing, not even a click.

In a sudden rush of memory, Jack counted every shot he had taken with the gun. It wasn't difficult to count to four—she was out of ammo.

Things took on that hated slow motion nightmare feel: unaware of her mother's situation, Cyn pulled her door closed. Father Paul climbed into the back of the ambulance, and was just reaching out to close the door when he saw Rebecca thirty feet away, staring at the shotgun in confusion.

The little girl demon with the big, gleaming pennies for eyes was much closer to her, just a few feet away. There was no way Jack, or anyone could save her. It was a fact, except in his mind it was a DAMNED fact. She was going to die; there was no getting around that, there was only acting like a crass unfeeling bastard and using her death to get away.

He scrambled for the front seat, digging for the keys, just as the monster, the little bundle of bones and dried flesh, leapt at Rebecca and latched its toothless mouth onto her neck. If she could have screamed, she would have, however she was feeling something beyond both pain and terror. Her mouth came open wide and her eyes were huge and filled with a misery that would forever haunt Jack's soul.

The demon fed on her as Jack tried to get the key seated in the ignition. It drank from her. It sucked her dry, pulling from her everything that made her human and that included her past and future. It was horrible to see. Jack and Cyn saw out of the side view mirrors, while Father Paul had a front row seat and was right there as Rebecca had her entire life pulled from her.

The skin of her cheeks sunk in and pulled tight, her eyes deflated and shrunk in on themselves, becoming strange pale raisins, her lips drew far back, stretching across her teeth until they split apart, her hair grayed in seconds and then began falling out, whispering down her back to land in an obscene little haystack and her nails grew three inches, curling at the ends into ugly looking bird claws.

She was sucked dry, but she didn't die. It would have been better for everyone if she had. Rebecca became one of the living dead.

"Jack!" Father Paul cried, pointing.

"We have to save her," Cyn said, hammering on Jack's arm.

"No," he answered in a soft voice. His eyes never left the terrible sight. But somehow his hands did what had to be done. They started the ambulance, put it in drive and sped away.

Chapter 24

Manhattan, New York City

They were blazing through red lights with the back doors swinging wildly, banging against the side of the ambulance, and there were undead corpses everywhere, and there were screams and sirens...and Cyn pointed her shotgun at Jack.

"Turn around." Her voice, quiet as it was, cut through the roar of the engine and the gun blasts that seemed to be coming from every direction and an explosion that sounded like it was just around the corner.

"I can't," Jack told her. "Your mom's dead, Cyn. I'm sor..."

She jabbed the barrel of the gun into the side of his head. "Turn around or I shoot." The barrel was as cold as her words.

He shrugged, but didn't slow the ambulance. He would deserve it if she killed him. He had given her mom an empty gun and told her to protect them; that was a straight up fact. It was his fault she was dead. The guilt was a brick in his gut.

"No," he answered. For a few seconds, she pressed harder, leaving a red circle imprint, preparing herself to kill him, he supposed with calm circumspection. He could afford to be calm since he really didn't care if she shot him or not. The guilt mixed with his exhaustion, made him apathetic to his fate, or rather *this* fate. Getting his brains blown out was an easy death compared to what was happening around them.

The streets were filled men and monsters and it was all Jack could do to weave in and out of the screaming people; it didn't help that Father Paul was yelling from the back for them to stop. Richards was laid out on the floor, either dead or unconscious with the priest draped over him to keep him from rolling out of the back.

Unbelievably, Cyn said: "This is my fault." He felt the metal bore wavering against his temple. A second later she withdrew the gun and he chanced a look at her. She was glass-eyed and staring out at the chaos without seeing a thing. Even when they hit something that had been long dead and a wet slop of decomposing flesh struck the windshield, she didn't blink or seemed to notice.

She went on: "I gave away the spell. I just gave it away like an idiot. My mum is dead because I was an irresponsible git. I wanted to be famous. That's why she's dead because I wanted to be *someone*, but what I was...what I am, is a damned child!"

"Stop it!" Jack snarled. "This is Robert's fault...or mine, really, but it's definitely not yours, so shut up." She glared and he deserved that, too. "I-I'm sorry, that came out awful, I know. The only thing you did wrong was to place your faith in your cousin. You believed Robert and so did I. That's not a crime, Cyn, so please, just stop blaming yourself and get that look out of your eyes. You can't give up. Your mom wouldn't want you to give up, would she?"

"No, she wouldn't," Cyn said after a moment's hesitation. "She would want me to get back home where it's safe. She would want me to get as far away from all of this as possible. And as far away from you as possible."

"Yeah, that sounds good, I suppose. I mean, I can see her point." He could see her point right in front of him where a platoon of uniformed policemen were running away from a single walking corpse. Jack could sense that it wasn't one of the powerful demons, so he aimed the ambulance right for it.

There was a satisfying crunch under the wheels.

He didn't slow to pick up any of the officers. As hard as it was, it was the right thing to do to leave them. They were crazed with fear and would more than likely mistake Jack for a demon and shoot him.

"Wrong, Jack!" Cyn snapped. She was no longer on the verge of being catatonic; her face was sheathed in anger and yet her blue eyes were misty. "You're wrong and so is my mother...or so was my mother or...you know what I mean. I can't run away, just like you can't. We can stop this. We're the only ones who can, I think. We just have to find the right spell."

"What you have to do is stop, please," begged Father Paul from the back. "I think Richards is dying."

Jack aimed the ambulance for an intersection that looked empty and skidded to a halt almost in the middle. There was a blare of a horn to his right and then a white Lexus flew past within an inch of their bumper, the driver waving a fist in true New York fashion.

"Take the wheel," Jack yelled to Cyn and then jumped out. He ran around to the back, climbed in and slammed the doors behind him. Immediately, the ambulance took off, taking a hard left, heading west, trailing after the speeding Lexus and causing Jack to stumble over Father Paul. "Sorry," he said to the priest and then he yelled to Cyn. "Be careful!"

Father Paul barked a short laugh. "Compared to you, Mister Jack, she is being careful. Now, help me get him on the gurney."

Richards, though still alive with a thready pulse, was dead weight. It took all of their strength to heave him onto the gurney and strap him in. Jack saw the O2 mask, stuck it over the detective's face, and then followed the plastic line to a valve. One twist got the gas flowing.

In the meantime, Father Paul poked another nitro-glycerine pill under Richards' tongue. "We must please get to a hospital or he will die. Go. Go make sure she gets us to a hospital."

Jack gave him a nod and then squeezed through the narrow opening to the cab of the ambulance. When he climbed into the passenger seat, he didn't hesitate to buckle up—there wasn't a law that Cyn wasn't breaking.

With tears still on her face, she drove down sidewalks, zipped through red lights, took a left on a one-way street and played chicken with thirty cars heading right at her. "Is this the way to the hospital?" he asked, his hands stiff on the dashboard.

"How should I bloody know?" she shot back as she shared paint with a plumber's van that was filled with people, all of whom were yelling curses at her. I was trying to get off this island. I'm sorry about the bobby back there, but if we don't get out of Manhattan soon, we may not ever get out."

They had left the first wave of undead behind them, but in front the traffic was beginning to snarl worse than anything Jack had ever seen. They had made it to Seventh Avenue only because of Cyn's crazy driving; the roads west were starting to freeze solid with the numbers of cars trying to get to one of the three exit points on the west side of the island.

Jack knew she was right. Once the creatures caught up, there would be pandemonium and then massacre.

"What about that ferry?" she asked.

"Cars aren't allowed on."

"Well, we aren't a car now are we?" she demanded and took a hand off the wheel to swipe away the tears on her cheeks. "As far as anyone knows, we're constables. Ok, maybe you could pass as one; you have a badge and a bloody big gun. They'll listen to you, I'd wager. You could get us on."

The mention of the gun reminded him of how badly he had messed up with regard to her mother. He glanced down at the shotgun Cyn had been carrying and then shook his head in wonder at what a fool he was. How many rounds were left in the thing? He grabbed the shotgun and started feeding shells into the port—it had been empty as well.

He was just about to mention how the ferries had been converted and there was no place for an ambulance to even park on one, when there was a roar from overhead. Fourteen army helicopters, each so full that they were practically spilling soldiers, flew west in two wedge formations, causing a smaller, red and white helicopter to swerve.

The lone helicopter played on his mind, giving him an awful idea, one that he refused to even contemplate until they hit 45th Street and the traffic fused into one great mass of metal and the air was filled with the blare of horns and screams of rage.

"Turn around," Jack ordered. "There's a hospital ten blocks north..." Cyn started to argue and he put a hand on her shoulder. "Trust me, ok? This may be the only way off the island."

She nodded, her exhaustion and grief taking over. Without caring how many cars she hit, she turned the boxy vehicle around and broke a great number of new laws in traveling the mile to Saint Luke's, where every entrance was taken up by ambulances; she parked dead set in the middle of the sidewalk.

Jack slung the shotgun over his back and pinned Richards badge to his chest. Cyn carried his 9 mm. "We have to get to the roof as quietly as possible and without arousing any suspicion."

This turned out to be relatively easy. The hospital was pure chaos; its fifty bed emergency room had eight hundred people waiting to be seen. Nearly all of them had been scratched or bitten by the undead and were in the throes of misery. Jack and Cyn knew the pain and they glanced guiltily at each other as they pushed Richards' gurney through the choked halls.

"I have to help them," Father Paul stated suddenly. He stopped pushing the gurney and stepped to the side to let Jack continue to push it. "I have it in my power to ease their suffering."

"No," Jack hissed in a whisper, his eyes flicking around. "You need to stay with us. We're going to need you, Father. You know that. This...this isn't about you healing people, this is you ducking your responsibility." The brick of guilt in his stomach had been shrinking, but now it was back and heavier than ever.

For the first time since they had met, Father Paul grew angry, his jowls shook and he waved a pudgy finger in Jack's face. "How dare you, Mister Jack? How dare you question my courage? Staying here is infinitely more dangerous and you know that. I think that you're using poor Detective Richards as an excuse to run away."

Jack began to puff up in real anger as well; however, the priest popped that bubble by adding: "Where is your cousin Robert? The simple answer is that you don't know. He's likely here in the city and yet *you* are doing your level best to run away. Don't tell me about responsibility until you learn to do yours."

The priest turned on the spot and went to the nearest person, a woman in the blue uniform of a fireman. He began to pray over her and in seconds the misery that had been lining her face disappeared and she passed out.

"Come on, Jack," Cyn said, pulling the gurney. "He doesn't know what he's talking about. We don't have the tools to fight Robert yet and until we do it'll be suicide to try to face him."

That was perfectly reasonable and Jack found himself nodding...but was it the truth? Were there spells somewhere in the world that could help him? And if so where? And why did it have to be him? Was he fooling himself into thinking that he was going to be some sort of savior, just so that he could run away, just so he could save his own life?

Indecision held him in place until Father Paul ran through his prayers. He took out the little bottle of Holy Oil, anointed the woman and then turned to Jack. "May the Lord bless and protect you, Mister Jack." He drew a cross on Jack's forehead with the oil and then stepped over to Cyn and repeated the same thing.

"Do Detective Richards, too," Jack asked, remembering a little too late, "Please...and, uh thanks for everything."

"It is nothing. It is my duty," Father Paul said. He seemed unsure of himself for a moment. "And...and I might have been too harsh with you just now. Maybe your job is to save the world. I hope it is. But you must know that my job is to save souls and I intend to save as many as I can before *they* come for me. Now go with God's blessing."

Slowly, feeling the guilt build to the size of anchors, Jack pushed the gurney away, knowing that the soft, chubby priest was a braver man that he would ever be.

Cyn was crying as she shoved ahead of people waiting on the elevators. "Police business," she mumbled a few times and then they were on the car and zooming upwards. "The top floor, please," she said to a man in white, a doctor, Jack supposed, who was standing closest to the glowing buttons.

The man gave them a sharp look—it turned dismissive when he saw how ill-fitting their outfits were. "That's restricted access. No one can go up there."

"We can," Cyn said, showing him the 9MM. The other passengers squinched away, suddenly finding the tops of their shoes of great interest. "Why don't you hit the next floor so everyone can get out."

"Maybe not everyone," Jack said. "What kind of doctor are you?"

The man in white swallowed loudly and pointed at himself. "Me? I-I I'm not a doctor. I'm a nurse." Jack lifted his chin to indicate the man's name tag, which read: *Jason Moore, M.D.* "Oh, right. Sorry the guns make me nervous."

The elevator dinged and when the door opened, the other passengers slid out in a sideways crab-like motion.

The doctor looked as though he wanted to edge out with them and Cyn stopped him.

"You were going to tell us what sort of doctor you were?" she asked.

"I'm a cardiologist."

Cyn looked over at Jack with her trademark smirk set under her teary eyes. "I think there might really be a God, and better yet, he might be on our side."

Chapter 25

Manhattan, New York City

They pushed out of the elevator, Jack in the back and Dr. Moore in front with Cyn keeping close, the 9MM partially hidden next to her side. With the helicopter's blades turning, it was surprisingly warm huddled under the downwash of the whipping blades.

"What's this?" a paramedic who was nearby, yelled. "We're filled already. We can't take any more." Cyn's gun came up and Jack fumbled his shotgun from his back. The paramedic shot his hands above his head and began backing away, only to trip on a pile of bodies wrapped in sheets that had been hauled to the side of the helicopter pad.

"Get up!" Cyn yelled over the noise of the engine which sounded as though it was throttling up.

Jack raced forward and pointed the shotgun at the windshield until the pilot took his hands off the stick. Once he did, Jack turned to the paramedic. "I need you to make room for us four. No! Don't shake your head. Clear us some room or I will!" He was altogether bluffing, or so he told himself, and yet he was keyed up and his finger was all over the trigger.

He remained at the ready until the two people who were on the verge of dying were pulled off. Jack took a look at their wounds—both bore the marks of being scratched by the walking corpses. The flesh around the wounds was black and dribbled grey pus that made his stomach turn upside down.

As Richards was being loaded, he yelled to the paramedic: "Get these two downstairs right away. Have them see Father Paul. Father Paul, do you hear me?"

Instead of answering, the paramedic glanced once at Jack's shotgun, which he had allowed to dip, and it couldn't have been more obvious that the man was thinking about grabbing it. "Don't!" Jack screamed and jumped back. "I'm not playing. Get these people downstairs, right now! Go!"

With his chance gone, the paramedic moved in a stooped cringe as he began hauling away the first of the dying patients.

"*Jack!*" He caught his name as if hearing it from a mile away. The rotors were speeding up and the engine was kicking into high gear. He glanced up and saw Cyn yell his name; he couldn't hear it, but he could read her lips.

They were ready to go. Jack made sure to keep the shotgun positioned better this time so that no one would get any ideas about trying to take it from him. It wasn't easy. The helicopter was almost entirely taken up by the stretcher and the mass of medical equipment that was normally a part of the aircraft.

Jack and Cyn sat at the back of the helicopter, facing across Richards' body toward Dr. Moore and another of the paramedics. They were both handed helmets and the second Jack had his, on the pilot asked over the built-in headpiece: "So where are you making us go?" His voice was sharp and angry.

"Huh?" Jack was momentarily at a loss, confused at the sudden voice in the helmet. "Oh, right. You're our hostages. Where were you going to go?"

There was a click and a scratch of static and then the pilot answered: "Princeton Surgery Center."

"Then go there. Oh, and pilot? I know that you can call people without me hearing, but I really suggest that you don't. Let us go our way and you go yours so no one gets killed. Got it?"

Another click and a scratch was followed by: "Roger that."

"I don't believe him," Cyn said through her mike.

Neither did Jack and yet, what choice did they have? He didn't see any other options open to them except to perhaps divert the chopper at the last second to land in some field or park. But what would happen to Richards? "Hey, Dr. Moore, can you hook my friend up to a heart monitor or something? He's had two of those little nitro pills. The first one seemed to help, but the second didn't."

The bird started to lift just as the doctor climbed out of his seat. He looked unsteady and a little green. "Let me get that," the paramedic said. "We don't need you getting sick all over the patient."

As the leads were being attached, Jack went on: "It's very important that you save him, doctor. He knows what's happening and how all of this started. In fact, if anything happens to him or to us, like if we get shot or something, you're going to have to talk to the FBI or the police or the army. You need to tell them that the man who started this is Robert Montgomery the Seventh. He's English."

"British, actually," Cyn said. "Really the family is from Scotland and the original name was Mac Gumaraid. But, I guess that doesn't matter much now does it? For legal purposes, we're British." She seemed pale and soft as talc; the gun in her hand pretty much forgotten as she looked out the window as the hospital seemed to fall away. Jack glanced out as well and saw that she was looking at the three lonely corpses.

"I never got to say goodbye," she said in a whisper, probably speaking to herself but accidentally announcing it to everyone. Jack thought she was going to cry again and took her hand in his; she squeezed his hand, hard, and didn't let go.

The chopper was loud but empty of conversation as they flew southeast over the Hudson River and New York Harbor. From their height, the world was serene. Jack thought about Cyn's mother and how he had screwed up. He couldn't get her wizened face out of his mind and nor could he get past the fact that the demon had made her into one of them.

That shouldn't have been possible. None of the others who had been killed by the creatures had returned from the dead—they just died, either by physical trauma or by the *dead disease* as he thought of it. Those three corpses that had been stacked up by the helicopter pad weren't going to suddenly spring to "life" at the next full moon. They needed a soul to enter their bodies for that to happen.

So how did the demon manage it?

There was no way to know, at least not without capturing it and torturing it for information. *Then, at least Cyn could say goodbye to her mother*, he thought. This little empathetic reflection on his part suddenly triggered a much greater thought.

Jack suddenly knew where he needed to go next.

He opened his mouth but then he saw that Dr. Moore had been checking on Richards; he looked especially grave when he scanned Richards' EKG readout. "Is he going to live?" Jack asked.

"Maybe," the doctor answered. He pulled off his helmet and stuck his stethoscope in his ears and started to listen to Richards' chest. As he did, his lips were fine lines of worry.

A voice suddenly spoke into his ear: "You know how this started?"

Jack jumped and looked around, trying to see who was speaking to him. It was the paramedic. "Yeah, I do, but you won't believe me, not until it's too late, not until one of *them* is crawling up into your helicopter."

"You don't know what I believe," the paramedic answered, his blue eyes going flinty. "Our radios get all sorts of signals from all sorts of places. We know something is happening out in Queens and Brooklyn. They say it's a terrorist attack, but none of us think it is. All of these patients are practically crazy and the necrotizing fasciitis isn't natural. Ronald, the other paramedic, thinks that it's an alien disease that's taking over people's minds."

"It is and it isn't," Cyn said. "It's actually..." she paused and laughed. It wasn't a normal chuckle by any stretch; the laugh was the sound of a woman who was tight-roping along the edge of insanity and knew it. "It's the undead," she finished.

The blue eyes were no longer flinty, they were crinkled with laugh lines. "Zombies? Ok, lady, sure."

Cyn was suddenly furious. She pulled out her phone and showed the paramedic some of the pictures she had taken at the Museum of Modern Art. "Look at what happened to that guard. The guy who did this cut that man open and used his body as an inkwell. Do you see the glyphs in his blood? Those are a proto-hieroglyph, Sumerian cuneiform mixture that indeed raised the dead. Do you see the sarcophagus? The *empty* sarcophagus? You see what I'm getting at here?"

The paramedic blinked at what he was seeing and then nodded slowly.

She went on: "Those same glyphs and another body just like this one, can be found on the third floor of the Brooklyn Museum in an exhibition called the *Mummy Chamber*. More of those same glyphs can be found at a home in Lindenhurst along with two dead police officers. So go ahead and laugh at the idea, but like Jack said, you'll only believe when it's too late for you."

The helicopter was quiet for a good, long time. They rocked back and forth as the chopper hit odd pockets of air and they were well over New Jersey before the pilot came on: "Part of their story checks out," he said and was no longer angry sounding. "I radioed a friend in the NYPD Aviation Unit and it took him a few minutes but there are...I guess it's now there *were* active investigations going on at those museums and in Lindenhurst."

"Well, I guess it's good that someone believes us," Jack remarked to Cyn. She gave him a smile; it was a tired smile and full of worry, but it was genuine.

"I didn't say I believed you," the pilot said. "Nor did I say I trusted you. There is an arrest warrant out for two people who match your descriptions."

Cyn's smile disappeared. "An arrest warrant? For what?"

"Murder and kidnapping," the pilot answered.

Jack thought that he would go on but there was only the lulling drone of the engines in his ear pieces. "Well they got the kidnapping part, correct," Jack said. "You guys are exhibit A, but the truth is we didn't kill anyone."

"Maybe," the pilot said. "That's not really up to me, though your story doesn't sound so good with you guys carting around that fella. You say his name is Richards? That's who you are supposed to have kidnapped."

"That's preposterous," Cyn said. "He is the one who detained us, and later, he came of his own free will. He's probably regretting it now."

Again the chopper was quiet as Jack and Cyn stared down at Richards. A few minutes later the doctor said: "I think I believe them. This guy, Richards hasn't been hand-cuffed or anything. He's not been hurt or knocked out. He even has a gun in an ankle holster. If he was kidnapped, why didn't he use it?"

Cyn shared a look with Jack and then lifted up the 9MM. "Maybe I should have the gun, what do you say? I don't want anyone getting twitchy."

"Sure, I don't want it," the doctor said.

"I just know what they tell me," the pilot remarked as Cyn took a very small black pistol from Richards' hidden holster. "And I believe my own eyes. When someone points a gun at an air-ambulance and pulls dying patients off it, I don't need the police to tell me they're the bad guys."

Cyn opened her mouth to retort, but shut it again. It was hard to argue with those sorts of facts. Jack saw it differently. "We probably saved their lives," he said, not adding: *For the moment.* He didn't think the two dying patients would live once the wave of creatures engulfed the hospital. "Call the hospital or radio them, I mean. Find out what's happening down in the Emergency Room.

They're going to say something about a miracle I'm betting. A friend of ours, a priest, stayed behind."

Again a pause and then the pilot came on. "This...this is crazy. He's not lying. They said that there's a priest curing people left and right."

"Holy crap," the paramedic said. His face was slack and his eyes kept wandering back and forth between Jack and Cyn as if looking for something miraculous about them as well. Abruptly the look changed to suspicion. "If this priest could heal people, why didn't he heal your friend?"

Jack shrugged. "My guess is because Richards' heart attack was natural. Yes, it was caused by the madness given off by the undead, but it was his own heart that gave out. Those people at the hospital are dying from something evil. It's some sort of magical poison and it's horrible, but thankfully a priest can cure it."

"This is crazy," the paramedic said a second time.

"Yeah," Jack agreed.

No one spoke until the hospital was in sight and the copter was settling down on the pad on its roof. There was crackle of the pilot's mike: "I didn't say anything," he admitted. "No one will bother you if you leave, but...but, I have to ask: what are you going to do? You know, about all of this? You know things. You know who did it and why. You should tell somebody, like the FBI or the army, like you wanted us to do."

"I'd like to," Jack said, "but we're wanted criminals. They're more likely going to believe someone like you or Dr. Moore."

"You want me to go to the FBI?" the pilot asked as if the idea was ludicrous.

Jack began nodding, but then remembered that the pilot was up front and couldn't see him. "Yes, I do. You have a way to fly over the creatures and get pictures, and you can go back to the hospital and video the priest curing people, and you can tell them my story."

The paramedic raised a hand. "Hey, why don't you come with us and tell your own story? With us as your, you know, your witnesses, they probably won't arrest you."

"I can't take that chance," Jack said. "There's something more important I have to do." Cyn gave him a curious look and mouthed the words: *Like what*? Jack pulled off his helmet and when she did as well he spoke into her ear: "I have to raise the dead."

Chapter 26

Princeton, New Jersey

"You can't," Cyn hissed as they skipped the elevator ride with Richards and Dr. Moore and headed for the stairs.

She had kissed Richards' cool cheek; Jack had squeezed his hand and whispered "Goodbye," and had missed the man the moment they stepped away. Richards had been steadfast, strong and levelheaded—he probably would have talked Jack out of his crazy idea.

"I can, and I don't really have any choice. We need information that only the dead can provide."

Jack began to speed down the stairs, knowing exactly what Cyn was going to say next. He was almost running, his boots clocking on each step, sending an odd echo bouncing along the cement walls. "And where do you think you're going to get the blood?" she demanded, exactly echoing his very thoughts. "You can't take it from me, because that could be construed as a gift."

He wanted to say: *I don't know*; only he did know. He was going to get the blood from the same place he was going to get the car that they needed to get them further west.

She knew it as well and repeated: "You can't, Jack. I know you think you're being all noble, but you're not. You're being a bloody git. The road to hell, Jack is not going to be paved in good intentions; it's going to be paved in the blood you steal...and the lives. This won't end with you taking a little blood from someone. You're going..."

He rounded on her, coming up short so that they almost crashed into each other. "I won't go that far, Cyn. No one is going to die, ok? Trust me on this."

"I don't trust you, Jack. You've taken blood twice now, both times from me. And I have to say it wasn't good. You may not want to hear this, but it felt awful. Maybe not to you, but for me it was horrible and disgusting, and...and draining a might bit. It made me feel sick when I was drawing those symbols."

"I'm sorry, I really am, but if you know a different way for us to find out what's going on, I'm all ears. There could be millions of people dying out there right now and that's partly my fault, Cyn. And it's partly yours."

She shoved him away and then pushed past, heading down the stairs at an even faster clip than he had been going. Over her shoulder, she hissed: "You don't need to remind me that I screwed up." They were at the bottom floor and standing in a busy corridor before Jack could apologize; she didn't listen when he did. She only pointed at the early morning crowd: the old, the sick, the hospital personnel going about their business.

"Who's it going to be? Who's your victim?" She was being loud and a number of people glanced over at them.

Jack glared. "Maybe you should go."

Cyn looked all ready to storm off, but then deflated and Jack knew why. Where could she go? To whom could she turn? She was wanted by the police. Her mother was either dead or in a state worse than death and her only relatives were sadistic killers, or Jack, and she seemed afraid of Jack.

"I mean it," Jack told her. "I don't want to be harsh, but there's no time for niceties or hurt feelings or...or worrying about some spilt blood. So far we've gotten by with just taking blood. There's no saying in any of this that someone has to die."

"And what about your soul? I never was big on religion but after Father Paul and what he was able to do, I don't know anymore."

He was right there with her in the land of spiritual confusion. He'd been so gung-ho about God at first, but then it seemed he had proven disappointingly weak. God wasn't the all-powerful badass that he had expected him to be and what did that mean for his soul? Was it up for grabs when he died? Was he destroying it by taking the blood of innocents?

There was no way to know, he only knew that he was already so ate up with guilt that it made him sick, and if Robert's undead army kept going, and kept killing at the rate they were and Jack didn't do everything he could to stop it, his soul would be worthless.

"I think I have to keep going if I want to save my soul. I haven't crossed the line yet...I don't think, and what we're planning shouldn't put me over the edge."

"What *we're* planning?" she demanded with wide eyes. "This is all you. And before you ask, I'll come and I'll help you if I can, but I won't kill anyone."

"What about kidnapping someone?" he asked under his breath. "Will you help with that?"

They needed a car and they needed blood. Jack adjusted the heavy helmet on his head, slung the shotgun and tried to walk through the crowd without arousing suspicion. Cyn followed and people stared openly at the two of them—mostly at their guns; Cyn didn't have a holster for hers and had to tuck it down the front of her jeans. They also stared at Jack's sword. It made no sense.

Some people asked them questions in low, conspiratorial tones: "*What's happening in New York? What's going on? What's with the army? Are we under attack? Is it true there are zombies in New York?*"

Jack refused to speak and kept his eyes down until they were outside, where the sun was shining but the air was sharp with an edge of frost. He gazed around at the parking lot, feeling his stomach knot up; what he was planning was odious, immoral and highly illegal.

A woman thick and dour walked by, glanced at them and then headed for the parking lot. Jack would have taken her, *but* she had a child with her. A middle-aged man came next. He was dressed in a suit and tie; he seemed in a hurry to be somewhere. *Probably important*, Jack thought and let him go.

A young woman came through the doors next. She took one look at Jack and Cyn in their odd ill-fitting gear and walked a wide circle around them. She paused forty feet down the sidewalk to light a cigarette. "What are you waiting for?" Cyn asked. "You've ignored everyone who's walked by and they've all been perfect candidates, seeing as they all have blood and she," Cyn gestured at the smoker, "wouldn't give us too much trouble if you ask me."

"She's engaged," Jack said. "She had a ring and, I don't know, it doesn't seem right."

"You can't use her to save the world because she's in love?" Cyn asked, and finally her pert little smirk was back, if only for a second. "You're not very good at kidnapping, which I suppose is a good thing."

Jack wanted to glare at her; however, his stomach was too knotted up and instead he just sort of looked "ill" at her. He thought again about going after the woman and then second guessed himself and ended up letting her go—just as he let the next five people go.

He would raise his gun, open his mouth, let it hang there open and useless until they were too far away and then he would sag. Cyn couldn't help but laugh at him and she was still laughing when an older man came up and asked: "You guys don't look like cops."

The man, greying and wrinkled with straying hair and a few days' worth of stubble on his thin cheeks, was alone and wore no rings. He wasn't particularly big and his voice had the rasp of a career smoker—he probably couldn't scream very loud, Jack thought. There couldn't be a better candidate.

"No, we're not," Jack answered in a high voice. His right hand slipped up the stock of the gun, fumbling for the trigger guard and somehow not finding it. When he did, he stuck his middle finger in it and quickly pulled it out again. He looked as though he was strumming the gun like a guitar.

Jack thought his nervousness couldn't be more obvious and yet the man seemed at his ease. He gave Jack a wink, leaned in close and asked: "So, you're what? CIA? Delta?" He jabbed a thumb at his own chest. "I was a *Seal* back in the day."

"A seal?" Jack asked, at a loss for what the man was talking about. Next to him, Cyn was jerking her head sideways, suggesting by the move that Jack was to stop messing around and get the old guy to the parking lot.

"Yeah, back in the seventies," the man said. "Lots of black ops. Lots of covert stuff that I can't talk about. Assassinations and coups. We done a lot of coups back in the day." He leaned even closer, whispering: "You don't want to know all the crap we done, all the illegal stuff we were into."

Suddenly, it clicked what the man meant. "Oh, you're a Navy Seal. Did you hear that, Cyn, he was a Navy Seal?" He gave her a knowing look that was also a warning look, suggesting that they should look elsewhere for their victim. "They are tough guys. No one messes with Navy seals."

"I just need to know if the Navy Seal has a car," she answered. "A lot of them don't from what I hear."

"Where'd you hear that?" the man asked. "Maybe the Seals in England don't have cars but in America we do. That's my ride right over there." He pointed down a line of cars in the front row of the lot, at a silver Honda Civic with a cracked windshield and rust eating up the under carriage. It was parked in the furthest handicapped spot, although the man seemed perfectly capable of walking.

Cyn gave it a long look. "Does it run proper?"

"Proper enough," the man admitted after slipping a suspicious look at Cyn. "Why do you ask? Who are you guys with? You with the government? I know my rights, young lady. I know my *American* rights."

She began walking toward the car, her hand on the butt of the pistol. The old man followed, as did Jack, who asked: "Cyn? What are you doing? He is a Navy Seal. Like I said, you don't mess with Seals, even ex-Seals."

"If you're going to do this, now's the time. We can't stand outside a hospital armed to the teeth or people will get nervous. Remember what you said: there's no time for niceties." She stopped in front of the car, looked inside and said: "Tolerable. Ok, Jack, let's get the show on the road." The 9MM was now in her hand.

"What she doing with that gun?" the man asked, stepping back into Jack.

Jack gave him a nudge forward with the shotgun. "We're, uh, commandeering your vehicle. You were right, we are with the government and because of...because of what's happening in the city, we have to take your car. Sorry. It's the law and uh, here's my badge. We're with the police."

He held out Richards' police badge. His hand shook, making the badge rattle. The old man didn't seem to notice. "I have rights," he stated, angry but also, uncertain. "You just can't take my car away. That ain't right."

"We won't leave you stranded," Cyn said. "You can come with us. Now, come on. Let's see those keys."

They found out his name was Carl and that he hadn't ever been a Navy Seal. He hadn't even been in the Navy. Carl had been a postal worker. "Of course he wasn't one of your Seals," Cyn said from the back seat. "You know how many blokes like to tell me they are SAS? I hear it all the time. They go on and on about their 'secret' missions. That's how you know they're fake. Real secret agents tend to be secretive. Your problem, Jack, is that you're too gullible."

"And your problem is that you're a pain in the butt," he replied.

She snorted at this. "So I've been told before."

"Uh, can one of you tell me where we're going?" Carl asked. He sat in the passenger seat with his knees clenched tight together and his head held perfectly still. They were heading west along with a few hundred thousand other cars; they putted along doing about thirty on average.

Everyone, it seemed, was heading west; the east bound traffic consisted of a steady parade of ambulances, fire trucks, police cruisers and military vehicles; Humvees and green trucks mostly, but there were also a number of boxy infantry carriers and a few tanks. Most of these were being carted on flatbed semis, but a few went roaring by, their treads adding to the pothole woes of the New Jersey road system.

"We're going to New Holland," Jack answered.

Carl began to splutter: "But...but wait. New Holland, isn't that in Pennsylvania? I can't go to Pennsylvania."

"Actually you can," Cyn told him. "It's right next door to New Jersey, if I can remember my geography of this bloody complicated country. You're practically neighbors."

The old man muttered under his breath until Jack snapped at him to be quiet. Jack was getting nervous. It was one thing to paint a protection ward on the ground; it was another thing altogether to raise the dead. There was no telling what would happen, especially without Robert's spell.

Both Jack and Cyn were operating under the assumption that there had to be a third spell, which Jack guessed was used to control the soul that came back. But that was only a guess. Not knowing made the entire idea of raising the dead very dicey.

Carl remained quiet right up until they entered Pennsylvania and then he began to mutter again. Jack ignored him until they were nearing New Holland. "We're going to need to lay low until night," he said. "I'm sure there will be some complaints if we're caught digging up a *you know what*."

"But I can go, right?" Carl asked. "You guys can trust me not to say anything. I know you're not cops, but that's ok. I never liked cops, so it's like we're on the same side."

That was pretty much the opposite of what Jack wanted to hear. He pulled the car off the road and down a side street. Finding a secluded and wooded area, he stopped the car and turned to Carl. "We are not on the same side and never think otherwise. In fact, turn around and face the door." Carl began to shake. The shakes swept right up his body and yet he turned but kept his eyes on Jack so that his head was spun almost all the way around on his shoulders.

Jack pulled out the cuffs he had taken from Richards. "Just a precaution, Carl," he said as he locked Carl's hands behind his back. "Now, I'd like to get some sleep, so no more mumbling or I'll put you in the trunk. Do you want that?"

Carl gave a quick head shake. He kept his word and remained silent unless spoken to. The three of them spent a long afternoon in the car. For the most part, they slept, even Carl slept as he had nothing better to do.

As evening approached, Jack allowed Carl to walk around and stretch. They then went into town, hitting a McDonalds for dinner. They ate while listening to the confusion of news reports—no one seemed to know precisely what was happening. Travel into the city was long ago restricted and now it was New Jersey's turn. People in city after city were being urged to "relocate" but no one was told where they should go.

The reports did nothing for Jack's guilt but they did steady his resolve. He sent Cyn into a hardware store for fine paint brushes, flashlights, a pry bar and two shovels. Then they went to a grocery store for bandages. Carl had big eyes for everything, but nothing more so than the shovels.

"I'm on your side, remember."

"One more word and I'll gag you, Carl," Jack warned and meant it. He had a strange antipathy for the old man. He disliked Carl almost to the point of hating him, and for Jack that was something. He wasn't a person who hated easily or at all. Other than his cousin, Robert and now Carl, Jack couldn't remember ever hating anyone.

The strange feeling made him nervous and he had to fight the urge to try to reassure Carl. Carl had to be against him or the blood offering wouldn't work and they would have to kidnap someone else.

Full dark was on them soon after, still Jack held them back. He knew the town of New Holland well. By nine the streets would be empty save for a few teenagers, none of whom would be messing around in a graveyard on that cold of a night.

The moment the clock on the dash flicked over to nine, Jack put the Honda in gear and drove to the town's only cemetery. He didn't need the flashlights to find the tombstone he wanted, but when he found it, he couldn't stop himself and shined the light and read the familiar inscription: *Jonathan Dreyden—Beloved Father and Husband*. It always gave him a queer sensation seeing his own name carved in the granite headstone.

Chapter 27

New Holland, Pennsylvania

Although they had bought two shovels, only one was used. Jack didn't trust Carl not to run off if his hands were uncuffed and Cyn had to keep a gun pointed at the old man practically the entire time. The moment they entered the cemetery grounds, Carl became a whiney, jittery mess and when Jack started digging up the remains of his father, Carl broke down in tears.

Blubbering, he begged them not to kill him.

"We're not going to kill you," Jack hissed into his face, "unless you keep making noise, that is."

Cyn, who had been extremely quiet once the sun had set, finally spoke up: "We should gag him. He's going to make noise. The uh, procedure is uncomfortable, if you know what I mean."

Jack knew or he guessed he knew. Carl would have to be sliced open; deep enough to bleed at least a quart of blood and, worse, he would have to have the wound constantly "dabbed" with the brush. It was going to be painful and frightening.

"Yeah. Gag him." Carl looked on the verge of a stroke and again, words of assurance sprang to the tip of Jack's tongue, but he bit them back; they were words that would waste the pain and blood Carl was going to give them.

Cyn found a shirt in the Honda that she ripped into two pieces; one to ball into his mouth, the other to tie it in place. Carl resisted the gag, until she brought out the 9MM and threatened him.

Feeling sick, Jack began digging. The first foot of earth was frozen, so that the shovel bit his hands and blisters began to form. After that, the dirt became easier to cut into. "Easier" was a relative term.

It took almost an hour of digging to uncover the casket.

When it was uncovered and Cyn shone the light down on it, Jack was so racked by shivers that his knees buckled, but he didn't allow himself to fall onto the lid. That would have been disrespectful and disgusting, squatting on the bones of his father. He fell against the side of the grave and let the cold earth hold him up until he could get his strength back.

Then came the arduous chore of getting his father out of the hole. In the movies these little things were never an issue. The camera cut away and *voila* the casket would be sitting right out where they needed it to be. Reality was far more difficult.

The casket alone weighed a hundred and fifty pounds, while Jack's father went into the dirt at over a hundred and eighty. There was no way that Jack could get the expensive, only to be seen once, box out of the ground by himself. Cyn was fashionably slim and relatively weak, while Carl was a shaking blubbering mess.

Jack's solution was to use the jumper cables in Carl's car to drag the casket out and into the night. There was a good deal of noise, but nothing compared to the high *screech* that occurred when they dragged the box along a sidewalk to the parking lot, which had a smooth enough surface to allow Jack to draw the symbols properly.

He got out of the car and stood, sweat freezing on his back, listening, certain that he would hear the wail of sirens coming their way. They had been both too loud and too obvious; someone had to have heard them or had seen them dragging the casket, but no one had.

Deep inside, Jack was disappointed. A part of him had wanted to be caught and now that he hadn't been, he had no good excuse to abandon the dreadful course he had set himself on.

A shaky breath left him as Cyn caught his eye. Her mouth opened and then closed and her lips twitched. "I guess it's time," she finally said.

"Yeah." He turned to Carl, whose eyes were just as big as could be; they bulged in their sockets and he was making a mumbly pleading noise. Jack pulled him forward and then pushed him to his knees next to the casket—the noise continued, grating on Jack's nerves.

"Shut up," Jack snapped, holding up a blade. "Unless you want me to make this harder on you." When he had pulled the knife, Jack didn't know, but it was suddenly in his hand and pointed at Carl's right eye. That eye was brimming with tears. They were the tears of the weak and they made Jack even more angry and disgusted.

The knife inched closer to the eye and might have kept going to puncture it had not Cyn put her hand on Jack's. "What's wrong with you?" she asked him.

"I don't know. I-I don't feel like myself."

"Then let's not do this. There's got to be a better way."

"Please, tell me one," he said and was a shocked at how scared and childish he sounded. "We have no idea how to destroy the creatures. Robert may not even know. Hell, for all we know they can't be destroyed. We need information and trust me, I don't want to do this anymore than you, but we're out of choices."

She dropped her hand and then her eyes. "I know. I...I just don't want to see anything happen to you. Without you, I'm pretty much alone."

"Then it'll be your job to keep me alive," he said, offering a smile. The smile felt good. It felt human and normal. "Ok, Carl, let's do this." He pulled up one of Carl's sleeves, exposing his forearm as the man suddenly bucked in fear. Jack grabbed him by the hair and shoved him back down. "I'm just getting a little blood, Carl. I'm not going to kill you. Now, hold still and I'll make this quick."

Jack intended to slice open Carl's arm in one quick motion; he botched it. The two times he had cut Cyn, he had been in desperate situations; there in the cemetery he had too much time to think, too much time to worry about the pain he was causing. This caused him to cut too shallow.

The cut was an inch and a half long and a fraction of an inch deep; Carl acted as though he had just been sawn in half. "Shut the hell up!" Jack seethed, the angry feeling coming back with a vengeance. He pushed Carl onto his belly and then knelt on his back.

"Careful, Jack," Cyn warned. "You're getting weird again."

"Maybe if he would just hold still." It was a pathetic excuse to be hurting Carl unnecessarily. Jack knew it and it made him feel greasy and ugly inside, but he didn't shift his weight off. What he was doing, stealing the blood of another person and opening a portal into hell itself was evil—why shouldn't he feel evil while doing it? Why shouldn't he *be* evil while doing it?

Perhaps evil was a component of the spell.

"Jaaaack," Cyn said, slowly, drawing his name out and raising an eyebrow.

Jack lifted off. He took a deep breath that did little to get the ugly feeling out of his head, and then cut Carl good and proper. Jack tried not to relish how easily the flesh parted and how quickly the blood welled.

Carl tried to go crazy again, and Jack crushed him with his knee again. "Hold still. We should be done with the knife. The thing is, I need your blood and if you keep spilling it I'll have to cut you again. So don't move."

Cyn was tight-lipped but said nothing. She handed him one of the paintbrushes and her phone with the pictures of the glyphs already selected. Jack worked, phone in one hand, the brush in the other, moving steadily around the coffin and with each dab of the brush his stomach heaved and the strength in his arm grew less.

The spells were draining something out of him.

He had thought it would affect Carl, but the old man skootched along on his knees, grunting or flinching whenever Jack stuck the bristled brush into his wound. Cyn checked each glyph as they went and in twenty minutes they were done and it was only a matter of speaking the words to the spells. He spoke Cyn's protection spell and there was a shimmer in the air that widened Carl's eyes.

But just as Jack started to speak the portal spell, he felt something catch in his throat. He could swallow but he couldn't speak. Opening his mouth, he tried to force sound out and ended up only burping—the smell of it was eye-watering and the taste was acid. He pointed at his throat and shook his head.

Cyn had been close enough to smell the burp; she knew something was wrong. "I'll say the spell," she said. "This is sacrificed blood so it shouldn't matter who says it." Jack wanted to say: *be careful,* but his throat was locked tight and growing tighter by the second; it was beginning to hurt.

"Ok, I can do this," Cyn whispered and then began speaking the words of the dead language. Her accent disappeared and her tone was flat until she came to the lettering that read *Jonathan Dreyden* and then her British sprang back. She repeated the words three times; the last with rising volume and her face cringed in fearful expectation.

But nothing happened.

The night was still cold. The coffin still sat there quietly. The blood began to dry. And Jack began to die.

The choking sensation grew and now he could hear his breath start to whistle a high note through his nose. He snapped his fingers at Cyn and then pointed at his throat.

"Why didn't that work?" she asked. "That should have worked." She went around the twin circles mumbling the words to the spell. When she got back to her starting point, she threw her hands in the air. "I said it correctly."

Jack was starting to see black spots. His knees buckled, so that he sank down behind Carl. He slapped the pavement with a feeble hand.

"Jack! Holy Christ, Jack. You...you you're so pale. It's the spell, right? I could tell something was wrong." She stared again at the circle and then asked: "What do I do?"

He pointed to the circle, twirled his finger round and round, and then pointed to his mouth. "Say it again?" she asked. He nodded and she began a second time, walking around the circle with her flashlight pointing at each glyph as she went.

After the first of the three repetitions of the spell, Jack knew she was wasting her time and killing him in the process. He was going to die. That was a fact. He wanted to yell at her. He wanted to scream profanities. That awful, angry feeling was coursing through him full bore—it was the only part of him that truly felt alive, as if the spell had energized it

Jack threw the bloody brush at her with all his force. It zipped through the air and struck her on the throat, leaving a smear of red and making her cry out. The useless words of the spell died on her lips and she stood there looking at him in an infuriating manner. She had the appearance of innocent fawn.

The look made the angry feeling inside Jack congeal into something worse.

"Why'd you throw that at me?" she demanded.

Because I want to live! he seethed internally. His fury was beyond him then and he saw next to Carl, discarded and half-forgotten, the knife. The blood on it was black as sin, while the steel glittered wicked and sharp in the night. He grabbed it, thinking that he would throw it at her as well.

The handle was warm, strangely inviting and yet the blade was beyond cold. Jack put a finger to it and then jerked his hand back. He wanted to curse, but his throat was still locked up tight...and yet he could breathe again.

And he knew why, just as he knew why the knife was the way it was. The knife was alive, or rather the knife held a part of *his* life within it. Perhaps it was his soul; he didn't know for sure. He just knew he felt empty and he knew that there was only one way to get that part of him back. He had to make a trade. A life for a life.

Blood was life and life was power.

The thought came to him unexplained and yet he did not need an explanation. A blood offering wasn't good enough to open the portal to the netherworld. That portal only opened when someone died. He would have to kill Carl.

It wasn't a surprise and it really wasn't very distressing. He had his anger and his growing hate. Jack couldn't feel love or compassion, not right then, and if he'd been asked, he probably wouldn't be able explain what either word meant. The spell he had begun was purest evil and it had stained his insides good and black.

It made killing Carl not only easy, but a pleasure as well.

Jack took a handful of Carl's grey hair and hauled back on his head. When he cut Carl's throat it was with a long, slow motion.

Chapter 28

New Holland, Pennsylvania

Carl spat blood from his neck. He vomited it out of his body in great pulsing gouts. It wet Jack's hand and it was so hot that it burned.

"Jack!" Cyn cried, horrified, stepping back, looking as though she was on the verge of running.

He ignored her. The angry, evil fever of the spell was on him and he spoke the ancient words that opened the portal between the worlds. There was the awful tin ringing that went right up his bones and drilled into his ears. He cringed but couldn't pull his eyes from the circles he had drawn. Within them and beneath the coffin the concrete seemed to melt into endless black, only deep, deep in that black were motes. They were souls or demons or whatever. They were things that had lived before and they were also the things that would live in a time that had not yet occurred.

Jack stared into the black waiting. It seemed a long time and he finally croaked: "Jonathan Dreyden?" Then came another wait, an expectant one this time. His father was coming. A single mote among the countless motes grew in size until it was a light that took up the entire darkness. Jack threw an arm up to shield his eyes.

There was a thump from the coffin and now Jack could feel again as he used to. He was himself once again and he felt like puking and crying and running away. He had killed a man, an innocent man. He had killed in the coldest of cold blood and now he was overwhelmed with grief and cried like a child.

"I'm sorry, I'm so sorry," he repeated over and over, his tears raining down. He crawled to the limp body of Carl and hugged it.

He had his face buried in Carl's empty chest when the lid to the coffin opened and a voice that was not created by human lips or tongue spoke: *What did you do, Jonny? What is this? Why am I here?*

Jack was afraid to look up. The voice was cold and choppy, speaking in quick sentences, unadorned by the least bit of human emotion. It didn't *sound* like his father, but no one else ever called him Jonny.

"I needed you, daddy. That's why I started the spell, but then it got out of control and I couldn't stop it. I didn't know it would be like this. I swear, I thought it was blood only." These were poor excuses, especially the first: he hadn't even tried to stop the spell; he hadn't thought it was even possible. "I didn't know that I had to kill. You have to believe me."

His father said nothing, which was worse than if he had berated Jack. There were a few seconds of silence and then Jack summoned the courage to look up from Carl's breast and saw his father sitting up in his coffin. Ten years in the ground had changed him. He was sunken and small-er than Jack remembered. His eyes were viscous pools the color of hawked-up snot. His skin was blackened by mold and sagged off his bones as though he was melting.

You used the spells. That was wrong, Jonny. That was, oh so very bad. You read my note; you were warned and now there is trouble. It's in the air. You were good. I remember you as being a good boy. What happened to you?

"Mom d-died," Jack answered, his voice hitching. "I-I don't know if you know that. Sh-she was killed and the spells were stolen. That's why I brought you here. Cousin Robert...he-he tricked me and now he's opened a portal to the netherworld. There are demons, Dad. Demons and all sorts of undead monsters are now here. That's why I used the spell. I need to know how to stop them."

I don't know the answer to that. He lifted a blackened hand and pointed a finger at Carl and added: *You have damned him for nothing.*

Jack wanted to apologize again and again, but what his father had first said dried his tears. "What? How do you not know?" he demanded.

Knowledge is not magically acquired in death. There is much I do not know and much I do not wish to know. I was happy.

"Can you tell us anything, Mr. Dreyden?" Cyn asked. She had inched back to the circle and Jack just noticed the 9MM in her hands—it was pointed at his chest. "Can you tell us about the spells? Are there more of them and do all of them involve blood?"

I know only a little, he admitted, *but I will tell you all I know. My grandfather and his father discovered the tomb of Rath-ara near the city of the dead. Rath-ara was a son in the line of early kings, of which very little is known. They were the witch-kings of Amanhaphala, ancestors of an earlier and much greater line called the Evean-na. They were sorcerers of great power. They had supremacy over life and death and could not be killed in the normal fashion. They reigned, father to son for eons. They built cities of fabulous wealth and were worshipped as gods but in truth they were not gods as we know the term. They were demon-like beings and lived for battle and they craved blood. They made war on each other, sometimes tearing the very fabric of existence.*

How they met their end, I do not know, but one by one their cities were turned to dust and their magic was destroyed when it could be or hidden when it couldn't. Only a weak few of their kind lived on and the line of Amanhaphala were some of these.

"But what about the magic?" Cyn asked. "What do you know of their magic?"

The corpse of Jack's father was silent for some time and then made a sound like a sigh. It was a long sound that shivered Jack's bones. After another moment Jonathan

Dreyden answered: *Their magic is blood magic. They offer the dead and the dying to the Gods of the Undead in exchange for power. I do not know their spells and I do not ever want to know their spells. And yet one spell was my birthright. The spell to open the portal was given to my line...to you, Jonny, so that it would never be used. You failed this trust, Jonny.*

Jack hung his head; his chin resting on Carl's stiffening shoulder. It was horrible to feel the corpse and smell it and to be so close to his victim, only Jack didn't have the strength of character to lift his eyes. His shame was beyond his ability to cope with just then.

"Thank you very much," Cyn said with a weak smile. "That was, uh, helpful, only I guess we could use some more information. Anything at all. Anything about our cousin or his plans...anything?"

I do not know. The world I left behind is insignificant to me now. It feels like a dream.

"Well, uh, is there anyone else we can talk to?" she asked. "I mean anyone here that knows about this sort of thing."

No one among the living that I am aware of. These secrets are heavily guarded. If the answers are out there, they will not be given up willingly.

Cyn and Jack shared an uncomfortable look. "Then I guess I should send you back," Jack said.

You cannot send me back because you cannot control me. Please, Jonny for the sake of your soul and your life, do not attempt to bring anyone back to this world of the living. The spell you have conjured is incomplete and had you made even the slightest error in my name, there would have been dreadful repercussions. The Gods of the Undead have been awakened and there are some who are angry at the loss of their souls, and they are vengeful creatures.

"I won't do the spell again, I promise. It was a big mistake, I know that now, and I..." Jack broke off suddenly as he felt a tremor of unease in the pit of his stomach. It grew slowly until he felt as though he was going to be sick.

Cyn had a hand on her stomach; her eyes were misted over and far away, looking east. "It's Robert. I can feel him. He's far away but I can still feel him. He's using the spell again."

Jack's father turned his head and something in his neck popped, adding to Jack's nausea. His father said: *Robert is opening another gate. He is very foolish. He will cause much misery and pain.*

Jack laid Carl's body down and stepped to the edge of the twin circles. "If I kill Robert, will that send the souls back?"

I do not know this answer; however I doubt it. These souls he calls do not come from the heavens, they come from the world below and they will not willingly go back. They will have to be forced back into their shadow world. I wish I could be of more help to you, Jonny, but now, I am to leave you. I cannot go until I tell you how sorry I am that you have been put in this position. You were burdened greatly while still so young and so alone, and for that I am at fault and beg your forgiveness.

"It's ok," Jack said. "I never blamed you."

You should blame me since my failings have led you here. But if you forgive me I am satisfied. Now, I must also tell you that your mother and I love you very much and do not wish for you to...

"You're with mom?" Jack asked, interrupting. "Don't let her know what happened here, please. I don't want her to know about him." He pointed at Carl, lying in a puddle of his own blood. "With all my heart, I wish I hadn't done this, but I can't take it back and I'm practically drowning in guilt already without mom knowing as well."

I keep no secrets from your mother. I buried the secret of your birthright and look where it has led. Do not worry about your mother, she will understand. This world is darker than it had been and I fear it will only get darker, still. Now, burn my bones. I do not wish to be called again.

Robert can force me against you and that would be a terror to me.

"I will," Jack answered. "Good bye, Dad."

Good bye, my son. Be strong.

Beneath the coffin, a black hole appeared for a blink, there was a rush of wind and then the body of Jonathan Dreyden suddenly slumped and fell back into the coffin. Jack and Cyn stood there staring for a few seconds before they both turned away. Jack had tears in his eyes. He looked east where he knew Robert was drawing his symbols in blood.

He felt utterly lost. He had murdered Carl for nothing. They hadn't learned a thing and they had nowhere to go and Robert was only getting stronger.

When he turned back to Cyn, he saw that she had crossed over to Carl. Unbelievably, she picked up the bloody paint brush and dabbed it into the pool of blood. Jack's eyes bugged. "What the hell are you doing?" he demanded, hypocritically judging her for desecrating the dead…the murdered.

She began painting over the glyphs, saying: "These are too dangerous to leave lying around for anyone to read."

"Yeah," he answered still too swamped to give a better response. Buried in guilt, he bent to the task his father had left him; Jack would burn his corpse. He had no idea how. Sure, he knew fire would do it, but how big of a fire?

Jack had never even barbecued a steak before, so his frame of reference was limited. He feared under-burning rather than over-burning and so he spent the next hour dragging over every log and bough he could find, until he had a great pyramid of wood twelve feet in height.

Then he went to the grisly task of hefting his father out of the coffin he'd slept in for the last ten years. There was a harsh smell of death around the corpse that he hadn't noticed before in all the excitement. It was too much. He had to walk away and even then he doubled over and blew out the dinner he had eaten hours earlier.

Cyn pretended not to notice and only stood to the side staring eastward, with lines creasing her forehead. Robert was working on the next of his four sets of spells. Whatever he had planned was going to be big. When Jack finally stood and wiped his mouth with the back of his hand, she asked: "What are we going to do?"

He wanted to answer: *Whatever we have to*, because that sounded tough and it was what a real man would say. Jack remained silent; the best he could manage was only a shrug. He had an anchor of guilt sitting square in his chest. Since he had sold his birth right for thirty pieces of silver, he had three times stolen blood and once stolen life.

If anyone was as evil as Robert, it was he.

"We'll figure it out," he answered in platitude and then went back to the dank coffin. His Adam's apple jerked up with a click and then he bent to the body of his father. Jonathan Dreyden had been a big man in life, in death he was a shrunken, loose thing, no longer the tough as nails descendant of the original Jonathan Dreyden who had been famously brave and strong. In death, Jack's father was sadly light. Jack cradled his lolling body, carrying it to the tall stack of wood.

"I'm sorry, Dad," he said, and then heaved the corpse to the top.

It took little to start the fire: some newspaper and a bit of kindling. In no time, the fire was reaching up to the stars and the heat baked into both Jack and Cyn. They stood close to each other, their shoulders touching. They took turns glancing at the other when they didn't think they were watching.

They pretended not to notice the smell, and they had no fear of the police. In spite of Jack's earlier paranoia, New Holland, just as every town in eastern Pennsylvania had, hours before, sent their law enforcement officers eastward. Jack and Cyn had heard the sirens and had seen the lights while waiting for the sun to drop.

Now, the townships were on their own and unprotected. No one would care about the fire or about the single upturned grave. They would worry, briefly, about the body of Carl, but with whatever Robert was doing, they wouldn't worry for long.

Jack carried Carl to the forest bordering the cemetery and arranged his body as nicely as he could: he folded Carl's hands in his lap, closed his half-cracked eyes, and put a stick under his head so that the huge slit in his throat stayed closed and didn't yawn open in a manner that was partly grotesque and partly an indictment—Jack hurt in his chest seeing the wound.

When he got back, he barely gave a glance to the bonfire. It was a monstrous thing now and his father had completely disappeared within its orange breast. "So," he said.

"So," she replied.

Neither wanted to put forth an idea about what to do next. Other than racing Carl's old Honda straight west until they hit California, nothing sounded good. What especially sounded like a crap plan was discussing Robert and what they should do about him.

They were silent for a good ten minutes, letting the fire's crack and snap fill in the blanks of their conversation. But even that had to end.

"So," Cyn said again.

Jack's shoulders slumped. He didn't have the luxury to stand there doing nothing. After blowing air from his puffed cheeks, he said: "I don't think we can run away. I-I guess we should find somebody in authority and tell them what we know."

"Which is what?"

That wasn't a good question. They knew only enough to sound crazy. "We'll tell them everything we know and everything we guess and, yes, they won't believe it at first, but maybe after they get a bellyful of the undead, they'll come around."

"And what will they do?" Cyn asked. "What can they do?"

Jack shrugged; it was as good an answer as any he could think of.

Chapter 29

Trenton, New Jersey

The roads east into New Jersey were blocked, not by traffic, but by the military, in what was a clear display of wasted manpower. There was only one car heading east and that was the stolen Honda. There were military vehicles on the road. They passed an entire convoy of forty trucks, but they were pulled over, waiting on orders, Jack guessed.

The lanes west and south and north brimmed with vehicles. They overflowed with vehicles; all of them piled high with goods in a most un-American manner. People had beds and dressers strapped to minivans. Televisions and computers and sofas tottered on Tercels. The beds of trucks had the contents of entire apartments roped onto them, making them tip alarmingly whenever they had to slip down an embankment to go around a stalled out car, of which there were many thousands.

Weaving through the traffic were people on foot. All of them were bundled against the cold and all of them carried a backpack or dragged a piece of luggage behind them. Some carried children along with their possessions. It was midnight and they were walking in twenty degree temperatures.

"They are refugees," Cyn said in shock. It was a chilling sight, one that no American had seen since the *Trail of Tears* and that was a line of ants in the sand compared to this. Every path, road, and highway was jammed by tens of millions of people all fleeing the greater New York area.

Cyn reached out a tentative hand and flicked on the radio. Earlier there had been what seemed like the same blathering DJ on every channel trying to sound both important and informed as they kept repeating *Details are sketchy at the moment* and *No terrorist group has claimed responsibility for the attacks as of yet* and *We urge everyone to stay inside and remain calm.*

The DJs had been replaced by a stern male voice. The reception was full of static and cut in and out "The following counties...be evacuated immediately. This is a mandatory evacuation order under sect...If you are in the follo...Atlantic County, Bergen County, Passaic County, Essex County, Hudson County..."

He went on and on, prompting Jack to remark: "Why doesn't he just say all of New Jersey?" It wasn't just New Jersey that was under the evacuation order, most of Connecticut and southern New York State was as well.

Filled up to his eyes with guilt, Jack clicked off the radio as Cyn asked: "Why would Robert do this? It makes no sense."

"Maybe he's not in control any more. Maybe one of those heavyweight demons is calling the shots now."

"Bloody hell," Cyn breathed and then turned to stare out the window at the long lines of people and cars. There were occasional gunshots and frequently cars tore the paint off each other to jockey for a better position—all for nothing. The traffic was snarled in an unbreakable Gordian Knot. Too many engines were simply stalling out for want of fuel and there was nowhere for them to be pushed to. The families in these situations would simply gather what they felt was most important and then begin walking.

Jack expected that to be his fate soon enough, except he wasn't going to be walking west. He would be walking into the thick of the mess that he had helped to create.

Just before the Delaware River, on the outskirts of Trenton, they came to the first military check point. Jack slung his shotgun and marched forward with Detective Richards' badge held up. His plan: to act as though he was a police officer with vital information, actually worked. Perhaps it was the dark hiding his ill-fitting gear, or maybe it was the youth and inexperience of the soldiers, but one way or another he was let through without them even glancing in the Honda at Cyn, who was doing her best to sit up tall and appear official.

The badge worked such wonders that they were even given an escort around the city to Route 1, which was a straight shot to New York. "Where can I find your commanding officer?" Jack asked when they reached Route 1 and were stopped at another check point. He made sure to pitch his voice as deep as it would go. "I have information concerning what's happening."

"What sort of information?" a sergeant asked. He was surprisingly old for a man with only three stripes and he lacked the bearing that Jack expected in a soldier: he was round in the middle, was "slouchy" in the way he stood, and had quick, watery brown eyes that darted out at the night every few seconds.

There were other soldiers nearby, but in the dark they were nothing but shadows or the whisper of conversations and the flare of countless lighters and the glowing embers of cigarettes that reminded Jack too much of demon eyes.

"You know I can't tell you that," Jack told him, hoping the cryptic response would suffice.

"Yeah, I suppose," the sergeant said. "Except the only problem is that no one is saying anything. Units come flying through here but where they're going, I don't think even they know. It's crazy."

Jack didn't know what to say to that and so he only stared at the sergeant in a knowing way and mumbled: "Hmmm," as though what had been said was intriguing.

"I think the C.O. is in Princeton, prolly," a soldier who was still in his teens said; he was so soft in the face that he made Jack feel old. "Last we heard, some general was going to set up shop in Princeton, but that was an hour ago, so who knows what's happening now? Before that they were in this place called Heathcote. Ever hear of it? I hadn't."

"I just know *they* keep getting closer and closer," said the sergeant. "An' I don't like it. Listen, you can hear the guns going like they're right over that hill."

The little group paused, most holding their breath to listen. There was a regular battle roaring northeast of them while all around them in a semi-circle were scattered pops and bangs of different caliber weapons. They would flare up in a mad rattle and then fade away to nothing.

The young soldier scratched up under his helmet and said: "That might be Princeton. I don't know. Our unit is from Maryland. Where all the Jersey boys are at, nobody knows. Rumor is they cut and run this afternoon. Can you believe that?"

Jack could very well believe it. "Did they have priests with them?" he asked, guessing that they hadn't.

"Priests?" the sergeant said, his watery eyes shifting from out in the dark to laser in on Jack. "So it's true? These are zombies we're fighting?"

Would they run if he told them the truth? Or would they be forewarned and thus forearmed? Or would it matter? "They are like zombies," Jack finally admitted. "In order to slow them down you need to basically dismember them; a head shot won't do the trick all by itself."

"Son of a bitch," the sergeant swore. "And the priests? Will they help?"

"Yes, but I don't know how. The creatures can poison you with just a scratch, but the priests can heal you. Also, they can do other things, so if you can find one, I'd do it. Now, that's all I can tell you, really. I have to find the person in charge."

The sergeant didn't answer except to swear a second time: "Son of a bitch."

It was up to the very young soldier to explain: "Like I said, we're not sure who's in charge or where they're at. We haven't been getting much from the radios 'cept a lot of weirdness. I just know that I wouldn't go up there if I was you. We've been here since five and we haven't had anyone come back to tell us what's going on, all 'cept guys runnin' away and our captain. He said that they're going to use this river as a fall back point. If you wait long enough, whoever's in charge will prolly come right here and you won't have to go searching all over the place for him."

It was a suggestion that was hard to turn down, but Jack's guilt made him shake his head. The young soldier only shrugged.

The sergeant, who was now jumping every time there was a new burst of firing said: "Unstoppable. You're basically saying that these things are unstoppable. Is that right? Because if so, that's crazy. I mean we're National Guard and I only have the bullets in this gun, you know what I mean?"

"Yeah, I guess," Jack answered, knowing that the sergeant would take one look at the creatures and run.

Another of the soldiers spoke up: "I heard that the line keeps breaking into pieces and that those things just keep coming and we keep getting these mentals roaring up here telling us, like, you know: *all is lost* and *Run away!* Like that. I thought that they were faking it, but now I agree with Sarge, it's crazy. Look at all them Hummers we've confiscated. We're supposed to lock those guys up for desertion, but it's sorta mean when you see how nuts they are. So we've been letting them go and they don't even care if they go on foot. They just book it on down the road. It's crazy."

Again, Jack agreed that it was crazy and nodded vaguely as the soldier went on about all the other things he was finding crazy, but Jack wasn't listening. At the first break in the man's list, Jack said: "I'm going to need one of those Humvees. I had to commandeer that Honda and it won't last."

There were six soldiers all told at the check point, and, other than the slouchy, nervous sergeant, none looked old enough to buy a drink. They deferred to Jack and he took the vehicle with the most fuel.

"Things are completely messed," Jack said to Cyn as they drove off. "Those poor guys are clueless. Whatever is happening with our cellphones is messing with the radios as well. They don't know what's going on five miles up the road. They have no idea where their C.O. is or anything."

"So does that mean we're just going to drive around in the dark?" Cyn asked. She had the shotgun cradled to her chest.

"I don't know if we have another choice," he answered, not adding: *no choice except to turn around and get out of here*. It seemed like the ideal choice. The further they went along the highway, the greater their fear built up. There was fear in the air, clogging their lungs.

They drove for twenty minutes and during that time the darkness of the night deepened so that Jack was forced to sit up straight with his chest against the steering wheel and squint to see the road. "The dark isn't natural," he said in a whisper.

Almost as soon as he spoke, their headlights, which seemed as dim as candles, just barely managed to pick out three men in camouflage who were running down the road towards the Humvee. The men immediately broke off into the forest, disappearing so quickly that Jack wondered if they had been an illusion.

He slowed and coasted along the "empty" road. It was only empty of people. The west bound lanes were crushed with cars, filling every single inch of the four lanes of asphalt. The east bound lanes were eerily quiet and wide open.

"You saw them, right?" Jack asked. "Those were real people, right?"

"They were soldiers and they were running away, Jack. How could they be running away? They're supposed to be fighting." She took a sharp breath as if just realizing something and then rolled down her window a few inches. "The battle...it's over." The fierce battle had died down and now there were just solitary bangs coming from here and there and... "They're all around us," she whispered.

Jack could feel *them* as well. His fear had hampered his strange ability to perceive the creatures, but now they were so close that he couldn't tune them out.

And Cyn was correct; they were all around them, even behind them. The creatures were streaming through the forest that ran on either side of the road, cutting them off. Jack slammed the brakes, shoved the Humvee into reverse and hammered down on the gas. They both stared back, using the side view mirrors and they both felt the demon before they saw it.

"Jack!" Cyn screamed. "Stop!" He was already braking and when the Humvee shuddered to a halt, there in the road was a very small and very familiar shape; the rear backup lights shining off the bright copper pennies where its eyes should have been.

Cyn began screaming for him to go, and he had the Humvee in gear and was straining the engine to get them out of there, but too late. There came an awful thump on the rear of the vehicle and then came the unnerving patter of tiny footsteps on the roof.

"Hold on," Jack ordered and then hit the brakes. Their momentum threw them forward and Jack hoped that the demon would go flying off the vehicle; however it managed to hold onto the hood of the Humvee.

The demon, toothless and horrifying, somehow warped what remained of its face into an evil grin.

Next to Jack, Cyn eased the shotgun up. She would blast the thing to pieces if it breathed its frozen breath as it had before. But it did not. It had learned its lesson. Instead, it raised one tiny fist and hammered down on the hood. That same hood that was designed to survive in combat was dented in five inches by the blow.

"Get the gun ready," Jack said, flooring the gas once again. "And make sure your seatbelt's tight."

"Why? What are you going to do?"

He didn't quite know. *Something crazy* was all he had in mind. He turned the wheel hard east aiming at the forest. His first thought was to ram a tree and hope that Cyn would recover quicker than the demon and that she would be able to blast it a few times with the shotgun so that they could escape—but that was a pipe dream. She'd never recover as fast as the demon; probably no one could.

Which left what? They were barreling through the forest just on the verge of careening into a ditch or into a boulder or a tree trunk that was too big to plow over. The Humvee was a beast of a machine and, within seconds of Jack entering the forest, it whammed directly into a young pine tree and bent it straight over.

They rushed on, taking out younger trees left and right and Jack saw that their only hope was to somehow scrape the demon off the front the hood without hitting something so big that it would stop them completely.

Unfortunately the forest wasn't a true forest at all. It was only a hundred-yard wide belt of trees designed to hide the ugliness of the highway from the surrounding suburbia.

Too quickly, Jack found himself in an alley of soft green grass with trees on one side and backyard fences on the other. The horror on the Humvee's hood lifted its bony little fist and smashed down again leaving another dent even deeper than the first and now there was a crack in the metal and the spinning engine could be seen.

It reached in up to its shoulder and Jack knew that if it grabbed the wrong part it could kill the Humvee in a second. In desperation, Jack turned toward the line of fences and took them on, not looking to punch a hole through one section, but looking to plow right along the fence line until either the Hummer died, the demon was knocked off or they ran out of fence.

There was an explosion of wood and splinters and for half a minute the Humvee tore down the length of fences that ran for an entire block. Jack couldn't see a thing. The windshield starred immediately and what he could see beyond the thousand cracks consisted of broken, splintered boards, crabapple tree branches, a whirlwind of leaves, and what he thought was a ghost, but what was really a sheet that had been left out to dry.

And then they were in another grass alley. There was no sign of the demon. Both Jack and Cyn tried to look back using the side view mirrors; however hers was torn off completely while his was bent and pointing at the ground. He heaved it up and saw that they had left a hell of a mess behind them. It looked as though a tornado had touched down and had ripped up the entire block.

He couldn't see the demon in all the mess, but Jack could feel that it was back there. He could also feel its anger. It set his nerves on edge and when he looked over at Cyn, she was practically in tears.

"It's been following us, Jack. That's the only way to explain the fact that every time we turn around that stinking demon is there. It's going to kill us, Jack. It's going to hunt us and kill us because nothing can stop it." Her voice was high and loud and her hand on the shotgun was gripped so tight that she was close to setting it off right there in the Humvee.

Jack put his hand out to her. She stared at it until he said: "I'll think of something, ok? I won't let it get you." Only then did she release the gun and hold his hand.

He had no idea what he could do to save her. The demon was relentless. They could drive to the ends of the earth and it would still come for them and would find them when they least expected it.

But I won't kill to save our lives, he vowed to himself. *I won't open the portal ever again.*

That seemed as though it would be the easiest vow to maintain. He had changed when he opened the portal; he had become everything he had ever despised. He had felt the evil in his soul well up and explode, taking over his mind and his body. It had been the sickest feeling imaginable and he knew he wouldn't go through it again just to save his miserable flesh.

And he wouldn't do it to save Cyn's either. As much as he cared for her, and it surprised him that he did indeed care for her as much as he did, he wouldn't murder for her.

Two people weren't worth it.

The question was, would two million people be worth it? He took the Humvee down a path and found himself heading northeast going straight through the city of Princeton, New Jersey, population: 2.

The streets were covered in bodies and blood ran in the gutters. Jack had to drive slowly along lawns and sidewalks to avoid running over the tens of thousands of bodies.

Many of the corpses were dressed in camouflage, but most of the dead had been civilians. They had packs on their backs and their faces were eternally stretched into insane grimaces. They had gone mad with fear before they had been pulled down and had their throats torn out.

It was heartbreakingly sad and then they passed the hospital they had landed at that morning; it was a blackened husk. There was no way Richards was alive in that building.

Chapter 30

Princeton, New Jersey

Had the hospital staff evacuated him before the creatures arrived? Or had he crawled out on his own when the screams and the darkness swept over the building? Or was he still up there, a charred corpse. Jack dearly wanted to go check, only the shadows were moving. The undead were near. He could feel the creatures plain as can be; dozens of them lurking, hoping that he would come closer. The ugly eagerness that Cyn and Jack could feel added to their discomfort and it was with a heavy feeling that Jack accelerated away.

"This is just wrong," Cyn whispered, squinting and swallowing loud and often. The all-pervasive smell of death was creeping in through the cracks of the doors and what they could see around them made Cyn hold herself. People ran here and there, chased by gangs of the dead, others screamed in the darkness as though they were being eaten alive—and they probably were.

They had left the demon with pennies for eyes far behind, but there were others like it, their evil standing out even among the sea of evil that Jack and Cyn found themselves in. They had somehow driven straight into the maelstrom and now that they were neck deep, there was nothing they could do but push through and hope some remnant of the army was making a stand somewhere ahead.

"Careful there." She held out a shaking hand to point at a child...a little girl in footy pajamas, dead as could be. She was whole and intact except for her head which was missing.

Jack was having trouble seeing because one of his headlights had a two-by-four sticking straight out of it as though it was a lance and he was a modern knight. To make matters worse, his windshield was shattered in a thousand places so that his vision was that of an insect's.

In truth, he thought the world looked better peering through the cracks. The death was blurred, the flowing blood was cut up in angles which looked less like the rivers that they were.

The real world was too hard to take in through clear eyes. It made him feel lightheaded and numb and he kept running a sleeve across his cheeks—he was sure he was crying and if he wasn't it meant that he was broken and he didn't want to know that, either. He feared that he was broken on the inside in a way that couldn't be fixed.

Slowly, carefully, he guided them through the ruined city and on the outskirts, where the bodies were fewer, there was an odd scene: a line of holes in the ground, carefully dug. He knew that they were foxholes…or that they had been intended to be foxholes, but they weren't foxholes anymore, they were graves.

Soldiers had painstakingly dug their own graves with two-foot long entrenching tools. They had sat in them with their bladders filling, uncomfortably and their hearts racing and their stomachs going silly until the darkness descended. There was enough gleaming brass around the holes to show that they had fought; they hadn't run off.

And there was enough blood wetting the ground to show that they had fought in vain. Jack kept his eyes straight ahead and refused to look down into the holes as they passed. What he saw in his periphery, the body parts and the heads spiked on rifles and the soup of blood and other unknown fluids filling the bottom of the holes was enough to make him grind his teeth to keep from whimpering.

Cyn had her hand in her mouth until they passed, but the ordeal wasn't over. There was a second line three miles further on and another after that just before a small river. It was here that Jack found a replacement for the battered Humvee they were driving in.

The replacement was, in fact, another Humvee. This new one was better in every way. Not only was it perfectly preserved it also sported a massive machine gun on top and, to make it even more perfect, it had extra fuel cans strapped to its side and in the back there was food, water and ammo.

Perhaps best of all there wasn't a dead soldier sitting in the front seat in a pool of his own blood with his throat torn out as Jack had feared there would be. Both doors were flung wide open and on the ground next to the Humvee was a fully loaded M4. Jack picked it up and stowed it in the back next to a case of bottled water. He grabbed two of the bottles.

"Here you go." He held out a bottle to his cousin. Nothing needed to be said or guessed about concerning the previous owners of the Humvee. The fear and madness had been too much for them. Jack had given in to it that first night he had fought Hor. It had been horrible and yet, ever since then it had become easier to overcome every time he'd been confronted by it. It was one of the few in-stances when the saying: *What doesn't kills, you makes you stronger* actually applied.

In silence, Cyn sipped her water as Jack drove the new Humvee on a northeast course. It was a marvelous machine that seemed unstoppable no matter what sort of ditch or hill or downed tree was in their way. When there was a blockage of cars, they went up embankments or plowed down fences or forded streams that ran nearly as high as their doors.

The land was an odd mixture of suburbia, nature and hell. They drove somewhat thoughtlessly, and it was twen-ty minutes before either of them even questioned where they were going. All they knew was that they wanted to "get away."

With the main axis of the undead attack heading southwest, Jack drove northeast, climbing into the hills until he had mounted a ridge that had a plaque situated nearby that read *City Overlook*. From the top of the ridge, they should have been able to see the glittering skyline of New York, instead the night had swallowed the lights and there was nothing but a deep, formless darkness engulfing the entire city.

The sight stopped them.

"This really isn't our fault," Cyn said, carefully screwing the lid back on one of the bottles. It wasn't easy to do since her hands were shaking so badly that the cap kept popping off and falling into her lap. "Right? We didn't know, is all. We're being too hard on ourselves."

Jack had no reply. Whatever Robert was doing was building to a crescendo and he could feel an unpleasant metallic zing in his teeth that went down his nerves. They waited, sipping water that sloshed in their twirling bellies and then *it* happened.

Robert must have finished his fourth set of spells and the darkness that held New York, exploded outward in a storm engulfing everything, damping out lights and erasing the world. The darkness swept along faster than they could have driven away and there was nothing either of them could do.

Cyn reached over and grabbed Jack's hand just before the darkness swept over the Humvee, rocking it on its springs. To Jack, Cyn, with her porcelain skin and blonde hair glowed faintly in the dark like a spirit or a ghost. She seemed so insubstantial that Jack felt as if he could blow her out of the Humvee with only a whistle.

Her cool hand in his, gripping him in terror was real enough. He pulled her close and, since they were both still in their tactical armor, he rubbed his cheek against hers. They sat like that, tense and afraid for some minutes and then the darkness settled like fog in the low places and gradually dissipated.

"How many did he raise that time?" Cyn asked, prying her hand from his grip and straightening up. She touched her hair and looked embarrassed, perhaps over her fear or perhaps over the fact that she had been clinging to her cousin; Jack didn't know.

Just then he wasn't sure of anything. "With no one to stop him?" he asked, rhetorically. "He raised as many as he could…as many as he dared to. There were other cemeteries right around Calvary, right?"

Cyn nodded miserably. "All told there are a few million people buried in Queens."

"*Were* you mean," Jack said. Again she nodded, but this time she remained mute. There really wasn't much to say.

The unnatural darkness that had hid New York faded and now the lights of the city, once so bright and gay, could be seen. It was no longer a pretty view from the ridge—parts of the city were without power and the buildings looked grey and forbidding, like tremendous tombstones, standing over a city of the dead. In contrast, other parts of the city were on fire. Flames ate up entire blocks, dancing merrily, destroying what the walking dead had not.

"It's not our fault," Cyn repeated, trying to convince herself. "We did everything we could have to stop this. Isn't that right, Jack? Say it. Say we did everything we could have."

Seeing as he had committed murder, Jack felt that he had. "*This* isn't our fault," he agreed.

Cyn had been on the verge of tears, in a snap, her demeanor changed. She glared at Jack. "What do you mean by *this*? Are you saying *we* did something else wrong? Because I told you not to kill Carl. Do you remember? I told you that it was wrong and evil, so don't try to drag me down with you. None of this, none of any of this is my fault. I was tricked and lied to. The glyphs I had could have said anything. I had no idea that it was a spell or..."

"Hey!" Jack snapped, cutting her off. "I'm not blaming you for anything. Yes, you were lied to and you were tricked, and you were entrusted with a warning and a puzzle that was so vague that it was too much for a curious mind. I don't blame you, I blame our great-great grandfather. If he thought the spells were so dangerous, why didn't he burn them?"

"Right," she said, confused. "That's right, he should have. So…so why did you empathize the word 'this' like you did?"

It was a moment before he could bring himself to speak. "Because we might still be able to stop Robert. If we can figure out what he's doing and where he is and what his game plan is, and, most importantly, the spell that he commands, we might be able to stop him."

Cyn's eyes narrowed. Cautiously, she asked: "How on earth are we supposed to find any of that out? Not even Robert's own father knew what he was up to and even if he knows now, how do we go about finding him in all of this?" She pointed at a world that had been turned on its head.

"I agree, we could never find Robert's father," Jack said, "and even if we did, I doubt he would have much to say. The power of the spells is so great that I wonder whether Robert would even tell his own dad his secrets."

Cyn lifted an eyebrow. "If he wouldn't tell his own father, then who would he tell? He wouldn't tell some chum he met in some pub, and he wasn't a bloke with a gob of mates," she pointed out. "So who does that leave? You heard your own father say that no one knows about any of this magic business."

"That's not what he said," Jack corrected her. "He said: *There's none among the living* who knows."

Cyn leaned so far back from him that she was pressed fully against the door as the implications of what he had just said sunk in. "You would do *that* again? Really? Do you know what you looked like when you killed that poor man? You looked insane, Jack. You looked evil and it was disgusting. It made me question everything I know about you and everything I…" She bit off the last of her words, and shifted her eyes away.

"I know what I looked like, or I guess I know, because I felt exactly what you were saying. I felt like a killer, Cyn. It was like I was born to murder and…and I enjoyed it on some level that I never knew existed. But I don't think that was really me. I think it was the spell because right now I'm like you, disgusted by the very idea."

"Then why even contemplate it, Jack? I know it's not you, but it might become you if you keep this up. This is black magic. It's evil and it will turn you evil, eventually, I know it. And you know it, too." She glanced at her watch. "Two hours ago you were crying like a baby. Do you remember that? You were so ashamed of yourself that you were practically blubbering."

Jack remembered and the memory sent a rash of heat into his cheeks. "Yeah, it's not something I'm going to forget so soon. But what we saw back there, the…the butchery and the blood and the bodies, I'll never forget that, not for a thousand years. And we both know that was just the beginning. Robert has unleashed hell on earth and, yes, it's not our fault, but if we can do something, anything to stop it, then what happens next IS our fault."

Cyn was quiet for a long time as the truth of their situation slowly burned through the wall of denial she had built around her. "It's going to get worse, isn't it?"

"A whole lot worse," he said. It would be unimaginable.

She knew it. Her lips sucked in and her eyes glinted as tears built up. "So who is it going to be? You want to…I know you don't want to, but you're going to bring someone back. I just don't have any idea who could help us. It would have to be someone who knew Robert; someone who knew his plans…"

"Someone who helped him?" Jack suggested. "Someone who was in the know only because Robert knew that he was expendable."

Her eyes shot wide. "Dr. Loret? But…"

Jack shook his head. "But he's on Robert's side? I really doubt it, not after Robert slit him open and tortured him."

Chapter 31

Central New Jersey

"Dr. Loret," Cyn said for the third time, shaking her head. Each time she said his name she sounded more and more confused.

"Yeah, he's the only one who's seen all three spells performed," Jack said as he climbed into the back seat of the hummer and worked a lock on the ceiling of the vehicle that popped up the hatch, giving him access to the gun mounted on top. It was one of hell of a big gun. "Do you know anything about fifty caliber machine guns?" he asked Cyn. The only reason he knew it was a fifty caliber was that it was written on a box of fat bullets that was hooked to the gun.

"No...no but, Dr. Loret? You actually think he knows Robert's spell?"

Jack looked over the gun—it was a puzzle. In the dark, not even the trigger was obvious and nor was it clear what the function of the little rod sticking out the side was for or the round knob protruding from the back or all the little metal gizmos on top. He knew what the handles in the back were for and so he settled in behind it and thumbed a button.

Bang! Bang! Bang!

"What the bloody hell!" Cyn shrieked.

"I found the trigger," Jack answered, pulling his hands off the handles. Not knowing that the weapon was "live," he had jumped higher than Cyn had. He tried to laugh off the shakes that struck him. "This thing is awesome." It wasn't awesome, at least not to Jack and not at that moment. It had been so loud that he was sure every ghoul within a mile was heading toward them.

Cyn pulled him down by the leg of his jeans. "Loret doesn't know the spell. You'd be killing someone for nothing, just like you did with Carl."

His gut turned where she had knifed the guilt into him. "Loret knows. I'm sure of it. Loret was there for at least three of the castings and sure, he was being killed for the third one, but he wasn't for the others. He was probably taking notes."

Jack started to clamber back up into the turret when she grabbed him again, asking: "How do you plan on controlling him? He's not going to tell you anything if you keep him penned up in a magic circle. That's what you were going to do, right? A circle outside the two conjuring circles to keep him caged?"

Actually he had been going to draw a protective circle around Cyn and himself, but her idea was far better. "Yeah, of course. And he will talk, I'm sure of it. He's going to want revenge. I bet he'll do anything to get it, too. Now, hold on, I'm trying to figure this thing..."

She pulled on his pants a final time and asked the question he didn't want to hear: "Who are you going to kill?"

Jack leaned on the gun. Who was he going to kill? That was the ultimate question before him. If Robert was standing there, he'd turn the machine gun on him and blast him to hell where he belonged. But that was his entire list of people he wanted dead. Even Robert's creepy father didn't make the list. As far as Jack knew, his father hadn't committed any crime, beyond being disgustingly proud of his son, that is.

"I don't know, Cyn. It won't be you, so don't worry about that."

He felt something below him and then, suddenly she pushed her way through the hole in the roof of the Humvee. There was so little room that they were pressed together, chest to chest.

"You'd let the entire world go up in flames rather than sacrifice me?" she asked. He was suddenly very aware of her lips and her breasts pressing into his chest. And she was suddenly aware of his manhood perking up.

"Ummm," he said. All this awareness was taking up so much of his mind that he was having trouble coming up with an answer. "Uh, I'd sooner let myself be sacrificed than let anything happen to you."

Her mouth came open, so close to his that he could feel her breath on his cheek. He was sure that she was about to kiss him; however, she started to blink in confusion and then she gave a little laugh and said: "That's nice and I-I think I would do the same for you, which means..."

He smiled. "Which means that neither of us are candidates. The blood can't be given. It has to be taken."

"Just like the life," she added. "Not that I want to die." Her smile came back, a brief light in the dark. "I'm just afraid of who we'll find to sacrifice. What if it's a little kid? Can we really do that to someone?"

Jack wanted to give her a little speech about the importance of being strong, of the need to do the difficult things in the face of evil, of sacrificing the few for the good of the many, but he couldn't find the words and if he had, he didn't know if he could have spit them out. There were no words that could make what they had to do, palatable or even right.

They were going to commit evil, far beyond simple murder. His father had pointed at Carl's corpse and said: *You damned that man*. He didn't say: You killed that man. He had used the word *damned*. If the words of the spell had been literal, then they had given Carl's soul away to the Mother of Demons in return for a few useless words.

And now they were contemplating doing it again. What if Loret was as clueless as Jack's father? How many more people would Jack damn for all eternity in order to stop his cousin?

"We should get going," he said, no longer concerned with his manhood. Even when Cyn wriggled down his body to get back into the Humvee, it didn't stir.

He took them down the ridge, heading for the city of the dead. Next to him, Cyn fidgeted with the shotgun and stared out the window. After a while she asked: "We're going back into the city?" She made it sound as if they were going back into hell itself.

It had that sort of feel to it.

"That's where Loret is. The way my father spoke, it seems that you need the bones of a person to bring them back, so we don't have a choice."

"Right, I get that, but what about the uh, 'person' we need? Where are going to find one in the city? I can't image anyone being left alive there. Oh, bloody hell! Look out, Jack!" In front of them was a bank of swirling darkness engulfing the road and within it were more of the creatures, seemingly waiting to ambush them.

Jack took the Humvee off road only to find their headlights illuminating more of the half-rotted cadavers. They were strung out in a long line that stretched into the dark. He charged through the trees at where he thought there were the fewest and just before he ran down a lady in a baggy, dirt-stained, brown dress, he felt his testicles draw up, and his hands went white knuckled on the steering wheel. Cyn gasped and grabbed her head with both hands.

They were passing through a cloud of fear and it seized Jack's mind making him want to slam on the brakes. His foot came off the gas. *Don't do it!* a voice...his own voice said into his mind. It was a logical-sounding Jack, and one that didn't fit in with their dire situation. *If you brake, then the ghouls will be on you in a flash and they'll kill Cyn. You don't want that, do you?*

"No," he whispered, holding onto a little portion of his thinking mind just long enough to crash into the lady in brown. She wasn't sucked under the wheels, she caught the Humvee in the chest and was struck with such force that her head flew off and smashed against the windshield. It broke open like a rotten melon, spilling a black mess onto the glass.

Cyn screamed and Jack's logic deserted him. He slammed his foot down, thinking that he was hitting the brake when in fact his foot had been hovering over the gas. The hummer leapt forward and by the time Jack found the brake, they were through the cloud of fear and bouncing up onto another road.

Jack didn't have a clue what the two-lane road was or where it went, he was just happy to be away from the creatures...well, most of the creatures, anyway. The headless corpse had survived the rough trip through the woods and was climbing onto the hood of the Humvee.

Now, Jack slammed on the brakes, screeching to a halt. The woman's corpse wasn't possessed by a demon; it was a run-of-the-mill ghoul and lacked the strength to hold on. She went flying and Jack gleefully ran her remains over as he continued down the road. He even grinned, feeling suddenly and strangely happy. He would even go so far as to call his mental state: euphoric.

The feeling had also struck Cyn. She grinned right back at him, although it faded when she saw the ugly smear on the windshield. "Could you do something about that?"

"Of course," he said and then searched for the lever to work the windshield wipers. At first the smear grew worse and Jack slowed to a crawl until the blades and wiper fluid did their thing and cleared up the mess. When it did, Jack was surprised to see a little town below them and within it was a building ablaze with lights. What was more amazing was that it was whole, unmarred by the evil in the night.

Jack would go so far as to call the building cheery and he raced down the road toward it, feeling a growing excitement in his gut. It was a church and not a very big one. It was simple in its construction: a rectangle with white clapboard siding and a steep angular roof that was dominated by a bell tower with a large cross atop it.

They pulled up in front and their strange, giddy feeling bloomed in their chests. There was singing coming from inside. The two of them jumped out of the Humvee and were so excited that they nearly ran into the church without their guns. Jack almost felt that they didn't need them.

"Hold on," he said and ran back to the Humvee. He grabbed the M4 for himself and the shotgun for Cyn.

"Do we knock, do you suppose?" Cyn asked as they hesitated at the front doors. Jack reached out and pushed the doors open easily. What was inside was wonderful at first; the light and the warmth and the voices raised in praise, baked into him, but he didn't step in. This was a church; a holy place and Jack was the worst of sinners.

He had made blood sacrifices to the Mother of Demons, twice in order to save his own selfish skin and once in a satanic ritual of murder.

When he hesitated, Cyn frowned at him. "There's power here, Jack. A power for good. You can feel it, right?"

"Yeah." It was a light that burned and threw his evil shade on the steps behind them.

There had to be three hundred people packed into the tiny church and most were turned around in their pews, singing, but also staring at Jack and Cyn. "Come in," a soldier said to them in a whisper. He wore a disheveled, mud and blood stained uniform. There were dozens of soldiers among the crowd and only a few possessed weapons.

Cyn pulled Jack inside and let the door close behind them. It clanged loud enough to make Jack jump. The crowd consisted of desperate, tired, but happy people. Most of them had lost everything but had found their salvation. Jack could see it in their upturned faces. They had lived through a night of terror and it had been a prelude to their discovering the Lord's saving grace. Jack envied them.

The two of them in their odd gear should have been a ten-second wonder, but for some reason they drew attention and the singing faltered.

"Why did we come here?" Jack hissed to Cyn. The euphoria was gone and his sins large in his mind. "We have a mission, an important one, and I don't think we can spare the time to sing a few songs."

"Maybe you were meant to come here," the soldier who had invited them in proposed; he was slightly older than the other soldiers; there was just the beginning of grey in his short brown hair. "Maybe the Lord has brought you to this place of worship to heal and rest. I hope you don't think it's rude that I say you look like you need both."

Jack knew they certainly did and yet he was afraid of what would happen if they stopped here and relaxed for a while. Not only would millions die while they dawdled, there was a great chance that they would become too comfortable and too content to go out and risk their lives.

"I would love to," Jack told the man, "only we don't have time. The mission is critical. Thank you, though."

Cyn looked crestfallen and for just a moment it seemed as though she was going to ask to stay behind— and he would have allowed it, lonely as that would have made him. However, she didn't ask, she grimaced and after a breath she turned for the door.

"I think you should speak to the Monsignor," the soldier suggested. He was eyeing them both closely and even gave them a sniff which seemed to confirm something. "Yes, come with me." It wasn't a suggestion.

He wound his way around the edge of the crowd, stepping over sleeping children and exhausted parents and those too injured to move out of their way. Jack and Cyn followed the soldier to a side door which opened into a short hallway where they found even more people seated against the walls.

There were three doors opening off the hall and the soldier went to the closest and asked a man in bib overalls: "I'm afraid I need to see the Monsignor, next. I hope you don't mind."

"It's 'k. I've been tryin' to get my thoughts in order and I'm afraid they just won't come."

"When it's time, just relax and let the words flow," the soldier said. "It'll be fine."

No one explained what was going to be "fine" or what words were supposed to flow from the man. And Jack didn't ask. He was growing more and more nervous with each passing second and he actually took a step back when the door opened, treading on Cyn's foot.

"It'll be ok," she said and nudged him forward after a girl of about seventeen came out of the room with her face streaked with tears. It didn't look like it was going to be "ok" to Jack, but he allowed himself to be pushed inside.

The room surprised Jack; it was basically empty save for a chair and an odd wooden partition that could be folded open or closed. The partition sat in the middle of the room, screening a man who said: "Please sit and know that the Lord our God is the Father of mercy."

The soldier cleared his throat and said: "Please excuse me, Monsignor. There are two people I think you should meet. They have been in contact with the dead."

Instead of getting up, the Monsignor pulled back the folding wall and stared at Jack and Cyn, taking in every detail of their appearance with shrewd dark eyes. Jack stared right back. The Monsignor was a tall man and old, angular and infirm. His eyes were grey but cloudy and the wrinkled flesh of his neck practically obscured the hard white collar he wore.

"Yes, they have," the Monsignor agreed. "They have both been touched by the hand of the dead and have been healed as well, and yet they have reservations about being in this room and in this chapel. Strange."

"How do you know all of this?" Jack asked. "I'm not denying it, I'm just curious."

The Monsignor waved for the soldier to answer. The younger man said: "Since we've come in contact with these minions from hell, there has been an *awakening* if you will within the various Christian denominations. Perhaps it's affected the other religions of the world in the same manner, but as of yet we don't know. We know only that many priests and pastors have discovered abilities of a biblical nature such as the healing of the sick, or the casting out of these demons. In this case, you project an aura that is unmistakable."

"Exactly," the Monsignor said, snapping his long, knobby fingers in excitement. "I believe that these God-sent powers have always been within us waiting on exactly this moment to blossom."

"This moment?" Jack asked.

"Yes," the Monsignor answered. "The second coming."

Jack was suddenly overcome with fatigue and he went and sat down in the empty chair. "It's not the second coming or the apocalypse or whatever. This was all started by a man...just a man."

"And you know him," the soldier stated with complete assurance.

"Yeah? How did you...wait, are you a priest of some sort?"

The soldier touched his own collar; on one side were the double black bars that denoted his rank as captain and on the other was a cross. "I'm a military chaplain. Strictly, National Guard. In everyday life I am a Lutheran Pastor. I am Pastor John Corley. Now you were saying how you know the man who started this?"

With Cyn's help, Jack told their tale—all of it, including the blood sacrifices and the misery of murdering Carl. Jack had wanted to hold back, to steer the story around the parts that cast him in the most vile light, but once he started talking, the words just flowed out of him. As much as he wanted to, he couldn't seem to stop himself. During the telling, the room was dead quiet and after, it became painfully so. Finally, Jack couldn't take it. "Are you two going to say anything?"

"You are heading down the wrong path, young man," the Monsignor said. "Darkness cannot be overcome by more darkness. It can only be overcome by lighting the world with God's love."

The platitude grated on Jack's nerves. "Perhaps what I'm suggesting is to fight fire with fire. As much as I'm amazed at this new power you priests seem to possess, I'm also a little disenchanted. The power of God's goodness wasn't enough for Father Paul to overcome even a few of the creatures and now we have millions to contend with."

"It is not the goodness or the strength of the Lord that should be in question," the Monsignor declared. "The failure of this Father Paul may be the failure of *his own* goodness and strength. Perhaps his faith was put to the test and he came up short. I don't know."

"No you don't," Jack snapped. "Father Paul was a good man."

Pastor Corley held up his hands to calm Jack and, unbelievably, Jack calmed. "I am sure the Monsignor did not mean to speak ill of Father Paul," the pastor said. "It was conjecture only. We don't know why Father Paul failed. Perhaps we aren't meant to stand toe-to-toe with these creatures in a battle of strength versus strength. Rarely has that been the way of the Lord."

"Where there is faith, the Lord will provide," the Monsignor said. "He has given us the strength to hold here. Satan's minions tried to tear down these walls, but they could not abide our light. Jack, you see this, yet you hold back. Why?"

Jack eyed the floor and shrugged. Pastor Corley said: "My guess is that it's because he still living under the weight of his sins and these ones are particularly heavy, aren't they?"

The floor of this empty room never looked so interesting; Jack couldn't seem to pull his eyes up off of it. He couldn't bring himself to look anyone in the eye just then, not even Cyn who had been with him during the worst of his atrocities. "Yeah," Jack said, in a whisper. "But I don't know if I believe in...in any of this, or how much I believe, or anything."

The Monsignor reached out and patted Jack's leg. "You may not believe in the Lord but he sure does believe in you. He loves you, Jack, and all that it takes to be forgiven for these miserable sins is for you ask for forgiveness. It's not an easy thing and yet you've admitted to murder and idolatry and that's the hardest part; opening up. Now that you have, just ask for the Lord's blessing and if you're truly sorry, the Lord will forgive."

It sounded too easy. Jack hesitated answering for so long that Cyn finally gave her opinion: "He thinks he's going to have to do it again, that's what I think. We talked about it, but now, I don't see why we'd have to. Jack, can't you feel it? There's a presence here."

There was a presence and a power; however, it was a new power, an untested power, the limits of which, if there were any, weren't known. It was sort of like the fifty-caliber machine gun mounted to the top of the Humvee. Jack knew it was a powerful gun, but didn't know how powerful, nor did he know how many bullets were in it and what sort of damage they would do.

He wasn't even sure how to aim the thing or how the weapon would react when he started firing it in a real situation. Would it jump or rise or would the barrel get so hot that it would melt?

"I feel the presence, I just..." he left off.

"You just don't trust it?" Cyn asked. When he half-shrugged, she glared, just a flash of anger before her face broke and she was practically in tears. "Jack, we can be done. We can be forgiven and we can let someone else take over the fight. It doesn't have to be us." When he hesitated, the glare came right back on her face and with it came a punch in the shoulder that turned his arm dead.

"Hey!"

She ignored his look of outrage and turned to the Monsignor. "Can I be forgiven for my part in all of this?"

"Of course, my child," the Monsignor said. "Come kneel in front of me."

In true Cyn fashion, she knotted up her blonde hair as if there was going to be something arduous about the act of penance, and knelt down in front of the priest.

"Good. Now, do you reject Satan and all his works and all of his empty promises?"

"Yes, of course," she answered immediately.

"Do you believe in the God the Father, almighty, creator of heaven and earth?"

She was slower to answer, but eventually said: "Yes, I think so."

"And do you believe in Jesus Christ, his only son, who was born of the Virgin Mary, was crucified, died, and was buried, rose from the dead and is now seated at the right hand of the Father?"

It was obvious that she hadn't been raised in a Christian home and this blanket statement of a faith that she was so new to caused her hesitation to be far more pronounced. The Monsignor gave her a benign smile and said, "Maybe we should do the short version. Some Holy Water, Pastor John, if you don't mind?"

The military chaplain hurried out of the room and was back in seconds with a silver chalice. The Monsignor dipped his fingers in it and wet Cyn's forehead in a cross, saying: "I baptize you, in the name of the Father and of the Son and the Holy Spirit."

Cyn grinned from ear to ear and there were diamond tears in her eyes. She opened her mouth to say something to Jack, but the Monsignor shushed her and then spoke in a rush: "God the Father of mercies, through the death and resurrection of his Son has reconciled the world to himself and sent the Holy Spirit among us for the forgiveness of sins. May God give you pardon and peace, and I absolve you of your sins in the name of the Father, and of the Son, and of the Holy Spirit."

Pastor John whispered to Cyn: "Say *amen.*"

"Amen," Cyn repeated.

The Monsignor crossed himself and then said, "You have been baptized and your sins have been forgiven, how do you feel?"

"I feel great," she gushed, grinning like a child. "Jack you have to do this. You have to."

"I will," Jack said. "When I know that the church is strong enough to take over, I'll be baptized and all of that. I..., uh, I promise." His words had caught in his throat momentarily. In all the singing and light and Cyn's smile, there was a sudden dark spot.

Pastor John sighed, his brown eyes drooping in fatigue. "Jack, please. Death is like a thief in the night. It comes when you least expect it and it's best to prepare your soul just in case."

"That's where you're wrong, Pastor. Death is coming for us right now. The demon is here, Cyn. I can feel it."

Chapter 32

Central New Jersey

The goodness radiating from the church and the people and the two priests had dampened Jack's ability to feel the undead. The creatures were just a shadow in his mind and their exact location had been vague. The demon was, as always, different. It was a poisonous knife cutting through everything and now that Jack could focus, he sensed that the little town with the little church was surrounded by the creatures.

It had been surrounded since before Jack and Cyn had arrived; he had felt it as they had come charging down the hill. But at that point, the ring around the town had been loose and distant. Now, with the coming of the demon, it was closing in tight; a noose around their necks.

Jack wanted to jump in the Humvee and get out of there before it was too late, only he knew that Cyn wouldn't leave with him. She had her new faith and trusted in the priests to protect her and to fight the monsters for her and to make everything normal again. It was a great idea, one that Jack wanted just as badly as she did.

But he had nagging doubt, eating at his insides. *The priests aren't strong enough*, it said. *Maybe someday, but not yet, and if you wait here with the others, you'll die like the others.*

It was such a powerful and logical doubt that he wanted to grab Cyn by the arm and drag her out of there. "It's coming, Cyn," he said. "It's coming for us. Do you understand?"

"You are safe here, my son," the monsignor said. "They have tried to get in before, only they cannot contend with our faith and the power of the Lord."

Pastor John had a faraway look in his eyes. "I can feel it now. It's coming from the southeast and it's powerful evil."

The monsignor closed his eyes and grew silent except for his labored breathing, which was surprisingly loud. "Yes," he said, swallowing. "I can feel it as well…but do not worry. The power of the Lord flows through me. Pastor John, help me up." The monsignor grunted and made quite a production as he was heaved to his feet. There was sweat in his hair from the effort.

"Pastor John, I will need the aspergillum, what you Lutherans probably call a 'sprinkler'. Also fill the brass container that it comes in with holy water. They're in the sanctuary, if you'll please run and get them. My dear Cyn, if you would be so kind as to fetch the crucifix on the altar. Don't forget to kneel before it. There's a good girl."

Jack was now alone with the man and they eyed each other. The monsignor's cheeks were red and his eyes bright. Jack thought that he was looking forward to the confrontation.

"The demon is going to use his ability to generate darkness and fear right off the bat," Jack said. "So far, they seem to lack imagination, but they do think and they do learn."

"If I were you, Jack, I would worry more about your soul than this demon. It is nothing but a fly compared to the power of the Lord." He clapped Jack on the shoulder and then pushed out of the room.

The people in the hall leapt up at his presence. The singing fell away and they pressed against the walls to let him through. A new fear was building and they looked to the monsignor. "Do not stop singing, my children. In fact, sing louder, sing stronger. Do not let this imp question your faith. Come! Mrs. Farnsworth let's have *Onward Christian Soldiers*."

An elderly lady began flipping through her hymnal. "Here we go," she said into a microphone. "Page 186 in the red books." She touched the keys tentatively, finding her finger spacing and then lurched into the song in a clunky manner as if she had never seen it before.

Pastor John came up with what looked like a brass bucket with a silver handled tool within it; the tool had a bulbous head with many holes. He was careful not to slosh the contents of the bucket. Cyn came next and with great solemnity, especially for her, she offered a twelve-inch tall crucifix to the monsignor.

"Thank you," he said. Jack could barely hear him over the singing which had erupted, yet still he thought that the monsignor's voice sounded strained. The fear in the air was heavier.

The monsignor walked to the front doors, paused and closed his eyes. He was praying, his lips moving and the sweat gathering even greater on his forehead and in his white hair. Finally, he pushed open the doors. Pastor John came behind him; Jack and Cyn came next, each holding their weapons, tightly; Jack the M4, Cyn with the shotgun.

"Check the load," Jack whispered and then he did the same thing with his rifle. There were twenty-nine rounds in the magazine and one in the chamber. He was a little embarrassed to see that the safety had been in the off position the entire time he'd been carrying it.

He left it off as the cold of the night struck him, creeping in through the layers of clothing he wore, going right for his heart where it started a trembling that slowly grew worse and progressed outward until Jack was clutching the gun in his hands to keep the shaking from being seen.

Not that anyone would notice. The coming demon had everyone's attention. For the moment it was hidden behind the great clouds of darkness that swirled and blew. The darkness blotted out the stars and the town and then the parking lot next to the church and very quickly the Humvee that Jack had found was half-engulfed.

"Father?" Jack said.

The monsignor's face had lost all color and only at Jack's word did he hold up the crucifix. It was trembling as well. A bad sign since the fear was only just starting to ramp up.

And yet the darkness stopped immediately.

It seemed to buoy the monsignor. "Be gone imp of Satan," he cried. It was a shrill cry, but there was power in it and the darkness retreated even more, revealing the cracks of the asphalt at the edge of the parking lot and un-covering the Humvee. Jack longed to jump in it and roar out of there.

There came a moment of hesitation from the darkness and then a voice as deep as the abyss from which it was spawned, said: "*Eta ah hror ey mota.*" A bleak wind swept out of the darkness and the shaking in Jack's body doubled and then tripled. The fear had come and it had the power of the demon and a thousand of the lesser undead creatures all working in concert.

The music faltered, a baby screeched and someone screamed. Jack's fear was a powerful thing, a huge thing. It was a snake writhing in his guts, making him want to piss himself. He almost did, too when the gun in his hand suddenly went off, sending a bullet zipping out into the darkness. In his fright, Jack's trembling fingers had found the trigger.

The shot seemed to jar Cyn who found her voice: "Do the prayer about the valley of shadow," she suggested to the monsignor. She was surprisingly calm, embarrassing Jack into pulling his finger from the trigger of his assault rifle when he really wanted to start spraying bullets everywhere.

"The Lord is my shepherd; I shall not want," the monsignor intoned. "He maketh me lie down in green..." He spoke the psalm by heart from start to finish and the more he spoke the stronger his voice became and the better Jack felt. The music in the church never restarted but the child stopped crying and there was a sense of victory and elation coming from within.

Then the demon showed itself; its copper eyes shin-ing, its gleefully evil child's face grinning. It stepped out of the mad, swirling darkness bringing with it its horrible stench. Jack had forgotten the smell as a weapon and it smote him worse than the others.

Again, Cyn seemed hardly affected. With the blessing still wet on her forehead, she blanched slightly and gritted her teeth, while Pastor John and the monsignor both gasped but otherwise stood the test stoically.

Jack was astounded that only he went weak in the knees. Since the terrible ordeal had begun—it felt like days ago—he had been the strongest of any of them, able to withstand everything that had been thrown his way, but now he was gulping back the vomit that was coming up his throat.

The demon had been gaining in strength and for some reason, he was the only one who was being affected.

"Enough!" the monsignor cried. "Go back to your dank hole, imp. In the name of the Father and the Son and Holy Spirit, I command you to depart from this world. In Jesus' name…"

Just as Jack knew it would, the demon wasn't going to sit still as it was banished. With fantastic speed, it rushed forward, it little legs a blur, its toothless mouth gaping wider than possible looking as though it wanted to stretch its mouth so wide that it could swallow the monsignor in one bite.

At the last moment, the monsignor held up his crucifix, stopping the demon in its tracks, causing it to hiss.

"*I will eat you, priest of the dead god*," it said, and then blew out a green fog and now Jack reeled back. His skin burned where the fog touched it and his lungs seized.

The others began to choke and cough, but they didn't fall over, gasping for air as Jack did, his M4 clattering to the ground as so much useless plastic and steel. Pastor John had the strength and the foresight to hold out the brass bucket and although the monsignor looked on the verge of toppling over, he was able to grasp the silver tool and with a flick of his wrist, he showered the demon with Holy Water.

The thing screamed and the sound didn't come from its mouth, it only echoed in their skulls. More madness for Jack, but only an irritant for the others as if this was only a drunken friend being overly loud in their ear. The monsignor flicked the tool again and again, dashing the demon liberally and wetting the ground all around them. The demon backed out of reach and stood glaring, somehow showing hate through the copper pennies of its eyes.

For a full minute, a wasted sixty seconds, the demon and the monsignor appraised each other. In that time, Jack was able to recover his strength and was able to stand and was able to look blearily down at the rifle.

Just as he stooped to get it, the demon spoke: "*Your God is powerful, but you are weak.*"

It was right, of course and Jack was about to nod in agreement, when he felt something pass between the demon and the monsignor. They were staring and silent, locked in a battle of wills. Everyone and everything watched in silence...all except Jack.

"No," he said, in a choked whisper. "This is wrong. Sing one your songs. You, priest," he said to Pastor John. "Make them sing. Hurry, before it's too late." The monsignor was weakening in the battle he hadn't prepared himself for. His lip was jerking up and down and there was a line of drool hanging like a forgotten and useless rope from a capsizing sailing ship.

The singing began uneven and weak, two or three different songs going at once. Jack stepped forward and grabbed the silver-handled tool from the monsignor's lax grip and splashed the little girl demon, breaking the connection.

The thing hissed, while the monsignor blinked, slowly before turning on Jack. "This isn't your fight. You are Godless, go hide someplace else."

"And you are a fool!" Jack cried. "Get into the church before it's too late."

"I have God on my side. I don't need to run away." The monsignor calmly turned back to his opponent...the creature that Jack knew for a fact would kill the man. He *did* have God on his side, but God wasn't there standing next to him with a shining shield.

The monsignor lifted his sprinkler to splash the demon if it dared to come closer, but it didn't—it didn't have to. It opened its mouth, its little girl mouth, and blew out a cloud of white fog. The ground grew hoary and iced. The sidewalk froze and grew slick and the monsignor's feet and legs became stiff as the intense cold swept up the man.

"May the light of the Lord shed his loving warmth upon us," the monsignor said and as Jack watched, the cold that was slowly freezing him in place, stopped and there was a hot breeze that swept down on them as if out of a desert night.

The monsignor looked on it with delight—and Jack wanted to scream at him in fury. The man of God was going tit for tat. He was reacting. He was in a fight for his life and he was utterly placid about it. The demon was there to kill.

Before Jack could plead with him to either run or fight for real, the demon spoke again in that dreadful, deep hell voice: "*Isha raha morte aff.*"

Like the fool that Jack had proclaimed him, the monsignor waited on this next onslaught. It seemed innocent enough; the demon lifted its bony, skin-rotted foot up as if it was going to throw a tantrum, but when it brought that foot down there was a sound like thunder and the earth moved beneath them, shifting right and left as if on rockers.

Jack was splay-legged and kept his balance. He grabbed Cyn to keep her from falling and she clung to him —feeling soft and fragile. Pastor John went to a knee and put one hand to the ground, looking ready to spring up as soon as the shaking stopped, which it did a second later.

Too late for the monsignor. He had taken a fatal step back and slipped on the ice the demon had created moments before. He was on his back struggling like an up-ended turtle. The demon grinned that evil rot-stinking grin of its and was just about to leap full on the struggling monsignor when something odd stopped it.

The church had shaken along with the rest of their world and now the bell in the belfry let out a far reaching *gong!* It was a strangely intense and stern sound that stopped the demon and its undead army in their tracks.

Then there came an odd, expectant pause as though everyone thought something of importance was about to happen. Only the monsignor moved in that long moment and he was barely to his knees when the bell swung back on its arc to strike the clapper a second time. This time the sound hung in the dead air with a muted quality that lacked any emphasis.

In Jack's eyes, it was the perfect metaphor for the battle. What started out with such promise was clearly weakening and by the time the bell rang for a third time, it would be a death knell.

Everyone had been staring up at the belfry; now they turned to see the demon child rushing at the monsignor. It moved with lightning speed, while Jack felt as though he was in slow motion. Too late, he hauled the M4 to his shoulder and sighted the gun—but the demon had already latched itself onto the monsignor's throat and was drinking his life.

Just as with Cyn's mother, the monsignor aged a thousand years in seconds. Jack was spared the worst of the display. All he saw within the sights of the M4 was the monsignor's hair as it withered, turned brittle and began to fall out.

And then Jack shot the man of God in the back of the head.

Chapter 33

Central New Jersey

Just as the bell rang a third time, a low sad tone, the monsignor toppled backwards to lay with the wrinkled remains of his eyes staring up at the night sky.

"What the hell, Jack?" Cyn whispered. She was angry, but then again, so was the demon-child; it turned the burnished coins on Jack and screamed in awful fury. It was a scream that froze the bones of those in the church and pinned them to their pews with fright. It even halted the army of undead; they hung back as though they were equally afraid of the demon.

Only Jack was completely unaffected by the power of that scream. The scream was vindication. In that split second between the sounds of the bell, Jack had acted when no one else had, and he had made an impossible choice that no one else would have dared.

He took another step down the darkest of paths with yet another murder, but he also kept the demon from stealing another soul.

It was with a malicious grin that he flipped the M4 to three-round burst and swept the demon off the monsignor's chest. The M4 didn't have much in the way of stopping power and the demon was up seconds later. It opened its mouth, perhaps to scream again or perhaps to blast them with its cold breath, but they never found out which.

There was the sound of thunder just to Jack's right and the demon went flying back, pieces of bones skittering everywhere. It was Cyn; her face was lined with grief, yet her eyes were ice. "Why'd you do it, Jack? I had a shot at the demon."

Just before Jack had killed the monsignor, her gun had come up, but she was too new to guns to know that a shotgun was not a precision weapon. She likely would have blown the monsignor's head right off and then she would've been the one adding dirt to her soul.

"You would have missed," Jack answered, "and the demon would have taken him. Now, the demon won't be down long and I think it's after me, so I'll draw it off. And uh, I guess I'll see you l-later." He faltered, knowing that this goodbye would likely be goodbye forever. Jack wasn't stupid. He had to try to raise Loret; this episode with the demon was proof that God's soldiers weren't ready yet to go toe-to-toe with a demon army, and Jack knew there was little chance of him getting into the city alone, or getting out alone either; and there was less of a chance of him overcoming the demon when it finally caught up with him again.

Cyn seemed to know it as well. She looked at Jack, then back at the church and then at the monsignor lying on the iced-over sidewalk, a hole through his head, and a coppery-smelling steam rising from it. "I'm going with you," she said after a shaky breath. "You need me."

He was so relieved not to be going into the hell of New York City alone that he almost wept. Instead, he grinned five feet from the corpse of the man he had just killed. It had been such a terrible, topsy-turvy few days that he didn't see that the smile was horribly inappropriate and neither did Cyn, apparently, as she returned it with a weak one of her own.

The demon's bones began to reform and so they hurried to the Humvee. Jack had just opened his door when Pastor John, suddenly rushed up and jumped in the back seat. In one hand, he held the monsignor's crucifix—there was blood splashed across Christ's face—and in the other he still held the shining brass bucket of Holy Water. He was grim and angry.

"If the demon is going to follow you, you're going to need me as well," Pastor John said. "The parishioners will be fine. The church is on sacred ground, which seems to stop the lesser...uh, what are they?"

Jack shrugged. "Ghouls maybe?" he answered and then felt around for the ignition button. Just as the Humvee's engine roared to life, the other back door opened, making them all scramble for their weapons and in Pastor John's case, the large crucifix which he brandished.

It wasn't a demon; it was the fellow in the bib-overalls who'd been just outside the monsignor's door. He had wide blue eyes that refused to blink and he had large hands that held onto the chair in front of him fiercely as though he was afraid they were going to try and kick him out of the vehicle.

"I'm goin' wit you guys," he said in a thick Jersey accent.

Jack's first inclination was to point his M4 at the man and order him out of the Humvee, but then he realized that here was exactly what he needed in order to complete the spell to resurrect Dr. Loret. It was almost a gift from God.

"Sure," Jack said, hating himself.

Next to him, Cyn's eyes widened and her mouth began to open. Before she could say anything, Jack hammered down on the gas and the Humvee leapt away. "Jack…" she hissed, glancing back at the man.

Purposely, he hit a curb leaving the parking lot. "Hold on," he yelled as she was thrown against her door. After that, there were too many ghouls around them for anyone to think about anything but survival. The living corpses converged on the Humvee, tearing at the reinforced windows with their bony claws or stepping in front of the roaring machine.

They were engulfed in darkness and swept with the maddening fear until the man in the back began raving. "Do something, Pastor," Jack ordered. He was whiteknuckling the steering wheel again, but other than that was holding it together better than the others.

"The L-Lord is m-my shepherd," Pastor John said in a voice struggling like a sputtering engine. "He-he maketh m-me lie down in green pastures. He leadeth me beside the still waters..." Gradually, his voice found strength and quickly their hearts were lightened as they broke through the ring of undead, leaving behind parts and pieces of the creatures; stuck to the grill was a black flap of cloth that flicked the remnants of grave dirt at them.

Cyn ginned at their escape and the man in the bib overalls, whose name they were to find out was Connor Randall, actually laughed and clapped his hands. Even Pastor John breathed a sigh of relief. Only Jack's heart wasn't lightened. He felt the shadow in it grow when he glanced back at Connor, remembering the horror of killing Carl.

"What happened back there with the Monsignor?" Jack asked, his voice a surprisingly angry growl. There was no getting around the fact that he felt profound disappointment; the task of stopping Robert had once again fallen to him and he was not happy about it. "What happened to the power of God and all that? Or was it again a failing of man?"

"Yeah, what about that?" Connor asked, turning aggressively on Pastor John. "I thought that old priest was supposed to be all powerful and then he gets laid out, just like that, and what were we supposed to do without him, sing all them monsters back into their graves?"

Pastor John's brown eyes blazed. "Do not talk ill of the dead, especially of the Monsignor. He was a good man and a courageous man. He went out and faced that beast alone."

"But how did he fail?" Cyn asked. "There was so much power in him. I felt it. It made me stronger. You don't understand, Jack. You couldn't feel it, but when the fear came, I could tell it was the worst yet, but I was barely fazed. And I was so sure that he would prevail...but he didn't...and I don't understand why."

"You have to remember, Cyn," Pastor John said, "the power wasn't the Monsignor's. It came from the Lord, so, yes Jack; the failing had to have been with the Monsignor."

There was a sharp accusation to the pastor's words as if he was daring Jack to say something concerning the dead man. Jack kept silent and regretted his earlier outburst.

He drove slowly through a street littered with vehicles and next to him he could feel Cyn growing antsy. She frequently glanced back at Connor, who started talking about himself and didn't stop until the planes streaked overhead to release their ordinance.

Connor's bib overalls weren't farm related as Jack had originally thought. He was a welder out of Hoboken and had been on the run from the flood of creatures since midday when they swept over the National Guard units trying to hold the approaches into New Jersey.

Everything had gone from: *Remain calm; we have the situation in hand, to Get out now!* "Then the shi…I mean the, uh crap had hit the fan, sorry, Father."

"It's Pastor actually, and as a military chaplain, I hear worse on a daily basis, or at least I…used…to…"

Just then the sky shook and there was a fantastic boom that caused everyone to crane their necks to see through the short windows of the Humvee. A second flight of jets shot overhead; in the dark, it was impossible to guess their type or their number.

Jack could only follow them once they went to afterburner and banked on a curve that would carry them out to sea in seconds, but before they got there, the northern skyline erupted in a string of fireballs each twenty stories in height. Nothing could have lived through it.

Nothing but the dead, Jack thought.

After the jets came attack helicopters which buzzed by in the hundreds. They spent an hour swooping in and out of the clouds of flames and smoke. And then the jets swept back and the earth rumbled. Jack had parked the

Humvee on an approach to a bridge that offered a great view of the violence, including a bombing strike on the bridge itself. It went up in a cataclysmic blast that staggered the air and made them gasp.

The four of them were mesmerized by the fantastic destructive power of the U.S military and, after half an hour when the planes and choppers were gone, the dead reformed and marched on, completely undeterred.

In the flames of a nearby burning Jersey city, Jack saw a bridge across the unknown river before them and took it much to Connor's amazement. "Why are we going this way? Huh? This doesn't make any sense."

They were driving just as fast as Jack could go; he was in fear of both the return of the military and what he would find when he got across the river—so far the sight in front of him was bodies upon bodies. They weren't the undead; they were the corpses of the people who had been ripped apart by the first wave of ghouls and demons.

From the height of the bridge, he could see the bodies, looking like discarded trash, as far as the eye could see, tens of thousands of bodies.

"No, none of this makes sense," Jack said, "but if we can do something to stop this, then we will…except you, Connor. I want you to fight it tooth and nail."

"Jack!" Cyn cried, glaring.

He glared right back. "If anyone has any better ideas give them to me now. And that includes you, Pastor."

"I don't know," Pastor John said in a whisper. They were down on the other side of the bridge and now Jack was blazing through the town, regardless of the bodies. His jaw was gritted so tight he was sure that he was cracking his teeth. Ahead of them was a great throng of walking dead.

The pastor stared at them and seemed unable to form complex thoughts. By rote, he said: "God loves us and is the ultimate power in the universe."

Jack heard a glaring "but" in the simple statement and asked it: "But what, Pastor? He's the ultimate power, but what?" There was a level of hysteria in his voice that was unacceptable as well as unavoidable. No man alive, not the bravest or the strongest could see what they were seeing and not be shaken to the core.

Even the pastor, a man of God with power flowing through his veins, was hesitant as he answered: "God is the ultimate source of power, but he leaves man in charge of man. He's given us our gifts and demands that we govern ourselves. Fortunately, he sent his one begotten son to guide us."

Cyn glanced back at the pastor, waiting for him to go on, to add something, anything that might help them and when he didn't she blew out a long breath. "I guess you keep driving, Jack. It may be the only way. If Pastor John is right, then I guess God has left this in our hands and we may have to get them dirty."

"It'll be me," Jack said. "My hands are already as dirty as they can get. You just keep the bad guys off of me, and Father, you get us through this mess. Your prayers work against the fear and the darkness, and the poison. We can't forget the poison." He laughed a miserable laugh as they banged over the bodies of the actual dead.

Most were cruelly contorted either through their death agonies or the rigor mortis that was setting in. They were also beginning to freeze, becoming hard as logs, and it felt as though the Humvee was coming apart with all the jolting and bouncing as Jack drove over them.

It was horrible and Jack felt that his mind was coming apart as well.

"Turn around!" Connor suddenly demanded. They were clear of the great majority of the actually dead while in front of them were the corpses that were "alive." Connor's eyes were just huge. He hammered on Cyn's chair and screamed: "Turn around, damn it!"

There would be no turning around, now. The silence by the others was tacit admission that they were out of ideas. They had tried the source of ultimate goodness and had failed. They now could only go down the road that would lead to hell…the road to Jack's hell. He knew that he was doing his damnedest to do the right thing; unfortunately he could only do the right thing by doing the most evil thing he could imagine.

"Just relax, Connor," Jack said as he revved the Humvee's engine and aimed it square into the mass. "I get the feeling we'll get through this with no problem."

Hell itself could not have been more terrifying.

This was the second wave of Robert's creatures. There were ghouls by the tens of thousands before them and fire and fear and there were demons lurking in clouds of darkness of their own making, but Jack wasn't worried. He had God on his side in the form of Pastor John and, what was more, he got the feeling that the devil was on his side as well, rooting for Jack to get through so that he could gut Connor and sacrifice him…so Jack could forever damn his own soul.

Chapter 34

New York, New York

Robert's second spell had awakened corpses that numbered in the low millions. They swarmed up out of their graves and swept over the city in a wave, bent on ferreting out anyone who still lived.

Jack could feel the creatures like a blight on his mind.

New York City was littered with bodies from end to end, and now the creatures were streaming into New Jersey. The military was unequipped to stop them; however, they could turn the "Garden State" into an American hell.

Jack drove through a landscape that was unrecognizable: the land had been tortured by thousand pound bombs, guided missiles, and cluster munitions that rained down hundreds of smaller anti-personnel "bomblets." Napalm and white phosphorus had been used so that half the state was on fire.

And Jack was sure that even then nukes were being discussed in some comfortable, air-conditioned bunker, hidden deep beneath the White House. He prayed to a God that he was sure was disgusted in him that the nukes wouldn't be used—they would be just as useless as all the rest of the bombs had been. The military was slowing the creatures, but not stopping them.

Above them the screech of jets returned and Jack cringed as the ground shook. In front of them the world went a brilliant white as hundreds of ghouls were evaporated in a single explosion—and then the Humvee was in the smoke and flames...and the bodies. The bodies were everywhere.

Too many were still moving.

The Humvee pounded into the next line of undead with a great jolt and their momentum was checked, first by the ghouls and then by a tremendous crater that sat square across the highway. Heedless of the danger, Jack gunned the vehicle right into it. Everything was smoke and dust and swirling ash. He couldn't see a thing until they were shooting up the other side and then they were back on the highway and a scream ripped from Connor's throat.

They were rushing through the black smoke of a chemical fire. The stench and the darkness were heavily laced with the demon fear. Jack and Cyn were veterans by now and shrugged it off, while Pastor John was practically shouting the Gospel of Mark at the top of his lungs. It was Connor who was bug-eyed and going crazy. He threw off his seat belt just as the land dropped straight out from beneath them.

A highway overpass had fallen in. They dropped ten feet, landed on the remains of a concrete span, and then skidded down onto another road, this one heading west. Jack kept the wheels turning as fast as he dared, looking for the first chance to get back to the highway.

A minute later there was a bent over sign and an on-ramp chugged full of the undead.

He spun the Humvee, that magnificent charger, straight into them, not daring to slow for even a second. They blasted corpses left and right, and in too many cases right over the top of the vehicle. With ghouls clinging to the sides of the Humvee, they roared right back up onto the highway and into the darkest cloud yet.

"More payers!" Jack yelled as he sensed the source of the darkness: a demon of great power straight in their path.

The ride had jarred the breath out of the pastor and it was with a hitching voice that he began: "Our Father who art in heaven, hallowed be thy name..."

Quiet as they were, the words were of comfort to Jack. His mind had been edging closer to the gulf of insanity and he went to the brink of it when he saw the demon. It seemed composed of equal parts straw, bone and stray twigs; its eye sockets were clogged with graveyard dirt and when it opened its mouth, black dirt fell and splattered wet on the highway.

Out of its mouth came a blizzard of white which swept the Humvee, finally causing it to falter. The engine coughed like an old man, weak and dying, and the interior lights grew dim. Slower and slower they went.

"...Thy kingdom come, thy will be done on earth as it is in heaven..." Pastor John said, his voice seemed to be gaining the strength that was draining from the Humvee. In seconds, the engine was dead and he was booming out the prayer: "Give us this day our daily bread and forgive us our trespasses as we forgive those who trespass against us and lead us not into temptation but deliver us from evil, amen."

By the time he had finished the prayer, the Humvee's momentum had carried them far past the demon and onto a stretch of open road. "Do you have a prayer for dead engines?" Jack asked. He could feel the demon coming.

"The Lord will provide," Pastor John said...and it seemed he did, either that or the heat from the engine block had unfrozen the gas lines. Jack tried over and over, hitting the ignition button and finally the Humvee started up, hesitant at first, then with growing power.

Close behind them was the demon hurrying to catch them and ahead of them were more ghouls. They were a raggedy bunch even compared to the usual ones and Jack guessed that they were the lesser creatures, those whose personal power barely allowed them to hold their borrowed bodies together.

Jack floored the Humvee and with a cry, blasted through, leaving the demon and all the miserable creatures in their dust.

He grinned at Cyn who grinned back. She clicked on the defrost to clear the windshield and then cocked her head to see through the side view mirror. "They're not following us," she said, her grin even wider than before. She began to laugh as she said: "Pastor John was right; God provided a way to get out of there. I really didn't think we would make it."

"Yes, trust in the Lord," Pastor John said, nodding and gulping air. He seemed giddy and his grin was even larger than Cyn's.

Jack had grinned, but he couldn't bring himself to smile. He didn't see their escape as a sign from God. The way in front was relatively clear and in fact it might as well have been paved in gold. He knew for a fact that they would make it into the city because once again he was bound to a path of damnation.

He was even "fortunate" in his choice of victim. Connor was splayed out in the back; he had been knocked unconscious when the Humvee had taken the plunge off the highway. "Don't touch him!" Jack snapped as Pastor John reached out to check to see if he was ok. "He'll be fine," Jack said and had the sinking feeling that he would be.

The pastor's grin dipped. "You don't know what the future holds, Jack. Your path is not set."

It was like the pastor had held his thoughts up to a mirror—right was left, good was bad, impossible was possible. *If it was only that easy*, Jack thought. His path was locked in iron and it seemed as though there was no changing it.

He drove through Northern Jersey as the night drew on. The lanes heading east were largely clear and before he knew it, they were at the George Washington Bridge— only then was their way finally blocked. Not only were the roads completely packed with cars, the bridge itself had been bombed into rubble.

Jack literally wept with relief. He had come through fire and death to stop his cousin and he would have committed a sin against God to end the war, but it seemed as though he wouldn't have to after all.

Cyn hugged him, reading his mood with precision. "You tried, Jack. No one can say that you didn't. I was getting pretty scared there for a while. I thought for sure we'd find the road wide open all the way into Queens, which is crazy. We saw how bad it was this morning...or was it yesterday morning?"

The eastern sky was dark, but not nearly as dark as it had been. "It was yesterday morning," Jack said, wiping his eyes. "And I was thinking the same thing."

"I find it strange that I was as well," Pastor John said. "I was simply sure that we would just zip along so fast that there would be no time to change your mind, Jack. But the Lord has again provided and we are balked." He pointed at the river. The Hudson was a dark strip, almost a mile wide between them and the city. The three of them turned to stare at it and just then there came an odd, echoey thump.

Jack's head dropped and his heart sank. He knew the sound—it was a boat thumping on rocks. Cyn rolled down her window, listened until the sound repeated and then asked: "Is God doing this? Is he trying to help us get to Queens?"

"I don't know," the pastor answered, looking shaken to the core. "And I really don't know what to do about you, Jack. I can't let you murder this man. It's one of the reasons why I came."

"I wish you would stop me," Jack said, and then got out of the Humvee. He stood for a moment; there were ghouls nearby, he could feel them further up the road. There were six of them feeding on the remains of a woman. "We've got to hurry," he said, shouldering his M4 and retrieving the rapier. He then went around to the back door and hauled Connor out of the Humvee.

The man began to blink. "What happened?"

Jack hauled him to his feet; he wasn't gentle. He was getting the same feeling he had with Carl. Jack didn't want touch Connor or even look at him and even the thought of him began to feed a brewing fury within Jack.

Cyn saw what was happening. "Here, I'll take him." She began pulling Connor down to the river's edge.

He was groggy and easily moved. "Like a sheep to slaughter," Pastor John said. It was an accusation, one that Jack ignored. "I will stop you if it comes down to it," the pastor said. He held up a 9MM pistol. Where he had gotten it from, Jack didn't know and he really didn't care.

"Then maybe it would be best if you shoot me now," Jack said and then turned his back on the pastor. Just like with their journey to Queens, Jack *knew* he wasn't going to die by being shot in the back. He led them down to the water and what he saw there had him turning to Pastor John.

"If you stop me, this will keep happening."

In the dark, Jack had first thought that the river was filled with ice flows, but it wasn't ice covering the river from bank to bank. The river was filled with bloated corpses.

Pastor John made a noise in his throat and began crying. And then he began blubbering. And then he fell down on his knees. Jack looked on the priest with cold eyes and saw himself in the display. He'd been a pathetic, mewling bitch after he had killed Carl. He vowed that he wouldn't be this time. What would be the point to sorrow and sadness and begging forgiveness? He was going into this with his eyes wide open this time. How could he kill someone in cold blood and then turn around and say: *woops, my bad, now forgive me.*

He left the pastor and made his way to the water where a boat was kicking up next to the shore. It was little more than an aluminum dingy, the kind a middle-aged man would take out on the weekends to get away from his nagging wife. There were dozens of bottle tops rusting little rings on the bottom of the boat.

Jack sent one skittering as he climbed in.

Cyn came next pulling Connor. He stopped at the water's edge and stared at the river of dead with his mouth hanging slack. "I'm not going in there," he said, pulling back.

"Then you'll die," Jack told him, matter-of-factly. "There are a whole mess of ghouls coming for us right now. It's either get in the boat or take your chances out there with them."

Connor, who had no idea the fate that Jack had in store for him, hurried for the boat. *Like a sheep to slaughter*...the words echoed in Jack's mind. Angrily he turned from the man and took a look at the outboard engine. It had plenty of gas and a new plug, but the props were clogged.

The propeller blades were imbedded in a person...a child, actually.

"Can you start it?" Cyn asked, nervously. The ghouls were coming closer.

"P-Probably," he answered, his stomach felt like it was coming up his throat. He looked away from the propeller and saw Pastor John standing just at the water's edge. "Push us out," Jack ordered, "and either get in or don't, but if you get in, get in with a purpose. Help or hurt us, just make up your mind."

The pastor shoved them out and hesitated before jumping in after them. No one asked him whether he was going to help or not, but he was no longer carrying the gun. He had the crucifix.

They only went twenty feet out into the river where the current, a sluggish underwater hand, grabbed them and slowly started pushing them down stream. The ghouls came up and eyed them from the bank; they were all dressed in black suits save for a single woman in a dingy grey dress. Only the woman had any flesh on her bones and that was stretched tight as a drum. The others were bone and gristle and grinning teeth. They looked like a wedding party of the damned.

They only paused for a few seconds before they waded in after the boat.

It was a bit of a shock to everyone that the ghouls turned out to be such good swimmers. They splashed straight for the boat. Cyn tried her shotgun on the lead ghoul and nearly toppled into the water herself when she blew the thing's head off. Pastor John barely caught her as she pinwheeled her arms to keep from falling in. They toppled into the bottom of the boat, disturbing the bottle caps.

"Give Connor your sword!" Cyn demanded. Jack had pulled it out and was using it to clear the body off the prop.

Not only was Connor looking as though he had just wet his pants, Jack wasn't about to do to clear the props by hand. "No. Use the priest."

Cyn turned to the pastor, who was trying to find a place in the boat that had any stability. "Come on, Pastor do something!"

"Of course, right," he said. "Just give me a second to get up." A bony hand clamped on the side of the boat, and then a second. Before the pastor could even right himself, let alone lift the crucifix, the grinning skull was hoisted up next.

Jack took it off its shoulders with one swing of the rapier. The extra seconds this afforded allowed the pastor to get to a secure squatting position. From there he recited Jesus' Sermon on the Mount, and as long as he spoke, the ghouls were kept at bay, splashing in the river fifteen feet away.

Finally, Jack got the last of the child—a little boy in onesie pajamas—off the propellers. To get the engine going was nothing more than a pull of the starter cord and then they were chugging away. They went slowly with Pastor John and Jack fending the bodies away from the prow of the boat with the butts of their guns. Connor sat in the middle of the boat and clung to the sides, while Cyn drove.

It was a slow trip around the southern end of Manhattan and when they turned north into the East River, the number of bodies only multiplied. They pushed through the dead, stopping twice to remove yards of spun skin from the props, and the sun was pinking the sky before they turned straight east onto a canal that ran deep into Queens like a dagger wound.

The southern edge of Calvary Cemetery sat thirty yards from the canal. Cyn pushed them up close and first Jack and then Pastor John climbed up onto a cement retaining wall. Connor came next, eager and grasping, afraid of everything: the water, the boat, the shadowed tombstones and the hundreds of thousands of upturned graves.

The one thing he was not afraid of was Jack, and that was a tremendous mistake. "What the hell are we doing here?" he asked.

Cyn turned away and Pastor John looked sick. Jack's ugly fury ramped up. It was the coming spell that made him feel such alien hatred, there was no other explanation. And that meant fate had a driving hand in all of this—the idea made it easier to answer: "I'm hoping to figure things out and you're going to help. Come on, it's this way."

Jack went first, feeling with that strange part of himself for ghouls and the demons. The only demon around was the one with the terrible half-penny eyes and it was away west, still in Jersey but hurrying their way. There were ghouls closer, not many and none seemed to be oriented on the little group. For the most part these close in ones were trapped in caskets of marble and would never break free.

The four crossed through the graveyard, the morning light guiding them around the countless holes in the earth until they found the one actually dead corpse in the entire cemetery. They all stared at Loret's mutilated body. Jack studied it for clues on how to cast the missing spell, the others simply looked disgusted.

"Who is this guy?" Connor asked.

Casually, as if he was secretly hoping that Connor would run away or fight him or even just scream, Jack unslung the M4 from his back. The welder did nothing but look at Jack with an infuriatingly dim expression. "He's you," Jack told him and then thumped Connor right between the eyes with the heavy butt end of the gun.

Chapter 35

Calvary Cemetery, Queens, New York

"How can Satan drive out Satan?" Pastor John said. It was a statement, not a question, and one filled with misery. He looked stricken as though the blow had struck him instead of Connor.

"What are you talking about?" Jack asked, his tone sharp and his eyes sharper. The fury and the hate were building.

Pastor John shrugged. "Just scripture. Just the Lord's word: *If a kingdom is divided against itself, that kingdom cannot stand.* It's the Gospel of Mark, 3:23."

"Ok, and what's it supposed to mean? Are you calling me Satan?" Jack certainly felt like Satan, he just didn't like the idea of someone pointing it out. As well, he felt as divided as was humanly possible. A part of him...a growing part of him had actually enjoyed the heavy *thunk* the rifle made when it had smashed Connor's face. The rest of him was appalled and on the verge of being sick.

The pastor shrugged again, an infuriating gesture of weakness in Jack's eyes, and answered: "No, you are not Satan. You're not even close, not yet at least. The scripture is Christ's warning against..."

With just a touch, Cyn stopped the pastor before he could get going. "Now's not the time, Father. The demon is coming and people are still dying by the thousands. Maybe we should wait over here."

She pulled the pastor away, hauling on the hem of his camouflaged shirt. Jack watched them go, divided once more by anger and jealousy, each eating into his mind until he balled a fist so hard that his nails bit into his palm. Only then could he concentrate.

"Why couldn't this be someone else's birthright?" he mumbled and then looked down on the two bodies: Loret and Connor. They couldn't stay where they were.

Loret was surrounded by the twin circles—Robert's used-up magic, and Connor was crumpled in a heap, too far from the cement. Jack dragged them both further up the wide sidewalk and then cuffed Connor's hands behind his back and tied his shoelaces together, just in case he woke during the ritual. It was an ugly thing to do and it was only just the start.

Jack pulled the knife he had used to kill Carl from his back pocket; the blade was black with dried blood. The paintbrush that he had used to create the glyphs was missing, lost somewhere in the last ten hours of fighting and running for his life. But it was no matter.

Fate kept him on course. The brush that Robert had used was lying just beside the sidewalk. It was revolting, the blood on it looked like tar and it smelled like a charnel house in summer. Jack grabbed it, smacked it against the cement to clear off most of the blood and then advanced on Connor.

"Be tough," he whispered as he slit open Connor's shirt, exposing his soft belly. But Jack was not tough. He winced and his eyes teared as he drew the knife along Connor's skin. The first cut was straight across his belly going deep enough to slice the muscles of his abdomen;

To keep him from running, a voice whispered in his mind. *But there's a better way, as you know.*

Jack knew. He had seen too many depictions of ancient sacrifices not to know that it would be best if he impaled Connor, "nailing" him to the earth, so to speak. A shiver went up his back and a second later a snarl appeared on his lips. He was torn in two, hating as well as loving what he was doing.

He wished he could feel nothing only that wasn't an option, sacrificing a man to one of the Gods of the Undead was too personal. He cried and he hated and he grinned and leered greedily and he felt the power swirling around him as again and again he dipped the brush into Connor's split belly.

Sometimes he stabbed the brush in, knife-like, with the strange hatred that he couldn't explain and sometimes he felt just the edges with the brush, afraid that he was hurting the unconscious man.

Gradually he went around the circle and with each glyph drawn; he felt something taken from him. His muscles began trembling and his breath came ragged in his chest. He was being drained. It was part of his soul that was being taken. After Carl, it was expected and so was the feeling of suffocation that clamped itself on Jack's throat the moment the circles were complete.

It was time to sacrifice Connor to complete the spell.

Jack was afraid to look straight at the man, fearing that when he did, Connor would be staring at him with wide eyes, and he was afraid to look over at Cyn, knowing he would see disappointment etched onto her face. Jack kept his chin down and approached Connor, making sure to focus squarely on the man's chest.

Hesitation was no longer an option; his head was beginning to go light and his hunger for the spell's completion was too great. At this point there was no turning back; either he would die or Connor would. Jack stabbed the blade deep and there was a tin sound ringing in the air and a surge of unholy power that ran up his arms, into his chest, up his throat and then out of his mouth as he spoke the ancient words that opened the portal to the world of the dead.

This time, Jack felt only a deep pang of remorse. He didn't cry or weep; there was simply a hole somewhere inside him where his soul hid and there was a pain that he tried not to think about.

With a sad shake of his head, Jack watched as beneath Loret's corpse a black hole, liquid and glassy, formed so that it appeared that Loret floated on a table of pure nothingness. Then came the motes of gauzy light; they were spirits coming to inspect the opening, looking to take advantage of any mistake Jack might have made.

When they saw that there were none, they hovered below, waiting again, hoping for an opportunity to escape hell. After a moment, when one didn't surface, Jack asked: "Dr. Byron Loret?" This didn't seem to help.

A full three minutes passed, and as the seconds drew out and Jack stood on the edge of the black circle, there came a sudden terrific screech ripping up the sky that made him jump. He squinted up and could just make out a tremendous metal dart cruising at *mach 2* a thousand feet off the ground. When it disappeared, there came an ever greater cacophony as a ripple of explosions on the Jersey side of the Hudson River shook the air.

It was the Navy firing from out to sea, Jack figured. The explosions went on for a good five minutes, crash after crash, and then silence.

Cyn and Pastor John had eased closer to the circles and Jack was still staring westward at New Jersey, which looked to be one tremendous bonfire, when he was suddenly jerked back to his sad reality: Dr. Loret finally made his appearance. There was a blast of cold from the black circle and then Loret sat up, suddenly, spilling his insides into his lap. He touched the knot of intestines and began trying to shove them back in place, hauling the loose flaps of his skin around him like an ill-fitting kimono.

Loret was hideous in death. For some reason, Robert had slit his eyes wide open and now they looked like two squished grapes; his tongue had been split down the middle and when it came out, which it did with unsettling frequency to lick his lips, it looked like a snake's tongues, except it was loose and flappy. Lastly, Loret was dual colored: the front of him was cadaver-white, while the back was a sick purple where the remains of his blood had pooled and coagulated.

"What a shame," he said, looking down at his open chest, the words sounding strange and wheezy as though his lungs were bagpipes.

"Dr. Loret?" Jack asked again. "I have some questions."

For the first time, Loret looked around himself. He seemed especially interested in the glyphs. He turned three small circles, like a dog readying itself for bed, and all the while his lips moved as he read and reread the glyphs holding him within the circle.

"You ass! Let me go!" Loret cried, stamping his foot and accidentally letting a cascade of intestines out to splatter on the ground. He scooped them up and then charged at Jack, but was stopped short by the invisible barrier that Jack's spell had created. "Let me out and I'll kill you!"

"And?" Jack asked. "Don't you mean, *or I'll kill you?*"

Loret tried to grin with his dead face and it came out as all teeth. "Yes, of course, sorry. What's wrong with her?" Cyn and the pastor had joined them; she was looking back and forth from the corpse of Connor Randall and the talking corpse of Dr. Loret. Her look was one of profound queasiness.

"I'm just feeling a little sick is all," she said, gasping and swallowing repeatedly. "There's so much ugliness everywhere I turn. No offense Dr. Loret."

Even in death, he could manage to raise a haughty eyebrow. "And how am I not supposed to take offense?"

No one had an answer to that and Cyn only shrugged. Jack, who was still feeling reverberating evil bouncing around his insides, and who was tired, both physically and spiritually, rubbed his forehead and said to Loret: "I don't want to be a jerk, but no one wants to hear your whining. We brought you back because we want answers. Where's Robert Montgomery? And what's his deal? What's he looking to accomplish with all of this?"

Loret's lips were grey worms on a slack mouth and when he sneered they bent into a bowed shape. "Maybe if you let me out, I'll tell you."

"Don't trust him, Jack," Cyn said quickly, lifting her shotgun. "Get your answer first."

"First?" Jack asked in surprise. "I have no intention of letting this snake out. He was a snake in life and I bet he's ten times as bad in death."

Loret sneered again. "Then we're at an impasse, because you don't have the third spell. You can't compel me to say or do anything. But…but that doesn't mean we can't strike a deal. Let me out and I'll tell you anything you want."

"Tell me first," Jack countered. "You're the one without honor. You're the one we can't trust."

"I'm without honor? What do you call that?" he pointed at Connor's corpse. "That looks like an infernal sacrifice to the Mother of Demons. That looks like you're selling off your soul bit by bit. Whatever you want to say about me, I never did that."

Jack dropped his eyes and felt the black spot on his soul like it was acid. Into the silence that followed, the Navy began lobbing two-thousand pound missiles across the city again.

"Ok, I admit it," Jack said, his words slow and measured. "I'm not a good person. I thought I was, but now…I guess not. Still, I won't screw you over, Doctor. I promise I will let you out if you tell me what we need to know."

Pastor John hissed: "Jack! Can I talk to you, please?" He tried to pull Jack away; however, Jack dug his heels in.

"I don't think so. I know what you're going to say: we can't release him. Right? You're going to tell me that he's a demon or whatever the smaller ones are. Guess what? I know that already, but he's a drop in the bucket. In the great scheme of things, he's the very least of our worries."

"Exactly," Loret said with growing excitement. "We have the same enemy. Let me out and I'll find Robert and drag him to hell. You can trust me. I'll kill him. I'll kill him a thousand times over. I owe that bastard."

Cyn shook her head in warning. "Get the information first, Jack," she said.

Jack closed his eyes, hoping to find a moment of peace, only Loret was so close, he could feel him like a torch. He had to turn away; in the west, the horizon was aflame and was as bright as the sun in the east. The Navy was laying down a curtain of shrapnel and fire in a desperate attempt to slow the second wave of undead.

"Information first," Jack said, without turning around.

"No," Loret said with equal finality. "You can't send me away, Jack. You lack the power and you don't know the spell, but I could teach it to you. Yes! I know the true reason why you brought me back. You don't care about Robert, I know it. You want his power. You want to be able to control the things you bring up from the pit." Loret's dead eyes were alight with a greed that Jack could feel echo in his own soul.

It was an effort for Jack to say: "I want the information first!"

"That includes the final spell, doesn't it?" Loret asked.

Jack was still staring at the flames, rising like a curtain in the west. He nodded his head.

Cyn marched around in front of him and glared up into his face. "Why Jack? Why on earth do you want to know that sort of thing? It can't lead to anything but more evil."

"I'm sure it will," Jack said, slumping, feeling tired and defeated. "That's the sad part about all of this. There's going to be more evil, no matter what we do, but if I can limit it then I will. In order to do so, I need to know everything and that includes the third spell. We don't know when it will come in handy. If we had it now, we wouldn't be bargaining with this creature, we'd be forcing it to reveal what we need to know."

"Exactly," Loret agreed. "Now, let me out and I'll tell you anything you need to know."

Jack shook his head. He had an urge burning in his gut worse than any crackhead had ever felt. It was a hunger that went beyond hunger and beyond lust, he had a *need* to know this last spell, and he knew that he would have sold his own soul to know it and, had Cyn not been there, looking at him with her beautiful blue eyes, he would've have scraped away the glyphs with his tongue and released Loret that second.

There was only one way to stop himself from giving in; he unslung the M4 and handed it to Pastor John, saying: "Shoot me if I accept any terms other than information first."

In spite of his words, Jack was a little shocked when the pastor…the US Army chaplain, snapped back on the charging handle of the M4 and leveled it at Jack's face. He said: "Finally, a request that makes sense."

Chapter 36

Calvary Cemetery, Queens, New York

For the first time in days, Jack smiled a genuine smile. It almost seemed that if the pastor killed him it would be some sort of redemption; as if his soul could be saved by this minor form of martyrdom. At the very least he wouldn't be alive to commit any more murders.

This change of attitude bolstered Cyn and the pastor and, at the same time, Loret shrunk. He turned his squished-grape eyes first to Jack and then to the resolute pastor, and did so with an air of petulant disappointment. "I will tell what I know, but you have to promise on your soul to let me out when I'm done."

"I promise," Jack said and when he did, a wicked gleam swept Loret's face.

"Stupid boy," Loret cackled. "Never promise your soul, not for something so insignificant. Now we are bound together. If you go back on your word, I will own you."

Cyn glared, not at Loret, but at Jack. "That's why you don't make deals with the devil, Jack." She made an angry sound and then turned her gaze on the animated corpse. "You have your promise, now start talking. Where's Robert?"

Loret turned to Jack. "My deal is with you, Jack; is that what you want to know first?" It was a sly question and Jack felt his hunger build. "No, you don't want to know about your cousin, you want to know about the spell, isn't that right?"

"Yeah," Jack breathed.

"That's what I thought. You're just like your cousin, so hungry for power that you'll do anything."

Cyn hauled Jack back and stepped right up to the edge of the circle, her toes throwing their shadows across it she was so close. "You don't know what you're talking about; Jack is nothing like Robert. He's only looking to end this and so am I. So, enough with the bloody mind games. If you want to start with the spell, fine, just get talking."

"Of course," Loret said and then glanced over her shoulder at Jack. "Are you sure you want her to hear the spell? Do you want to share the power?"

Jack hesitated in answering. The honest truth was he wanted the spell all to himself. He was ashamed of the fact and yet he couldn't fight it. He shook his head and Cyn's eyes widened in shock.

"You don't have anything to worry about, Jack, I don't want to know the spell," she said. "Not after seeing what all this is doing to you. You should see yourself. It's not pretty. When I first saw you, you were this shy, bumbling boy and now…you've changed in a bad way."

"I know," he answered without meeting her eyes. "The spells are evil; I know that, but…but…" He gestured at the empty cemetery. "I don't have any choice. You do, though."

She stepped back and said: "I won't listen."

Pastor John did not make the same promise. He stood nearby with his arms folded across his chest, his eyes going wider and wider as Loret explained the spell and showed Jack the glyphs that were used, drawing them on the ground using his own thick blood.

Jack had him smear each one before he went on to the next—there was no need for Cyn's phone this time and not once did he ask Dr. Loret to repeat the glyphs or the words of the spell; they were imprinted on his mind, seared there in fact. He couldn't forget them even if he wanted to.

At certain points, Pastor John clucked his tongue and at the end he pronounced the entire thing as: "Disgusting."

There was no point in disagreeing, "Yeah," Jack said and had trouble swallowing. For the first time since all of this started, he felt a form of empathy for his cousin. The spells at his command weren't just inherently evil; they almost felt alive, as if there was an insidious force behind them or within them that could manipulate the caster.

Even then, Jack felt an unearthly desire to strike down the pastor and use his life's energy to open a portal to the netherworld. The desire was nearly a compulsion. Jack stuck his hands in his pockets.

"Ok…Ok, we know the spell," he said through gritted teeth. "What about Robert? What's his game plan? And where the hell is he?"

"So angry, just like your cousin." Loret let his split tongue fall out as he smiled. "And I don't know where Robert is or where he's going. Though if I had to guess, I'd say Washington DC. You see, he didn't have a game plan, as you put it. He brought back Hor just to see if he could, just to see if the spells really worked."

Pastor John's face somehow registered even more disgust. "This is the year 2016, no sane person murders a man in the hope that a magic spell will work, even if it is written in hieroglyphics and on some ancient scroll."

"Robert wasn't acting on a whim," Loret explained. "There's way more to these spells than a whim. There's a craving and a calling, right Jack?" When Jack refused to answer or even look his way, Loret went on: "And Robert wasn't just guessing that they would work, he was almost certain. He had some proof."

Cyn had been angling closer and now she asked: "What sort of proof? Was it something from our great-great grandfather?"

"No," Loret answered. "Lord Blackburn was too smart to leave the clues to something so dangerous in writing. I've read his notes. They were usually quite floral in their presentation, but the notes on his final dig were all very short and to the point and the point couldn't be stated clear enough: they found nothing!"

"So, what's that mean?" Cyn asked. "How does finding nothing point to proof of something?"

Loret, annoyingly superior even in death, grinned and the effect was awful. Cyn blanched, which only made Loret's grin go wider. "They were on that dig for seven months! No one digs for seven months without *any* findings, but he didn't claim a single piece of pottery or a chip of stone that *might* have been part of a tool or a toilet brush. Clearly, he was hiding something, but it was only clear in hindsight. At the time, people thought he was a fool."

"This is your proof? Perhaps he..."

"I wasn't done," Loret hissed and then tried to attack the barrier again. He only stopped when his belly spilled on the ground. Sulking, he hauled the mass up in armfuls and went on: "My proof stems from the one Egyptian who lived through the expedition: Baqir Sharma. He was remanded into an insane asylum in 1925 and wasn't released until 1978 and died the next year."

"Did he say anything during that year?" Jack asked, afraid of the answer, afraid that whatever had driven Baqir mad was already at work in his own mind.

Loret forgot about his intestines for a moment. "He said a lot and he wrote down even more and somehow Robert found it all. Sixteen handwritten books. Robert had them all translated—and the translator he hired? Ended up dead, ran over by a truck...that should have been a warning to me, huh?"

"Go on," Jack said with a roll of his eyes. "You made your bed."

This earned Jack a sneer and there wasn't anything like a sneer from cold dead lips. "And you are making yours, Jack. But let me help by tucking in another corner of the sheet. Baqir described the entire expedition in perfect lucid detail. Your great-great grandfather uncovered a sorcerer of such power that even death could not stop him." Loret's blown eyes were now suddenly alight.

"How did they kill it?" Jack asked, quickly.

"I don't know if they did," Loret answered, his zeal gone. "Baqir did not stay to find out. The second he could, he ran away. He was in the desert alone for three weeks before he was picked up and shipped off."

Pastor John made a face as if he'd just sipped curdled milk. "That's still not enough to kill a man over. I've seen evil in this world and if Robert killed a man over what you've said then..."

"It's more than that," Jack said, interrupting. "I know it now. Once Robert had all three spells translated, I don't know if he could have helped it. There's something in them...a pull or a desire, or a need. There is a need to use them. Whoever wrote the spells wove something within them, like a psychic demand to use them. Now that I know the third spell, I feel it."

Cyn touched his arm as if expecting to be shocked. "Can you control it?"

That was a question he didn't know the answer to. "Yes, so far." It was just a guess, he could feel the urgent demand in the back of his head and he wondered how he'd be able to sleep, and if he was able to there was the question of whether he would kill in his sleep? He shook his head to clear it. "Ok, so we know why he raised Hor, but why the others? Why did he destroy the city?"

Loret grinned again, his grey lips pulled all the way back. "That's all on you, Jack. You hounded him. You forced his hand. That's what he said, at least, but that wasn't the truth. But I think you know why you're being targeted, don't you?"

"The birthright," Jack said. "It's mine isn't it?"

"It's all yours," Loret replied. "It was Jonathan Dreyden who first possessed the spells. He gave them to his father, Lord Blackburn, who divided them to keep them from being used. As the true hair to Blackburn, Robert is jealous of you and your birthright. He tried to kill you with Hor and then he tried with the other mummies and when that didn't work...well, Robert got angry."

Cyn asked: "You said you think he's going to Washington, what's that have to do with Jack?"

"Oh, my sweet, it's not just Jack who he was trying to kill. He was going after you and your mother as well, but he lost track of you and then we had the police all over us. I have to say, it was quite a shock when they showed up at my house. It sort of put Robert in a tough spot. He had to do *something*, or he would've been arrested for murder."

"So he raised a zombie army?" Cyn asked, appalled.

Loret lifted a single shoulder in a shrug. "It's not like he could've gone home at that point. He also said that destiny had provided him with an opportunity."

Cyn slumped. "To rule the world?" she asked, and when Loret nodded, she shrunk even more. "Since we've been little, he has always been going on about the inherent right of the British to rule the world and how his family peerage should have been an inheritable one. Now he's looking to make himself king. But why the king of the dead?"

"He won't be just king of the dead," Jack said. "He'll be untouchable. He'll be feared by the entire world and he'll wield great power with that fear. He'll go for DC first, but he'll go for the Vatican as soon as he realizes there is still power in the church. Speaking of which, Loret, can you be killed...I mean can you be killed again?"

The corpse looked down at himself, ropes of intestines dangling from both hands, blood starting to pool, both in his feet and on the ground beneath them. "I don't think so. Since, I've been called without the third spell, I can't be forced back by my master, since I don't have one. I will live forever as you see me. Though I do fear the priest and can't say why...but we are straying from the only topic I am obligated to discuss, and I have exhausted my knowledge on the subject, so release me!" Loret leaned into the barrier, excitement playing in his blown orbs.

Cyn brought up her shotgun and Pastor John did the same with the M4. "I'll take that," Jack said holding out his hand for the gun. "You have your crucifix and your God."

The pastor gave over the weapon, saying: "He's our God, Jack. He forgives all those who bow before him with the courage to beg forgiveness."

Jack wondered if that was true for him. He felt as though he was slung with a yoke. On one side he had the guilt and pain weighing him down and on the other he had the hunger of the spells—the need to kill, the need to grow in power. For the moment the two balanced themselves out and it almost felt as though he needed the guilt to keep from him gushing blood out onto the ground and sacrificing anyone close to himself.

"You two can discuss theology later," Cyn said. "I don't want Jack losing his soul over a technicality, which, I would not put past this piece of scum."

"Step back, Loret," Jack ordered. "And I'll release you." He didn't care for how close the creature was. Loret seemed bigger in death and a thousand times hungrier.

"No," Loret said. "That wasn't part of the bargain. Let me out, now!"

Jack felt a fire of hate radiate from his chest that burned as bright as the flames that were turning New Jersey to ash. The yoke was tilting toward the dark anger. "You'd be wise not to anger me, Loret," he said with such malice that the creature actually stepped back and appraised Jack. "That's better," Jack said. "I release you Dr. Loret. Go your way and I will go mine."

The circles were still intact and yet, the barrier was no longer between them. Cyn kept the shotgun ready and Pastor John held his cross; only Jack didn't raise his weapon. There was great power in fear, but there was even greater power in courage. "Go," he said and Loret left with his intestines slung around his neck like a curled garden hose.

"So what do we do?" Jack asked when Loret was picking his way toward the cemetery wall.

"Here's what you should do, Jack," the pastor said. "You should get down on your knees and beg the Lord for forgiveness. It's not too late, even for you."

The words *even for you*, sunk in and Jack understood this on a level where the soul gripped the body. *Even for you* meant even for a murderer like you. He shook his head, feeling the yoke tip from one side to the other. He wanted it to fall all the way over to the side of his pain and misery, but the other side wouldn't let it.

A part of him, perhaps the wrong part didn't know if he wanted to apologize. Yes, he was hurting inside and wanted to run away from the body of Connor Randall as fast as he could, but all the same, he wasn't exactly sorry. What he had done, *had* to be done. What was there to apologize about?

"Maybe later," he said, causing Cyn and Pastor John to share a look. "I mean it, I guess. I do feel bad, but we all agreed beforehand that there really wasn't any other way, so it seems pretty hypocritical to get all teary eyed now."

"You're a pretty cold sod, Jack," Cyn said, shaking her head. "You have to stop doing these spells, they're changing you."

They were indeed. Twelve hours before he was blubbering over the body of a strange old coot he had never met before and was probably better off dead. Now, he had raised a ghoul and when he had ordered it to be gone, it left—even without the spell of command.

"Probably," he said, with a shiver, only it wasn't cold he was feeling. It was the heat of hatred starting to tip the yoke in the wrong direction. "Not yet," he whispered and didn't know why. Nor did he know why he knelt down next to Connor and touched the man's face. It was cold, miserably cold. It sent a shock of grief through him that immersed the hate and he was able to mutter: "Sorry," so that no one heard.

Chapter 37

The Atlantic Ocean

Captain Corley, A.K.A. Pastor John, proposed that they find the nearest intact military unit and explain the situation on the ground as best as they could. Cyn not only seconded the idea, she acted as though her vote was the only one that counted.

"Then that's what we'll jolly well do. There you go, Jack. Look lively. Get your gun and that sword of yours and let's be off." She didn't wait for him. With the shotgun hoisted on one shoulder and her blonde hair blowing in the breeze, she headed straight away for the boat, fully confident in her decision, likely because it didn't involve anymore murders and because it foisted their responsibility onto an authority figure: the US Military.

Jack dragged his feet. Going to the military was almost certainly a waste of time. Up until the day before, the US military had been the greatest power on earth, capable of laying waste to the planet if it so choose. Now, it wasn't even a close second. Despite all the fire power they possessed, they could not kill the ghouls or the demons.

He was afraid that going to them would lead to a confrontation with Robert, who they could easily kill, and yet no one knew what sort of mayhem his death would cause. At least Robert had a plan of sorts that had to involve keeping a significant level of the population alive and functioning in a form of pseudo-civilization.

Releasing the demons would undoubtedly lead to mass chaos and perhaps the eradication of humanity.

Unfortunately, the only way to stop Robert was through magic. Magic had started all of this and only magic could truly end it—but what sort of magic that entailed or how many murders he would have to commit, Jack didn't know.

There was no use suggesting this to Cyn or Pastor John; both had leapt on the idea of foisting their problems onto the military, and had fast-marched away from the corpse of Connor Randall and were at the boat in under a minute.

The chaplain had managed to get into the unruly thing without a problem; however, Cyn acted like she was a cat about to be dropped into a full bathtub, and had to be lowered down by Jack. She was soft and warm, and for that moment, he felt like a normal person. He wanted...no, he needed to crush her to him; he needed to feel something besides the craving for darkness that was eating him up.

"Don't let me fall!" Cyn hissed, gripping Jack around the shoulders as she reached out with a dainty foot for the prow of the boat. She was feather-light and Jack held her tight and only reluctantly let go once Pastor John had a grip of the stiff tactical gear she wore.

When she was safely in, Jack eased into the boat and then came the ungainly dance as the three of them tried to change their positions without capsizing the boat or falling in to join the endless parade of corpses.

Eventually they found their proper seats: Cyn in back working the outboard, while Jack and Pastor John sat in the front so they could push the bodies out of their way.

"What sort of power do you think the Pope has?" Jack asked the pastor after they had cleared the canal and were in the river of the dead and heading south, passing between Manhattan and Brooklyn.

"None at all," he answered and then pointed at the sky. "Any and all power is derived from the Lord."

Despite that the answer wasn't much of an answer at all and grated on Jack's nerves to no end, he had followed the pastor's finger and was still looking up when the sky rumbled and a train of planes could be seen rushing their way. They were monsters, the dragons of their age. They were B52s and B1s whose bellies opened wide to rain destruction. Each of the hundreds of planes held upwards of seventy-thousand pounds of explosives. In minutes all of New Jersey was covered in a cloud that stretched for miles from north to south.

Cyn stared into the west, long after Jack had to turn away. He faced the sun and let it warm his face. It was a pretty morning, cool and sharp, the sky a fine blue and the puffy clouds hanging over the ocean looked as though they had been painted on simply for his enjoyment. He did his best to focus on the clouds and not the death behind them —there had certainly been people still alive in New Jersey, hiding in cellars or holed up in banks.

In his mind, he saw the military was simply finishing what the ghouls had started, or rather, what Robert had started, with Jack's help. But he did not blame them; it would have been the height of hypocrisy to blame them for sacrificing the few in order to try to save the many.

The planes never stopped coming and the helicopters continually buzzed.

It was an hour long slog before the crossed beneath the Verrazano Narrows Bridge and the waters opened up. They were able to pick up speed and soon they were in the Atlantic with a fine spray in their faces. Cyn aimed the boat at the horizon where dark smudges were the only visible signs that the navy was still in position.

As they got closer, the ships loomed huge, monuments of steel and strength. There were dozens of ships and all were just about as useless in the face of the undead horde as the Air Force, and Jack had zero faith in them.

Jack tugged on the pastor's green shirt. "Ok, what sort of God-given power do you think the Pope has?" He wanted to be reassured on at least one front. The ships were making him nervous, especially one of the smaller ones that was kicking up a white wake as it sped right for them. By its size Jack guessed that it was some form of a destroyer.

"I wish I knew," the pastor said. "For my entire life I saw the Pope as simply the Bishop of Rome, the head of the Catholic church. A holy man for sure, but not one with powers greater than any other priest, unless you count his infallibility, which is unlikely to be able to help us against the demons."

"Maybe he has some supernatural powers that we don't know about," Jack said.

It felt like wishful thinking and Pastor John didn't reassure him with his terse answer. "Like, I said, I don't know." He then he turned to Cyn. "Cut the engine, and don't touch any weapons. We don't want to get shot out of hand." The destroyer had turned sideways on to them and was much bigger close up. It loomed like a grey wall and part way up was a sailor manning a 25MM chaingun. It was pointed right at them. Pastor John lifted his hands over his head.

Before Jack could get his hands in the air, a metallic voice boomed: "Turn around and head back to shore. We are not taking on refugees. I repeat: turn around."

The pastor stood up in the rickety aluminum boat, pointed to his uniform, and yelled: "I'm not a refugee. I'm Captain Corley, Army National Guard."

There was a long pause and then the metallic voice returned: "This is Commander Cyrus Taylor of the USS Orion. You are ordered to return to your unit with all possible speed."

"I can't," Pastor John, yelled back. "My unit was destroyed. Now please let us board, we have valuable information. We know how all of this started." This pronouncement was followed by an even longer pause and John added: "I'm a military chaplain. What I know has to go up the chain of command as fast as possible."

The reply was a curt: "Proceed aft. Leave all of your weapons in the boat."

"Aft is the back of the ship," Pastor John said to Cyn, pointing.

"Is that right?" she asked, sarcastically, giving Jack a wink. "Is that where they put it?" The pastor was too preoccupied to answer. Jack thought it strange that while Cyn looked relieved at being allowed to board, the pastor was suddenly grim and seemed to be under a great deal of stress.

A webbing of rope was slung down from the back of the swaying destroyer. Jack boosted Cyn up toward it and only when she was halfway up did he notice that she had disobeyed orders and had the shotgun slung across her back. He went next and he too brought a weapon: his rapier.

Only Pastor John went up weaponless; he had his crucifix stuck in his belt and that was it. Though he was last to man the rope and he was fifteen years older than Jack, the captain climbed so quickly that he was on deck first. He snapped to attention, saluted first the flag at the back of the destroyer and then Commander Taylor, who was a stern-faced officer with flinty eyes that were the exact match in color as the ocean that the destroyer was rolling on.

"Permission to come aboard, sir?" Pastor John asked.

The commander dropped his salute, replying: "Granted." Taylor seemed to enjoy his long pauses and they suffered through another one as he gazed at the three of them. Finally he turned to another officer who stood just behind him: "Get us back on station while I figure out what this is about."

The other officer left and then Taylor beckoned them to follow. Quietly he led them through a ship that was so tight that there were times that even Cyn had to plant her back against a bulkhead to let a scurrying sailor move by. Everything was steel and hard and dreary; once below decks there wasn't an ounce of natural light and a heavy feeling of oppression descended on Jack as though his yoke was weighted down with the mass of the ship as well as his pain and guilt.

Behind them walked two sailors, each armed with pistols, and when they finally came to Taylor's office, Cyn and Jack were disarmed by the men and then all three were frisked before they were allowed to enter. When they did,

Pastor John stood at attention in front of the commander's desk, and again Taylor appraised them; he looked like a poker player about to call a bluff. "Start talking," he said simply.

Although the order was directed at the pastor, Corley glanced to Jack to begin, but Jack found himself tongue tied—telling the story would involve admitting to acts that were so appalling that he didn't know if he could bring himself to say them out loud.

When he hesitated, Cyn took over, telling the story from beginning to end. As she spoke, the commander's eyes narrowed until they were slits. In response to what she thought was skepticism, Cyn's voice grew sharp: "If you don't believe me, I have proof." As evidence she showed the commander the pictures on her phone of the first two sacrificed men, and then she had Jack's rapier brought from the hall.

When Taylor touched the darkened blade, his eyes shot open. "What the hell?" he growled, pulling his hand back. He was no coward and a second later he forced himself to handle and inspect the blade more thoroughly.

"It's what happens when you cut one of them," Jack said, not looking past the blade and into the commander's eyes. There was a sense of ugly judgment emanating from the man that Jack certainly deserved, but didn't care for. "They spread their filth through contact."

"Well," Taylor said, finally placing the rapier on his desk. He glanced once at his hands and then wiped them on his khaki pants. He didn't say anything more for at least a minute and when he spoke, he didn't speak to any of them. He picked up a phone, hit a button and said: "I'm going to need a ride over to the flag ship and get someone on the line over there, I need to speak to Admiral Owens ASAP. Tell them it's a priority."

Cyn gave him a look of mild surprise. "So you believe us? I have to say I'm a little shocked."

Taylor grunted: "You haven't seen my briefings. The footage of what's going on is sick and it jibes with what you told me. Really that damned sword is enough to merit a meeting with the admiral, and he'll want to hear all of this. I don't know what he'll do about it, but he'll want to hear it."

Things moved with military precision and speed; in eight minutes the four of them were boarding a helicopter. As soon as they were buckled in, the beastly craft shot straight up into the sky, sending Jack's stomach into his throat. Cyn's hand found his and he gave her a smile, not knowing if he was comforting her or if it was the other way around. Either way, he was glad for the touch; it calmed his nerves.

He wasn't afraid of any admiral, not after the crazy crap he'd lived through over the last few days. What made his stomach go wonky was the idea that they would have to tell their story yet again and that they would be judged yet again and who knew how many people would be in attendance this time? A dozen? Two dozen? And how many of them would say: *You did what you had to do* or *We should be hanging a medal on your neck for going above and beyond.*

Jack guessed the number would be zero.

Instead, they would look at him out of the corner of their eyes with disgust, but that was only if he was lucky. If he wasn't, they would sneer openly in contempt and talk about murder charges and prison sentences.

The idea grated on him and fed the anger and the hate that had been with him since Loret gave up the third spell —and the yoke started swinging over—Jack was suddenly very aware of the proximity of the rapier, that elegant killing machine.

"It'll be ok," Cyn said, and then glanced down at their locked hands. He had been gripping her hand far harder than he had meant to.

"I'm sure you're right." He didn't believe it.

They buzzed across open ocean, never climbing more than a hundred yards off the white caps. Then before them was the most massive vessel Jack had ever seen. The carrier was a monster, a marvel of man's ingenuity, capable of destroying a city, of ruining a country, of changing the course of history.

Jack found himself sneering at it.

The yoke upon him was hard over to the wrong side. Within him was a power beyond even the carrier. "Hey!" Cyn yelled over the roar of the helicopter's engine. "Relax. You're breaking my hand."

She gave him a grin, but there was worry in it. He liked it, but not in a perverse way. No one had worried for him for years…no one had even cared about him for years. The closest he had to anyone considering his well-being was the finance lady back at NYU; she was very quick to call if he was late with one of his checks.

Cyn pulled her hand away, shook it, and then grabbed his again. He didn't think she would and that little thing, her taking his hand, had the heavy yoke swinging back and finally he felt a warmth that he'd been longing for. It lasted right up until he saw Commander Taylor looking at their hand holding with a touch of contempt. They had told him that they were cousins; they hadn't told him that they were very distant third cousins.

The look made Jack's teeth snap together and the yoke swung once more heavily back into a bad place. He was very much aware of it now, that terrible hateful feeling and he was able to keep from crushing Cyn's hand but he wasn't able to stop the hate from hanging like a cloud over his mind. He was still dwelling on that hard feeling when they landed on the carrier and before he knew it, they were being rushed off the chopper, yanked along by sailors in bulbous helmets.

They crossed a flight deck that radiated so much heat that the air shimmered and then they were down in another maze of steel corridors. Stairs led up then down and up again. Jack was quickly lost which didn't help his mood and he wanted to just stop and cry: *Do you know who I am?*

When he heard the voice—his own voice in his mind, he laughed aloud. It was preposterous. He was no one at all. He was less than worthless. The yoke was spinning now.

Jack went into the meeting with a bizarre feeling completely taking over his mind. He was drunk with power and at the same time as humble as an ant.

They left the cramped maze where everything was strictly utilitarian and entered a suite that was uber manly in its theme: dark mahogany walls, leather reclining chairs and matching couch, a wet bar with a bottle of thirty-year old scotch sitting out. They sat there in silence, just the four of them, until a lieutenant opened the door and called the room to attention.

Admiral Owens, a buffalo of a man with a ruddy face and iron-grey hair, swept in, followed by six captains, none of whom were introduced and all of whom seemed far more senior to Captain Corley, leading Jack to guess that a captain in the army wasn't equal to a captain in the navy.

Next to Jack, both Captain Corley and Commander Taylor stood ramrod straight and snapped up stiff salutes. They extended military pleasantries with the admiral and then came a long moment—military officers seemed to enjoy long moments, it appeared to Jack—and then the admiral said: "Well, let's hear what you have to say."

Jack kept his eyes down as Cyn again told their story. She didn't sugar coat a sentence of it. Jack came across as a monster looking to cut or kill people without a qualm as long as he could get their blood or steal their life. Of course, she mentioned the extenuating circumstance, the river filled with corpses, the road paved with the dead, the knowledge that this was just the beginning, but all Jack felt was shame and guilt...and anger.

Always anger.

He stewed in it until he couldn't follow the conversation that began around him once Cyn's story was done.

Questions were asked, perhaps of Jack, he didn't know. He kept his eyes down and his mind closed.

The only thing that brought him around was when Admiral Owens waded into another lengthy pause. The pause was as wide as it was long and no one spoke or even moved much—except Jack, who stirred as if coming awake. He wanted to ask: *Are we done? Can we go?*

Cyn nudged him with her arm and then told him with a down turn of her brows to remain quiet.

Finally, the admiral stirred: a long sigh, a shake of his head and then a shrug was followed by: "This is quite a lot to take in. Really...really I'm not sure if I believe you and if I do, I'm not sure what I should do about it. One man started all of this? We thought it was the Muslim Brotherhood."

"No," Cyn said. "It was just Robert."

One of the captains, a small man, neat and trim with almost no lips, spoke up: "I believe this information is fortuitously timed, especially concerning our new orders. It gives me hope at least."

"May I ask what orders you're referring to?" Pastor John asked.

"The orders are *need to know* only," another of the captains said, dismissing the junior officer. He then faced the trim captain. "I think I have the exact opposite take, Blaine. You heard what became of their monsignor; he couldn't take on a single one these demons."

Captain Blaine didn't bat an eye. "This is different, Brewer. This is bigger! We've all heard the reports, but this is first-hand information. Yes, this monsignor couldn't hold his own, but we don't know him, we don't know how *Godly* he really was. But I don't think we can doubt..." He stopped before he could give away his secret, but he needn't have worried, Pastor John's eyes were widening.

"You're bringing in the Pope?" he asked, breathlessly.

Jack knew they were, the second every officer clammed up and began shifting their eyes back from one to another. Finally, the admiral admitted: "*We're* not bringing him in. He's here already, at the White House, I mean. Since everything on the land side of the war has been one giant cock-up right from the start, we will be providing air coverage for the Holy Father. He's going to attempt to put a stop to this."

"I need to see him!" Jack cried, stepping up to the desk. "He can't face the creatures until I talk to him. He doesn't know what he's getting into."

The admiral leaned back, calmly folding his hands over his belly. "Settle down, son. You're wrong on all accounts. The Pope knows the score. I'm not a rosary-rattler, but I got to hand it to him, he volunteered right off the bat. He flew in last night with a whole mess of cardinals. Our mission is to provide aerial reconnaissance and support as well as emergency evac if needed."

"He needs me," Jack said.

"I doubt it," the admiral replied with narrowed eyes. "All that blood and body of Christ stuff, that's metaphorical. It's not real, so you can cool your jets. The Pope doesn't need some sort of satanic advice."

"But he needs my advice," Jack insisted, ignoring the word "satanic" as well as the somewhat snide way the admiral was looking at him. "I know why the monsignor lost. He was too righteous. He was too much a man of God. He wasn't willing to get down in the dirt and really fight and if the Pope won't get mean then he won't stand a chance, either."

Chapter 38

The Atlantic Ocean

Jack pounded the admiral's desk and demanded that a helicopter whisk him off to the White House so that he could confer with the Pope. When that was answered with a grunting laugh, he begged on his hands and knees and there were real tears in his eyes.

The Pope was Jack's last hope. If he failed, then who would the world turn to? Jack supposed that there were other holy men and women and guessed that other denominations had their leaders, but if the Pope was killed, would they step up? Would they rush forward, eager to take on millions of ghouls and demons, single-handedly?

Unlikely.

This made the Pope's success all the more important. If he failed then it would be up to Jack to figure out a way to deal with his cousin—and that meant more death and murder and more guilt. It meant digging up grave after grave in an attempt to find someone with any answers. It meant the yoke sliding permanently to the wrong side.

In truth, it meant the end of Jack Dreyden. He was already changing. What would another twenty murders do to him?

"Save the crocodile tears," the admiral snapped, "and get your hands off of me."

Surprisingly, Pastor John came to Jack's aide. "I think you should listen to him. The monsignor was a good man and a valiant one. He had complete faith in the Lord and yet that wasn't enough. Jack has fought these creatures. He knows them better than anyone. The Pope needs to hear what he has to say."

"I agree," Cyn said, pulling Jack to his feet. "Feel that sword of his, Admiral. This has been going on for two days, have you heard of anyone fighting them with a sword? Have you heard of anyone fighting them and actually coming out alive? He's done it time and again and if he has advice then it should be bloody-well listened to."

Admiral Owens glanced at his assembled officers; two were noncommittal, issuing only shrugs, two, Blaine and Brewer nodded, though reluctantly, and the final two shook their heads: The last saying: "This is the Pope. I don't picture him riding a white charger into battle and brandishing a flaming sword."

"That's immaterial," Jack shot back. "He's going into battle and whether he is armed with a sword or with some sort of spiritual power doesn't make a difference. The concept of fighting is the same. He should know what the demons are capable of. He should know how they react. He should know their strengths and weaknesses."

"That actually makes sense," Admiral Owens said. "Forewarned is forearmed. It's what we preach in the military on a daily basis. Brewer, find out how much time we have. Blaine, prepare a chopper. The rest of you return to your stations; you have your orders."

In proper military fashion, there was a flurry of activity and then a long wait. Jack and Cyn ate and drank and then fell asleep leaning against each other on the admiral's couch, and they were both too tired to care that they looked more like lovers than cousins.

It took two hours for even a man as high-ranking as the admiral to get hold of someone on the Pope's "protection detail." The detail consisted of a battalion of marines, each of whom volunteered to be baptized and blessed.

Once they reached the officer in charge, Colonel JT Abrams, there was another long wait as the situation was explained up the chain of command within the Pope's entourage.

At noon, the request was denied. "The word is that the Holy Father has the power of God on his side,"

Colonel Abrams said over a radio that cracked and hissed. "I'm to tell you that it will be enough."

"Then we take the helicopter and go anyway," Jack insisted, scratching the side of his face and looking around for his sword. He was a touch bleary from the long nap and it was a moment before he saw the sword leaning against the wall.

Before he could get it, Owens stood up and walked the length of his office three times before he finally shook his head. "He's the closest person to God that we have on our side. I won't gainsay him."

"Maybe he's right," Cyn said. "Maybe we should have faith." Her eyes were tired and twitchy; Jack could tell that she didn't believe the words that came out of her mouth.

The admiral left to oversee reconnaissance operations. Two unmanned *Fire Scouts*, which were dreadfully ugly little helicopters that were jammed with electronics, and a *SH-60 Seahawk* helicopter that could stay on station for three hours were sent over Philadelphia, which had been evacuated the night before, along with Delaware, eastern Maryland and half of Pennsylvania.

The Pope, his squadron of cardinals and his battalion of US Marines were shuttled to the edge of the expanding Dead Zone: Philadelphia, the *City of Brotherly Love.* It was eerily dead. Its streets strewn with empty cars, its buildings dark. It looked as though it had already been lost in battle.

With rockets and bombs flying overhead, a Mass was conducted by Cardinal Michael Tuccillo, Archbishop of Vienna, who, at sixty-eight, was the youngest of the clergy in attendance. He had a lilting Italian accent and an oratory style that was both fluid and enticing, and, by the end of the Mass, all eight-hundred marines that had packed into Saint John's Evangelical Church, glowed with a heat that they had never felt before.

Jack and Cyn watched the feed from the three recon birds on a tremendous television hanging from a wall in the admiral's office. What they saw didn't make sense: two companies of marines marched in formation straight across the Benjamin Franklin Bridge, the last intact bridge over the Delaware River. Behind them came the Pope, carrying a tremendous wood cross high in the air, and leading a phalanx of cardinals. Behind them came the last two companies of marines.

"Why aren't they taking their tanks and stuff?" Jack asked. They had left behind millions of dollars in valuable military hardware: tanks, armored personnel carriers, and Humvees loaded down with fifty cals and machine guns. "This doesn't make any sense," he said and then picked up the phone that sat on the admiral's desk.

A woman answered: "This is the bridge, Commander Turner, speaking."

"Hey, my name is Jack Dreyden, is uh, the admiral there? We have a problem already with the Pope."

"The admiral is very aware of the situation, thank you," Turner replied, coldly. "Please refrain from using this line. Out."

She hung up so quickly that Jack stared at the phone in confusion. "She was rude," he said. "She basically hung..."

"Forget that Jack," Cyn said, jumping up and pointing at the screen. The marines in front of the papal procession had cleared the far side of the bridge.

They were technically in Camden, New Jersey, though it looked more like the ruins of Beirut in the eighties. It was a tumbled land of bent steel, shattered glass and dust. Not a building had been left untouched by the constant bombing, while the streets were no longer streets; they were cratered and tortured. Everywhere there were mounds of rubble alive with stakes of rebar and spears of glass.

The undead had been held back by firepower alone and even as they watched, bones began skittering across the ground as the bodies of the ghouls and demons were being reformed.

The leading companies of marines advanced, spreading out, moving into this hell on earth and, as they did, the warm glow on their faces drained away to be replaced by grim lines of reality. They were few while their enemies were legion. The dead city of Camden slowly came alive as the shelling ended and the planes disappeared over the horizon. The fires burned low, consumed by the cold and the smoke mixed with the coming darkness.

It was midday, yet a great bank of darkness hung over the city and it slowly came to engulf the marines and the priests. It surrounded them as deep as the sea. The men faltered, but the Pope led them to one of the greater mounds of debris and toiled up its slope. He stood, an old man in white, leaning on his cross and his breath came in gusts, like little clouds.

The cardinals, struggling against age and the weight of their chin-to-toe vestments pushed up the mound to stand around their leader and the marines surrounded them with their all but useless weapons pointed out; so far, none had fired. So far the undead were content to gather round, growing their numbers.

"This is wrong," Jack said. "They shouldn't be just standing there, they should be attacking. They should be driving their enemies away, before their numbers grow too great."

"Maybe it's not about numbers," Cyn suggested. "Maybe it's about faith. Maybe you should have more faith in them."

The ugly in Jack wanted to lash out at Cyn in sudden violence. A part of him despised her just then. A part of him wanted to scream into her face and tell her that what she had just spilled out of her mouth was so profoundly stupid it was embarrassing.

He hated this feeling and he hated himself for feeling it.

"It's not about numbers," he said after taking a deep breath and forcing a smile onto his face, "and it's not about faith. It's about *power* and who has it and who doesn't.

And it's about who knows how to use their power and I'm afraid that the Pope doesn't know how yet."

Cyn flicked her eyes at Jack, but said nothing.

For a full minute they were quiet and then Cyn gasped. The darkness surrounding the marines had surged forward as though a hole had appeared in the ocean of darkness and the water was rushing in to fill it. Their feed was silent, but they could imagine the screaming and the crash of automatic weapons.

The darkness washed right over the marines and all that could be seen of them were hundreds of pricks of lights going off in a circle around the mound. The darkness ran right up to where the cardinals formed their uneven perimeter. The old men backed up as the Pope raised the heavy cross and looked up, past the circling helicopters, past the sky of blue and beyond any boundary of space.

Jack could see his lips moving...right up until the darkness spilled over the grey cardinals in all of their flowing finery and surged up the Pope in white.

"No," Cyn said in a feeble whisper. She grabbed his hand and stared with wet eyes as the blackness swirled and pulsed.

In those seconds, Jack felt the hate in him grow stronger. What he was watching was validation that hate was stronger than love. That evil was stronger than goodness. He was seeing that there wasn't much power in God, after all.

But then the screen lit up in a brilliant white light that exploded outward and they could see ghouls blasted back, some flying in pieces. Next to him, Cyn was jumping up and down, pumping her fist, screaming: "Yes! Yes! He did it! He did it!" She slammed into Jack and hugged him so hard that he thought his ribs would snap.

Cyn was crying with joy and at first Jack was feeling the same and the evil, hate that had been eating him up was banished. The Pope was untouched, as were his cardinals. They had held firm and their power was undeniable.

The same could not be said of the marines. Cyn sobered as the cameras swiveled away from the Pope and to the men that were supposed to be protecting him. Half were dead or missing and the other half was sheeted in ice and shivering, their fingers frozen to their assault rifles.

Some were horribly injured, missing hands and arms, their bellies torn open. They rolled on the ground in mortal agony and Jack knew their pain, he knew the pain that hell inflicted. It was a pain that drew compassion from the hardest of hearts and it drew it at the worst possible time.

"No," Jack whispered. "Leave them."

The cardinals were coming down from the mound, some slipping on the demon-ice and some tripping on the unevenness of the ground and some just gimpy from their advanced age. Slowly they made their way among the marines and when they touched the injured, the men appeared to wilt in relief.

"Leave them!" Jack yelled, thumping the desk. Cyn gave him a look of disbelief and he pointed at the television. "The battle's not over! The demons aren't dead. Look you can see the darkness creeping forward again. Now's not the time for this, or they should have brought priests. It's not a job for cardinals. All it's doing is weakening them."

"But they..." Cyn began. Then her eyes caught the slow insidious motion of the demon-fed darkness—it was creeping back, little by little, and within it hid the countless ghouls. "You're right," Cyn said. "We should warn someone."

She had the phone up to her ear before Jack could stop her. "They'll never hear. You can't use radios or phones in the middle of a horde like that, remember? Besides..."

Jack paused as the noise outside the carrier, what was a constant thrum and whoosh of planes taking off or landing, suddenly spiked as a dozen or more helicopters throttled up their engines. "Now's not the time for that either! What is wrong with these people?" The anger and the hate, which had been swept away just like the darkness had been, were creeping back.

"They're just doing what they think is right," Cyn told him.

"Listening to me would have been the right thing to do. Look." The darkness was at the base of the mound once more, only this time it was the black of the abyss. Impenetrable. It was about to surge again and this time the good guys were in disarray.

The marines no longer held a unified front. Their lines were in shambles. They were practically unarmed. Most had discovered that their M4s were useless against the bone creatures and while some had thrown their weapons away, the rest had turned the guns around to use them as clubs.

It showed that they still had a fighting spirit and Jack thought it good that they would at least go down swinging. The same could not be said of the cardinals. These old men were arrayed all over the mound and most looked beyond their age as they healed the wounded and cured the diseased—noble as these actions were, it was a waste of time and energy. They were at war and what was needed at that moment was firepower.

Just as Jack knew it would, the darkness came on again, engulfing the mound, running right up over the Pope and his great cross. There were flashes of light and explosions of flame in the darkness and the cameras picked up the valiant struggles of marines swinging their rifles and of cardinals in red and black shooting light from their hands.

It also showed them being overwhelmed and brought down by sheer numbers. Then came another violent blast of white light and the cameras were able to center on the Pope...alone.

There was no cheering this time. Cyn wobbled in place and Jack put out a hand to steady her. They could plainly see the hundreds of bodies. None had been left alive this time; there was no reason to have. The injured had been used to weaken the rest.

Now there was only one.

The Pope turned and saw the death all around him and what he was thinking Jack could not imagine. Should he retreat and live to fight another day? Should he make a stand and test the limits of his God-given power? Should he leap down among his enemies and scatter them to the wind or die trying?

The choices were taken out of the Pope's hands.

Out of the ringing darkness stepped a demon that Jack had seen before on a road in New Jersey. It was a tall bone-monster that was strung together by mildewed straw and in its eye sockets was graveyard dirt. The creature dragged a man behind it—one of the cardinals.

The cardinal had a gaping wound in his chest and both hands had been either torn off or bitten down to the wrists. As they watched, the bone-demon stabbed a finger into the cardinal's right eye and worked it around in circles.

"Oh God," Cyn whispered.

The demon then beckoned for the Pope to come down. "Don't do it!" Jack screamed at the television. The Holy Father stood his ground. They could see him talking, his eyes angry and his gestures threatening. The demon only grinned and pointed to his left where a second demon emerged; another one that Jack recognized.

This one's head was covered in a worm-eaten burlap sack—Jack never wanted to see what was beneath the sack; he was sure it would send him over the edge and he was very close to the precipice even then.

The burlap sack covered demon dragged forth, not another cardinal and nor was it one of the marines; it was a child, a stunned and pale child. From the high angle, Jack couldn't tell if it was a boy or a girl, but it didn't matter, the sight of the child staggered him.

It was clear that when the Pope dropped his chin to his chest that he had the same reaction. Seconds later, he began to nod to an unheard request. He pointed a wrinkled hand at the child and the demon let it go. But the child didn't run. It stood there in a fugue until the demon shoved it, and only then did it wander off. The child had been traded for the life of the Pope.

"No," Jack whispered. Inside he felt the yoke suddenly weighted down on the evil side by a thousand pounds of hate. It was a fire inside of him that grew hotter with each step the Pope took into the waiting darkness and when he finally disappeared, Jack exploded.

"Son of a bitch!" he screamed and in one move, he picked up one of the heavy leather chairs and flung it at the television set. It broke with a crash and then came off the wall to hang, suspended by a black cable.

Unfulfilled by this outburst, Jack picked up the phone. "This is your fault, Admiral! You did this! You killed..." he stopped and stared at the phone as the line went dead in his hands. He looked at it in confusion until he saw that it was Cyn who had disconnected him.

He was about to scream into her face when she stopped him with a single word: "No."

"No what?"

"It wasn't the admiral's fault, and it wasn't the Pope's either. And I'm sorry to say that even if you'd been allowed to go, the outcome wouldn't have been any different. They have an army, Jack. We had a bunch of very brave but very ill-prepared men."

Jack was holding in his anger by the barest of margins. "That's why they needed me. You even said so."

She shrugged. "It wouldn't have mattered. We had eight hundred and they had eighty-thousand or two-hundred thousand or two million. The battle might have lasted longer, but it wouldn't have ended any different, except you would be dead as well."

"So we need an army of our own," Jack said.

Cyn sat down and dug the heel of her palms into her weary eyes and without looking up, said: "Yes. We need every priest, rabbi and witch doctor in the world. If they can stop the darkness and the fear, we have a chance."

"No," Jack said.

She ignored him and went on planning: "And on top of that, we'll need an army of soldiers who are armed with shotguns and swords and battle axes." She sighed heavily and added: "We'll lose millions, but we can beat Robert. That's the lesson we should learn from today."

She was wrong. "And what happens when he raises another army. I hate to break it to you but there are now tens of millions of bodies out there just waiting for a demon to take up residence. And do I need to remind you that we don't even know how to kill the ones we have already?"

Cyn jumped up and stared angrily into Jack's face: "Then what do we do? Huh? You can throw a tantrum and blame everything on the admiral, but you just admitted that we don't know how to kill them. So what do we do? Give up? I don't care if they have an unstoppable army, giving up is a coward's way out and I never pegged you for a coward, Jack. You may be a second-rate necromancer and a hack with the sword, but you're not a coward."

Before he knew it, his hand shot out and grabbed the collar of the white shirt she wore beneath her tactical vest and for a moment the yoke was so far over that he was tempted to punch her in the face. He held back, but couldn't hold back the sneer.

"Second-rate necromancer?" he asked in a soft, evil voice. "That's where you're wrong. I'll show you what a real necromancer can do."

Chapter 39

The Atlantic Ocean

The mood on the carrier, from the greenest sailor right on up to the fleet admiral, was one of total defeat. When the Pope went under the darkness, there was a full two minutes of stunned silence before Admiral Owens sent in the fourteen SH-60 Seahawks he had hovering nearby in order to execute whatever evacuation could be accomplished under the conditions.

To the pilots, it was as if they were hovering over an alien world. The darkness could not be swept away by the powerful downwash of the blades. From the air, nothing could be seen of the ground except for the tips of a few buildings and three of the birds crashed with all hands while trying to find the point where the darkness ended and the land began.

One had a rotor clip the side of a building and in a second the machine was on its side and falling like only 17,000 pounds of metal could. There was a single alarmed cry of "Mayday!" a flash of orange light within the darkness, and then nothing.

The other birds carried on with their mission, but were called off when first one Seahawk and then another dipped slowly beneath the roiling darkness and never came back up.

Twenty minutes later, the Admiral was given the order to begin bombing and missile attacks once more. To Jack it was a declaration of defeat. The bombing announced to the world that the military, the White House, and even organized religion were all out of ideas; all they could do was slow the attack, but they couldn't stop it.

The Navy's targets were now the west bank of the Delaware River and a line along highway 76 cutting across Pennsylvania, though this was gradually moved south again and again as somehow the creatures kept advancing.

Jack and Cyn were alone together for over an hour and in that time they didn't speak or sit near each other. Cyn leaned back on the couch, staring at the ceiling, while Jack sat on one of the comfortable chairs; though he didn't do much sitting. The idea brewing in his head had him pacing half the time.

He couldn't sit still. Now that he had decided to use his power, it ate at him. The spell demanded to be used. Something inside of him demanded blood. It was the ugliest feeling in the world. Thoughts of murder continually lit upon his mind like blowflies on a dead coon lying in a ditch.

The spell drove him to distraction. He paced and he balled his fists and he pulled at his hair until Owens finally came back into his office; he was more alarmed at Jack's appearance than he was angry over his destroyed television set. He was accompanied by only two captains this time, Blaine and Brewer. Both were too stunned by the loss of the Pope to dwell on a broken television, either.

"You were right," Owens said to Jack, taking a seat behind his desk, seeming to use it as a barrier between him and Jack.

"I wasn't, actually. I know that now. If I had gone, nothing would have changed, but...but we have a new plan." He tried on a disarming smile, but it sat as crooked on his face as the television sat on the wall.

Cyn waved a finger at Jack. "Don't say we. I'm not a part of any plan of yours. I can tell what you're thinking, Jack and it's bloody awful. I don't want any part of it."

The blowflies were back in an instant and the growing evil in Jack wanted to teach her a lesson in manners. It wanted to break her. It wanted to hurt her and he was half turned around in his chair when the phone buzzed and a male voice said: "Sorry, Sir, but Captain Corley and Commander Price would like to see you and your guests."

"Send them in," Owens replied, with a voice as dry and old as sand.

Price was obviously a preacher of some sort. To Jack, he had the look: white hair, soft hands, a bible clutched in them of course, and a sad, kindly smile.

It was a look that Pastor John had never mastered and now he was even further from it. He had changed in the last few hours: his eyes were red from crying, yet they were also hard and mean. His mouth was small and set grim. His lips were so drawn in that they no longer looked as though they were capable of speech; however, after a very quick salute to the admiral, he asked Jack: "What do you know? You were going to share ideas concerning fighting these monsters with the Pope, what were they?"

"Excuse me, Captain," the admiral growled. "Since when does an Army captain barge into an admiral's office and start making demands? Jack was actually about to discuss a new plan. We can deal with you in a second."

Pastor John turned his newly hardened eyes to the admiral. "Sorry to say this, sir, but today, I outrank you."

The two men glared at one another and into the silence that dragged on, Jack wanted to say: *I outrank you both*. It was no exaggeration. Cyn had called him a second rate necromancer and even if that were true, it still gave him strength beyond any of the men in the room.

"I will answer Pastor John, first," declared Jack, taking the power of leadership away from both men and claiming it as his own. "The Pope made the same mistakes as the monsignor. He did not treat the battle as a battle. He marched into the middle of tens of thousands of ghouls and basically figured that God would do his fighting for him. I'm sorry, but God stopped doing personal appearances eons ago and even then, when did he ever fight man's battles for him?"

"Never," Pastor John replied in a heartbeat. "The closest I can recall is in the book of Joshua in the battle against the Amorites, the Lord 'rained down hailstones' on the enemies of Israel."

The evil part of Jack reared up and put a smirk on his face. "Hailstones," he said with a little grunt of laughter and then immediately regretted it. How on earth, after everything he'd gone through and had seen, could he mock God? He closed his eyes and again balled his fists, fighting the evil down into the pit of his stomach where it burned and frothed the acid, unpleasantly.

After a breath, he went on: "The point is God helps man, he doesn't live his life for him or step in every time things get hairy. The Pope didn't fight. He didn't wage war. His cardinals healed and blessed, both good things of course, but neither can win war."

"So what would you have us do?" Commander Price asked and then gestured to where Jack's rapier sat leaning against the desk. "Do you want a bunch of priests to beat our plows into swords and fight these monsters toe-to-toe?" He seemed outraged at the idea.

"Yes," Jack answered, staring the man right in the face. "Some of you, like the good pastor here, are fully capable of fighting. If you can't, then you can fill an auxiliary role. Did you see the marines yesterday? None of them seemed to have been affected by the fear. I've seen firsthand a priest counteract both the fear and the darkness. Just think if the priests were trained to hold back the darkness."

The admiral nodded with bright eyes. "And what if the marines had better weapons? M4s won't cut it, but 242s might and shotguns and grenades would definitely slow them down and ruin their day."

"And better tactics," Captain Blaine put in. "From what I saw, it was every man for himself. They need to work in teams."

"And they need to meet force with overwhelming force," Captain Brewer said. "They were ridiculously overwhelmed…and what about the stronger ones, the demons? How do we fight them?"

This brought on a silence, one that Jack could appreciate. They were finally thinking, properly. They were analyzing their enemies, looking for weaknesses and strengths. They were planning—all so much better than walking in to hell with only a faith in God as armor. Faith only went so far. It had to be backed up by good works and hard blows.

The admiral broke the silence. "The question is, how do you kill them? That's what really needs to be answered here, Jack."

"Yeah, Jack," Cyn said. "How do you kill them?" Her look was crystal over granite; beauty with a deadly ice to it. "You've got all these military men plowing through stratagems, but there's something you aren't telling them. These monsters are unkillable. They are souls or the perverted twisted shadows of them, and how do you kill shadows?"

"Only light destroys shadows," Pastor John said with confidence.

Cyn looked to Jack. "Is that your idea as well? Using light?" The naval officers and the one army chaplain leaned it towards Jack, expectantly, but it was Cyn who answered her own question. "No, he is looking to destroy the shadows by drowning them in darkness. I know it Jack. I know what you're thinking."

He shrugged because what could he say? "She's right, I don't know how to kill them, at least not yet. Has anyone tried silver bullets?" He meant it to be an offhand joke, more to deflate Cyn than to garner an answer.

"Yes," the admiral said. "Silver, platinum, palladium, every metal that could be grabbed on short notice. We've had teams of Delta operators try them all. They even had some of the bullets blessed to see if that would work. They tried everything. They dipped bullets in Holy Water and in Holy Oil. They even tried different kinds of wooden projectiles thinking that stakes would do the trick. Nothing worked, none of the teams returned."

Jack glanced at Cyn; she was blinking slowly, her eyes on the floor. The rest of the room was looking to Jack. They knew he had a plan, but it was such an awful plan that he was slow to give it up. "If we want to win...if we want to defeat the creatures, I'm going to need a man...someone dispensable," he said in a whisper.

The admiral's face lost color as he asked: "Why?"

"I think you know why," Jack answered, not looking up. There was a quiver of excitement inside him. He knew they would hem and haw over his idea but they would agree in the end. And they wouldn't just agree to let him sacrifice a man to the Gods of the Undead, they would help him. The idea sent a queer shiver up his back.

He loved the feeling and hated it. It made his nerves crawl and his stomach wanted to puke up his very spleen —and at the same time, he started to get an erection. He swallowed back the bile and the nasty feeling growing in his loins and threw out a last life line. "I guess there may be other ways...exorcism. It'll be a one at a time thing but, you never know."

Admiral Owens seemed put off by the idea. "Exorcisms? That would take years."

In truth it would take forever, Jack knew. There were always more undead for Robert to create, an entire plane of un-existence filled with the damned. "You can also lock up the pieces," he said in a desperate gamble to save his own soul. "If you hacked off the limbs and encased them in iron boxes..."

"Oh stop it, Jack!" Cyn seethed. "These ideas might work against a stray demon or two, but against an army of them, never. So why don't you spit out what you really want to do? You want to create your own army, don't you? You want to replace Robert!"

Yes! he wanted to cry. In fact, he wanted to scream it at the top of his lungs. It was his birthright. The power of the three spells was his to command and had been since before his father's father was born. He knew it deep in the rotten part of his soul which ached and seethed. He didn't know if that part of him had remained hidden or unknown or unexplored all his life, or if it had only just grown like a weedy, unkillable form of hemlock or arsenic in the last few days.

He didn't know and it was hard for him to care.

"I don't know about replacing Robert," he said at last. "I just know that death begets death. Does it not? I know that only a stronger demon can kill a weaker one. I know this may be our only chance."

Cyn wouldn't back down; in fact, she stepped forward, challenging him. "You should see yourself, Jack. You've changed. You're asking us to agree to replace Satan with Lucifer."

Jack was glad that he couldn't see himself. He hated what the power of the spells was doing to him and yet he didn't think he could stop it even if he wanted to, and really, he didn't know if he wanted to.

All he knew was that it was eating him up from the roots of the soul out and before he knew it, he was on his feet and the rapier that had been leaning against the desk, just another piece of metal, was suddenly in his hand and he was lunging at Cyn, that ugly part of him in full control, the sword raised.

He was fast, but Pastor John was closer; he stepped between Jack and his cousin. "Stop," the pastor said, just a soft word. Jack didn't just stop, he bounced back as though the pastor's outstretched hand was the wrong end to Jack's magnet.

The little scene spanned all of two seconds and yet it cast a pall in the room. Eyes flicked around: the admiral to the commander, the pastor to the captain. Eyes flicked and yet no one looked into Jack's face, perhaps afraid of what they would see there.

The silence was like a murderer's wake, it went on and on so very uncomfortably until Commander Price spoke. "The analogy is not without merit," he said, slowly as if dipping his toe in the water, as if the sword wasn't still in Jack's hand. "Lucifer was an angel."

"Ha!" Cyn laughed, cruelly, seeming to want to hurt Jack. "An angel!" She was either on the verge of tears or a volcanic explosion. It was hard to tell which.

Jack was in his own volcanic state and could barely contain himself. Through gritted teeth, he said: "You shouldn't mock." It was a warning and she was lucky to get it. Had she been anyone else...he bit back the black thought and turned to the admiral. "If you want to stop the creatures, you'll do as I say. I need a man or a woman. I don't care which. It's not going to be pretty, so the more despicable the better. If you have a killer locked away in the ship that would work."

The full impact of what was being asked of the admiral struck him so that he went from a great bull of a man to a soft, wavering mushroom. "I-I don't know if we have anyone like that. This is a military ship. We have honor...and integrity. There are a few cases of insubordination and two or three guys busted for drug use, but no one like what you're asking for."

He turned to the other captains, both of whom shook their heads. Blaine said: "We could maybe try to get a prisoner released from a federal prison. It would take some time..."

"That'll take months," Jack said. "We don't have months or even days. We have hours, maybe. If Robert decides to make more of *them*, he may become unstoppable. So, right now I need you to do the unthinkable and give me someone. I don't know...an orphan, or someone without a wife and kids. The more unloved the easier it will be on everyone."

When the admiral hesitated, Cyn said: "Don't worry, Admiral, I know someone who fits the description and what's more, he is on this ship."

"Who is it?" the admiral asked. He was so undone by the revelation that from three feet away Jack barely heard the man's words.

"What we need is a murderer and an orphan, right? Someone without a wife or kids or loved ones...someone despicable, isn't that what you asked for, Jack?" She was staring right at Jack Dreyden. "He's closer than you think, Admiral."

Jack fit his own description perfectly.

Chapter 40

The deep black part of him was furious, ready to kill, only Jack was so hurt by the truth that a wave of depression washed over the anger and he shrugged in defeat; Cyn was right. He was fast becoming a monster. "Even if I was a candidate, who would kill me? Who would offer me up as a sacrifice? Would you do it, Cyn? Would you, Commander Price? Admiral? Who wants to step up and become a murderer?"

When no one answered, Jack said: "That's what I thought. Now, if you're done being nasty, Cyn, we still have an undead army to deal with. I need someone, Admiral, and don't bother volunteering. The life has to be taken."

"I can't believe I'm hearing this," Commander Price said. He cast a hard look at Pastor John. "Are you going to stop him or will I?"

"The enemy of my enemy," Pastor John answered, stiffly. Just as Jack had foreseen they did hem and haw and went back and forth over morality and all that business— he barely listened. They were going to give him a soul to sacrifice.

"That's what I wanted to hear," Jack said, trying to quell the excitement growing in him—he preferred the depression, only the wicked part of him was too strong and awful. He wondered if he was feeling the same sort of excitement that 16th century villagers felt before they filled their baskets for a fun-packed day of picnicking, socializing and witch-burning.

All he knew was that he felt disgusting, but when it came time to be baptized he backed away. "Don't bother.

I'll just get dirty again." Commander Price was only too happy to move on to the next member of the team.

Jack had asked for a live body to sacrifice and had received one and he'd asked for a team of Navy Seals to protect him and he'd gotten them as well. The platoon members of *Seal Team 8* were all tall, hard men who walked into the briefing room like military automatons, ready to carry out any mission without question...supposedly. During their briefing, Jack caught each of the men looking at him out of the corner of their eyes, some with their lips curled in revulsion.

He didn't care what they thought of him as long as they did their job. He was sure that they would. They became laser focused as they changed out their preferred weapons for weapons better suited for their mission. Soon they were festooned with grenades and draped in bandoliers of shotgun shells. Their canteens were filled with Holy Water and at their sides each carried a newly sharpened saber.

The sabers had been ceremonial "weapons," strictly for parades and full-dress occasions; still they were made of metal and after grinding stones were found, it was discovered that they could hold a very keen edge. Jack's rapier was cleaned, sharpened and, though he wouldn't allow himself to be blessed, he was happy to see the silver of his blade glistening with Holy Oil.

It was two hours from the moment he asked the admiral for a person to sacrifice until the helicopters lifted off. Just before they did, when the Seal team was lined up on the windswept flight deck, newly baptized, their weapons blessed, and looking ready to take on the army of undead single handedly, Jack noticed that there was one slight problem.

"There's one too many of you," he said. "We have two Seahawks and both can only carry eleven people. Do the math. Me, Cyn, Pastor John and our..." He didn't want to say *sacrifice*, but there really wasn't a better word. It was a man, as Jack expected it to be, and he stood against the wall swaying under the influence of an opiate of some sort or another that was being pumped into his system through an IV line. Jack didn't care what was in him just as long as he wouldn't struggle when the time came.

"...And our friend," Jack went on, gesturing in the direction of the sacrifice without actually looking at him. He hadn't really looked at the man yet and didn't plan on it until he absolutely had to. Nor did Jack know anything about him and he didn't want to know. "There are nineteen of you, do the math."

The Seal team, as quiet a group of men as Jack had ever seen, only glanced around at each other and then at Cyn. "I'm not going," she said. "These men are trained to fight and I'm not. I'd just get in the way."

He was strangely hurt that she didn't want to come, but instead of asking why or trying to understand as he would have only days before, anger swept him. It was petulant, childish and he snapped: "You are coming and that's final!"

Cyn was used to getting her own way and she squared her shoulders and marched straight back the way they had come—he caught her at one of the high-stepped doors that led into the bowels of the carrier; he was too rough as he yanked her around and she stared at him with such a cold look that even the hate within him took a step back.

"I'm not going, Jack! I'll jump out of that bloody helicopter if you..."

"I need you," he said interrupting.

The three words melted her hard-as-ice look and there were the beginnings of tears in her eyes only she dropped her chin to try to hide them. "I just want there to be another way," she said. "I want someone else to be the bad guy, not you." She tried to laugh away her tears as if they weren't important, as if they didn't mean anything. She ran a sleeve across her face and said: "Also I can't help but believe that bringing in more evil into the world will only make things worse. What if you can't control them?"

"Then we all die, but that was going to happen anyway." He was profoundly affected by the tears. They washed away the fires of his anger and turned the pillars of his hate into mud. They made his insides feel loose and his head giddy.

"Well, that's good," she joked and then her smile faltered and her tears sparkled. "How do you need me?"

He hadn't yet tried to put it into words, exactly why he needed the slip of a girl. She was his anchor, the one thing that kept the evil from taking over...really, she was the one thing that kept him from *allowing* the evil to take over. She had been right about him. He had basically been friendless before he met her. He had no family except her and no one to love, but her.

Without her, he had no reason to fight Robert other than the selfish desire to live and the even greater desire to wield his birthright and to conquer the world, to reshape it the way he felt it should be.

But he couldn't say any of this. She was his cousin. They barely knew each other. She was fine and beautiful. She was from the upper crust of British society. He was a dusty bookworm with a ferocious evil side that longed to kill.

He turned a shade of pink and made stuttering, vowel sounds: "I-I uh, uh, we-we...you-you were uh..."

The smirk that he loved to see came back and she said: "It's ok. I get it, at least I think so. I'll come with you. We'll do this together." There came an awkward moment where they grinned at each other. Jack wanted to take her hand and walk her back to the flight deck, but he feared that he would see judging looks on the part of the men and he feared even more the rage that would come when he did. He knew he was close to the edge of sanity.

The closer to the edge of hell he got, the closer he came to going stark raving mad. Or closer to becoming like his cousin: coldly insane.

The Seal's commanding officer, Lieutenant Jason Neilson, wasn't happy about losing a trained operator in favor of an untrained girl barely out of her teens. He looked to the admiral for support, but didn't get it. "Mr. Dreyden is in charge. What he says, goes."

"Yes, sir," Neilson said in a voiced drenched with anger. He turned to Cyn. "Ok, let's see what we have to work with." He walked a circle around her. And then took two bandoliers from one of the sailors. "Sorry McCullough, you're out and she's in." He handed the bandoliers to Cyn. "Good luck," he said, coldly. "You're going to need it."

"Sod off," she said right back.

This caused him to laugh. "That's a little better. Ok, men, let's mount up!"

Parked sixty feet down the deck from them were two SH-60s, already whipping their blades in a blur. The team was split into two groups. Jack rode with the sailor he was supposed to kill and nine Seals, including Lieutenant Neilson. Cyn, who had a second, unspoken reason for being with the team, rode with Pastor John.

It had occurred to Jack that if he was killed, someone would have to finish the job of stopping Robert. Cyn was the only one capable of doing this. Not only was she a linguistics major, specializing in ancient Egyptian, she also knew the first two spells and Pastor John knew the third.

The thought that someone else could wield the power of the spells made Jack a little edgy. He couldn't look at her without feeling the yoke on his shoulders lean to the dark side unless he took her in piece by piece: her worried blue eyes, her small, quick hands, her smile.

He wouldn't stop staring at her even when the choppers lifted off. He felt as though he could stare at her forever. Her blonde hair and the white oval of her face stood out among the swirls of green camouflage. She was captivating and she was also the only view that didn't make his stomach haul over like a capsizing ship.

In the SH-60 was the sacrifice—Jack couldn't even look in his direction—and the view below was terrifying. From the air it looked as though all of New Jersey was on fire, while New York City, once a glittering beacon of light, was hung in a pall of smoke and ash and within the gloom things moved, roaming and owning the streets.

"Tell them to slow down," Jack yelled into one of the crewmen's ear after they were well over the city. "I'll let you know when I see a good spot." The helicopters swept across Queens and crossed over Manhattan. Jack was forced to take in the view, horrible as it was. Bodies were everywhere; most were still, the blood around them dry and dark brown.

Their first landing point was at the north end of the island, Jack spotted an open field just south of the Harlem River and pointed to it. By happenstance it turned out to be Trinity Cemetery. "The more the merrier," he said under his breath.

Because of the trees and buildings, there wasn't room for both choppers to land simultaneously and so Jack's went in first. The moment it touched down, the Seal Team was out and moving in a crouch. They made the transition from the helicopter to the firm earth look easy. Jack's inner ear failed him as he hopped down; the world felt as though it was tipping and before he knew it, he was lurching sideways only to be caught by Lieutenant Neilson.

Cyn was out of sight while the sacrifice was right there, looking pale and oily. He had the air of a man who liked his girls young; not quite out of the first grade kind of young. Seeing him was all it took for the yoke to fall off into the dark. Jack was suddenly seething. The momentum of the spells so close to being called was too much for him. He tore his eyes away from the sacrifice and saw that he held a short piece of silver in his right hand, which he drove into Neilson's midsection for no other reason than because the Seal had the audacity to touch Jack's shirt.

The knife drove in and struck nothing but air. Neilson sidestepped the knife, easily tripped Jack and then clubbed him on the back of the head. He went limp, unable to stand or make any sense of what was going on around him.

There was a great deal of noise and wind that kicked up cyclones of black ash.

Hands grabbed him and spun him to face the sky and there was Cyn, leaning over him. "You ok, Jack?" Jack gave a weak nod and she said to Neilson: "This is my fault. I should have warned you that he gets a little crazy when he's doing the spells, they affect him, but he's actually a good guy."

Neilson didn't look at all as though he believed Jack was a good guy or anything close. "Let's just do..." One of his men fired his shotgun, the first of many shots. "Let's do this and go!"

Jack was hauled to his feet and then pushed to an open spot of concrete in front of a mausoleum; a second later the oily man with the pedophile eyes was rushed in front of him so that they were nose to nose. Neilson thrust the knife into Jack's hand and then everyone stepped back as if they expected Jack to slit the man's throat right there.

That wasn't how the spell worked. "Lay down," Jack growled.

The man was stoned on whatever the military was piping into his system and he said: "I am lying down, man." He swayed in place, looking placidly at the onrushing creatures. There were dozens and dozens.

The evil feeling in Jack was back stronger than ever, egged on by the thumping in his head where Neilson had pounded him. Jack yanked the man to the ground and without warning tore open the man's shirt, sending buttons flying.

"Hey," he said, confused. He had a tattoo on his hairless chest that had the word: *Mom* sitting in a red heart right over where his real heart was. The tattoo, as silly and clichéd as it was caused Jack to hesitate and just then he saw that the man wasn't much of a man—he was likely just a few weeks over eighteen; he was skinny, afraid, and tripping bad. He was someone to be pitied.

More gunfire, rapid and fast, woke Jack and killed any feeling but hate within him. In a quick move, Jack sliced the boy's chest open, cutting an inch deep into the muscle. The boy cried out and tried to sit up.

Savagely, Jack punched him square in the jaw, knocking him back down.

"Jack," Cyn said in a soft voice. "Do what you have to, but no more, please." He seethed, gripping the knife with a shaking hand, until Cyn held out a fine brush. It was new and unblooded. "Give me the knife, Jack," she said. Unafraid of him, she stared directly into his eyes until he nodded and switched out the tools of his trade.

The firing was becoming urgent and he saw that all around them ghouls were charging. They were the dreaded bone monsters woken from their ancient pits in Queens. The sky darkened from their amassed power as though night had come four hours early. The magical fear came with it, setting up a tremor in Jack's chest.

He was the only one affected by the fear. The newly blessed soldiers stood their ground and fired at point blank ranges, and Pastor John held out his crucifix and called forth a light that was harsh and unwavering centered upon his outstretched hand.

"Go on, Jack," Cyn said, nudging him. He found himself glaring at the light and the priest in unvarnished hate.

"Right," he said, remembering himself. He looked down at the blood welling from the wound he had caused. It called to him. It made him hungry. It made him hurt inside with a need that was appallingly evil. Dipping the brush, he began drawing the hieroglyphs; with each symbol, he would whisper the word as well.

No longer did he need to be urged on. The glyphs almost felt like they were painting themselves and in a minute and a half, he had drawn a single circle of glyphs—this was a variation of "Cyn's" spell, the first of four. It sat on the axis of the compass and directed the boundaries within which the dead could be raised.

That was the easy spell. The next spell, "his" was harder and drank from his soul.

When it was done, a tone sounded in his mind, like that of psychic bell ringing and it echoed deep and loud, setting off vibrations within him that pulsed and never quite died away. Jack stepped back, eager to get moving to the next, eager to finish the spells, eager for the power. Cyn began to read the glyphs, perhaps just checking his work, but he didn't need anyone to check. He *knew* it was right; that sound within him told him so.

It was the same sound and feeling he'd had when Robert had used the spells, so it was a good guess that Robert was even then sensing the same thing. His cousin probably knew exactly what they were trying to do, which meant they didn't have time to waste.

Standing, he pushed Cyn away. "It's good. I can feel it. And I bet Robert can to."

"Which means he's going to do all he can to stop you," Cyn said, her eyes shifting around as if she expected flying demons with tremendous batwings and claws like daggers to suddenly appear. "We have to get out of here." She waved to Neilson and gave him a thumbs up.

Neilson spoke into a throat mike and a second later one of the helicopters that had been hovering, pitched down and came at them so fast that Jack thought it would crash. At the last second, it flared up and landed as if it was settling down in an open field instead of tree-lined cemetery that was being attacked from every direction.

The boy with the bleeding cut across his chest and the "Mom" tattoo was still unconscious and so Cyn grabbed one arm and Jack the other. Together they dragged him to the helicopter. He was out cold, dead weight, but Neilson picked him up as if he were stuffed with feathers, and flung him into the copter.

Jack was shoved in next and found himself almost on top of the door gunner on the other side of the bird. The gunner was rock and rolling his weapon, blasting back the waves of ghouls, tearing them apart, littering the cemetery with bones. Hands and arms flew and skulls cracked like tea cups. The gunner wore a madman's grin and his eyes were huge and his hands like iron on the handle of his gun.

Then Jack felt his belly go light and they were lifting off, going straight up, allowing the second helicopter to land. And all the while, the gunner never let up. He kept up a steady firing until the moment the second copter lifted and then he sat back, his face breaking into a wide smile of relief.

All the men shared the same look and some were joking and some were high-fiving each other. Jack didn't want to burst their bubble and yet they had to know. "That was the easy one," Jack yelled into Neilson's ear. "We have three more and each is going to get harder. My cousin knows. Look!" Jack pointed down at the ghouls. Where before they had glanced up at the passing helicopter with only mild interest as they flew overhead, now they were turning in mass in the direction of the copter's path.

"That's not good," the lieutenant exclaimed, staring over the edge of the doorway. He punched his throat mike and said in a voice that was unbelievably calm: "We have to go faster."

Chapter 41

Manhattan, New York City

Either Robert had more spells that Jack didn't know about or he was a very good guesser. The helicopters raced along the narrow streets, keeping low enough so that the entire city of dead couldn't track them, and just high enough to avoid the traffic lights and still, they were mobbed just as soon as they landed on the front lawn of the UN building—the eastern boundary of Jack's spell.

Even before they touched down, the door gunners were firing like mad to keep the wave of bone-creatures back. Fearlessly, the Seals leapt from the chopper and charged at the dead, putting themselves between Jack and a thousand of Robert's creatures that were hell-bent on killing him.

It was a swirling fire-fight as more ghouls raced in, while those that had already been practically obliterated by the chopper's guns reformed, sometimes under the feet of the Seals. Jack couldn't watch. He dragged his sacrifice out of the copter and didn't waste a second moving him any further. Out came the knife, the old blood on it still wet; he slashed the man open a second time, the blade sinking deeper than he had expected.

The blood was dark. It was mesmerizing. It sent a hunger through Jack that had him licking his lips. He reached out a shaking hand and put his fingers in the wound; it was warm and good; good in what way, he didn't know, he only knew that it was good for him. The fingers went deeper, penetrating so that he felt the pulse of the man's heart so close...

A sudden blast of hot air as the helicopter lifted off, was like a slap to Jack's face. It brought him around to his duty and not a second too soon.

Pulling his hand away, he began dipping the brush in the dark blood and drawing his symbols as fast as he could, only dimly aware of the second helicopter landing, or the blasting guns, and the explosions as grenades were being used in a sign of desperation or the screams...someone was hurt.

Jack knew the pain of the poison; it was a horror.

A second man began screaming and another. In the middle of the battle, one of the helicopters appeared to leap like a frog. It had been hovering low about a block away, trying to get the ghouls to come after it, but to no avail—the ghouls were after Jack and raced around the copter, ignoring it.

In one great bound, it lifted off and landed twenty feet from where the Seals were fighting. This time the landing wasn't the least bit graceful. It came down with jarring force, crushing an unknown number of the creatures, while from its sides, fire and lead flashed outward in a torrent but too late to save a Seal who had his eyes driven into his brain by stiff, bony fingers.

Jack barely paid attention to any of this. The only thing he cared about were the symbols and the soft hand on his shoulder. Cyn was there, standing next to him, holding her shotgun, one-handed, braced against her hip, pointing at the sky.

The glyphs and the mumbled spells took all of three minutes to complete. And as before the "sound" erupted in his mind, louder now and the vibrations were worse. His heart became a dark, sore hunk of coal in his chest and had he been performing the spell under different circumstances he might have gone off the deep end right then. However, he wasn't alone. He was surrounded by brave men fighting against outrageous odds, and as he watched, one of the Seals was dragged down by sheer numbers as he tried to reload his gun. The man's vest was ripped off of him and he was torn in two. Nearby two more were slashed by the raking claws and poisoned, their screams adding to the din of battle.

All around them was a wall of bones and decaying scalps and the filthy remains of funeral suits and the flapping remnants of burial dresses.

"Holy crap," Jack breathed and then frantically waved the helicopters in.

"The injured first," Neilson ordered. Jack stepped back and watched as two of the men who couldn't walk were dragged to the chopper and hauled in, while another three staggered in under their own power. Next the bloody sacrifice was put in and then Pastor John climbed in and went to work right away on the injured. Two more Seals came up, each hefting a corpse over their shoulders.

One of the Seals jumped onto the helicopter and the other did a quick count. "There's ten," he said to Jack. "Get on."

Jack hesitated. The wall of bones was edging ever closer and he didn't see how the next helicopter would be able to land in the middle of it all, especially since the remaining men were spread so thin. And if it couldn't land, everyone left behind would die a gruesome death.

The spell had such a hold over Jack's mind that he almost got on the chopper. He almost left Cyn behind to die, but then she looked at him and he saw the fear in her eyes. Just the look damped the ringing tone. She was his anchor and he knew if she died it would be better for everyone if he died as well.

She was facing out from the chopper, in a crouch, her shotgun at the ready. Cyn was such a slim, elegant figure that it was surprisingly easy for Jack to pick her up, one hand gripping the seat of her jeans, the other on the back of her tactical gear.

"What the hell?" she cried, as she went sprawling half on the dead, half on the poor boy with the "Mom" tattoo. She tried to scramble out again, but he stopped her, grabbing her shoulders.

"I'll get the next one; it'll be ok."

She was so close that he could have leaned forward an inch and kissed her; he wished she had. She licked her lips, wanting to say something, only there was no time. Jack slapped the metal hide of the bird and screamed: "Go!"

The pilot needed no further orders. His bird was full and there was no sense waiting even a second longer. It went up like an elevator, leaving Jack blinking as the ash swirled. Then it was just Jack, Lieutenant Neilson and nine men surrounded by an army.

"Keep the LZ open!" roared Neilson. "Hold them back!" He then turned to Jack and said: "You should have kissed her and you should have gotten her weapon."

Jack had only his rapier, and was just then realizing what a ridiculous weapon it was for the situation. Though perfect for a one-on-one battle with a single monster made of bone, it was too slim for the hard-bitten melee which faced him.

The only other extra weapon at hand was Neilson's ceremonial saber. It was nothing like Jack's fencing weapon. Its blade was heavy but fine in its balance. It was a cavalry saber and had been perfectly designed for exactly this sort of fight. It was loosely tied to the back of Neilson's Kevlar vest.

"What the hell are you doing, Jack?" the lieutenant yelled, as Jack snatched it and then ran to the weakest point in the line. "Get back here!"

Jack was filled with a lust for blood and death, and with these beasts there was no need to hold back. He could give in and hack and maim with impunity. He could even have fun. The sword was surprisingly light in his hands and the blade was clean and pure. It heaved the head off the first creature, passing through bone and gristle like they were nothing.

He then hacked off a reaching arm with a back hand stroke and then brought the blade back to leave the ghoul standing useless and limbless. He turned to the next one and went at it with two hands in a swing that was all muscle and no technique. The creature, partially caught up in her own burial dress, exploded as if she had been made of kindling and string.

Another met the same fate and Jack suddenly realized he wasn't feeling the ugly, electric evil sensation he had felt when he had used his own swords against the creatures. Not only that, the saber felt impossibly light in hands as though he was flicking a willow wand back and forth.

It was the blessings and the Holy Oil. Against the undead, they made the sword magic. He waded in slashing back and forth, hewing them down like weeds, the blade shining brighter and brighter. He found himself grinning when he saw that those he struck down weren't reforming. Their parts wiggled or jumped like landed fish, but they weren't slipping back together.

The power of the priest's magic on the blade had unwound them, destroying whatever bond kept the bones knit together. "The swords!" Jack cried. "Use the swords!" His grin grew from ear to ear—here was a way to defeat the army of undead! For just one second, he let himself forget that Robert could call another army if this one was destroyed.

Eagerly he swept the creatures back and there was a malignant joy in him.

What brought him around was that a touch of reality began to force itself into the unreal battle. The sword might have been magical, but so were the creatures. They came on, armless and even headless, and even a touch was debilitating. Jack's tactical armor saved him from being killed time and again, but one touch had him gasping in pain and reeling away.

And this brought on a new focus and understanding. There were too many of them for the little group to stop. They would all die if the second helicopter didn't land soon. The problem was that the tiny circle of Seals was being pushed ever inwards and there wasn't room.

The helicopter was almost directly overhead and even with the door gunners pouring hot brass down on them like rain from a squall, it couldn't make up for the thousands of beasts clawing to get at the eleven men. It was stuck fifteen feet off the ground.

In between swings of his sword, Jack could see Cyn in the first copter staring across a space of seventy feet. It was as if they were again nose-to nose and he was looking right into her eyes. She was afraid for him and she was afraid for herself—when he died, she would have to finish the spell and she would have to give up her soul.

He knew this for an absolute fact and it made him crazy and it made him evil. He roared something. It wasn't English or any language spoken by man. It just came up out of his perverted soul and it stopped the ghouls in their tracks, but only for a second and then they came on fiercer than ever and Jack fought harder than ever.

All in vain.

There was no power on earth able to stop the tide of the creatures...only Robert could and, in his paranoia, he did.

The dead were within the tight perimeter when Jack suddenly felt the death knell of a human sacrifice. He knew it now and understood it. He had slain Carl, stabbing him with a bitter hunk of faceless, factory forged metal and he had killed Connor with the same ugly, inelegant blade. He knew when someone was using *his* spell.

All three of the spells were *his* birthright and it galled him somewhere unspeakable whenever they were used by someone unworthy.

Around him, the ghouls suddenly stopped attacking. Time seemed to stop for them. They stared west. They stared in the direction where the gate of hell had opened.

Lieutenant Neilson and the other Seals, couldn't feel a thing. They didn't know that Robert, in his fear of Jack, had brought something *big* into the world. They were just happy at the unexpected reprieve in the fighting and while the ghouls stared, the Seals blasted them into pieces.

In seconds, there was enough room for the copter to land among the bones and grave-clutter. The air was suddenly a hundred and ten degrees and whipping ash all around. There was a crunch of breaking bones and then, right behind Jack was a great gray metal beast. Just like the ghouls he stared west and had to be pulled into the copter.

When he blinked, they were cutting through the streets once again, the mood aboard the helicopter somber. The men went about reloading their weapons in a state of grim anger. Jack, on the other hand wasn't anywhere near somber. He was downright freaked out. What Robert had brought through the gate was greater than any demon they had yet faced.

He tried to "feel" for the creature, and even though there were so many of the lesser creatures around them and their evil was a huge burst of static, he could feel the new one. It was horrible, like a mega-watt transmitter of evil. And worse, not only was it a transmitter of dark energy, it was a receiver as well.

It knew Jack was searching for it and it knew right where Jack was.

Neilson nudged Jack, making him jump. "Where are we putting down?" he asked.

"What? We're here already?" Jack asked looking out of the chopper's door. Sure enough, out the right window was the Hudson River. They were at the western edge of the boundary Jack had chosen. He had wanted to land in a strip of a park that ran along the West Side Highway; however it was already overrun with the creatures, all looking up eagerly.

Unfortunately, there was nowhere else to land. The roads and sidewalks were packed with cars. Even if they could land, there wasn't ten feet of open space to draw the glyphs. The helicopters slowly made their way along the highway in five minutes of fruitless searching. Those were precious minutes that shouldn't have been wasted.

The dead were racing towards them, including the latest monster Robert had called up. The thought of it ate at Jack and he finally said: "I guess we land in the park and take our chances." They were terrible chances, he knew. He could envision the fight: the door gunners would blast a landing zone and they would set down in a litter of bones which would reanimate practically under their feet as Jack tried to draw his glyphs and the others fought and died.

"No way!" Neilson yelled. "We'll be shredded. What about on top of that building?" He pointed to what looked like a warehouse—its roof was flat and empty, and perfect.

"Yes! Do it. We might have to get down to ground level, but at least we'll be able to land."

Since they didn't know whether the roof could hold the weight of the helicopters, they couldn't actually set the 17,000 pound birds down. They leapt out from about four feet up. The Seals spread out, racing for the three exits while Jack waited for the second helicopter. He could pick out Cyn's frightened face as if she was standing right in front of him.

Then he was blinking and holding up an arm as the wash swept him. The second team, minus four Seals jumped out and then helped Cyn down. Jack's sacrifice was newly awake and looking around in a groggy, barely lucid state. He too had to be helped.

Cyn ran right for Jack, her eyes going wild in their sockets. "It's coming! It's coming! I can feel it. We can't stay here." There was no use questioning what the "it" was.

"Block it from your mind, Cyn. Block it out. Just don't think about it at all." She tried. Her mouthed formed a little "O" and her brow furrowed, but the fear never left her eyes.

The Seals, holding the sacrifice, keeping him from crumpling to the ground, were standing near, waiting for orders. Jack pointed to the closest stairwell door. "Get him down to the ground floor and I'm going to need him unconscious. I don't care how you do it, just make sure he's not moving."

The Seals trooped away and Pastor John, looking strangely frail and worn, started after them. Jack grabbed him and pointed him toward Cyn, who was almost hysterical from the fear of the coming creature. "Fix this and then get downstairs."

"I can feel it, too," Pastor John said. "It's big. It's a-a fiend from the lower hells. I know it. I don't know how I know it but I know it."

"And you also know that your God is bigger than any fiend. Now fix this. Bless her or whatever, and get downstairs!" Jack turned and raced for the stairs. They were three stories up, but Jack practically threw himself down the flights until he was on the ground floor.

The warehouse held brown boxes Stacked on shelves all the way to the ceiling; what was in them, Jack didn't have a clue and didn't care. What he cared about was just being laid to the floor with a large knot swelling on the side of his temple. "Good, good," Jack said, feeling the eagerness of the spells coming back. By the way one of the Seals glanced at him with disgust twisting his handsome features, Jack was sure that he looked demented—he didn't care about that either.

He laid aside Neilson's half-forgotten saber, and out came the knife and with an even deeper cut than before he added another layer of blood to the blade. He began painting and the Seals began fighting.

Three of the tall rolling doors of the warehouse were attacked and the metal was no match for the strength of the thousands of beasts. The doors bent in, further and further until there were three foot gaps at the sides and the walking skeletons began to slip in. They made easy targets and at first the battle was controlled and even easy by the standards that they had been fighting under.

Then the fiend arrived, casting a pall upon the fight. Even the ghouls stepped aside in favor of the monster, and the warehouse grew eerily silent. They could hear the heavy clacking steps as it came right up to the warehouse walls where it cast a shadow that was as tall as the thirty-foot ceiling and as wide as a city bus.

It was big and the fear that flowed from it made even the blessed soldiers retreat almost to the stairwell, while Jack practically withered into a shaking ball.

"It'll be ok," a soft voice said—and suddenly it was ok. Pastor John had touched him and the fear was gone. "God loves you, Jack."

For Jack it was an odd thing to hear and impossible to answer if an answer was even needed. "I need time," Jack whispered. The circle of glyphs was only half-completed. He needed the pastor to hold out against the creature for two more minutes; the only problem was that John looked tired and worn. His spiritual labors in the running fight had taken their toll. "Remember, your God is strong," Jack said.

"The Lord is all-powerful but his vessel is weak," the pastor answered and then walked through the echoing warehouse towards where the fiend stood with a wall of metal and glass between them.

Pastor John crossed himself and then said in a carrying voice: "Leave this place, fiend. The Lord is here. The Father of all resides in me and his power is absolute. Be gone!" A blast of white light shot from the pastor's upraised hand outlining the shadow of the bone-monster.

It screamed in a rage, shattering glass and causing the humans to cringe. Jack's hand slipped as he drew, causing a glyph to smear. Quickly, he wiped away the blood, so that it was a dull brown stain. He spat on the ground and swiped at it with his left hand until the spot was clear enough to begin again.

Jack dipped the brush just as the fiend reached out with its clawed "hands" and tore down the wall. The brush wavered over the unconscious man, blood dripping onto the leg of his jeans. Jack should have been writing, but the fiend drew his eye. It was an alien horror, built of bone—

built of thousands of bones that were tied together with a deeper darkness than was physically possible.

The beast was formed in the likeness of a man; legs of bound bone, a chest like a cage, shoulders that stretched wide and arms fifteen feet in length ending with fingers that seemed extraordinarily long even for a thing as massive as it was.

From there it degenerated into something more alien in design. Its head, again a cage in form sat atop a short neck. Around the head were three mouths shaped from human bones and seven eyes that glistened wetly. Jutting from its back were two wings that were hideous, more vulture-like than bat-like. They were "feathered" in the flesh from a thousand corpses. The skins were fresh and there was a rain of blood when it shook out its wings.

It was an absolute horror to behold and it shook Pastor John so badly that the hand holding the crucifix faltered.

From the three mouths laughter boomed that grated on the nerves and hurt the ears. Jack had to force his hand back to the task of painting the glyphs while twelve feet away Pastor John gathered his courage.

"Go back to your pit, servant of Satan!" John cried in a high voice. "The Lord commands you." Again, a white light rolled outward from the pastor; it was a diffuse wave and though it crumbled the ghouls, leaving them little more than piles of bleached bone, it only caused the fiend to shake and roar.

But the light did not last and Pastor John staggered and went to one knee from the effort. His strength was failing and wouldn't be enough; he would be killed, torn into pieces so that each of the mouths would get their bite. Jack saw it in a blink that there would be no saving the man unless he grabbed him right then and ran.

That would mean leaving his sacrifice lying there; a wonderful treat for the fiend. As well, it would mean the end of their mission. With his teeth grit, Jack turned from Pastor John, a brave and true man. "Get this guy out of here," Jack said to the Seals through his clenched jaw. He pointed at the unconscious young man, the bloody thing whose only purpose left was to die.

The Seals hesitated until Jack picked up his saber and started smacking them with the flat of it. "Go! Now, before it's too late."

Pastor John had his crucifix raised and from it came a weak glow. The fiend stepped into the warehouse, its long arms thrusting aside the stacks of boxes and the industrial shelving as if they were made of toothpicks, and yet it moved in slow motion as if it was wading against an invisible river. It came at the pastor and with each step John's face grew more and more strained.

It was good verse evil. It was man against the unkillable embodiment of evil. It was mortal against immortal. It was an unseen battle that everyone felt pulse around them. The ebb and flow caused a wind to surge back and forth around the vast space.

It was a battle of actual dark versus light with the shadows growing, filling in every corner, blotting out the sun. It was a battle that ended with the fiend standing high above the man of God in triumph. Pastor John was beaten down. He was sprawled with only the crucifix raised, the glow from it no more powerful than a candle.

The fiend loomed over the pastor, its ugly wings stretched wide, its head spinning like a carousel, each mouth opening greedily but before it could bite down it would spin again to the next mouth. Jack couldn't take his eyes from the spectacle and he hesitated, just steps away from the stairwell door.

"Don't watch," a soft voice said into his ear. It was Cyn, pulling him to the stairwell where the Seals had retreated.

Jack tried to resist her small hand and the light pull she affected. He felt it was his duty to watch. He had chosen Pastor John for this assignment and he had allowed the man, weakened as he was, to go up against this prince of demons.

But he also had an obligation to make his own kill, to fight his own fight. He wasn't God's warrior; he was just a man trying to do the best with what he had to work with.

He turned away just as Pastor John's light failed him.

Chapter 42

Manhattan, New York

Jack slammed the heavy fire door closed and turned to see the staircase filled with the platoon of Seals looking at him expectantly as if he had the answers to everything.

As if on cue, Neilson asked: "What do we do?" His God-inspired courage apparently slipping, now that their spiritual leader was even then being ground into bloody chuck by the bone-teeth of the fiend—the door was heavy, but not so heavy to block the screams of the pastor. Nothing could.

"Get up to the roof and prepare to go," Jack ordered. "That thing might be too big to fit into the staircase and I can do the spell on the landing." He didn't add: *I hope*. He was afraid that raising the angle of this circle would change the parameters of the spell, lifting it too high so that he wouldn't be able to reanimate as many of the monsters as he needed.

And he would need a lot.

All the Seals except for Lieutenant Neilson hurried back up the stairs. The lieutenant stood next to Cyn with a look that was bordering on panic. "You two should go. I got this," Jack said. They didn't budge, though Neilson kept glancing upward as sweat rolled down from beneath his helmet.

Jack had a sense of déjà vu as he laid the sword to the side and brought out the knife. It now had an evil, hungry feel to it, but Jack was able to control it this time and sliced only deep enough to bring the blood running. He began painting the glyphs as fast as he could.

The fiend played with its food, giving Jack time to get three-quarters of the way around the circle. Then there was a roar that shivered the warehouse and turned the air to ice. Jack gasped and threw an arm across his face. Cyn did the same thing; however Lieutenant Neilson, maybe the toughest of the Seals began to back away, his fear becoming too great for even him to control.

Now that he was dead, all of Pastor John's blessings were coming undone and the Seals were being subject to a fear that was simply beyond them. It was sad to say that Jack was getting used to the feeling; it was like getting used to cancer. It made him sick and nauseated, but he kept going right up until the fiend tore down the fire door.

It would have taken Jack a sledgehammer and an hour's worth of swings to get through the door but the fiend tore it apart in twenty seconds, bringing down part of the wall with it.

It then brought its huge head down and stared at Jack through the opening with one of its tremendous eyes. The eye itself was a horror. It was made from hundreds of individual human eyes smushed into a ball the size of an oven. Jack found himself staring instead of finishing the circle. Seconds past and yet he couldn't force his eyes away; it felt as though he was being held against his will.

A high girlish scream broke the moment, jarring Jack to his senses. He thought it was Cyn, but it was Neilson; he had reached his limit and with his mind snapped, he went racing up the stairs, screaming his throat to ribbons.

The fiend laughed at this, a booming, echoing noise that caused Cyn to retreat up another stair; she was on the verge of coming apart as well.

Jack wasn't even close. In fact, he was furious. When the fiend had laughed it showed its long, sharp bone teeth and hanging on them were the bloody remains of Pastor John. In an unrestrained fury, Jack snatched up the saber and flew down the dozen stairs separating him from the creature. He meant to stab that awful mouth, but at the last second the fiend felt him coming and stuck a hellacious eye in the doorway instead.

That'll work, too, Jack thought, as he drove the sword up to the hilt into the orb with all the strength in his arm and shoulder. The sword must have been blessed by Commander Price; it still held its power. If it hadn't, Jack would have died right there.

There was a *crack* like a whip snapping, a flash of light, and then there was the hateful, dark power racing up the blade and into Jack. The fiend roared in pain, while Jack staggered back and fell onto the staircase. His right arm so completely numb that he was sure that if he looked down on it he would see that it was dead and rotting, hanging by just a few tendons.

He forced himself to look: the arm was intact. It looked the same as it always had except there was dirt and ash upon his palm and the fingers were curled in what looked like a claw. He didn't have time to marvel; Cyn was suddenly there, next to him, pulling him up the stairs. He stopped her at the landing.

The boy was laid out there, seemingly at peace, seemingly just waiting on Jack to finish this third set of spells. The cold had closed his wound—Jack would have to cut him again. Each spell needed its own cut, its own opening in the body, its own channel to the soul.

Jack knelt, his dead arm forgotten. He was overcome by the hunger to kill. It was such a huge need in him that he could block out the noise of the fiend's anger as it roared loud enough to be heard for miles. The world echoed with its sound and yet Jack couldn't care less.

But he couldn't block out Cyn. "We have to go. Come on, Jack!" She was trying to haul him out of there—the stairwell was filling with clouds of darkness and quickly the air had turned black as sackcloth and cold as the deepest winter night. The fear was heavy as well; it was as strong as Jack had ever felt it. It gripped his heart and threatened to explode it.

In spite of all of this, he wouldn't move.

The craving was too great. He had to get to the blood. He had to dip the brush into the body where the meat hit the metal and above all, he had to paint the glyphs. It was a need too strong for Jack to resist—he would give his life for it.

Taking the knife in his left hand, he made a cut across the man's throat. In his unholy eagerness he very nearly slit too deeply which would have ended things right there. The blood ran quickly, running onto the landing; wasted in Jack's opinion. "My fault," he said, and then felt around in the growing dark for the brush.

"Jack!" Cyn screamed. "Forget it! We have to go."

He grabbed her, left-handed and pulled her close, snarling: "Give me light. I have to do this." It was a lie. If every demon in the city suddenly turned to dust, he wouldn't have stopped.

Cyn brought out her phone and shone the harsh light. Normally, it was annoyingly bright. Just then it barely cut the murk and though she was inches away, all he could see of her were soft lips. They were blue and every time she breathed, she puffed out a little plume of steam.

"Hurry," she begged through chattering teeth. He was so consumed that he didn't feel the cold. It was nothing to him.

It wasn't exactly by memory that he painted, now. His hand was directed by something greater than the patch-work of neurons and micro-synapses that constituted memory. His hand felt guided by fate. It was an altogether heady feeling and when he was done, he bellowed the words of the spell in a direct challenge to the fiend.

The tolling bell that could only be heard on a level by the dead and their masters rang out stronger than ever. It sent a vibration through Jack, one that he knew wouldn't stop until the final spell was cast or until he died. It made him feel unstoppable and he cried out: "You cannot defy me! Go tell my cousin that you failed."

"*You are not done yet,*" the fiend replied in a triple voice from its three mouths, the words harmonizing strangely as if three separate creatures were speaking. "*You have to come out. You can do little in there. You cannot finish what you've started in there. You must come out to where I await. You must come out to die.*"

"Maybe we shouldn't," Cyn said as Jack stood. She was only a vague outline; the electronics in her phone were failing and the dark was becoming absolute. He felt closed in, trapped.

He had to run his hand over her in order to find her arm to help her up. "Weren't you just begging to go?" he asked her, his hand gripping her sharply—he couldn't seem to help it; there didn't feel as though there was anything gentle in him just then. Everything was splintered and hard. "Besides, we have a destiny."

She pulled her hand out of his grip and then punched him in the chest. With the dark, it was completely unexpected. And, as usual with her, it was such a strong blow that it caused him to step back, where he almost tripped on the unconscious, bloody sailor.

"Hey," he said, rubbing his chest. "Why'd you do that?"

"You don't have a destiny, Jack. You have a job to do and nothing more. You'll do the spell. We'll figure out how to get rid of all these bleeding monsters and then you'll be done. Do you hear me? This ends tonight."

The yoke was so far over and the spell had its hooks so deep into him that he felt as though he was going to crack in two. He nodded, agreeing with her and yet at the same time the other part of himself hissed into his own ear: *That's all very easy for her to say. She's rich and beautiful. She isn't the one who's a mass murderer. Her hands are barely dirty and her soul is clean as new ice. It must be wonderful to be able to be so condescending.*

And what do you have to look forward to if you can even find a way to live through all of this? At best you can go back to being an absolute nobody. Your career is over before it ever started; your doctorate is finished. You are facing a possible prison sentence and she wants you to give up the one reward for putting your life and soul on the line?

I don't think so.

Jack touched his head, feeling it as if it belonged to someone else. Where had that voice come from? It seemed very much like a harsh voice and not his at all, but he couldn't be sure. The truth was that just then, Jack really couldn't remember who he had been. He'd been a student, yes, but who was he beyond his books and his classes. What sort of person had he been? Just a regular one? He really couldn't remember. He wanted to think he had been a nice guy and wanted to blame this hate in him on the spells but just then he didn't know. It made him feel crazy

A strangled, frightened laugh escaped him which he quickly turned into a cough before Cyn could ask what he was laughing about. "Let's…let's get this guy out of here," he said, breathlessly. "Grab a hand." He went to reach out with his right hand, but the arm didn't move and so he switched to his left, wondering what he was going to do about his arm. It wasn't like a hospital was going to be able to fix it. The newly high-powered priests might, but the question was would they after he was in command of his own undead army.

And if they would, there was the question of whether their fixes would work on someone like him? He was so far down the rabbit hole that he had to think that if a priest touched him there would be a flash of light and the smell of brimstone.

He forced his imbalanced mind away from the thought and concentrated on dragging the young man up the next few flights of stairs. They went as fast as they could and near the top they cleared the darkness and stood under the yellow glow of a naked bulb.

Cyn was afraid of what they would find out there, Jack could read the fear easily. It was oddly quiet beyond the door. There should have been machine gun fire and the blast of grenades and the roar of the helicopters. Instead there was only a single muffled engine going.

The fiend was out there as well.

They could both feel it against a closing ring of darkness. "They're all coming aren't they?" Cyn asked.

"Yeah."

Robert had reversed his armies. They were racing back to New York because it was now obvious that this was where the real fight was going to take place. To Jack it felt like he was standing in the middle of a ring of dark flames that was closing in on him.

He was hating and cocky and there was a snarl twisting his lip; he didn't want to go out unarmed—that seemed pathetic. "Hey, Cyn? Do me a favor and put my sword in my hand. My—my hand doesn't seem to work, not after… you know. I just don't want to go out there unarmed."

She drew the rapier that he had taken from Dr. Loret's wall and shoved it into the claw of his hand. Jack knew a blade in his hand would give the fiend pause. Its pain had been very real, perhaps greater than any mortal could have endured and Jack wanted every advantage, real or illusionary, that he could get.

But the rapier was more than a prop. The moment Cyn had fitted the pommel into his dead claw, there was a glow and a shock ran up the arm. It was warm and beautiful…and disappointing. Jack could suddenly use his hand again. The sword had been blessed by Pastor John; his last blessing. It was a weak, fading charge and once it had slipped into Jack, healing him, it was forever gone.

The rapier was now just a chunk of metal. Against the fiend, it was useless.

Although his arm now worked as well as it ever had and he was just as deadly with the sword, he let the blade clatter to the ground. The fiend wouldn't be fooled by it.

Strangely, Jack wasn't exactly happy that his arm was alive again. What he felt was bitter disappointment, because he knew that's how Pastor John would feel if he was there and knew what Jack was thinking. And that's how the Monsignor would feel if he knew what his sacrifice had been for. And Father Paul as well. And Detective Richards…and even Carl and Connor Randall.

And his father.

They had all died in one way or another, simply to get Jack to this point and it was a hard fact that they would all be disappointed that he was bending under the power of the spells…that he was wasting the gift of their sacrifices to him, that he was hungering for a chance to usurp his cousin as *King of the Dead*.

That was the title that whispered in the back of his mind…and now the title was stained, discolored by the taint of disappointment.

"They don't know how it is," Jack said, not quite as under his breath as he wished. Cyn glanced at him and he was damned sure that he saw the same disappointment in her eyes. It wasn't right on top. No, it was buried deep where she thought it was hidden. It wasn't hidden from him; he saw it just fine and it hurt…which only made him angrier, hateful and broken.

The yoke in his mind had broken—it had snapped in two. He was both good and evil. He wanted to destroy the world as well as save it. He wanted to rule the remains like a king and he wanted to go hide away on some island. His right arm was strong and righteous but his hand was tacky with drying blood. He wanted to scream in frustration, but all he did was whimper.

Shaking in confusion, he reached down and took the young man by the hand and burst through the door and out into the horrible world beyond. What he saw made *him* disappointed. The Seals, those badasses, were, for the most part, cowering in the shade of their leader. Lieutenant Neilson had rallied his courage and was screaming into a radio. Around him were the bravest of the Seals, guns pointed out, their faces stamped in fear.

These were the eight bravest.

The rest had broken, succumbing to the hell-fear that turned ordinary men to jelly. They were clawing their way onto one of the helicopters, overflowing it, weighing it down; they were beyond rational thought, as was the pilot who took off with men still clinging to any hold they could get.

Jack tore his eyes from the scene. What was happening as a backdrop to the helicopter was far more eye-grabbing and terrifying. The entire city was blanketed in the unnatural darkness; it stood three stories high from river to river impenetrable to the naked eye.

Standing a head above it all was the fiend. It was blowing great clouds of the darkness from its three mouths in huge jets, filling the city streets.

The head and its seven eyes turned as the SH-60 slowly lifted off. The chopper seemed to move in slow motion, straining to get lift, straining to get the hell out of there. It was far too slow. The beast's seven eyes were filled with ten thousand human ones and they were all looking at the chopper with an aching hunger.

With a grunt, the fiend leapt into the sky, its flesh wings slapping the air, creating a wave of stench that sickened anything left alive for miles. Jack cringed and Cyn fell against him. She didn't see what came next.

The beast could fly.

It launched itself directly into the path of the helicopter, catching the machine and pulling it down into the darkness. The engines revved and whined and the men screamed. The pilot did everything it could but the fiend was too strong and gradually the chopper was taken and all that was left were those screams which went on and on.

Chapter 43

Manhattan, New York

The crash of the Seahawk was surprisingly low-key. There was a metallic thud, a few strange *whoo-whoo-whoo* noises as the blades whickered away and then came the sound of glass crashing down. There was no fireball or earth shattering explosion.

Muffled as the crash was, the screams rising up from the sea of darkness were just the opposite. They were magnified in the dead city. There were no traffic sounds, no honking of horns, no babble of people on cell phones, no pitiful group of survivors making a desperate last stand; the city of the dead was dead quiet—all except the screams.

They echoed for miles.

And they went on for an oddly long time. The screams were doing a number on the eight Seals. Already drenched in the terror of the fiend they shrank even further back from the building's edge. Some begged for the lieutenant to call in the second helicopter which was circling a half a mile away.

"Don't do it," Jack ordered. "That thing is down there waiting for you to do just that. I can feel it." The fiend was watching, waiting, lurking beneath the darkness, ready to spring on the chopper once it was loaded and slow. To Jack it was a sign of weakness.

It had been stung by the blessed sword and wanted no more of those sorts of wounds.

Jack glanced down and saw a discarded pack. One of the Seals, in his panic, had thrown away his best weapon against the bone creatures: there was a saber slid down along one of the buckles. He drew it, feeling the warmth and goodness emanating from the steel.

"I say we fight it," Jack said.

"I say: no way!" one of the Seals blurted out. "That thing is...is too much. It's too big. Our only chance is to get the hell out of here."

"Coward," Jack seethed, conveniently forgetting that he had fled, screaming in his first encounter with a far less terrifying demon. "You'll die if we just sit here. The fiend is afraid of us. Think about it. It's down there, hiding."

"It's n-not hiding," the Seal replied. "It's eating."

Jack grabbed the much bigger man by his chest rig and started pulling him along, saying: "And we'll be eaten next if we don't do something besides cowering. Come on, Neilson. Have you forgotten our mission?" As his only answer, Neilson shook his head. "Ok, then let's get moving," Jack said. "Swords out."

Cyn stopped him, whispering urgently: "You can't do this. It'll be a suicide mission."

She was right of course, however, in Jack's broken mind it was the only way to escape. He would send the Seals down to be killed and then he, Cyn, and the boy would call down the helicopter and slip away in all the confusion. It was a cold plan, he would admit, but it was also the only plan.

"It is what it is," Jack told her. "And it's our best play." He turned to Neilson. "Come on, Lieutenant. It's time to earn your pay. Let's see if the military can come through this time."

"This time?" Neilson demanded, outraged. He grabbed Jack by the shirt and unexpectedly started pulling him back to where the others were. "Everyone, get your asses down!" he barked, dropping to his knees and pulling Jack along with him. "You too, ma'am," he said to Cyn.

Not three seconds after she knelt there came a roar and suddenly a grey jet appeared flashing down 50th Street just above roof top level. A quarter mile away, it dropped two CBU-87 cluster bombs which appeared to come apart in midair and four-hundred grapefruit sized bomblets rained down all along the street in front of the warehouse.

The explosions took out the entire street, and shook the building. Flames, orange in a roiling black plume stretched high overhead and the heat made everyone cringe. Jack's ears were ringing from the noise and he still had his head down when the last helicopter came to hover a few feet above the warehouse.

"Come on!" Neilson ordered, hauling Jack to his feet. The sacrifice, still limp, was literally tossed in like a bag of potatoes; Cyn was helped in next and then Jack climbed up. Only then did the Seals jump in and the helicopter beat the air with its four rotors and climbed away.

Both door gunners had their M242s yanked as far to the rear as they would go—they had seen what the fiend could do. But the fiend did not suddenly piece its ten-thousand bones together and jump at them; the surface of the dark below them remained still.

"Yes!" Jack cried. "That's what I'm talking about! Neilson, that was great and you Seals did a great job, too." He was feeling huge, as if nothing could stop him from drawing the last symbol. "We have one more, just one and then it'll be our turn." By that, he meant that it would be his turn and his alone. The Seals could all go jump off a bridge for all he cared.

"It won't be easy without a priest," Cyn cautioned.

"We should go back and get Commander Price," one of the Seals advised.

Everyone thought this was an excellent idea, all save Jack, who thought it was not only stupid but a sign of cowardice. "We don't have time. My cousin is bringing everything he has to bear on the southern tip of Manhattan; I can feel them coming by the millions. We can't spare even a minute."

"But without a priest..." Neilson said, leaving the end of his sentence hanging.

"You have Holy Oil," Jack said. "Say a prayer and anoint yourselves. And use the swords when they get close. There's magic to them." The men followed his instructions and for the next ten minutes as they flew south, the chopper was filled with mumbled prayers.

Cyn broke the near silence. She started pointing out the door of the helicopter. "Are...Are we sinking?" she asked, her eyes wide.

Robert was pulling out all the stops. They weren't sinking, the darkness was rising. The Seahawk was cruising at a thousand feet and now the darkness was at five hundred feet.

"How are we going to land?" Cyn asked.

Lieutenant Neilson unbuckled and made his way to the cockpit to confer with the pilots who both agreed they couldn't land in the darkness. They would crash for certain.

"What about that building?" Jack asked. He had pushed in next to the lieutenant and was pointing at a fifty story building, the last floor of which was an island in the dark.

"You'll be way up, but sure," the pilot answered.

"We'll be fine," Jack said. "Just tell me which way Battery Park is."

The pilot pointed west and said: "It's about four hundred yards that way...somewhere. If you want, I can drop some flares in a line from this building to approximately where it is. I can't guarantee they will land where I want them to but it'll be better than nothing."

"Yeah, do that."

Again, the helicopter couldn't risk landing on the roof and so they hovered just above it and by the time they were all out and on the roof, the darkness was at their knees and the cold was shriveling their testicles, all except for Cyn, who was shivering so badly that Jack worried that she would accidentally fire her shotgun.

"Let's do this," Neilson said. "Kendrick and Stern lead the way. Skelly, hoist that boy on your shoulder. Adams will take over when we hit the street level."

The fear was heavy on them and the cold made their joints ache and the darkness was simply impenetrable. Cyn's phone lasted three floors; after that they walked in the dark, each keeping hold of the person in front of them. Down and down they went and even though they knew they were progressing through the inside of a building, it felt as if they were heading deep into the bowels of the earth—as if they were going down into hell.

In the dark, Cyn found Jack's hand. Hers was like ice. He gave it a squeeze to make sure that he was holding the hand of a person and not one of the dead. "I'm here," she said in a whisper that set off an echo of whispering.

"What the hell?" one of the Seals in front of them almost screeched. "What was that?"

"It was me, sorry," Cyn said, louder now.

"Keep it together," Neilson said. "We have to be close to the bottom. When we get out we go left. That'll be west. Use the swords like Jack said. They'll kill quietly and hopefully will keep us from being found."

There were grunts of agreement from everyone but Cyn, who didn't have a sword. She had her shotgun and a few bottles of Holy Water. "Stay near me and you'll be fine," Jack said.

It took twelve minutes to get to the lobby of the building where everything crunched and crackled underfoot. It was glass. "Why don't we just do the spell here?" someone asked.

"Because I can't see a damned thing," Jack said, giving the obvious answer. "Not only that, who knows if this place has even a single actual wall left intact. The second I start the spell, all hell is going to break out and we're going to need some protection. In Battery Park there is a place called Castle Clinton. It's not really a castle like they have in Europe. It's more of a heavy brick fort laid out in a circle and there's only one door we have to guard."

He didn't add that it was completely open, without any sort of roof, and if the fiend got there before he was finished with the spell, they would all die very quickly.

Although it took them twelve minutes to slip down fifty stories, it took fifteen to find their way outside. They had to go by feel alone; not an easy task when every wall felt the same. Eventually, they made it out onto a sidewalk where things slowed down even more.

The city streets this close to the Staten Island Ferry station were piled with dead. Not just one or two here and there or a few stacked in neat little bundles. No, they were three or four deep and they seemed to go on forever in every direction.

This was Jack's army, really just a tiny fraction of it; that is if he could bring them back from the dead. He guessed that there had to be between five and ten million corpses within the boundaries of his spell. It was why he had insisted on heading all the way down to Battery Park.

But it was turning into a nightmare. In no time they were exhausted from going up and down the mounds of bodies, feeling each, deathly afraid that one would be "alive", one of Robert's bone-creatures. They were quickly covered head to toe in blood.

Nothing could have been so horrific than crawling over the dead. They kept as close as they could to each other. Cyn and Jack called to one another in whispers and touched each other when they could, absolutely uncaring what part of the other's anatomy that they were touching; they simply needed each other.

The lack of ghouls was a mystery that was solved a few minutes later when they saw the first flare. Its para-chute had been caught up by the second story of a build-ing. The light it gave off should have turned night into day. Instead it was dim and showed more shadow than light; however it did illuminate the area well enough for them to see that more than a hundred ghouls were gathered beneath it.

It also showed them an easier way to travel. The sidewalks were heaped with bodies, while the streets were clogged bumper to bumper with cars. They saw that it would be far easier to scootch over the cars than the bodies. And two of the cars were police cars. Jack went right for them; in the trunks of both were boxes of hand flares; they each took three.

There was no whispering now. No one dared. The group of eleven slipped and slid over the cars, moving as silently as possible, but it didn't seem to matter that they frequently thumped hoods of cars with their boots, or scraped their swords on windshields. The creatures were too absorbed in the light.

They found the same scene a hundred yards on and a third in Battery Park where the light was enough to display the grim outline of Castle Clinton itself.

On the grounds of the Castle, the bodies began to grow in number and at the tall wooden door itself they were piled seven high, the ones at the bottom, having died of asphyxiation. They had been trying to find a last refuge in the castle, but the stout doors had been locked against them.

After pulling back the bodies, Jack's team began a whispered conversation about different methods of blowing the door quietly. "We could use these bodies to dampen the sound and then..." began Lieutenant Neilson.

Jack interrupted: "Just blow the lock! *They* are coming. I can feel them." The noose was closing in on his guilty neck. He tried to block them out and failed. *They* knew he was trying to send them back to hell; they would fight that with everything they had.

With the flares dying, the dark became all-consuming once again so that they couldn't see their hands flap in front of their faces—in order to prepare the charge they would need light. The Seals formed a wall around Neilson, who lit off a flare and in the red light, he assembled an explosive charge in eighteen seconds. Four more seconds were spent as everyone dove into the piles of dead for cover and then one more was spent waiting for the blast.

The door bounded inwards with a flash and a crash. There was no use being subtle now and everyone popped flares. Jack raced through the door first, a flare in his outstretched left hand, his sword cocked in his right. The interior of the castle, a wide round space, was completely empty. Jack dropped the flare, uncorked another and dropped that too.

"Right here!" he said, snapping his fingers at the Seal who had been lugging about Jack's sacrifice. The Seal laid the man down with what Jack thought was excessive kindness.

It was time for the final act; the final spell, or rather the final portion of the final spell. That part would entail Jack marking his own body. He would paint his own flesh with his victim's blood. It was why there was never any sign of Robert's spell. He carried it around on his body, possibly forever.

Jack laid aside the sword and then, strangely, made the shallowest cut yet. Something within him, a last cry for help perhaps, had staid his hand. The boy bled well enough that Jack didn't waste even a moment for a second cut. He went right in, starting with arch-glyph, the one that described the spell as having fout parts.

From there he sped through the first circle of glyphs, going faster than possible. The undead army was at the gate. For now, *only* a thousand or so, but more were coming. The Seals fought with all the bravery, skill, and honor that they were known for. And yet they were overmatched, not only by sheer numbers, but also in power.

The ghouls were strong and unflinching. They charged regardless of the holy swords and quickly forced their way into the castle. Cyn grabbed Jack's saber and rushed into the battle screaming at the top of her lungs. In one hand, she held the sword and in the other she held a bottle of Holy Water, which she splashed about.

The water alone had the ghouls backing away and her sword crumbled creature after creature into piles of bones.

But there were countless of them and even Cyn's sudden appearance and her use of the Holy Water, which was taken up by the Seals, wasn't enough and they were forced back away from the door a second time.

Jack saw the fight out of the corner of his eye as he dipped and drew in blood. It was a fight cast in sinister red shadows, marked by the slash of shining silver and flying, pale bones. Time and again, a man would be raked or bitten and their cries were torture to the ears. Thankfully, they still had their Holy Water which they doused on their wounds, easing their pain, allowing them to continue to fight.

Somehow, just as Jack finished Cyn's spell, defining what could come through the gate, the Seals forced the ghouls back to the door and even managed to shut it once again, piling against it—there were only five of the Seals left standing and in the courtyard were the bones of a hundred of the ghouls.

They stood, braced and ready to fight again, breathing heavily and for some unknown reason the ghouls backed away. Jack was busy going onto the second circle—his spell, and didn't have time to guess why.

Cyn knew. "It's here, Jack," she said in a whisper that carried across the courtyard. He thought that she meant the fiend and he cast his face up into the darkness expecting at any second to see the seven-eyed beast from the lower plane.

Then Jack felt the presence of something nearly as awful. It was *the* demon. The little girl with the copper pennies on her eyes. Its cold evil was a force that smote him and Jack had to take a breath before going on. He had to hope that the others could hold the thing back for thirty more seconds.

They lasted ten.

Lifting its tiny foot, the creature kicked in the door, sending the Seals flying. Cyn had been to the side and managed to splash it with the last of her Holy Water. It recoiled, momentarily and then opened its mouth impossibly wide as if it was unhinged. It was going to breathe its deadly ice breath on her and she did the only prudent thing: she shrieked and ran.

The demon turned its grinning skull head on the Seals who were charging it, swords raised. Somehow they were able to overcome the fear and the nauseating stench of the beast. It opened its mouth again and blasted out a blizzard in a great cloud of white that enveloped the men, obscuring them, momentarily.

When the cloud cleared, Jack saw the men crawling on the ground. Two were dying, their lungs frozen, having breathed in the icy air; two others were blind, their eyes frozen shut. Only Lieutenant Neilson could still fight.

He climbed to his feet and faced the demon; he was completely over matched and using a weapon that took years of practice to become proficient with. The demon wasted no time and attacked. Neilson did his best. He swung the sword with all his strength; however he did so in such an obvious manner that the demon dodged the blow easily.

It leapt inside the return swing, jumped on the lieutenant's chest, and jabbed its hand into Neilson's open mouth.

When it yanked its hand back out, it pulled with it a length of Neilson's spinal column. The lieutenant collapsed in a pile.

Then the demon turned to Jack who had been frozen in place just as surely as if it had covered him in a foot of ice. The only actual weapon close at hand was the three-inch knife he'd been using to carve up the poor sailor. It was worse than useless.

Slowly, he reached out for the only thing near him that had any chance against the demon: the flare. It burned at 1500 degrees Fahrenheit. The demon laughed when Jack pointed the red fire at it and then it opened its mouth to test its ice breath against the flame.

Jack didn't think the fire would stand the test and too late he remembered his bottle of Holy Water. He turned to run, knowing he'd be too slow, but then he saw a flash of silver streak out of the dark—it was Cyn, swinging his blessed sword in a heavy two-handed chop that should have split the beast in two.

The demon was too quick; it dodged to the side and Cyn ended up striking the cement with all of her strength. There was a great *clang* and then the sword was bouncing, jarred out of her weak grip by the force of the impact.

She watched it tumble away, while the demon watched her neck—hungrily. Jack was already moving, slashing at the demon with the red fire in his hand. He knew that it couldn't really hurt the demon, but that didn't matter because he also knew the demon.

It turned away from Cyn to meet the new attack, which wasn't an attack at all. It was a feint, only a distraction. "Get out of here, Cyn!" he yelled, dancing first to his right and then back to his left. She stumbled backed into the darkness with the demon foolishly eyeing her with its cold penny eyes. It gave Jack a chance to reach around and grab one of his bottles of Holy Water.

"Want a sip?" he asked. The words were another feint. Another way to buy time he couldn't afford. The ring was closing. The ghouls were coming by the millions and the fiend was in the air, soaring at them on wings feathered with human skins. Jack only had minutes to kill this thing and finish the spell. He took another step back and another, shaking the bottle for the beast to see.

And then his foot struck what he'd been after all along: the sword.

Dropping the flare, Jack snatched up the saber, and unlike the others, he was deadly with it. The demon was no fool. It seemed to guess that Jack had the advantage and very slowly it began to back away into the dark—it had all the time in the world, and it had the darkness as an ally.

"Hey!" Jack shouted and then kicked the flare at the demon, something it hadn't expected. It was lit, perfectly and Jack charged—another feint. The demon had many weapons, many tricks; however it had its favorites. It opened its mouth to blast Jack, who was already bounding away, having lobbed the bottle of Holy Water at the demon.

In a millisecond, it froze solid and in the next millisecond, it exploded like a bomb. The demon was shredded by the shards of ice; its ugly, tight skin was in tatters and it was missing one of its copper penny eyes.

Jack waded in with the sword as fast as he could, hoping to catch the demon in a state of confusion. It was not to be. His first strike was like lightning and hacked off the thing's right arm. It howled in pain and then, as if it was throwing a tantrum, it stomped its foot, shaking the ground and nearly throwing Jack off his feet.

By the time he'd regained his proper fencing stance, the creature was gone. It had fled into the dark. Jack edged back to the flare, turning his head this way and that, keeping the sword up and at the ready. Then he remembered Cyn.

"Cyn! It's out there. Be careful."

"I can feel it," she yelled from the darkness. "It's to your right"

He spun and when he wasn't immediately attacked, he grabbed the flare and charged. He found the demon coming forward, a grin on its misshapen face. *You've lost*, was all it said, speaking directly into Jack's mind.

"I don't think so," Jack said, and then attacked. No feints this time. He had the beast wounded and with the flare in hand, he hounded it back and forth until it tried to use his breath once more, and then Jack dashed forward in a picture perfect lunge and skewered the thing, sending the blessed saber deep down its throat.

It tried to scream around the gleaming blade, but Jack only thrust deeper and deeper, a malicious grin turning up the corners of his mouth. "I will be your king," he whispered, feeling the heat of the Holy sword burning into the creature.

Jack gave the blade one last twist. There was a final scream that ran up the blade and then the demon died on the end of his sword, and Jack gloated until Cyn called his name.

She did so in a strange manner. There was fear in her voice but also defeat.

He ran to her and saw that she was standing over the sailor, the boy with the "Mom" tattoo—his throat had been torn out in the dark. The demon had been right: Jack had lost. He could feel the power of the spells in him. They were a storm of hate warping his soul.

His mind was pure anger and his heart was very nearly as black as the hell he wished to be king of. He had lost. The spells demanded a life and there was no one but him and Cyn. He turned to her and his soul must have been on full display because she took a step back.

"No, Jack, don't do it," she said.

Don't do it—by that she meant: don't kill me—three words that sealed her fate. The spell had to be powered and the greatest power that Jack knew was from blood stolen and a life taken against its will. If she hadn't said anything, she would have been perfectly safe from him.

The demons and the ghouls and the fiend would've gladly killed her, but Jack wouldn't have even considered it. He loved her, but that was with the "good" part of him, only that part felt like a distant thing, a voice far away screaming for him not to give in.

Unfortunately, the voice couldn't hold a candle to his overwhelming *need*.

He was so hungry for her soul that for a second he understood the demons perfectly. He understood the rich, blackness of their evil with a degree of empathy no human could. The demons had cast away their light, denying God and now all they did was crave the light. That same craving, that same need was in Jack, and it was practically impossible to fight against it. He was to become one of *them* and all it would take was one flick of his sword.

Understanding struck his cousin; Jack saw it in her eyes. She saw her coming death and saw that it was unavoidable. On one hand she had the demons and the ghouls and the fiend from the lower hells, and on the other she had Jack who was coming apart at the seams and felt as though all he had of himself was the tiniest kernel of his soul, a hard little diamond that clung to his old self.

She smiled her last smile and even in those circumstances managed to put a bit of her old devil-may-care attitude into it. "Please," she said. "Just don't be like him. Kill me if you have to, but don't be like Robert. Remember, people love you."

Maybe she was going to tell him who these people were, but Jack's urgency was too great. He had to act; the ghouls were at the gate and the fiend was soaring south as fast as it could. For good or for bad, he had to do something. He had only two choices: kill Cyn and become a demon himself, but possibly save some part of the world— a world he would rule. Or let her live…for a few seconds more and then watch as she was ripped apart and her soul pulled down into hell.

The choices: love or life seemed obvious.

With a soul-tearing cry, he lashed out with the sword, drawing her blood and stopping her words.

Chapter 44

Manhattan, New York

Cyn began to make a strange noise in her throat as if the air was caught there and couldn't get out. Her mouth worked soundlessly and her eyes bulged wide. She looked like she was dying, and she was.

Jack, on the other hand felt great. The power of the spells over him had suddenly and completely vanished. He almost laughed aloud…but then Cyn fell to her knees, still making that strange noise.

He bent down next to her and at first he didn't know what was wrong, the cut hadn't been all that large, just big enough to do the job. Then he remembered the poison. "We'll get some Holy Oil on that in a sec, but first draw your spell and hurry." He pushed the brush into her hand.

"M-my spell?"

"Yes, your spell. We got to keep ourselves safe until we can figure a way out of this."

"You mean you're not going to kill me?" She looked amazed and happy, but also cautious.

Jack didn't have time for this, not right then. The ghouls were only just realizing that the demon was dead and were starting to surge toward the door. "No, I could never kill you. I always knew that, but I think I forgot it for just a second there."

When he had looked into her eyes at that last moment, he had wanted to kill her with nearly every fiber of his being—and she should have been terrified, and she was terrified, but she wasn't wholly consumed by her fear. Somehow she managed to retain some greater feeling deep in those beautiful eyes. She loved him even though he was a monster.

It was a shock.

He was on the verge of killing her simply to save his own skin and yet, she still loved him. Even after the horrible things he had done, she loved him. It seemed impossible. He had not felt love in years, truly it hadn't been since his father had died. His mother had gone into mourning *and* into hiding. His father's murder and the subsequent warning note had consumed her and gradually fear had supplanted love.

And then she had been killed as well and Jack was alone.

He had not asked for Cyn's love or begged for it. It had been a gift freely given and it was strong enough to stay his hand and save her life.

"I could never kill you," he said again. "But we're going to die if you don't do your spell. Can you?"

She nodded and with gritted teeth, went to work drawing her spell, while Jack ran, not to the door, but to the dead Seals. The demon had killed the last two, probably to make sure that Jack couldn't use them as sacrifices, something he likely would have done if they had lived.

Now, there was no danger of that. The power of the spells over him was gone. Now, all he had to worry about was surviving the next minute, destroying an army of ghouls, fighting off a fiend from the deepest pits of hell, and finding a way to stop his cousin.

Step one: survival.

It's why he ran to the Seals. He was a master swordsman but there were too many of the creatures barging through the door for him to fight. What he needed was the power of the military. In the confined space of the doorway, a grenade would wreak a lot of havoc and ten grenades would wreak ten times as much.

The dead soldiers were still covered in weaponry and Jack started pulling the pins from grenades and throwing them as fast as he could. The explosions: *Bang! Bang! Bang!* went off one after another in a deafening string.

Jack went from corpse to corpse, thankful that they were so close. He had thrown twelve grenades, each one lighting up the doorway in a strange shutter, like the worlds slowest strobe. He had the thirteenth in his right hand, the pin pulled and the fourteenth in his left, ready to go when his mind caught up to what the last grenade had shown him when it exploded—nothing.

There had been piles of bones scattered everywhere, but there hadn't been a single intact bone-monster in sight. They had backed off again and certainly not because of the grenades. Jack spun and saw in the glow of the flares something tremendous standing on the other side of the wall, towering above it.

It was the fiend.

Without hesitation, Jack threw the two grenades in his hands. He lollypopped the throws, timing them so that the grenades exploded on the creature itself. Bones blew out in a rain of fragments; however compared to the size of the creature, the explosions were disappointing and the effect, tame.

Jack hadn't expected more. He had hoped that after the drubbing the Navy jet had given the creature earlier that the explosions would give it pause. It did, long enough for him to glance around and find one of the blessed swords.

He swept it up and brandishing it, he screamed: "If you step one foot in this castle, I will send you back to hell! I am more powerful than ever!" And he was, too. In spite of everything that had happened, Jack felt pretty good, in fact, he felt great.

Physically, he felt as strong and quick as he ever had and mentally, he was a great deal tougher. The fear rolled right off of him now and the cold and the stench were hardly issues. He had faith in his sword that it could at least hurt the monster and he had faith in himself. He had passed the test with the three spells, something few people on earth could have done.

On the flip side, he knew he had no chance against the fiend. It was impossibly big and impossibly strong. Thus, his words, perhaps his last, were one more feint, a last gambit to buy Cyn time in order to finish her spell.

You are nothing, the fiend said in its three voices. *You are weak and your soul is forfeit. It is mine.*

"Not yet it isn't. I..."

"Jack!" Cyn said in a whisper. The circle was finished. All the spell needed for completion was for Jack to get within it and speak the words. Facing any other monster, it wouldn't have been a problem. Against something that could shoot ice a hundred yards, however, there was definitely a problem.

He needed ten seconds—a long span of time in this situation. But he had a weapon and no other options. Cocking his arm back, Jack threw the sword at the fiend. It glittered silver and bright as it flew through the air right at the thing's breast; he wasn't expecting a lucky stab through the heart, if the monster even had a heart. No, he was buying seconds and didn't bother to watch the flight of the sword, which the monster batted away, easily.

In that short time, Jack had raced to join Cyn within the circle, and began speaking the words to the spell as fast as his lips could move. The beast, seeing what Jack was doing, gulped in a huge breath from its three mouths and then blew ice and snow in a great gout that kept going and going. It created a vortex, sucking air in through two of its mouths while blasting out the super-cooled air with the third. The creature was so powerful that even the darkness began to roil and spin around it.

The fiend stood in the eye of a storm of its own making and high overhead, Jack could see the light of day—it was wonderful. Jack and Cyn watched from within the magic circle, completely unharmed. They weren't even cold. The snow and ice rushed right past them and built up in drifts on the far side of the castle.

When the fiend saw that its magic was being wasted, it stopped its icy breath and in a fit of rage tore down the wall of the castle and hurled thousand pound chunks of mortared brick at the two of them, also in vain. The rock blasted against nothing. The air shimmered and the hurled rocks cracked and splintered, rebounding away. They could not be harmed by the undead as long as they stayed within the bounds of the circle.

"Now what?" Cyn asked, when all around them was frozen rubble and the beast finally quit. "We're at an impasse. They can't get in and we can't get out."

"Well, now we fix that cut of yours," Jack told her. He had a tiny vial of Holy Oil. It smelled like a cross between cedar and roses. They both drank in the scent and then smiled at each other. He touched her wounds with the oil and she sagged into him, limp with relief from the pain. He didn't let go.

"So you couldn't kill me," she said wearing her trademark smirk. "What's that about?" He shrugged and felt his ears begin to go red. "I couldn't kill you either," she added. "I thought about it, you know. The spells have been calling to me all day; promising things. It was scary. It's like there's *something* out there demanding that we cast these spells."

For a time, Jack was silent, thinking. Eventually, he answered: "I agree. Something does want us to unleash hell on earth and who or whatever it is, is trying to make it easy. My first thought when I saw the spells was that they just seemed so simple. You would think that the ritual to open a gate into hell would be more intricate, that it would take much more time and effort, that it would take much more power than one sacrificed life."

"Well, it also took a working knowledge of a dead language that no one has been able to read for the last five-thousand years." She grinned at this and he grinned back, but slowly, his smile faded. They were trapped. It was hard to get beyond that.

He looked around; most of the flares were under tons of debris and the one closest was dying; the darkness was gradually folding in on them. "I think it's time we start praying."

She smiled. "You are all on board believing in God, then?"

"After everything that's happened, how could I not be? I completely believe in him. It's not even a matter of faith. I'm just afraid of what he thinks of me after everything I've done."

"What was the last thing that Pastor John said before he died? *God loves you.* I believe it. Look how his followers sacrificed themselves for you, over and over. And, if you ask me there is a reason you couldn't kill me. I think you love me. And love is greater than any evil."

"Light drives away darkness," he said, feeling as though an even greater idea was just outside of his reach.

There was a new rumble, not far away. The fiend was out there in the dark, doing only God knew what. "So...do you even know how to pray?" she asked. "Father Paul and Pastor John both knew scripture. I don't know any."

"Neither do I," Jack said. "I guess you just ask God for stuff and promise to be good?" She shrugged and so they both assumed what they hoped were subservient positions: heads bowed, hands clasped. "I'm praying that he sends angels," Jack said. "That's something I'd like to see. A big battle royale." They were both silent for a minute, praying and then Jack looked up—the dark was unchanged. The heavens hadn't opened and a host of angels hadn't come bursting forth with shining brass swords and white feathered wings.

"I don't think it's working," Cyn said. "Maybe we're doing it wrong. Or...or maybe there is something to all that sacrificing. Jesus died for our sins. Maybe we have to sacrifice, or give something up?"

The strange near-idea was back. So close to the surface. Jack squeezed her hand. "I'd give up my life for you. If that's what it takes to get you out of here safe and sound...and I want to defeat Robert, of course," he added quickly, looking up.

"And I'd give my life for you," she said in a whisper.

He suddenly felt ridiculously happy, even though he had no right to feel happy—he was surrounded by death and blood and outrageous evil, and yet there was a bubbly feeling in his chest. He'd been alone for so long that he couldn't even put a name to the feeling.

Around a smile, he said: "Let's hope God doesn't answer both of our prayers. We can't both die for the other. What good would that do us?" She smiled, her teeth bare glints in the dark. He smiled back and could only hope that she saw. "No," he said, going on, "we both can't die for each other and since I thought of it first, I will die for you." *A gift freely given is greater than any that is stolen*— was that the idea that had been just skimming the horizon of his mind. And if so, what did it mean?

Her smirk twerked in confusion. "What? What do you mean? You're not thinking of going out there, are you? Because that's not dying for me, that's just dying. That's suicide."

"No, I'm not going out there," he whispered, suddenly catching on. "The spell. I'm going to do the spell. It'll be different this time, I hope," he said, thinking on the fly and letting his mind and his tongue run: "It has to be different. Before, I envisioned my own army of undead. I envisioned myself ruling the world—for everyone's own good, of course. That's how I justified myself, but it was all a lie. Evil to beget evil. But I think there may be a better way. A life to save lives!"

Cyn held up a hand. "You can't save lives if you're dead."

He ignored her. It felt as though his mind was running down a steep slope, going faster and faster. "Do you remember what Dr. Loret said?"

He didn't wait for her to answer: "He said that no one goes back to hell willingly. They have to be forced. And he also said that he was going to go find Robert and drag him down to hell. What if that's a real thing? I get the feeling that it is."

"Maybe it is, but you can't raise an undead army using your own life. It won't work, Jack. You can't sacrifice your own self. The blood has to be *taken*, remember? The life has to be stolen. All you're going to do is make a bloody big mess."

What if she was wrong? What if there really was great power in self-sacrifice? The spell read: *Take this sacrifice...* But what if he changed it to: *Take my sacrifice...*? The only question was: did he have to die to open the portal? So far they had been working under the concept that a life had to be taken, but nowhere was the word "life" found in the spell.

It was a soul that was the ultimate sacrifice, the ultimate power. When he had done the simpler protective spells, he had felt something drain from him—that had been his soul's power being drained. It had been an ugly feeling and yet he had recovered. So the question was: *What if he could open the portal and still live?*

There was no way to know.

"And only one way to find out," he said, talking to himself again. "And if this works I can atone for what I've done and save her at the same time." He wasn't quiet enough and Cyn opened her mouth to sputter out an argument, but Jack threw caution to the wind and ran the blessed sword across his left arm, drawing blood. "Scootch back, I need all the room I can get."

He began to draw the first symbol—the arch—linking this spell with the others he had drawn and there was an immediate surge within him, a running of power through his innards, racing along his bones and out through his hands and down the brush. It felt electric. "Huh," he said, his mouth hanging open as he looked down at his palms.

"Huh, what?" she asked. "What's happening?"

Jack didn't answer her—her words had zipped right past his ears. He stabbed the brush into his wound a second time and went on, feeling the power in the brush grow with each symbol he drew.

"Strange," he whispered. It was indeed a bizarre feeling, and, after the first thrumming of power, not a good one. He began to feel weak and thin, sort of drawn out like a watery soup. After a breath, he started again.

"Stop," Cyn said, taking his hand.

He pulled it back. "No. It's working. I need light." He had a last flare stuck down in his armored vest but the buckles were too difficult for his trembling hands to undo.

"Whatever you're doing, is not working," she insisted. "I don't feel anything. And you're doing it wrong. It's all wrong. *I* have to take the blood from *you*. And I don't think I can. I can't kill you like that. I don't think I could even cut you."

"Light, please," he whispered, moving onto the next glyph, his hands shaking and beginning to slip into claws. Pain was coming along with the electric surge of power. He was doing too much too early. This was not an entry level spell. "There's a flare in m-my v-vest. And m-maybe you won't have to do anything."

Finally, she got close and peered in at his face. "What's wrong? Why are you sweating?"

"I'm sweating?" He touched his forehead and felt the fever cooking in him. "It's the spell. It's strong."

Cyn backed to the edge of the circle she had drawn, her back to the wall of darkness. "Can you control it? Jack, please. I'd rather starve to death then have you turn into a monster like our cousin."

"This is different," he said, swallowing loudly and then forcing himself back to the task of drawing the portal spell. The glyphs were getting blurry as sweat began dripping into his eyes. "This isn't the same power. It's not evil and...and it's not Godly, excatly. It's coming from me. I'm using something inside and it doesn't feel good at all. I can stop, but th-then w-where would we be? So please, get me the l-light."

She unbuckled the heavy vest, pulled it off his torso and set it aside. He immediately felt better. He felt lighter, less constrained. Gulping down air, he went back to work.

The blood from his arm flowed easily and in the red glare it looked odd, as if there was a shimmer of white to it.

When he finished with the second spell, Jack fainted. He thought he was just going to take a breather before starting on the final spell, but the next thing he knew, he felt a hand shaking him. "Jack? Hey, wake up. You're almost done."

"What happened?" he asked, blearily. Cyn was just a hazy figure and the flare was no brighter than a candle on a birthday cake.

"You were acting completely trolleyed and I wanted to let you rest as long as possible only the torch is burning down."

"Trolleyed?" he asked.

She grinned: "What you yanks call getting hammered. You know, drunk? Now come on. If the light goes out..." She didn't need to finish. There'd be no drawing the spell and there would be no getting out of there.

The short breather had done him a world of good and he had enough energy to last him through half the remaining glyphs. According to Dr Loret, the third spell was to be painted on the person who would control the demons— Jack painted them on his chest and no longer was his hand guided like before. Whatever force wanted the gate into hell opened, didn't want it opened in this manner.

Jack, with Cyn's help steadying his hand, drew the first six glyphs readily enough, but the last six were intricate and not just exhausting, they were *depleting*. The brush went into his wound easily; however it became a nightmare pulling it back out again. It felt as though the brush became snagged on something vital, something he couldn't live without and there was always less and less of this substance until at last, he felt the well was dry.

He shook and swayed and his eyes kept opening and closing. He was on fire, but at the same time his limbs were like ice.

"One more, Jack," Cyn said. "You can do it."

"I don't think I can," he said in a whisper. "It's too much." It was way too much. He knew it now. He was a beginner. Perhaps if he had only tried one spell he might have been able to pull it off, two spells might have put him in the hospital. Three spells were going to kill him. He felt himself fading in and out, just on the brink of consciousness, and what lay on the other side? Who knew?

Cyn kissed him awake. His eyes fluttered and he could barely make out her smirk. "It's now or never, Jack," she said, and for the life of him, he didn't know what she meant by that. She pulled him back into a kneeling position, picked up his hand and stuck the brush into the wound.

That was just fine. There was a little discomfort, but nothing one wouldn't expect—then she pulled the brush out. Jack screamed. It was a long sound that ended in a croak and smack on the face. "Come on, Jack!" Cyn yelled. "The hard part's done. The brush is out, now paint!"

Jack drew the intricate glyph and there was a tolling bell inside his head and in his hollow chest. He mumbled the words to the spell and then all hell broke loose.

The cement within the twin circles went suddenly jet black, looking wet and deep, so deep that the mind couldn't comprehend. It was a hole that was a thousand years deep. Jack could fall into that hole and drop for a hundred lifetimes and never see what was at the core and he was sure he never wanted to.

It was a hole of such evil that the individual spirits and demons that came rushing out of it looked like light particles compared. There was no wait this time. Jack had been preparing this spell for the better part of the afternoon and literally millions of spirits shot out the second that he uttered the final word of the spell.

They blasted straight up, but not straight out.

Cyn's protective spell worked both ways and now there was a roiling column above them that went for miles and miles. More would have come from the gate into hell;

however something big was heading toward the opening. It was greater than the fiend and darker, impossibly dark. And it was larger; physically it was an order of magnitude so vast that Jack's mind couldn't comprehend.

It was one of the Gods of the Undead. It could be nothing else. Only one of these fell creatures could affect both worlds as it did. The gate expanded going from the size of a manhole cover to the size of a Buick in seconds, while the cement courtyard beneath them mounded and swelled like a tremendous pustule ready to spew venom that would poison the entire planet.

The flat courtyard drew itself into a hill that was fifty-feet tall and the cement was being held together by bonds that were unearthly. Cyn somehow found a way to tear her eyes from the sight. Jack could not. The beast of beasts came at the gate with its mouth wide, a mouth that was pure insanity and from which came the screams of the damned.

Jack would have stared until his heart exploded and his mind turned to water and washed right out of his ears, but thankfully, Cyn managed to retain some part of her. She saw the vial of Holy Oil that Jack had set aside and threw it into the gate.

For one second, everything was pandemonium and chaos. For one second, the world teetered. For one second mankind was on the brink of extinction. And then the second passed and then the gate snapped shut with a last withering blast of cold evil.

Jack fainted again and when he came to, he found himself staring up at the countless spirits he had released from hell. In his chest his heart stuttered and lurched like an engine on its last legs, drinking gas that was three parts water and two parts rust. His vision went in and out and if he had fingers he didn't know. It felt as though his arms ended at his elbows.

He was dying. His soul was a smokey wisp that any stray breeze or simple breath could whisk away—and then he'd be done. Above him the host of the damned waited to see if he would die. If he died they would be free on earth to do as they pleased. If he died his cousin would win.

It was hard to care.

"Jack!" Cyn screamed into his face. "Stay awake, Jack. I need you." Staying awake wasn't the issue, Jack thought. Connecting each breath to what was left of his soul was the issue. If he couldn't do that then the breaths would become only a whistling, useless sound and he would fade straight away.

"Jack!" Cyn screamed again, growing desperate. "Hold this, Jack. Feel it. Can you feel it?" It was the Holy Sword. It had been a fancy, piece of show-off three days before. Now it was a real weapon, one with God's stamp of approval on it. There was a warmth to it both metaphorically and physically.

It burned Jack—not his flesh—it burned his sins and there were many and they were nasty and they went deep like a rotten tooth. He could only stand the feeling so much before he thrust the sword away.

"That's enough," he said. It wasn't, not really. His sins were so great that he should have been forced to hold the sword, burning into him for years. But he had other things he needed to do.

He needed to save the world.

Epilogue

Manhattan, New York

As much as his body wished to die, Jack wouldn't let it. He struggled into a sitting position, only just then realizing that he had been lying in Cyn's lap. He had a vague recollection of tears on his face and her hand in his hair, but had thought it had been a dream.

He wished he could focus on those soft hands and what those tears meant; however, he had crippled his soul for a reason and now it was time to make every sacrifice that had been made on his behalf worthwhile.

"Go," he said to the millions of spirits above him. "Find the nearest uninhabited corpse and report back to me." He dared touching the blessed sword once more. The pains of his sins made him wince, but he ignored the truth of the pain and drew the sword across the circle of glyphs that Cyn had drawn, breaking the spell.

There was a rush of air and a stench that had Jack swooning a second time as the spirits and the demons sped to do his bidding. They were strangely eager. Crossing through Jack's gate had put them under his unconditional control. It was a contract that they could not break under any circumstances and, as much as they wanted to turn on Jack, who was weak as a kitten and lacked the spiritual strength to light even a candle, they carried out his orders to the best of their ability.

The Navy Seals were reanimated first, standing slowly, their frozen bodies creaking, and then came the hundreds of thousands of corpses of the people who had tried to flee by way of the Staten Island ferry. One by one they stood and came to Jack. And then came the millions of people who had come streaming out of Queens and Brooklyn and who had been trapped and slaughtered on their way through Manhattan when the bridges and tunnels had been closed.

In no time, Jack had his army. Manhattan had been layered five deep with corpses and now Jack's army overmatched Robert's by sheer numbers. As well, his corpses were fresher, made of actual flesh and meat instead of riddled bone and ancient tendons. His army was better in every way, including the strength and numbers of demons Jack had under his control.

He didn't know it, but among the undead he held the title of Vahl Necron—*Demon Slayer*. He had killed the copper-eyed demon in direct, hand-to-hand combat, a feat that hadn't been accomplished in a millennium. It meant something to the undead and so when he commanded his legions to: "Drag them back to hell," they surged forward under his victorious banner.

With just his mind he could control his army. He could control them easier than he could control his own fingers. With just a thought he had a thousand ghouls attacking the fiend. When a thousand only angered it, he sent ten-thousand after it.

They tore it apart, bone by bone. It roared and cursed and blasted the air with its darkness and ice, but these did not hurt fellow ghouls and, what was more, the fiend was earth-bound. It could not fight without a physical body and eventually it was nothing but a pile of bones and then the cement beneath the fiend turned smokey. There was a loud crack and the bones of the fiend collapsed.

"Destroy the rest of them," Jack ordered

With Jack's army spreading out, everywhere victorious, the veil of darkness around the city drew back. "It's still light out?" Cyn asked. She smiled and laughed and then cried. It was nearly impossible not to cry when so many corpses were battling still more corpses. The fresher ones—Jack's army—were stronger, but they were also tremendously sad.

It was one thing to be repulsed by a "living" pile of bones, but to see a child in her bloody pajamas, her eyes popped right out of her head and her lips chewed off, fighting with a fiendish grin on the hideous remains of her face, was too much.

Jack pulled Cyn close to his chest and breathed her in. The world stank of decay but Cyn was a flower in a desert and her heart beat added to his weak one, feeding it. He grew stronger, slowly recovering his strength, though his hands still shook and his legs wobbled.

She closed her eyes as the battle raged and only Jack saw the unspeakable things that occurred: demons tearing apart demons, packs of ghouls setting on one another, eating each other. The carnage was nightmarish. The blood that ran, maddening. The sound of molars on bone was the sound of reality warping into a cartoon world where Jack wanted to stuff his fingers in his ears and scream to drown out the sound.

Jack forced himself to watch. It was a reminder of what he had caused and what he had almost become. It was a hard penance to watch the horror.

Gradually, the battle around them ended as Jack's army swept forward in victory and from then on the fight consisted of only psychic echoes in his mind and the horrible mounds of flesh and the scatter of bones. Death was ugly. Jack wanted to flee from it as fast as he could, but he wasn't done, not yet.

Slowly, stumbling and weak, Jack and Cyn made their way up town.

It was a long walk, kicking through millions of bones and stepping around the occasional remains of one of Jack's undead soldiers. Everywhere there was broken glass and burned out buildings and over-turned cars. And there was blood in pools and puddles and splotches and sprays. The blood was dry as paint and ugly as rust, and in the fading afternoon light it looked like a disease attacking the city.

They refused to look at it. Both Jack and Cyn, arm in arm, stared up at the sky as they walked. It was golden and there was a new touch of warmth to the air.

They were heading to the Waldorf; in the direction they could feel Robert…well, truly, it was Hor that Jack had honed in on.

Hor was a blight on his mind. Jack sent four of his nastiest demons ahead to hunt down Hor and, of course, Robert. Even before they got to the hotel, footsore and exhausted, Jack knew that his beasts had failed. Hor was strong, but not strong enough to take on four demons, not even with Amanra's help. It made Jack wonder what sort of nasty surprise was waiting for them.

Regardless, they mounted 42 stories to the top floor. Winded, they stepped out into what used to be an outrageously beautiful and opulent hallway. It wasn't the same.

Blood sprayed the walls; scattered bones were like autumn leaves and tatters of flesh were the tell-tale signs of a demon battle. In a pile of bone and dust next to the elevator, Jack noted the ancient remains of one of the Egyptian mummies, while strewn down the hall were the blackened bones of the Incan.

The rest of the bodies in the hall were what was left of Jack's four demons. It wasn't pretty and yet Cyn and Jack only glanced at the mayhem. What held their attention was the dead cleaning lady splayed out in a circle of glyphs just before Robert's door.

She had been sacrificed. And she was only the first.

Inside the suite of rooms were more. In the living room were three tiny bodies. They were children, sacrificed to the Mother of Demons. One had been butchered to bring forth the fiend that had killed Pastor John and the squad of Navy Seals.

They had no idea what the others had died for. Jack stared down at a circle of strange glyphs, committing them to memory. Then he knelt and touched the child who lay in the middle of it. She was dead and hollow—he understood the feeling. She wasn't like a normal corpse where there was a lingering warmth, a touch of memory. She was gone inside.

"I wish God had answered our prayers," Jack said to Cyn.

"How do you know he didn't," Cyn asked. She kept her arms folded across her chest, hiding her hands. She wasn't going to touch anything. "I prayed for us to be saved and we were. I prayed for Robert to be defeated and he was. That was pretty spot on if you ask me."

"I meant I wish he had sent angels...and don't even suggest that I'm angelic in any way." Jack rubbed his chest where there was only the tiniest whisper of his soul left. It was like a flickering match trying to catch a log on fire. Given enough time, he knew that it would and, unlike the girl, he wouldn't feel so hollow. "I'm not an angel. Right now, I'm barely a man."

"Just be thankful that we've won."

Going to the window, Jack looked down at the destroyed city and thought that nobody had won. There were the dead and there were the survivors, but no winners.

He turned his mind to his army, knowing that he had let his concentration wander and that he was losing control at the edges. Some of Robert's demons and the craftier spirits were escaping, throwing off their corpses and hiding among the people, among the living, where Jack couldn't see...at least from this distance.

In spite of his exhaustion, he concentrated on encircling and hunting down the last of Robert's army. It took two days to destroy them all and in that time Jack did not sleep, and hardly ate. When at last it was done, he gathered his army on a farm in western New Jersey and then forced the demons and spirits under his control back to hell.

For an hour, Jack walked among the dead, among the millions of unstirring corpses until he passed out.

He woke to the smell of honeysuckle and was dimly aware that Cyn knelt over him; he was being washed in a river and she was kissing his lips. Unashamed, he cried as he felt his soul once more. It was a warm spot in his chest

Cyn, clean and beautiful, cried as well—tears of joy at first but when Jack said: "It's not over," her tears were of sadness. Hundreds of demons had escaped and would have to slain one by one, but worse was that Robert had pulled a Houdini and disappeared.

"It's a big world," Cyn said. "He could be anywhere."

"Egypt," Jack said, his mind on the strange glyphs that had been written in blood in Robert's suite. What were they and what did they do? There was no way to know, but he knew where to look for answers. Five-thousand year old riddles could only be solved in the ancient sands of Egypt. He had to go where all of this had begun. And he knew that Robert would go to Egypt as well. Robert was more than half demon now and he craved the power of the eldest beings. He would go to Egypt and Jack had no choice but to follow.

The End

****

Author's note:

As always, I hoped you enjoyed the book and as always I humbly beg for an Amazon review and a quick mention on Facebook so that I can continue to write what I think are pretty good stories(Most people agree, except for those whose chests seize up over the occasional errant comma.)

The second book in *The Gods of the Undead* series is being written right this moment(Yes, even if you are reading this note and two in the morning, chances are that I am up and writing!) If you would like your name to appear in it please contact me at petermeredith07@gmail.com. I try to use as many fan names as possible, but if your name is Willy Willoughby maybe just write to say hello.

Now as you desperately wait on book 2, how about you take a look at some of my other works. I would suggest my seven book series: The Undead World. Here is chapter 1 of *The Apocalypse* to wet your whistle:

The Apocalypse

Chapter 1
June 27th
Rostov-on-Don, Southern Military District, Russian Federation

Under the neon lights, Yuri Petrovich seemed a sick, pasty white, however since this was normal for almost everyone at the facility, it went unremarked if it was noticed at all. From his office, he passed through the agriculture research section—what once was the façade of the operation, and took the secure elevator to the lowest sub-basement.

There he grunted a 'hello' to the aged guard, Beria, and signed his name on the log board. "Time for my monthly checks," Yuri said affecting a bored voice despite the tremor in his hands.

The guard didn't look up from his magazine, a German rag that was two months out of date. "Better you than me," Beria replied, as he always did. Though the man wore a gun at his hip, he was extremely disinterested in anything concerning the facility and no one knew who or what he actually guarded.

"Key me?" Yuri asked.

Once upon a time it would have been a sharp-eyed and sharply dressed political officer who had to match keys to get into the *White Room*. Now it was only fat, put-upon Beria. He sighed heavily as he heaved himself out of his creaking chair.

"On three," he said, taking up his position on one side of the door. "One, two, three." They both turned their keys and the door opened with a hiss. Beria beat a hasty retreat to his beloved chair, where his fat rear had only wiggle room left.

Yuri went into the next room and donned his bio-suit, ran down his checklist, inspected his filters twice, and then went first through one air-lock and then a second. Despite his years on the job, the *White Room* always gave him a shiver down the spine when he entered however today the shiver went to his guts and wouldn't leave.

"Five hundred million rubles," he whispered to himself. "Five hundred million fucking rubles…"

This helped. And so did the fact that he knew Beria was completely ignoring the cameras. To be on the safe side however, Yuri went through the dull routine of cataloging the various strains of bio-weapons stored there and he did so as slowly and methodically as he could.

Though it was called the *White Room* by the sad few who knew of its existence, it was officially unnamed and not at all associated with the Department of Agriculture housed in the building above. Instead it had grown as an offshoot of the Stepnagorsk Scientific and Technical Institute for Microbiology. It was what the Soviets had called a Biopreparat facility and thus very illegal in the eyes of the world–for good reason.

Yuri glanced down the rows of steel and glass cabinets that were clearly marked: Anthrax, Ebola, Marburg Virus, Plague, Q fever, Junin Virus, Glanders, and Smallpox; each had to be numbered and their dates checked. He worked, with clipboard in hand, in the tedious manner he had cultivated ever since he had become chief of scientific research at the facility.

The term 'research' made him want to gag. There hadn't been a *kopek* of new research money in a decade, and every year his budget shrank. There was even talk of ending the bio-weapons program altogether.

And then what would Yuri do?

The struggling Russian government wasn't hiring many scientists, and the private sector wasn't eager to be associated with a man who had made his living producing and maintaining weapons of mass destruction. His legal options were few, and his illegal options were even fewer, but they were oh, so lucrative – Five hundred million rubles worth of lucrative. The promise of the money was the single reason he had taken to going to the one locked drawer in the room on every visit.

With a quivering in his chest that wouldn't stop, Yuri undid the stout combination lock, opened the door to the locker, pulled back on the stainless steel slab, and then forced himself to breathe in a normal manner: in and out, in and out. The body lay beneath a sheet and as always, Yuri uncovered it with gritted teeth, while his gorge rose in the back of his throat.

The body was that of a man, or rather it used to be a man, now it was something else.

He took the right arm of the thing, it was grey and stiff, and set it to hang as far as the handcuffs would allow, letting the black blood pool in the extremity. Yuri then went through what had become a routine and completely unnecessary check up. The thing on the slab should have been dead. It was quite literally ice cold since the refrigeration unit was kept at a constant zero degrees centigrade. And yet it was already moving.

The hands spread and the muscles around its mouth began to work, opening and closing. It was in the eyes where it was most "alive". Somehow they were hungry and furious, but also glassy and empty of any intellect. Lately, Yuri had begun to dream about those eyes, and lately Yuri had become an insomniac. He couldn't sleep, knowing that those nightmare eyes would be worn by everyone he knew—if things went wrong.

Still he had a job to do and after a deep breath of stale bio-suit air, he began his check-up, starting with the hated eyes. He then peered into its ears, and nose, and its horrid, dank mouth. Then, making sure his body was completely blocking the camera, Yuri pulled a syringe from one of the zippered cargo pockets that adorned his suit and jabbed the needle into the crook of the thing's arm where a fat vein had begun to bulge.

The thing didn't flinch. According to every report the creature that once had been a man, couldn't feel the slightest pain.

Yuri filled the syringe with black blood, and then very carefully pocketed it. The virus was blood born and though he could bath in it if he wished, a single prick from the infected needle would kill him in hours.

With sweat running down his back, he covered the body, slid it back into the freezer where it belonged and then went on to his next chore which was to switch out the attenuated viruses in their little plastic pipettes. There were a total of twenty doses of the vaccine—he took six, leaving normal saline in their place. No one would notice, not until it was too late for them.

Of the six doses, he would inject himself with one of them that night, just in case; three were part of the bargain that would make him rich, and the final two he would keep for himself.

These last would guarantee him a position of power if his clients, the North Koreans, were ever foolish enough to release the virus. Given the right conditions he could churn out vaccines in as little as four months, while he had to wonder if the Koreans would ever figure it out. They were pathetically behind in all aspects of technology, as everyone knew.

Yuri closed the last glass case and breathed a sigh of relief. He was done and not a single alarm had gone off, which meant that one wouldn't. Beria had been as poor at his job as ever. Moving quickly, now that the toughest part of his job was past, Yuri breezed through both air-locks, and with the utmost care he transferred the syringe from his bio-suit to his jacket pocket. It felt like he was carrying a bomb with a hair trigger as he made his way up to his office, however nothing untoward happened and he was able to take the needle off the syringe without mishap.

The now capped syringe and the clear pipettes he bagged and then placed inside his thermos, while the needle he dropped onto the open face of the sandwich his wife had made him for lunch; it would go to waste anyway, he could never eat after a visit to the *White Room*. Very carefully he wrapped it back in the brown bag it had come from and this he gently put in a medical waste container.

One last item: Yuri took the container, which was nothing more than a plastic bag, and walked it personally to the incendiary chute and tossed it in. Now he was done. He went to his desk and sat there picturing everything five hundred million rubles would buy, sighing happily.

Enjoy the rest here:
The Apocalypse: The Undead World Novel 1

Fictional works by Peter Meredith:

A Perfect America
The Sacrificial Daughter
The Apocalypse Crusade War of the Undead: Day One
The Apocalypse Crusade War of the Undead: Day Two
The Horror of the Shade: Trilogy of the Void 1
An Illusion of Hell: Trilogy of the Void 2
Hell Blade: Trilogy of the Void 3
The Punished
Sprite
The Blood Lure The Hidden Land Novel 1
The King's Trap The Hidden Land Novel 2
To Ensnare a Queen The Hidden Land Novel 3
The Apocalypse: The Undead World Novel 1
The Apocalypse Survivors: The Undead World Novel 2
The Apocalypse Outcasts: The Undead World Novel 3
The Apocalypse Fugitives: The Undead World Novel 4
The Apocalypse Renegades: The Undead World Novel 5
The Apocalypse Exile: The Undead World Novel 6
The Apocalypse War: The Undead World Novel 7
The Edge of Hell: Gods of the Undead, A Post-Apocalyptic
Epic
Pen(Novella)
A Sliver of Perfection (Novella)
The Haunting At Red Feathers(Short Story)
The Haunting On Colonel's Row(Short Story)
The Drawer(Short Story)
The Eyes in the Storm(Short Story)
The Witch: Jillybean in the Undead World